A PROMISE TO CHANGE THE WORLD

"I just want to fix what is broken. That's what a Mechanic should do. Will you help me, Alain?"

As he listened to Mari's earnest words, Alain thought of the storm in his vision sweeping down upon the second sun in the sky. What happened now would either help Mari fight that storm, or perhaps put an end to the future only she could bring. What happened now could perhaps doom the world illusion to the eventual fate of Tiae and worse.

It did not matter, his Mage training told him. The world illusion did not matter. What mattered to him was the young woman who knelt by the door, the shadow who called herself Mari. A shadow the storm would utterly destroy to prevent her from bringing the new day of hope to this world...

PRAISE FOR THE PILLARS OF REALITY SERIES

"Campbell has created an interesting world... [he] has created his characters in such a meticulous way, I could not help but develop my own feelings for both of them. I have already gotten the second book and will be listening with anticipation."

—Audio Book Reviewer

"The Dragons of Dorcastle was a fantastic read. From the very first page I was drawn into a world filled with an almost steampunk feel but that's heavy in magic too. It was an action packed and exciting book and one I can't recommend highly enough."

—Book Lover's Life

"I was so pleasantly surprised by how much I enjoyed The Dragons of Dorcastle... I can already tell that Mari and Alain are going to be characters I'm going to have a good time following... I'm so eager to see where their story goes next!""

—Not Yet Read

"The intense battle and action scenes are one of the places where Campbell's writing really shines... Campbell's years of military experience help him write realistic battles."

—All Things Urban Fantasy

"The Dragons of Dorcastle... is the perfect mix of steampunk and fantasy... it has set the bar to high."

—The Arched Doorway

PRAISE FOR THE LOST FLEET SERIES

"It's the thrilling saga of a nearly-crushed force battling its way home from deep within enemy territory, laced with deadpan satire about modern warfare and neoliberal economics. Like Xenophon's Anabasis – with spaceships."

–The Guardian (UK)

"Black Jack is an excellent character, and this series is the best military SF I've read in some time."

–Wired Magazine

"If you're a fan of character, action, and conflict in a Military SF setting, you would probably be more than pleased by Campbell's offering."

–Tor.com

". . . a fun, quick read, full of action, compelling characters, and deeper issues. Exactly the type of story which attracts readers to military SF in the first place."

–SF Signal

"Rousing military-SF action... it should please many fans of old-fashioned hard SF. And it may be a good starting point for media SF fans looking to expand their SF reading beyond tie-in novels."

–SciFi.com

"Fascinating stuff ... this is military SF where the military and SF parts are both done right."

–SFX Magazine

ALSO BY JACK CAMPBELL

THE LOST FLEET

Dauntless
Fearless
Courageous
Valiant
Relentless
Victorious

BEYOND THE FRONTIER

Dreadnaught
Invincible
Guardian
Steadfast
Leviathan

THE LOST STARS

Tarnished Knight
Perilous Shield
Imperfect Sword
Shattered Spear

THE GENESIS FLEET

Vanguard
Ascendant
Triumphant

THE PILLARS OF REALITY

The Dragons of Dorcastle
The Hidden Masters of Marandur
The Assassins of Altis
The Pirates of Pacta Servanda
The Servants of the Storm
The Wrath of the Great Guilds

LEGACY OF DRAGONS

Daughter of Dragons
Blood of Dragons
Destiny of Dragons

NOVELLAS

The Last Full Measure

SHORT STORY COLLECTIONS

Ad Astra
Borrowed Time
Swords and Saddles

* available as a Jabberwocky ebook

THE DRAGONS OF DORCASTLE

THE PILLARS OF REALITY: BOOK 1

BY

JACK CAMPBELL

Published by Jabberwocky Literary Agency, Inc.

This paperback edition originally published in 2015 by
Jabberwocky Literary Agency, Inc.

Originally published in audiobook format by Audible Studios in
2015.

Cover art by Dominick Saponaro.

Map by Isaac Stewart.

ISBN 978-1-625674-21-0

To
my son Jack

For S, as always

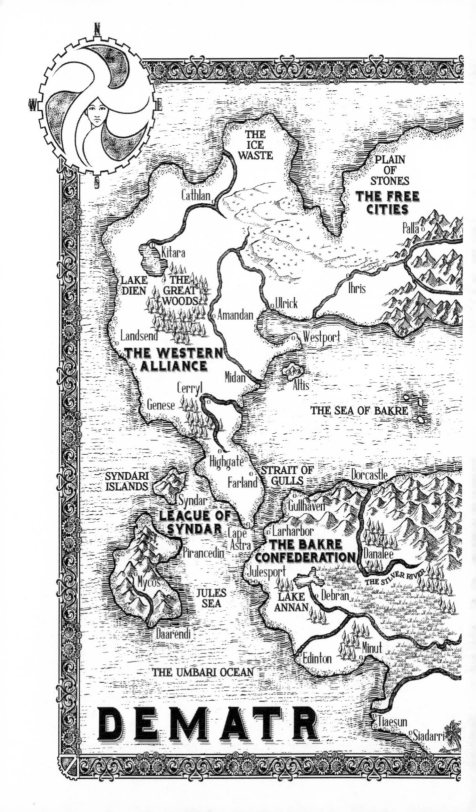

DEMATR

Acknowledgments

I am indebted to my agent, Joshua Bilmes, and to Steve Mancino and Eddie Schneider, for their relentless championing of this series and their ever-inspired suggestions and assistance, and to the rest of Jabberwocky (notably Lisa Rodgers and Krystyna Lopez) for their tireless labors, and to editor Betsy Mitchell for her enthusiasm and editing. Thanks also to Catherine Asaro, Robert Chase, Carolyn Ives Gilman, J.G. (Huck) Huckenpohler, Simcha Kuritzky, Michael LaViolette, Aly Parsons, Bud Sparhawk and Constance A. Warner for their suggestions, comments and recommendations as Dragons took the long path from draft to reality.

CHAPTER ONE

The heat, the dust, the mountains rising ahead were all false, as much illusion as the mirages wavering with the fake promise of water.

Mage Alain of Ihris focused inward, denying the dry, hot wind which had just flicked a cloud of fine sand off the crest of a dune and dusted it over the caravan. Denying the grit which settled in his eyes. None of it was real.

Mounted caravan guards rode alongside the open carriage in which Alain sat, their horses plodding with the same weary gait as the oxen pulling the long line of wagons. Those guards were here for the same reason he was, to protect the caravan from the bandits of the Desert Waste, but that in no way made them equals.

He was a Mage. At seventeen years old he was the youngest Mage in the history of the Mage Guild, but to the common people in the caravan and among the guards, Alain's age did not matter.

They did not matter, either, Alain reminded himself. Those other people, like the desert about him, like the carriage in which he rode, were all illusions, mere shadows created by his own mind. Only he was real. Ten years of harsh schooling in the Mage Guild had taught him that he was always alone, no matter how many shadows his mind imagined seeing.

Alone.

A memory intruded despite his best efforts: a vision of two graves near Ihris, where the remains of a man and a woman lay buried side by side. His parents had never been real and had never mattered, the Mage Guild had taught. It didn't matter that his parents had died at the hands of raiders off the Bright Sea after Alain had been taken from them and isolated within a Mage Guild Hall. It didn't matter that he had not learned of their deaths until a few months ago, when he attained Mage status and could finally leave that Guild Hall.

It did not matter, Alain told himself, trying to deaden all feeling as he had been taught.

But the stab of pain the memory brought served as a reminder of what Alain had successfully hidden from his teachers in the Mage Guild. Despite his best efforts to deny all feeling, to see others only as shadows with no value, deep inside emotions still tore at him. All of the Mage Guild's teachings, all of the elders' ruthless discipline, had not caused his mother's last words to fade in Alain's memory as the Mages took him away. *Do not forget us.*

At least there were no other Mages here to detect Alain's failure, to constantly watch him for signs of weakness.

There should have been, though.

This was his first assignment since earning his status as a Mage. He did not know why he had been sent to protect the caravan alone. Normally, two Mages would have been assigned, as some insurance against failure. And even though the Mage Guild saw everything as illusion, the elders had always shown a fondness for gold, real or not. The protection of two Mages cost the common folk twice what one Mage would.

Alain peered ahead, where the track the caravan had been following for days wound up out of the wastelands and curved toward a pass surrounded by rugged hills. Despite his denial of the dust and the glare, a moment of weakness caused him to wish that he had a pair of the odd headgear some of the caravan guards wore, a sort of bandana with two pieces of dark glass set in it that protected the eyes. But those "goggles" were made by Mechanics, and the Mechanics who claimed the ability to change the world illusion in their own ways were frauds.

His elders had never wavered in that. Common folk might be fooled into using and paying for the strange gadgets of the Mechanics, but no Mage would be taken in by their hoaxes. The goggles could not actually work, and as a Mage Alain could not touch them.

Perhaps the pass would finally bring them out of the blazing desert, or at least provide momentary shade as they passed between the higher ground on either side. Between the glare of the sun hammering down from above and the reflected heat from the ground below, Alain felt like a loaf of bread being baked in an oven. It might be just an illusion, but it was a very warm illusion. Regardless, he had to take no apparent notice of the heat. He had to maintain at all times the stoic indifference of a Mage to physical hardships, no matter what those hardships were.

That pass, though. He should not remain indifferent to that. A narrow way between looming walls of rock. If bandits did lurk here, they would surely choose such a place for an ambush.

Alain denied the unease that thought brought to life. He denied any hint of nervousness that he might soon face his first deadly test outside a Mage Guild Hall.

The commander of the guard rode not far from Alain's carriage. Alain raised one hand slightly, turning his head just enough to look at the commander.

Common folk avoided looking directly at Mages, but they knew to respond when a Mage beckoned. Tugging at the reins, the commander brought his horse over to trudge next to Alain's carriage. The commander pulled down the scarf protecting his nose and mouth, then slid up the goggles covering his eyes so that his face was visible. Only then did he bow as deeply as permitted by his position in the saddle. "Yes, Sir Mage."

Alain watched him, knowing that his own expression revealed no feeling at all. Merciless training had taught that skill to the young acolytes of the Mage Guild. But with the ability to hide all feeling came a corresponding proficiency at spotting emotion in others, even when they tried their best to hide it. On those few occasions when he had spoken with the commander before this, the man had revealed beneath an impassive face and respectful tone of voice the usual fear of Mages. Now within the commander's eyes and voice lurked a greater worry.

After most of a childhood spent obeying Mage Guild elders in all things, it felt odd to be addressed with so much respect and fear by a man of the commander's age. It would have felt awkward, that is, if that were not one more feeling to be denied.

Gesturing ahead, Alain spoke in a voice with no feeling in it. "We approach a pass."

"Yes, Sir Mage." His voice hoarse, the commander used the back of his hand to wipe his dust coated lips, then raised a leather water flask and drank to clear his throat. "We are entering difficult territory."

"More difficult than this waste we have spent so long crossing?"

The commander hesitated, anxiety flaring in his eyes as he tried to guess what Alain had meant by that comment. "Yes, Sir Mage. The pass threatens worse than heat, thirst, and dust." He pointed up the road, to where the hills loomed over either side of the pass. "Bandits rarely operate far into the waste, and once beyond those hills there may be patrols out of Ringhmon to help keep the peace. But if we are to be attacked, if there are any brigands out and about, that pass is where they'll make their try at us. It is called Throat Cut Pass for good reason."

He hesitated again, not quite looking at Alain. "Sir Mage, do you know of any...?"

"No." Alain let the flat word stand alone. Some Mages did have occasional flashes of foresight warning of what was to come, but never reliably, and he had never felt that gift himself. The elders said that stress or danger could bring foresight to life in a Mage, but Alain would not explain any of that to a common. "Why does Ringhmon not garrison the pass?"

The commander licked his lips nervously before replying. "A garrison here is too much trouble and expense as far as Ringhmon is concerned, Sir Mage. Keeping a strong garrison supplied out here wouldn't be cheap, and a small garrison would too likely end up victims to the bandits." He pointed ahead again. "See that column of stone, Sir Mage? Ringhmon claims its borders out to here, but that's nonsense. They're not half so big as they like to pretend."

"Ringhmon is over proud." Alain made it a statement, not a question.

"That is very true, Sir Mage," the commander stated bluntly, though he seemed surprised that a Mage was showing interest. "I've had to sit and listen while they claim that only the might of Ringhmon has served to check the southern advance of the Empire."

Alain kept his face and voice expressionless, hiding the inner flash of amusement that he felt. "It is the great desert waste that has stopped the armies of the Empire."

"That is so, Sir Mage." The commander gestured behind them. "You saw the wreckage we passed on the road days ago. That's all that's left of more than one Imperial expedition. Heat and thirst and the dust storms are what has stymied the Empire's march south. That and the will of the Great Guilds." The commander's eyes flared with open fear. "I mean your Guild, of course, Sir Mage. The only truly great Guild."

Alain did not acknowledge the man's words or his apology. He had heard references to the "Great Guilds" since leaving Ihris, and had come to realize that the commons were referring to the Mage Guild and the Mechanics Guild. Odd that the commons should believe that the Mechanics had real power, but then the Mechanics, like the Mages, had Guild Halls in every city. Alain's elders had told him that like the Mages, the Mechanics hired their work out to those with the money to pay for it. While at this moment Alain was contracted to this merchant caravan treading a narrow line of neutrality between the Empire and Ringhmon, his next contract might be with the forces of the Empire, and the one after that to the enemies of the Empire. His only loyalty was to the Guild, and all that mattered to the Mage Guild was a client's ability to pay, as long as none of the clients dared to raise a hand against the Guild or failed to heed the wishes of the Guild in any matter. Anyone who tried to attack Mages, whether the minor towns of the Syndari Islands far to the west, the loose-knit cities of the Bakre Confederation in the lands beyond Ringhmon, the forest-bounded cities of the Western Alliance to the northwest, the Free Cities that held the great mountains far to the north, or the old cities of the mighty Empire that ruled the east, would find the Guild's services denied to them, and many Mages offered in the service of their enemies. Mighty the Empire might be among the commons, but even the Emperor had no choice but to do as the Mage Guild demanded.

Only the Mechanics defied the Mages, and they were beneath notice. Or so Alain had been told. The Mechanics believed that they also ruled this world. The idea would have been amusing if Mages ever allowed themselves amusement.

"What numbers and sort of bandits might we encounter?" Alain heard the continued lack of any emotion in his voice with satisfaction. This might be the first time that he had actually faced danger of this kind, but no common would be able to tell that.

The commander lost his fear in the need to offer a careful and correct response. He rubbed the stubble on his chin thoughtfully, gazing into the distance. "Not too many nor too well armed, I'd think. Any group of more than a dozen has all it can do just to survive out here. Nor is this area rich with pickings. Caravans such as ours are too infrequent. It's doubtful that bandits out here can manage any rif— any weapons beyond sword and crossbow."

Alain bent another impassive look on the commander, who seemed to be sweating more now after almost saying the name of the weapons the Mechanics claimed were so superior. "I can deal with any weapons."

The commander gulped, plainly trying to find diplomatic words. "Yes, Sir Mage, of course. We have no doubt of that. I will go prepare my guards now, Sir Mage, if you no longer require my presence."

"Go," Alain said, his own gaze back on the road ahead of them.

"By your leave, Sir Mage." Bowing again, a wash of relief visible on his face, the commander urged his horse to a quicker pace, anxious to put distance between himself and Alain. "Bows!" the commander called in a powerful voice that echoed across the empty land. "At ready!"

The chain-mailed guards loosened the straps holding their crossbows to their saddles, pulling back the cords to ready them and setting bolts into place. When that was done, and the crossbows resting across the front of their saddles, the guards also loosened their sabers in their scabbards.

Alain settled back, gazing ahead and feeling the power around him. A Mage never knew until he reached it how much power an area might hold, but Alain had been told to expect that all portions of the wastelands would hold little power to draw on. He wondered if bandits knew this, and if it played in their decisions to favor ambushes in this place. Commons weren't supposed to know such things, but Alain had been informed that Dark Mages would sell almost any knowledge for a price.

The sluggish pace of the oxen slowed even more as the wagons of the caravan reached the slope and began toiling up the rise. Alain glanced around, trying to appear uninterested even though there was a strange kind of excitement in waiting for a possible battle, a thrill he could not completely suppress at the idea of finally using his talents in a life and death struggle. There was some fear there, too, though he couldn't tell whether it was fear of failing this test or fear of being harmed. Alain could see no signs of threat ahead, but he noticed all of the caravan guards were scanning the rocks as they held crossbows ready to fire.

Alain kept looking up at the rocks, but as the time went slowly by and the caravan crawled up the road toward the pass he found the glare of the sun bouncing off the bare stone was causing his eyes to water. He looked down, blinking several times to rest his eyes, then started to look up again.

Light flashed off something high up on the wall of the pass. *Armor or a weapon,* warned Alain's lessons in the military ways of the commons, but before he could react in any way the earth beneath the front wagons of the caravan erupted in a colossal bloom of dirt and rocks. Alain gaped at the sight, Mage composure seriously rattled, as rocks rained down from the sky and the thunderous sound of the explosion echoed through the pass. He had barely time to realize that the leading parts of the caravan had simply vanished in the explosion, along with the portion of the guard force around them, when the walls of the pass began to ring with repeated crashing sounds, far less massive than the first blast but still loud enough that it was as if a thunderstorm had come to rest around the caravan. Alain blinked again, staring at bright, sudden flashes of light winking into existence among the rocks.

The driver of Alain's carriage had been staring open mouthed at the crater where the lead wagons of the caravan had once been as he fought to control the panicked oxen pulling it. Now the driver jerked backward as if he had been hit with a crossbow bolt, then flopped forward. All around, Alain could hear people shouting and screaming over the strange thunder, and see dust or splinters spurting up where some sort of projectiles were hitting. Oxen bellowed with terror and pain, dropping to the dust to lie limp in their harness. The guard commander was roaring out orders, his goggled face impossible to read but his voice frantic. Sudden gouts of dust erupted from his clothes, and he fell to lie motionless while his horse stampeded away.

Alain pulled his eyes away from the blood spreading out from the center of his driver's body. He had to do something. A growing surge of anger and fear channeled into his spell, drawing from and building on the weak reserves of power around him. He held up his right hand, feeling the warmth gathering above it as he willed the existence of heat. *The heat I feel is an illusion. I can make that illusion stronger. I can make the heat here, above my hand, so hot that it will melt rock. It is only a temporary change to the world illusion, but that is all I need.*

The heat in the air above his palm bloomed into visible brightness, then Alain swung his palm to point it toward a cluster of those winking lights and willed the heat to be there.

The fireball didn't really fly to its target, though that was what common people always thought they had seen. He had the illusion of heat here, and he could put that illusion somewhere else. In an instant, it went from being near Alain's hand to being at the place he had aimed it. The superheated ball of air appeared at its target and rocks flew in all directions while a different kind of thunder filled the pass.

The attack on the caravan paused for only a moment, as if shocked, then resumed with even more fury than before. Alain, seeing no signs of attack from the place where his first fireball had landed, gathered another ball of heat to him. A moment later, a second big explosion marked the destruction of another nest of bandits.

Wood splintered around Alain. It took him a moment to realize that the bandits must now be trying to kill him. A moment's fear was submerged by his training as he jumped down from the wagon and willed another spell into being, making light bend and curve around him. He looked down, seeing himself waver and then vanish from sight.

That done, Alain paused to seek more targets. Another guard screamed and dropped nearby, causing Alain's concentration to falter. He stared at the dead guard, then all around. He could no longer see any caravan guards still fighting, just bodies lying in the dust. A couple of wagons lay on their sides, overturned when their teams panicked. One of the drivers was still fleeing on foot, but jerked and fell as Alain watched.

Am I the last? Dust flew in spurts all around him, telling Alain that the attackers were hurling their projectiles at where they thought he was. His stomach tight with fear, Alain focused on his spells again with a great effort. *If I am to survive this, if I am to save anyone left alive in this caravan, I have to keep fighting.*

Calling up power, Alain created fireball after fireball, placing them on the heights above the caravan. A series of explosions shattered ancient stone to cascade onto the attackers. His barrage finally caused the onslaught to falter. Clouds of dust rolled down, covering the area of the caravan and blocking Alain's view of the devastation around him as well as the walls of the pass where the bandits were positioned.

Alain stopped, his breathing heavy and sweat covering his body. He looked down to see his hand trembling with exhaustion, and realized that he had so depleted his strength that the protection spell had failed. A foolish error worthy of an acolyte. Until he rested a little he would not be able to defend either himself or the caravan. Even then, almost no power remained here to draw on. Under his robes he carried one of the long knives Mages bore, but that would be of little use against whatever weapons these bandits were wielding.

Not that defending the caravan seemed to matter any longer. The attack continued from the front and sides, the bandits hurling death blindly into the haze of dust. More and more crossbow bolts thudded home into the dirt or the sides of wagons, as if the ambushers were running low on the deadlier, unseen projectiles. But Alain could hear no movement nearby, or sounds of any guard returning the fire.

Alain staggered back, spent from his spell work but trying to reach the wagons in the rear. Perhaps some guards still survived there. His own flurry of attacks might keep the bandits from advancing for at least a few moments longer, giving time to muster some other defense.

He stumbled through the slowly falling clouds of dust past several more wagons, all abandoned or with their former occupants dead. Tired and scared, Alain could hear his Guild elders lecturing him that a Mage must not show weakness, must not show human frailty. Alain repeated the lessons to himself, trying to block out the thunder of the bandits' weapons, taking long, calming breaths while he attempted to deny any feelings of fear.

But along with the fear he could not totally eliminate, one thought kept intruding. What other weapons were the bandits using? The thunderous weapons which had wiped out the guards were not crossbows. They were far deadlier.

He reached one of the last wagons, a large one with barred windows whose door had been kept locked since the caravan had left on its journey. Alain had not mingled with the other members of the caravan, of course, since all were commons, but he had overheard some speculation about the occupant of this wagon possibly being a spoiled Imperial lady who had remained unseen throughout the journey. If so, and if the lady still survived, he might still be able to do something for someone.

Alain came around the side and saw that the wagon door sagged open. How could the bandits have reached it before he did? Forgetting caution and weariness for a moment, the Mage rushed forward to look inside the wagon.

A figure rose up before him, holding something in one hand that glinted dully in the dust filtered sunlight. Alain checked his own lifted hand and the two stared at each other for a long moment. *A Mechanic?*

There could be no doubt. Even in the scorching heat of the waste the woman wore the dark jacket which marked the members of the Mechanics Guild as surely as Alain's robes marked his own. Unlike the garments of the Mage Guild, though, which bore symbols and ornaments to mark their ranks and special skills in a form only other Mages could read, the jackets of the Mechanics were aggressively plain, just leather stained dark. Those unadorned jackets sent a message to everyone that Mechanics thought themselves so important that they did not need to impress with their clothing or show any visible sign of rank. Her trousers were also plain, though made of tough and high quality material, and her boots dark leather like her jacket.

It took Alain a moment to overcome his shock, then look past the raven black hair cut short so it fell just to her shoulders and the frightened, angry expression, to see that the Mechanic was about his own age.. Her youth startled him, but then it surely would not take the Mechanics that long to teach even elaborate tricks to their members.

"What are you doing here, Mage?" the Mechanic demanded, pointing the object in her hand at his face. That thing she carried had no blade, nor any visible bolt like a crossbow, instead looking like an oddly shaped piece of metal with a hole in the end facing

Alain. But the way the Mechanic held it made clear it was a weapon of some kind. "I've seen you occasionally during the journey, so I know you're not among the attackers. Otherwise you'd already be dead!"

He could hear the fear in her voice, barely concealed beneath the bravado of her words.

"I am charged with protecting this caravan!" Alain yelled back over the crash of the bandit weapons.

"They depended on a Mage for protection?" she shouted. "What was the caravan master thinking? Who's attacking us?"

Under normal conditions Alain would have turned his back on her, adopting a Mage's lack of interest in anyone and anything in this world. Under normal conditions he would not speak with a Mechanic at all. But he was badly enough rattled that Alain answered instead. "Bandits, the guard commander said. He said there would be only a few, and poorly armed."

"Bandits!" The Mechanic shook her head, eyes wild. "Impossible. There are dozens of rifles firing on us. No bandit gang could afford those."

"Rifles?" Mechanic weapons?

"Yes." The Mechanic held up the thing in her hand. "Like this pistol, but bigger and longer ranged. Where are the caravan guards?"

"Either dead or fled. I believe most have died. I found no one alive until you." He had spent years being told of the evil nature of Mechanics, and wondered for just a moment if Mechanics were behind this attack. But the fear in the eyes of this female was real.

Alain realized suddenly that the thunder of the Mechanic weapons had fallen off a great deal and the thump of crossbow bolts had also subsided. He stared toward the front of the caravan. "The bandits must be advancing."

He looked around, not knowing what to do. His training had covered such circumstances, but to actually face them, to be desperately tired and surrounded by the dead while weapons he didn't understand hurled death over long distances, left him momentarily paralyzed. For a moment he felt his youth and inexperience so heavily that he could not even think.

The Mechanic spoke again, her voice sharp. "We need to get out of here." Then she looked startled. "I mean..."

Alain understood her hesitation. He could not imagine spending time in her company, either, even under these conditions. "I will try to stop them while you flee. I was contracted to protect this caravan and those in it. That means I have an obligation to protect you."

"You protect me? A *Mage* protect me?" The Mechanic seemed to forget her fear momentarily as outrage bloomed. "That's—"

Hoarse shouts sounded a short distance away. Alain licked lips dry with dust. "They have reached the front of the caravan." He had regained some control now and kept all feeling from his voice.

"Aren't you scared, Mage?" she asked. "You sound bored. What are you planning to do?"

Alain gazed down at his hands, then shrugged, feeling overwhelmed. "I will have to stand here and fight. There is nothing else to do."

"Yes, there is. We can run."

"We?" The single word made no sense.

"You and me. I won't let anyone, even a Mage, die if I can help it! I don't leave anyone! Not even you!"

Alain, baffled by her words and feeling fear bloom inside him again at the thought of death, fell back on his earliest training. "This world is not real. Dying is but the passing from one dream to another."

The Mechanic stared at him as if his words had been just as incomprehensible to her. "You intend dying here because you think it doesn't matter?"

"I know it does not matter," Alain stated in as calm and emotionless a voice as he could manage.

The Mechanic's eyes narrowed in thought. "Fine," she said. "Your Guild contracted you to protect this caravan? To protect me? To do that, you'll need to stay with me. We seem to be the last two alive, and if you stay here while I go, then you'll be breaking your contract. Now, whether you like it or not, come on!"

Alain hesitated a moment longer as the Mechanic turned to go, then followed. After so many years of obedience to authority, it wasn't easy to shake off the Mechanic's commands, and her argument did seem reasonable.

As soon as the Mechanic was sure Alain was behind her, she started running off to one side, beckoning him to follow. Now that he was behind her, Alain could see a large pack on her back. He wondered what it contained that could be so important the Mechanic didn't abandon it so as to flee faster. Treasure of some kind? The elders had always said that Mechanics were ruled by greed and deception.

They scrambled over rocks and up a steep slope, dust clouds still concealing them from the bandits. *Why did she insist I come with her? Why am I following her?* But he stayed with the Mechanic as she climbed.

The shouts were coming slowly closer, showing the bandits had kept moving forward but were being cautious, probably because the dust kept them from seeing very far. Only an occasional crash from one of the Mechanic weapons could be heard now.

As the Mechanic reached a long ledge and swung past a cluster of rocks, some figures suddenly emerged. Two had crossbows and the third a strange weapon with a hole in the end like the Mechanic's hand weapon. All were pointing their weapons at her.

The Mechanic had frozen in the act of bringing up her hand weapon, staring at the bandits, clearly realizing that she was trapped. The bandits had not yet noticed the Mage lagging behind her.

CHAPTER TWO

Alain was once again calling forth heat above his hand, his own remaining strength and the residual power here both draining like water into the spell. He had a moment to realize that he could have run again while the bandits were occupied capturing the Mechanic, but rejected the idea before it fully formed.

In the time required to create the spell, one bandit's finger twitched on the trigger of his crossbow. The Mechanic might have died then, but the bandit with the strange weapon struck aside the crossbow so that its bolt flew harmlessly away. "Fool! If any harm comes to her—"

The heat above his hand peaked. Alain placed it upon a boulder directly beside the man in the center of the group. An instant later the surface of the boulder exploded with the sound of shattering rock.

The man closest to the fireball uttered a single sharp cry as he was flung sideways, then collapsed. Ripped by sharp fragments of stone, his two companions were thrown outward and fell in tumbled heaps.

Alain bent over, then fell to his knees and sagged against the nearest rock, gasping for air and hoping no more bandits lurked nearby. Fighting off a blurring of his vision, Alain managed to look up, searching for more danger, and found his eyes focusing on the dead bandits. His earlier attacks had been at a distance and he had not seen the results. Now he could see that the side of the bandit nearest where he had placed the fire had been burnt black. Trails of red blood trickled away from the other dead bandits. Alain looked away from the bodies, feeling a sudden odd hollowness at seeing men he had killed. *They are only shadows*, he kept repeating to himself, but the words brought no comfort. Nausea rolled through him and he was grateful that he had not eaten for a while.

Alain gradually became aware that the Mechanic was staring at him with wide eyes. She took three steps to him, going to one knee and reaching out, then stopping her hand just before touching him. Even Mechanics, it seemed, knew that no one touched a Mage without a Mage's permission. "Are you all right?"

He struggled to nod, unable to speak for a moment.

"What did—?" Rising again, the Mechanic ran to the rock Alain had just struck, avoiding the bodies and running her fingers above the crater on its surface. "It's hot. Much hotter than the sun's heat could account for. Superheated steam could do this, except that there's no way you could have a steam boiler hidden under those robes. But there's no apparent residue, either." The Mechanic came quickly back to him, her expression determined. This time she reached to grab one arm and help Alain to his feet. "You can't do this without burning something, using some accelerant. What is it?"

Startled by her touch on his robes, Alain took a moment to think through what she had said. His mind couldn't concentrate, fuzzy with fatigue and fear, so he shook his head. "I do not know your words."

"You have no idea what I'm talking about?"

"None." More shouts came from behind and below, where the wreckage of the caravan lay. "We had better move from here. They may have noticed the sound of my spell breaking that rock."

"Just a moment. Can you stand?"

After Alain nodded the Mechanic let go of his arm, spun around and picked up the strange metal object longer than her arm. Alain gazed at the thing, noting that it bore a superficial resemblance to a crossbow, except that it was longer and lacked the bow portion. The metal of the weapon gleamed under a sheen of dust. A pungent smell came from the thing, sharp and almost stinging to the nostrils but with an undertone of something deep and oily. He felt an urge to examine it more closely, but since it was obviously of Mechanic make he knew that would be foolish. His teachers had warned him of the traps Mechanics placed on their so called devices.

The Mechanic held the weapon, turning it in her hands as she hastily examined it. "Standard model repeating rifle. Made by Mechanics Guild workshops in the city of Danalee in the Bakre Confederation. This one's new. Only been fired a few times." She looked at Alain, then tossed it onto the ground. "But the lever action has been broken, so it won't do us any good." Glancing quickly toward the crossbows still clasped in the hands of the other two dead bandits and then averting her eyes, the Mechanic shuddered. "I don't want a crossbow that bad."

The shouts from the caravan came again, this time clearly expressing disappointment and carrying the tone of command. From the direction of the sound, Alain guessed the voices were coming from the area of the wagon the Mechanic had occupied. "The bandits have discovered that you are missing."

"Blazes, we've got to get out of here. Can you climb by yourself?"

"Yes," Alain said, not understanding the reason for her question but unwilling to admit to his continued weakness.

"Good. Let's go." With a lingering look of regret toward the long Mechanic weapon lying discarded on the ground, the Mechanic turned and started climbing higher along the walls of the pass. "Thanks for saving us from those guys, Mage," she called back in a low voice.

Alain watched her for a moment. She obviously intended for him to stay with her. He could not remember how to respond to her last words. *Thanks.* That had meant something to him once. He had said it...to Asha. Only once, the night they had both been brought to the Mage Guild Hall with the other new acolytes. He had been punished for it. That had been...twelve years ago? What had the word meant?

He climbed after the Mechanic as she toiled up the slope. Alain took each step, each pull upward on a handhold, one at a time, refusing to collapse again. The dust was gradually thinning, but down around the caravan it still blocked vision enough that Alain could not see what the bandits were doing, and hopefully they could not see the fleeing Mage and Mechanic. The climb was steep and difficult now, leading ever upward, and Alain felt his lingering strength being quickly consumed as they went higher.

The Mechanic looked back at him and then stopped, crouching behind an outcropping of rock that screened her from below. "How are you doing?"

Alain had to pause to get enough breath to answer. "Why do you ask this? Why do you keep asking such things?"

She looked aggravated at his response. "Do you think there's something weird about being worried about somebody else?"

He could not think of an answer to that.

"Stars above," the Mechanic said, "what's the matter with you? We're in this together, like it or not. And, no, I don't particularly like it either, but we do what we have to do, Mage."

Alain caught up with her, hauling himself up behind the same rock outcropping. He wished he were not so tired from the effort of casting his spells. "I neither like it nor dislike it. It is. But you are foolish to risk yourself for another, to worry. It does not matter."

Anger flared on her face. "Everybody matters, Mage. Don't lie to me. You must have feelings one way or the other, even if you hide them behind those robes and a face that shows nothing."

"You do not seem to know Mages very well." Alain looked away from her. After his years around impassive Mages, and then around commons who sought to hide their reactions to a Mage, the emotions on the Mechanic's face were so clear and strong that it was if she were shouting the feelings at him, their intensity almost painful. Grateful for the chance to rest, Alain peered from behind the rock to search the slope behind them for signs that the bandits had realized which direction their quarry had fled.

"You're the first Mage I've ever met," the Mechanic said. "Do you believe that there's something wrong with helping others?"

"Helping?" That had meant something once, too. He had been punished for that, and now shied from remembering.

"Yes." The Mechanic gazed at him, some other emotion he couldn't identify showing on her face now. "You don't know what helping others means? You don't believe people should help others?"

He did have a reply to that. "There are no others, and I do not believe this. I know it. Mages believe in nothing."

His frank statement seemed to startle her. "Nothing? And that makes you happy?"

Another easy answer, drilled into him countless times during his years as an acolyte. "Happiness is an illusion."

"I don't believe that, and I can't believe you do." The sound of shouts down in the pass came again, distance rendering them vague but still menacing. The Mechanic took another deep breath. "We can't afford to rest any longer. Ready?"

He finally realized that she had waited here, she had spoken with him, to give him time to rest even though it increased the danger for her. Alain took a moment to answer as he tried to understand the Mechanic's actions, which were even more confusing than her words. "Yes."

The Mechanic started climbing again, toward a crest that seemed tantalizingly close now.

Alain kept waiting for more thunder that would signify that the Mechanic weapons were launching their projectiles at him again, but they reached the top and slid over without any sign they had been spotted. The Mechanic was sitting below the ridge line on a slope that dipped down a short ways before rising to join more hills looming behind her. She was obviously waiting for him again. "They didn't see you?" she asked.

"I do not think so."

"How you can be so calm and unemotional about this, I don't know," the Mechanic said.

"A Mage has no interest in the world," Alain explained.

"Not even when it's trying to kill him? At least you're consistent." She rubbed one hand across her face, smearing sweat and dust into a dirty, wet mask. "You said that everybody else in the caravan died?"

"I believe so. All I saw were dead. I heard no sounds from anyone fighting or calling out offers to surrender."

"Stars above." She blinked away tears. "We were lucky to escape with our lives."

"They do not want to kill you. They sought to capture you," Alain said, offering the obvious explanation.

"What? Me?" She stared at him. "Why do you say that?"

"The attack destroyed the front of the caravan. Your wagon was at the rear. None of the weapons were aimed at the area near your wagon. The bandits did not immediately kill you as they did all others in the caravan, and before I killed them, their leader stopped one from harming you. I could hear the shouts when the others reached your wagon. They were discontented."

"No, that's..." She swallowed as her voice choked. "Bandits. They wanted to loot the caravan. That's what bandits do."

"They destroyed the wagons in the lead. Why would they destroy so much if they desired to loot it?"

The Mechanic ran one hand through her hair, haunted eyes gazing now at the nearby rocks. "Yeah, but...they shouldn't even have known I was with the caravan. My Guild insisted I stay locked in that wagon so no one would know I was on my way to Ringhmon." Her face darkened with anger. "They made me stay *locked* in there. If I hadn't figured out how to take apart that lock I'd have been trapped in that wagon when the bandits got to it."

"I would have gotten you out before then," Alain said tonelessly.

Her eyes shifted back to him. "That's why you were coming back?"

"Yes." There was no reason to deny that. "I had been contracted to protect the caravan and I thought whichever shadow was in the wagon might still need my protection."

"I never imagined a Mage would do that. The Senior Mechanics always said...*you* said that Mages didn't care about people."

"I did not do it because I cared about you. You are nothing," Alain said impassively.

It did not take a Mage to see the resentment that statement aroused in the Mechanic. "Thanks."

"I do not understand."

"I'm being sarcastic, Mage. What's your name?"

Alain eyed her, trying to guess why the Mechanic had asked for that information.

"If we're going to depend on each other to live I deserve that much," the Mechanic insisted. "And I need to know what to call you besides 'Mage.' "

His elders would be angry if they knew he was even talking to a Mechanic. They would be angrier yet if they knew he had accompanied her this far. Even though the elders, like all Mages, were supposed to feel no emotions, every acolyte learned to fear the anger the elders would never admit to.

Many of those elders had also made clear their belief that he did not deserve to be made a Mage so young, despite his ability to pass the tests.

And the elders had sent him here, alone, as if wishing for him to fail.

The defiance he had kept carefully buried in recent years rose close enough to the surface to bring the words to Alain's lips. "I am Mage Alain of Ihris."

"Mage Alain of Ihris." The Mechanic studied him for a moment, her nervousness fading a bit as she examined him. Now, resting close to each other, he could see clearly how young she was. "Ihris is a long ways north of here. I'm Master Mechanic Mari of Caer Lyn."

"Caer Lyn." Islands, to the west of the Empire. "That is also north of here."

"Not nearly as far as Ihris." She closed her eyes, breathing deeply.

"We need to keep moving, but I think we should rest a little longer. Climbing in this heat is very tough and we'll kill ourselves if we push it too hard." After he said nothing, the Mechanic opened her eyes to glare at him. "Well?"

"What?" Did all Mechanics act in such strange ways?

"I expressed an opinion. What is your opinion?"

"It does not matter."

Her expression changed from disbelief to anger to resignation so quickly that he barely had time to recognize each emotion. "Fine. I'm in charge, then. Why does everybody always want me to be in charge? Have you ever been in anything like this situation before?"

"No. This is my first contract."

She frowned this time. "Mine, too. What's such a young, inexperienced Mage during out here by himself?"

He knew no Mechanic would catch any bitterness leaking through his control of his voice as he answered. "My Guild has declared me a Mage, but being inexperienced, my price is less than that of older Mages. The caravan could not afford more."

"If you're so inexperienced, they should not have sent you out alone to face this kind of danger!" Strangely, the Mechanic's anger now seemed aimed at his own Guild's elders.

"The commands of the elders are not to be questioned."

What did her expression mean now? But her brief gasp of laughter did not sound like she was happy. "I never expected to hear something that made your Guild sound like my Guild."

This talk was treading onto dangerous ground. Guild secrets. If there were another Mage here...

If there were another Mage here, he would never have spoken to this Mechanic. He would not have gone with her. He would never have known anything about her or any other Mechanic.

If Mechanics were enemies as he had always been told, then he had a duty to learn more about them. And perhaps he would learn that this Mechanic, at least, was not an enemy. She did not act like an enemy.

But she was not a Mage. What was she then? "Why are you here alone, young, inexperienced Mechanic?"

She flushed slightly at the question. "I wish I knew all of the answers to that. I asked for some of those answers, but Senior Mechanics aren't in the habit of giving explanations when they issue orders. The short answer is that I have some unique skills that Ringhmon needs." Her voice held undeniable pride as she spoke that last sentence.

Alain almost frowned, too, barely catching himself in time. If everything the Mechanics did was a trick, why import this girl when more experienced tricksters surely lived in Ringhmon? How could she have unique skills? But it was obvious now that what he had been told about Mechanics, or their weapons at least, was at best incomplete. "Are these unique skills of yours the reason why the bandits seek you?"

"No. No, that's impossible. They'd have no possible use for my skills, unless they were thinking of ransom," she said. "But kidnapping a Mechanic? The Guild would never stand for it."

"The attackers had many of the weapons made by your Guild," Alain pointed out.

"Yeah." The Mechanic's lips twisted, her feelings once again hard to read. "A bandit gang with as much firepower as an army could afford."

Twelve years of Mage Guild training had never been able to suppress Alain's curiosity. "Why would your Guild elders permit that?"

"I told you that my...elders...don't provide reasons for what they do. They don't listen and they don't explain." Her feelings didn't seem so much anger as frustration now. "I wish—" The Mechanic's eyes went to him, startling him with the intensity of her gaze. "I'm sorry. I shouldn't be talking about things like that with a..."

"I am a Mage," Alain said. That was not a matter for the comfort or discomfort of others, whose feelings did not matter anyway, but he understood the Mechanic this time. There were things that should not be discussed with any outsider, and especially not with a Mechanic. But perhaps there other things she would explain. "I have been trained in tactics, since my work would involve the military forces of the common people. Perhaps that is why I was thought able to handle this contract alone. Tell me your thoughts on your tactics. Why did you choose to run up the side of the pass instead of back down the road along the way we had come? Why did you choose the harder path?"

The Mechanic slumped, then to Alain's amazement began laughing softly. "That's who I am, I guess. If I'm working on a piece of equipment, say a locomotive or a far-talker, I do things the best way I can. Not the easy way. And I'm like that in everything. I don't do what's easy. The Senior Mechanics, my elders, haven't always appreciated that." She sighed, her eyes gazing bleakly at nothing. "From what I'd seen of the road to the pass, it was wide open. We'd have been spotted and run down in no time. So going up the side of the pass was the harder road, but the right one."

"You were correct," Alain said, then wondered why he had felt any need to tell her that. "Once I had the opportunity to think it through, I realized that you were right."

Her gaze went back to him, puzzled. "Why is a Mage telling a Mechanic that she was right?"

"I..." *do not know.* "Because we survived and have a chance to reach Ringhmon."

"Yeah. A chance." The Mechanic closed her eyes again. "Do you have any food or water? I don't."

"I do not, either."

"How long can we survive in the Waste without water?"

It took him a moment to realize she was not expecting him to answer that with some exact number of days. "The caravan master's map showed wells farther up the road once we had cleared the pass."

She opened her eyes, looking at Alain with hope. "You're sure? How far?"

"I am sure, but I do not know how far." Mechanic Mari nodded wearily, leaving Alain wishing he had been able to tell her something more hopeful. *She is a shadow. Do not forget. Nothing more than those you have fought today.*

He felt a cold hollowness inside himself. He had never fought in earnest before today, never killed before today. The common folk he had seen among the caravan now lay dead themselves. People who had depended upon him for protection. All of them were shadows, so none of that should matter, but it did.

He sensed something then, and turned to look back at the crest of the ridge. A black haziness floated there, the sort of thing that might drift into vision when physical stress was so intense that a person was in danger of passing out. He knew that type of thing all too well from years of intense training to teach him to ignore what non Mages called reality, but this haze was different.

It did not waver, and suddenly Alain realized what the haze represented. *Foresight, warning of danger. That skill has finally come to me, in a time of great stress as the elders taught. But the elders also said foresight was an undependable gift at best.* He inched upward cautiously until he could see back down the slope they had climbed. There were figures visible down there, above the dust now as they clambered up the heights, their Mechanic weapons shining in the sun.

Alain crawled backward rapidly. "They are coming up in this direction," he reported without letting any betraying feeling into his voice this time.

CHAPTER THREE

Mari's heart jumped at the Mage's words. Her right hand went to the pistol she had holstered, then she took a breath to calm herself. *All right. Time to go. Which way?* "There," she said to the Mage as she pointed. "Farther into the heights." She had stopped questioning their weird alliance, which after all was going to be as temporary as she could manage. The Mage was unnerving, with his emotionless voice and face and his strange attitudes. But the fact that these so called bandits were still chasing them made teaming up with him a simple matter of survival, even if she didn't feel responsible for his fate.

The Mage gave her one of his impassive glances. "To the west? The ground is more difficult that way and the original attack came from that direction."

"Exactly! They'll think we're running in panic and taking the easiest route, which is in the other direction."

"And you always take the more difficult route," the Mage said.

"Well...yes." She hadn't expected a Mage to remember that. "Because it makes sense this time. Besides, it'll be easier to stay hidden up there." Mari paused, thinking of how Mage Alain had fallen after whatever he had done to the bandits on the ledge. "Can you manage it?"

What would she do if he couldn't? Leave him? *No. Nobody gets abandoned. Not by me. Not even one of them.* Touching him earlier to help the Mage to his feet had felt...peculiar, after all that she had heard about Mages. But if he needed assistance again, she would grit her teeth and do it.

Despite his usually successful attempts to hide his emotions, Mage Alain gave her a look which communicated a trace of wounded pride. For that brief moment he seemed more human, more a boy close to her own age. "Of course I can manage."

She lurched to her feet, wishing tools weighed a lot less. Leaving them behind was unthinkable, though. Being a Master Mechanic had qualified her to have one of the limited number of portable far-talkers. It was in her pack, but the range on the device was so limited that Mari figured she would have to be within less than a day's march of Ringhmon before she could use her far-talker to contact her Guild for help. Until then it was simply a heavy object in her pack.

"Why do you not leave your treasure behind?" The Mage's bland tone made the question sound as if the answer held no interest to him.

"Treasure?" She gave him a baffled glance, then realized the Mage was looking at her pack. "This isn't treasure. My tools are in here."

"Tools?"

"Mechanics use tools. Didn't anybody ever tell you that?"

"No."

"I don't have time to explain," Mari said, wondering if she should be explaining tools at all to a Mage. "But a Mechanic never loses or abandons her tools. It's one of the most important rules of my Guild." Taking a deep breath, Mari started off, scrambling along the slope at an angle until it merged with another rise before climbing. Mari didn't know why the young Mage was so tired. He looked strong and healthy, even *tough*, but he had almost collapsed after whatever he had done to take out those bandits, so it must be related to that. But how? The engineer in her kept puzzling over the answer, a welcome distraction from the fear she still felt.

Despite his obvious weariness, though, the Mage stayed right behind her, displaying a stubborn determination to keep up that she had to admire.

They rolled over another, higher crest, once again blocking their view of the way they had come. Mari tried to swallow and then coughed, trying to muffle the sound with both hands over her mouth. How far into these hills would the bandits search for them? How close behind were they now? "Did you see any sign of them, Mage Alain?"

He shook his head. "I saw nothing of the bandits. I heard a few faint cries, but they seemed far distant."

Maybe she had made the right decisions. *I'm only eighteen years old, and ten years of studying engineering isn't exactly the best preparation for running for your life from bandits. Knowing how to fix a steam engine isn't likely to be too useful out here.*

The Mage had approved of her first decision, and left other decisions to her, so he must think she knew what she was doing. She wished she had the same confidence in herself. Why had she been sent to Ringhmon this way? Sent alone on her first contract, contrary to normal procedures, and told it was too urgent to wait for the winds to shift so she could take a ship from the Empire to Ringhmon's tiny coastal port. With the Empire and Ringhmon not at war at the moment, that would have been the safest way to travel. If this contract was so blasted important, if getting her there as fast as possible were so critical, then why had they put her into this kind of danger?

And why had Professor S'san, who had always shown the greatest interest in Mari at the Mechanics Guild Academy in Palandur, insisted on giving her as a graduation gift a very expensive and hard-to-acquire semi-automatic pistol? Every weapon and every machine was made by hand, their quantities strictly limited by the Mechanics Guild, and the allotted production of pistols like Mari's was only a few a year. What had worried S'san enough to justify that gift?

As much as she had always chafed at authority, Mari found herself wishing that a more experienced Mechanic was with her. Someone who might know what to do and how to survive.

Of course, if there had been another Mechanic with her, she never would have spoken to the Mage. She surely would have been overruled on telling the Mage to come with her.

And Mage Alain would have died, and she would have been captured by those bandits on the ledge.

Not a better outcome.

At least for the moment they seemed to be safe. Mari tried to draw in a deep breath but ended up hacking painfully. Her throat was a dry wasteland to match the ground they were surrounded by. "We're going to need water soon," she croaked.

The Mage nodded. "Do even those from the stars need water then?" he asked in that empty of feeling voice.

She gave him an annoyed look, unable to tell if he was joking or giving her a hard time. "Mechanics have special skills, but we're still as human as anyone else when it comes to things like food and water. Don't Mages need water?"

"Of course. We also share those same needs." The Mage appeared thoughtful for a moment, as if recalling a memory. "Perhaps all people came from the stars."

"Very funny."

"Funny?" The Mage asked as if not knowing what the word meant.

He couldn't be that cut off from emotions, could he? Mari wanted to snarl a reply, but her dry throat caught and she coughed again.

The Mage considered her, then spoke slowly. "There is a place nearby where water lies."

Mari felt hope flare as her head came up. "Where?"

"The caravan."

The hope vanished like a burst bubble. "Are you crazy, Mage? We can't go back there."

"Not at this moment. But you said they expect us to flee in panic. This is so. They will not expect us to stay near the caravan, to creep down when opportunity offers and find water there."

Mari took shallow breaths, lost in thought as she considered the idea and how dry her mouth felt. The plan was insane, but somehow the totally emotionless way in which the Mage had outlined it made it seem almost possible. "It's our only chance, isn't it?"

"I can see no other action which would offer any chance."

She could be too impulsive. Her teachers had warned her of it many times, but her impulsive decisions so far today had kept her and the Mage alive. "Then let's go a little higher up before we start bearing back toward the pass. We'll wait until it gets dark. Hopefully the bandits will be done looting the caravan by then."

"The bandits did not seem concerned with loot," the Mage pointed out again.

Mari nodded wearily. "That's right. They blew up the front wagons. Why destroy loot? Even if they wanted me, why throw away the chance to pick up some loot on the side? And those weapons. And the explosives. How could any caravan carry enough loot to pay back those expenses? Mage Alain, I don't expect you've priced out the cost of repeating rifles and bullets, but the Empire itself wouldn't field an attack force like that unless it had a very good reason. There was an army's worth of rifles there, and a treasure chest's worth of gold used up in the bullets they've already fired today."

"So you said. Capturing you must have been worth such a cost to them."

Mari's laugh once again turned into a choking cough. "Me? I'm skilled at what I do, but I'm not that conceited."

The Mage watched her intently. "Perhaps your value is greater than you know, greater than any treasure spent in pursuit of you."

The sort of statement any girl wanted to hear from a guy, and she had to hear it from a Mage with an expressionless face and a toneless voice. "I'm not that special. I have special talents, and the job in Ringhmon will be worth a lot to my Guild, but—" Mari realized that the Mage was now staring at her. "What?"

"Do you know of foresight?"

"Foresight? You mean fortune-telling?" Mari asked, not bothering to hide her automatic scorn.

"No," the Mage replied with no sign of being offended. But then he wasn't showing much sign of any feelings, so that didn't mean anything. "True foresight tells what will happen and cannot be summoned reliably, nor is it easy to understand what can be seen or heard." The Mage was looking directly at her, his expression somehow serious despite the lack of visible emotion. "I have developed a small gift of foresight. Some new danger awaits you in Ringhmon."

Mari felt herself stiffening, rubbing her left arm slightly against her body so that she could feel the pistol resting in its shoulder holster under her jacket. "Please tell me you're not threatening me." Every warning she had ever been given about Mages came back with renewed force.

He gazed at her for a long moment before replying. "No. This danger does not come from me."

Of course, Mari thought. It was a come-on. The Mage wanted her to offer something in exchange for more information. The oldest con game in the book, and he actually had the nerve to pull it while they were being chased by bandits. "What is it you want? How much money would it take for you to see more about this danger you claim I face?"

The Mage's expression didn't waver. "No sum of money or other favor would make a difference. What my foresight provided has no value to me. What little I know I will tell you."

Surely he wanted money. Her Guild seniors had never wavered in their assessment of Mages. *Money-grubbing frauds, fakes, liars, never to be trusted or spoken to.* Or touched. How many rules had she broken today? "You don't want any payment?"

He shook his head. "You made no contract for my services. Warning you may fall under my contract with the owners of the caravan. Either way, you owe me nothing, and I do not care for money."

"How can you be so cold-blooded about everything?"

She could have sworn that one corner of the Mage's mouth twitched upward for just an instant as he gestured toward the sun beating down upon them. "I am actually quite warm at the moment."

Even though delivered in a voice without any feeling, that sign of humanity, or an actual sense of humor, caused Mari to forget her anger. There really was a boy behind that face Mage Alain used as a mask. He seemed absolutely sincere, and his refusal to consider payment was the opposite of what Mari had been told of Mages by her Guild. This Mage Alain was weird, but he didn't seem to be evil. "So, all you know is that there is some danger for me in Ringhmon."

"I heard words that hold no sense to me. *Beware that in Ringhmon which thinks but does not live.*"

Mari stopped breathing for a moment, certain that she had betrayed her shock. She inhaled slowly, trying to get herself back under control, wondering how a Mage could have acquired knowledge of the secret contract for which she had been ordered to Ringhmon. "Why are you saying that?"

"It is what I heard. I do not know the meaning. I know of nothing which thinks but does not live."

"Not even any Mechanic device?" Mari pressed.

"I know nothing of any Mechanic device of any kind." The Mage paused to look at her, his eyes the only thing alive in his face. "I have been in a Mage Guild Hall since I was five years old. There I was told that all Mechanic devices were tricks."

Was he lying? He had to be lying. But why? And why declare he knew nothing more if the Mage was trying to extort something from her? "That's what I was told about Mages, that everything you did was fake."

Mage Alain appeared to think on that for a moment before answering. "We were both misinformed, then."

He wasn't making a joke this time. Or was he? Mari couldn't tell. She wasn't that good at understanding boys, who weren't nearly as easy to figure out as a balky steam locomotive or fluid dynamics equations, but this Mage seemed far harder to understand than the apprentices and full Mechanics she had grown up around. "I can't figure you out," she said. "What do you want?"

"What I want does not matter." He said it mechanically, if that description could ever fit a Mage, the words coming out as if they had been drilled into him.

Remembering some of the harsher harassment she had endured in her Mechanics Guild apprenticeship, Mari wondered what things had been like for this Mage. What had been done to him to make him seem so inhuman? "Why can't you just act like everyone else?"

He gave her an inscrutable look. "I am not like everyone else."

For some reason that sounded sad to her. "I ask your pardon, Mage." The formal words almost stuck in her parched throat, but Mari forced them out, seeing real surprise flashing for a moment in the Mage's eyes in response. "I'm a Mechanic, but I'm not closed-minded." *Which has got me in trouble already more times than I can count.* "Thank you for your warning."

The Mage shook his head. "Thank...you," he repeated, the words sounding almost rusty as they came out, an intentness again showing in his eyes. "Thank you," he repeated in a murmur to himself, a hint of understanding appearing in his voice. "I...remember. Asha."

"Asha?"

"Long ago. I do not remember what to say." He gave her a look in which no feeling could be seen. "What do I say?"

"Um...you say...you're welcome," Mari replied, feeling oddly anguished by the Mage's reactions.

"Yes." He inclined his head toward her. "You...are...welcome, Master Mechanic Mari."

Mari averted her eyes, not wanting him to see her feelings, and wondering who he might once have been before the Mages got their hands on him. But now he was a Mage, too, and there was nothing she could do about that. "Um...let's go, just in case those bandits are still tracking us. We've rested as long as we should."

The rocks on the heights kept slipping under her feet, the sun beat down mercilessly, their path seemed to always lead either up a steep slope or down a steeper slope, and her pack felt as though it weighed more with every step.

The dryness in her throat had become a constant source of distress. But she kept moving, trying to pick a path that kept a screen of rocks or ridges between them and where the bandits might still be climbing up. A small ravine opened before them, leading down and back toward the site of the attack on the caravan, so Mari eased carefully down the walls of the gap and followed it until it ended in a sheer wall. Muttering curses, she climbed, her pack seeming to be trying to pull her down with evil intent.

It almost succeeded, as a handhold crumbled and Mari began sliding downward past the Mage, who simply watched her falling. "Help!" Mari got out as she slid past. The Mage just stared again for a long, heart-stopping moment, then at the last possible instant shot out an arm to lock his hand on her wrist.

She could swear he looked remorseful for an instant, then the Mage mask was back in place. He waited until she had a good grip on the stone again, then let go of her wrist as quickly as if the touch burned.

Mari didn't know what to think of this boy. Part of her felt sorry for him, part was grateful for his aid, but part of her remained worried and suspicious. *Why can't he show what he's feeling? Does he really feel anything? Why didn't he help me right away? How could he have known anything about my contract in Ringhmon?* "Thanks."

"You...are...welcome." The Mage had a far off look in his eyes. "Help," he whispered to himself, as if trying to remember what the word meant.

The afternoon wore on as they labored over the heights back toward where the front of the caravan had been, the sun slowly sinking in a red haze born of the fine dust thrown up by the battle, dust which would take hours yet to settle. Mari finally made her way along a narrow rift that gave out on a rock screened ledge.

From here they could look down into the pass and see the wreckage of the caravan spread out beneath them. Mari couldn't help wondering if some of the bandits had used this spot as a firing position earlier in the day. If they had, they hadn't left any brass lying around from bullets that had been fired, but even bandits would want the discount on reloads offered by the Mechanics Guild. The sun had sunk far enough that the entire pass was now in shade, providing a small measure of relief from the heat that had been plaguing them. Groups of figures in the robes of desert dwellers could be seen moving around the pass, gathering up swords and crossbows and ransacking wagons but apparently not taking much from them.

"What are they doing?" Mari whispered.

The Mage studied the scene for a while. "They are trying to create the illusion that the caravan was looted without actually looting it. See, they're setting fire to that wagon after pulling out the goods within, but the goods are so close they will also burn."

Mari slid down behind a rock and tried not to think about water. Her shirt under her jacket was soaked with sweat, but she was determined not to remove that jacket. It was a symbol of who she was, of all she had done to earn her status, and it also felt like protection, even though the leather wouldn't stop much. Protection against bandits, and protection against this strange boy even though he had shown no signs of threatening her. "We'll have to wait until dark to have any chance of getting down there without being detected."

"Can you conceal yourself?" the Mage asked.

"What?"

"Can you conceal yourself?" the Mage repeated. "Use a spell to make yourself hard to see?"

"You've got to be kidding," Mari said. But the Mage appeared to be perfectly serious. "No. I've got dark clothes on. That's as good as it gets."

"Then I should go alone. I can hide my presence, though with effort, and have a better chance of succeeding."

Mari regarded him. She was less concerned about being spotted than she was about physically collapsing during a climb down from here. That would make so much noise the bandits would hear it for certain. But if she stayed up here, the Mage would have a free hand down there. "How can I trust you, Mage Alain?" she said bluntly.

The Mage stared outward. "I would not expect you to take the word of a Mage."

The word of a Mage. She had heard that phrase often. Mechanics, and common folk, used it to mean something totally worthless.

"I cannot think of any assurance I could offer you," Mage Alain added.

"You're telling me there's nothing that could make me trust you?" Mari asked.

"No, I am saying that there is nothing I could say that could make you trust me."

She got it, then. He was telling her to judge him by his actions. But even those actions could have been driven by a desire to survive rather than good will toward her, which would make betraying her an easy thing for the Mage to contemplate. "I need to hear some words, anyway. Just give me one reason to trust you."

The Mage gazed back without visible emotion. "I want to...help." He said the word again as if it were an unfamiliar thing, and she remembered his hesitation when she had been falling earlier, as if he were unsure what "help" meant.

Mari nodded, trying not to show the wave of pity that hit her. "All right, I can understand wanting to help someone. But why do you want to help me? Our Guilds have been enemies for their entire histories, as far as I know."

"I do not understand it myself." The young Mage looked down. "You saved my life. When I was ready to stand at the wagon and die because I could not think of anything else to do, you made me come with you. If you had not led us up the side of the pass I would have passed from this dream into the next already."

Her memories of those moments were obscured behind veils of fear, but Mari remembered the Mage seeming lost and indecisive, having to be ordered to follow her. "I thought you said dying didn't matter. That everything is an illusion. Why do you care about living now?"

The Mage almost frowned as he pondered the question. She was sure of it, even though the expression barely appeared. Finally he looked back at her. "There are many illusions I have not yet seen."

Though delivered without apparent emotion, the open humanity of the statement won her over. "All right. I'll trust you." *That will make a nice saying to engrave on my tombstone: She trusted a Mage. But it's that or just give up.*

Between the lingering heat, her thirst, and exhaustion, Mari found herself drifting in and out of consciousness as they waited for it to get fully dark and the movements of the bandits to subside. At one point she saw her best friend Alli sitting nearby, fiddling with the broken rifle that Mari had left on the ledge with the dead bandits. She didn't seem to have changed in the two years since Mari had last seen her, aside from the fact that Alli was now wearing a Mechanics jacket like Mari's. *What are you doing here?* Mari silently asked Alli.

Fixing this rifle. You need it, right?

Yeah. If anyone can fix it, you can. You always loved weapons, Alli.

Weapons are way safer than boys, Mari. What are you doing here with one?

He's not a boy. He's a Mage.

He's a boy Mage, Mari. Why are you hanging out with him?

I have no idea. It must make sense somehow. Why didn't you write me more than a couple of times after I left the Mechanics Guild Hall in Caer Lyn? Why didn't you answer my letters?

But Alli didn't answer and when Mari roused herself enough to focus, she was gone.

Most of the bandits rode out just before sunset, many back to the east along the track the caravan had taken but some to the west toward Ringhmon. The pass, already murky with shadow, grew rapidly darker as the sun fell below the horizon.

"I will go now." Mage Alain's voice was cracked with dryness that sounded as bad as that which tormented Mari, but he moved surely as he crawled over the rock barrier and began heading downward.

Mari hitched herself up far enough to watch him for a while. She had been right in guessing that he was physically tough. Even after the exertions of the day and the lack of water, Mage Alain didn't seem weak now.

He also wasn't particularly hard to see in his Mage robes, even in the gathering darkness, but as the Mage reached the floor of the pass he vanished. She blinked, wondering if fatigue was affecting her eyesight, then slumped back down, half-delirious with thirst and hoping she had done the right thing by trusting the Mage.

He could be selling her out right now. Telling the bandits where she was in exchange for his life and enough water and food to reach Ringhmon by himself. *Who would be fool enough to trust a Mage? You, Mari. Not like you had any choice. But if he does try to sell me out, those scum won't take me easily. I can't run, but I can fight.*

Mari propped herself against the rocks so she could see down the slope, then drew her pistol. She lay there, trying to rouse herself occasionally to look for anyone coming up, but the slope stayed empty.

The weapon in her hand was a deadly thing, but in this case far overmatched by the numbers and firepower of the bandits. Using it even once would bring the bandits upon her.

The words that Professor S'san had spoken as she gave Mari the pistol remained engraved in her memory. *"This weapon I am giving you is a tool, an emergency tool. It is not to be depended upon as a first resort, or a second, or even a third. Your greatest assets will always be your mind and your ability to act on wise decisions. Fail to make proper use of those assets, and the weapon cannot save you. Remember that, Mari."*

Great advice, Professor. Just how do I use it now?

Mari turned the weapon, thinking that if she had simply fired when the Mage loomed out of the murk, she probably would have killed him. Then, when she fled, the bandits on the slope would have caught her or killed her. Thinking, instead of firing, had saved both of them, at least to this point. *What a strange tool this pistol is. Normally a tool exists to be used. But it's as if this one is best not used, unless absolutely no other option remains. I guess that is what Professor S'san meant. But if she gave it to me, she must have thought I might face that kind of situation. I really hope I never end up in that kind of mess.*

She had no idea how much time had passed when a dispassionate voice whispered, "Master Mechanic Mari." Mari blinked. The Mage had appeared close to the ledge. She hadn't seen him coming up, which was odd since the slope was so open. But he was back, and no bandits were with him, so she breathed a sigh of relief and holstered her weapon. Even through her daze, Mari couldn't help noting that the Mage had an easier time remembering her Master Mechanic rank than Senior Mechanics did.

Mage Alain slid over the top of the rocks, several bundles cradled in his arms. "The large water barrels have all been smashed, but some of the wagons were untouched as of yet, so I was able to get supplies from them." Opening one of the packs, the Mage pulled out several clay bottles and worked the cork free from one. "Here. Water."

Mari's hands trembled as she drank. It took all of her self-control to keep from gulping down the entire bottle at once. Finally she lowered the bottle, gasping for breath but feeling a tremendous sense of relief. "How can I ever repay you?"

"Repay?"

"You know," Mari said. But Mage Alain looked back at her as if he didn't know at all. "I'm in your debt," she said. "For the water. So I asked how I could pay you for it."

"Pay." The Mage shook his head. "That is a matter for elders to deal with."

"I wasn't talking about giving you money."

He eyed her with that unrevealing expression. "I have no use for money."

She felt a twinge of fear, and let her expression harden as she gazed back at him. "I hope you don't think you're going to get anything else from me."

Was that puzzlement in the Mage's eyes again? "I do not want anything from you. Why do you prepare to fight?"

Mari realized that one of hands was gripping her pistol. She let go of the weapon and forced herself to relax. "I— Sorry." That earned another blank look. "You don't know what 'sorry' means?"

The merest hint of a frown line appeared on the Mage's brow, as if he were struggling to remember something. "It is forbidden," he finally said.

"Forbidden," she repeated. "Why?"

The Mage shook his head. "The teachings of my Guild."

"Guild secrets?" Not too many hours ago she would have laughed, thinking that the only secret the Mage Guild had to keep was the fact that it was all a fraud. But she had seen some inexplicable things since then. "It has something to do with that heat you created?"

He gazed back at her silently, no trace of emotion visible.

"Guild secrets," Mari answered herself. "Fine. I understand that you can't talk about that. Whatever the reason is, I wasn't trying to insult you or hurt your feelings. 'How can I repay you' is just an expression, another way of saying thanks."

"Oh." The Mage sagged back against a rock. His expedition seemed to have exhausted him again, as if whatever he had done to stay hidden had cost him a lot of extra effort. "I am unused to different ways of... of saying thanks."

"I'd noticed," Mari said. "What's it like down there?"

"There are still some bandits present. I got close enough to overhear their conversation."

"I'm not sure I would've had the courage to do that," Mari admitted frankly. She saw a hint of surprise on Mage Alain's face, then a trace of embarrassment. *When the Mage gets tired, he doesn't hold his mask as well. Good. I prefer being with someone who acts at least a little human. Too bad being exhausted and getting out of this alive are mutually exclusive.*

Mage Alain pointed back down the way the caravan had come that morning. "They believe you must have stolen a mount from one of the guards and fled down the road. Most of them have pursued on their own mounts, feeling sure they will run you down by morning at the latest."

Mari inhaled deeply, trying to suppress a shudder. "They are after me. Did you hear why?"

"No."

"They didn't track us up the side of the pass, then? They didn't find where you had killed those three bandits?"

The Mage nodded. "Yes, they found that place. But since it was clearly the act of a Mage, and none of the weapons were taken, their leaders believe that is the way I fled. They believe I will soon die alone in the desert waste, and assume since I went that way no Mechanic would willingly have taken the same path."

She smiled at the chance that had misled her pursuers. "It wasn't entirely willingly, I have to admit. We were under some pressure."

"I do not understand why you keep saying 'we' or 'us' when you speak of you and I," Mage Alain said. "The two of us are together, but hardly companions."

Mari bent her head, resting her forehead on one hand and feeling incredibly weary now that her thirst had been dealt with. "I'm just being efficient. 'We' is a lot easier to say than 'you and I.' "

"I see."

"I wasn't being serious. I was using sarcasm."

"How can I tell when you are being serious?"

Mari raised her head to look at the Mage. "I start speaking in short sentences, my voice gets loud, and my face gets darker."

"I will remember that," Mage Alain answered with no emotion but apparently perfect sincerity.

Exhaustion, tension, the relief of getting water, the Mage's safe return, and the simple absurdity of it all finally got to her. Mari started laughing, holding her hand over her mouth to muffle the sound but unable to stop for a while. The Mage eyed her, waiting silently. "Sorry," Mari finally managed to gasp. "I just...what do *we* do from here? Do you think the road toward Ringhmon will be safe if those bandits are searching for me the other way?"

He thought about that, then shook his head. "I doubt the road will be safe. From what we know," he paused after the phrase and gave her a dispassionate look before continuing, "they have more than enough numbers to scour the road in both directions for you."

"Then what do we do? Strike out overland?" She waved at the rough terrain. "We could spend weeks trying to get through this, and unless I'm mistaken there's only a few days' worth of water here." Mari tapped the bottle closest to her. "You said you saw the caravan master's map? How far do we need to go to reach someone who can help?"

The Mage frowned very slightly, not to reveal emotion but in thought. "There were wells along the caravan route, but I cannot recall their locations. The first place where any were marked was, I would guess, about halfway from here to Ringhmon."

"We were supposed to be in Ringhmon in six more days. So, on foot, at least three or four days' travel to reach these wells?"

"I would say so. It could be as much as five days on foot. Along the road."

"And we have to avoid the road. Any ideas?"

Mage Alain shook his head. "Not right now. Why do you ask me my opinion? You are a Mechanic. I know Mechanics do not respect Mages."

Mari shrugged. "You seem to understand some of this stuff, things about fighting. You said you were taught about it. That kind of material wasn't part of my education. And...I like knowing what other people think. Even if they want me to make the decision, I want to have their input. I hate it when people make decisions about me without asking me about it, so I'm not going to do that to other people."

"Why not?"

Could that question possibly be sincere? "Because I want to treat them right."

"You speak of how to act toward shadows? They are nothing." She, too, was only a shadow, the Mage Guild's teachings told him. She, too, was nothing. But he felt a strange reluctance to say that to her again. "What is 'right'?"

She took a deep breath. "Look...I don't like being treated badly myself, and I don't enjoy treating other people badly. I tried being rough on people who were junior to me a couple of times when I was an apprentice, because that was expected of you when you got some seniority, and I really didn't like doing it, so I haven't since then. That's what I mean by treating people right."

Mage Alain spent a while thinking before he spoke again. "Why does that matter?"

"Because it does. To me." She wondered why she wasn't getting angry at the Mage's attitude, and realized it was because he appeared to be genuinely puzzled.

"This is how Mechanics think?"

Mari had to look down, biting her lip. She didn't want to admit the truth, not to a Mage, but it was a truth everyone on the world of Dematr already knew. "Not all of us. Many Mechanics treat common people badly, because...because the Guild says they don't matter."

He nodded. "I had not expected any wisdom from the Mechanics Guild."

"It's not wisdom! I don't think it's wisdom."

Mage Alain studied her, then nodded again. "You do not lie. You have not treated me badly, even though you are a Mechanic."

"Yeah...well..." Mari looked down, feeling embarrassed. "My instructors used to complain that I didn't listen to everything they told me."

"Even when they disciplined you?"

Mari paused before answering this time. Even though the Mage's robes covered most of his body, she had spotted the marks of scars on his hands and face. "I don't know what you mean by discipline, and I don't think I want to know. Life as a Mechanic apprentice can be pretty harsh, but I'm getting the feeling that you went through a lot worse."

"It was necessary," Mage Alain said.

"If you say so," Mari replied, not willing to debate the issue right now. "But getting back to your question, I ask your opinion because that's what I do, and you seem to be pretty level-headed even if you do believe crazy things."

"This was...praise." Mage Alain watched her intently. "From a Mechanic. Am I supposed to ask how I can ever repay you for saying that?"

She grinned even though her dry, cracked lips made the gesture painful. "That's up to you. Listen, we're both worn out. I can't think straight. Let's get some sleep and see how things look in the morning."

"Do you feel safe sleeping here?"

"I won't feel safe until I get inside the walls of the Mechanics Guild Hall in Ringhmon," Mari replied. "But for tonight, hopefully this is the last place those bandits will be looking for us."

She had closed her eyes before it occurred to her that the Mage might actually have been asking about whether she felt safe sleeping near him.

Was he being honest with her? Mages were notorious for their lies. And the way he implied that not revealing his feelings was somehow tied in with that heat thing felt ridiculous. She could build a machine that would create heat, and it wouldn't matter if she were frowning or smiling the entire time she was at work. Despite the jokes about machines mockingly refusing to work when they knew you needed them, engineering had nothing to do with feelings.

But he had done something. Somehow. A Mage had done something that she couldn't explain.

A Mage here with her. Her too exhausted to stay awake and alert for anything he might try. Bandits below, so that she dared not struggle or cry out if the Mage attacked her. Situations didn't get much uglier.

Her last thoughts as she passed out from fatigue were that if she had misjudged Mage Alain, if her decisions to trust him had been wrong, this night could get a lot worse.

CHAPTER FOUR

The dream came, as it usually did after a difficult day.

Eight-year-old Mari stood in the doorway of her family's home, staring at the Mechanics who had come for her. Her father protesting, her mother crying as the Mechanics led her away. *You did very well on the tests. You will be a Mechanic.*

The dream shifted, Mari watching the streets of Caer Lyn glide by as if she were floating down them. The city watch in chain mail and bearing short swords, common folk watching impotently as the Mechanics passed with Mari and one other child they had collected. Sailing ships crowded the harbor, their masts and spars forming a spiky forest that swayed slowly to the rhythm of the low swells undulating across the water. A single Mechanics Guild steamship headed out to sea, trailing smoke in a long, spreading plume. Then the Mechanics Guild Hall rising before her, the group passing through the gates into rooms where Mari gawked at her first sight of electric lights and the Mechanics carrying their strange weapons.

Another dream-shift, and young Mari was standing before the mail desk at the Guild Hall. She was taller, and wore an apprentice's uniform with the ease of someone accustomed to the trappings of the Mechanics Guild. On her sleeve was the mark of a second-year apprentice.

The retired Mechanic occupying the desk shook his head sadly, as he always had. *Still nothing for you, Apprentice Mari. The common folk do that, you know: you become a Mechanic and they can't accept that you're better than them. They've probably even forgotten that today's your birthday. They just leave you behind. Not like the Guild. We're your family now.*

They can do that to me, that younger Mari said, fighting back tears, *but I will never forget anyone. I will never leave anyone behind.*

On the desk a letter appeared, but as she grabbed it to look at the address she knew it wasn't for her.

Mari's eyes flew open to see the brassy blue morning sky above her. The familiar nightmare born of her memories faded into the waking nightmare of here and now. As her mind brushed aside the cobwebs of sleep, Mari remembered her last waking thoughts the night before and tensed. She looked down at her body. Her clothing hadn't been disturbed.

Cautiously turning her head, Mari saw that the Mage lay on the other side of the small ledge, as far from her as he could get, head concealed under the cowl of his robes. Just as his feelings lay concealed, she reflected. Maybe he had been as tired as she last night, too tired to act on any male cravings. Or maybe Mage Alain wasn't like all of the Mages she had heard about.

She lay still for a little while longer, trying to banish the last traces of the all too familiar dream and listening for any sounds from the caravan below them. Finally she fumbled for one of the water bottles, carefully removing the cork and drinking far less than she wanted before resealing it.

Her movements woke the Mage, who sat up gradually and squinted his eyes against the glare of the morning sun. He said nothing, getting water and drinking sparingly, then opening another pack to bring out trail food salvaged from the caravan. He handed some to Mari before taking a bit for himself.

Mari ate slowly, not feeling very hungry as she thought about her dilemma. Yesterday had left little time or energy for thinking, but in the harsh light of morning she was stuck in the desert with a Mage and had no idea how to reach safety. As Alli's hallucinatory presence had helpfully reminded her, male Mages were infamous for predatory behavior toward any female who took their fancy, and Alain was a male Mage and she was a female.

Still, last night had passed without incident. During the day he hadn't grabbed at her even when unsteady ground would have offered a convenient pretense. From what she had been told, Mages didn't even worry about giving excuses for that kind of behavior. But Mage Alain had done nothing to cause her alarm aside from being strange. Strange and dangerous was one thing. Strange and helpful was another. *I wonder if he thinks I'm strange? There would be plenty of Senior Mechanics, and more than one Mechanic instructor at the academy, who would agree with him on that count. The same Senior Mechanics and Mechanics who think all Mechanics should act the same and look the same and think the same.*

Give this guy a break, Mari. We can't be friends...wow, that was weird that I even thought of that...but even if every other Mage is scum, until Mage Alain gives me cause to think of him otherwise, and until we find help, I'll consider him an unusual ally.

Moving very carefully, she raised herself up to look over the rocks. Figures still walked about the remnants of the caravan, perhaps a half dozen by a quick count. There was no telling how many couldn't be seen, or might have gone off but still be within hearing range of a gunshot. Slumping back, she shook her head at Alain. "They haven't left yet."

He nodded. "I have an idea." After his silence so far this morning, the lack of any feeling in his voice sounded particularly jarring again.

But Mari gave him a brief smile anyway. "Good. That's one more idea than I have."

The Mage looked at her for a moment as if once again trying to understand her words. "I suggest we stay here through the day, resting as best we can. When night falls again we make our way down to the road and walk it toward Ringhmon. In the darkness, we should be as safe as possible if we remain alert."

"Yesterday you thought the road wouldn't be safe," Mari said. "What if those bandits are lying in wait for us along it?"

"We will be better able to escape or fight if it is dark. You have your Mechanic weapon and I have my spells, so we are not helpless. There will be some chance, anyway. The road will have its dangers, but I do not think we have any chance of survival at all if we try to go overland through these heights."

She rolled onto her back and gazed up at the sun-blasted rocks around them, remembering their painfully slow progress of the day before. "I hate to admit it, but you're right. That road is our only chance. Unless your Guild comes looking for you. Do you think they will?"

"No."

She should have guessed that. Mages didn't seem to waste much time on things like optimism, and any Guild that went to so much trouble to convince its members that nothing mattered wouldn't be highly motivated to care about one Mage whose caravan was overdue.

"What of your Guild?" Mage Alain asked.

"The Mechanics Guild Hall in Ringhmon will eventually send someone to find out what happened to me, but by the time they decided we'd be dead," Mari said. Wait the mandated period before marking someone overdue, fill out the proper paperwork, get it approved, get authorization to spend Guild funds on a search effort, and so on. The old joke claimed that you could die of old age while waiting for the Guild to officially approve your birth.

Mari looked up at the sky, nerving herself for what she knew she had to do. "All right, Mage Alain. These bandits are after me. Maybe we should split up, so you'll have a chance." He said nothing for a long moment. Mari looked over and saw the Mage gazing outward, his eyes unfocused. "Hello?"

The Mage drew a long breath, then shook his head. "I choose not to do that."

That had been the last thing she had expected. Why would a Mage choose to remain with a Mechanic when his chances would be much better without her? "Why not?"

"If all is an illusion," Mage Alain said in the slow manner of someone thinking through each word, "it would not matter what path I took. Therefore, I will stay with you."

"Gee, thanks, you sound so enthusiastic." Mari glared at him, trying not to show how scared she was at the idea of being alone out here with the bandits searching for her. "Listen, this is real."

"Nothing is real."

"Stars above! I'm trying to give you a better chance to survive. Take it, you blasted fool Mage. Yesterday, you came with me to survive. Today, you need to leave me to live. So *do it.*"

Mage Alain looked back at her without expression. "You are giving me orders, Master Mechanic Mari?"

"That would really be effective, wouldn't it?"

"No. It would not. Was that your sarcasm again?"

Mari gave an exasperated sigh. "You're as stubborn as I am. How old are you anyway?"

She saw him tense. "I am a Mage."

"No question. Not a doubt in my mind. So, how old are you, Mage Alain?"

She thought he wouldn't answer, but then Mage Alain met her eyes. "Seventeen."

"Really? Is it unusual for a Mage to be that young?"

His eyes searched hers for a moment, as if trying to determine her reason for asking, then the Mage nodded. "I must prove myself," he added.

"Oh." Mari sighed again, her anger at his stubbornness fading into guilty relief that he hadn't accepted her offer. "I know that feeling. I'm eighteen. Youngest Master Mechanic ever. I made Mechanic at sixteen. Unprecedented." She hated bragging, but her inability to mention what she had accomplished without seeming to boast had worn on her. At least when speaking to a Mage she could talk about it without anyone thinking she was trying to impress. "I passed every test. I know my job. But every Senior Mechanic I meet thinks I've been promoted way too fast."

"Many of my elders think that of me," Mage Alain said. "Perhaps they are right." He gestured toward the caravan's remains. "I did not succeed here, in my first test."

"Do you think any Mage, any person, could have saved that caravan?" Mari asked. "The people who attacked us had overwhelming force. The caravan never had a chance."

"But it was my responsibility to protect it. That was the contract."

She looked at him. "I thought you told me that Mages believe nothing matters. You just said that you would stay with me instead of going off alone and maybe living through this because it didn't matter."

"That is so."

"Then why does what happened to the caravan matter?"

Once again Mage Alain almost frowned, the merest creasing of his brow, but said nothing.

"Actually," Mari continued, "I agree that it does matter. But I also think you did the best anyone could've done. I mean that. You were willing to stand and die. What more can anyone ask?"

The Mage considered that, then met Mari's eyes again. "It matters because the commons must remain in fear of Mages, and failure by a Mage might cause the commons to feel less fear. As for asking, more can always be asked of someone."

Mari felt herself smiling at the irony of that last statement. "It sounds like whoever runs the Mage Guild has some things in common with the people running the Mechanics Guild." The Guilds were enemies. Hate wasn't too strong a word for the way Mechanics were taught to think of Mages. Yet she kept hearing things from this Mage that she could identify with.

Before she could say anything else, Mari heard the sound of a voice shouting below and felt a surge of fear.

The Mage peered over the rocks. "They are preparing to leave, I think. We were not overheard."

"It would probably be better if we kept quiet from now on, anyway."

He nodded, settling back and closing his eyes, seeming so calm that she couldn't doubt his earlier declarations of belief that nothing mattered. Mari watched him for a minute, wondering why she had felt an impulse to confide in a Mage of all people. It had been a long time since she had any friends she could talk to freely. Maybe the sun was making her tongue too loose. After all, what did it take to qualify as a Mage? She had been told it merely involved learning enough tricks to fool the commons. But that was wrong. Mage Alain had clearly been put through physical challenges far worse than those which Mari had faced, and there was that superheat thing he had done.

They can't really do anything, more than one Senior Mechanic had told her dismissively. No one had ever contradicted them.

Mari stared up at the sky, thinking. *I've been in Mechanics Guild Halls or the Academy at Palandur since I was barely eight years old. I haven't actually seen any Mages during that time except at long distance when I was out in Palandur with groups of other Apprentices or Mechanics. But if Mage Alain can do something like that heat thing, someone else must have seen other Mages do it. Some older Mechanics, who've been out in the world.*

Why does every Mechanic say Mages are only fakes?

Regardless of the answer to that, Mage Alain wasn't exactly a trusted co-worker. Whatever he had been through had obviously been brutal, but she couldn't give him back his humanity or his childhood. She would have to keep her thoughts to herself from now on, unless they were about reaching somewhere they could find help.

By the time the sun had hit its highest, turning their hiding place into a veritable oven, the last group of the bandits had departed, heading west toward Ringhmon. They had torched the last undestroyed wagons of the caravan, leaving thin columns of smoke spiraling into the air behind them as they rode off. Mari and the

Mage waited a while longer, despite the discomfort of their hiding place, but finally Mari decided that if she were going to die she would rather be killed by bandits down on the road than be broiled alive up on the ledge.

The climb down wasn't easy, even in full daylight. Mari examined the remains of the caravan and its former guards and drivers as best she could stomach, looking for anything else that might help them. But in the time since the Mage's search last night the bandits had done a thorough job of destroying and despoiling everything that was left.

She met Mage Alain again at the edge of the crater which marked where the first explosion had shattered the front of the caravan. Somebody had used a lot of explosives to produce a blast that powerful, and the Mechanics Guild charged plenty for explosives. This "bandit gang" had a great deal of money behind it.

If Mage Alain was right about what the bandits had said—and the lack of bullet holes in the ruin of her own wagon would seem to confirm his guess—they had spent all of that money and killed all of these people in order to get their hands on her.

Why?

Mage Alain shook his head as he looked down into the crater. "The caravan master did not escape. I believe a few guards may have made it out of the pass, fleeing east, but they could not have outrun the bandits."

"I'm sorry to hear that." Just common folk, her Mechanic training told her. Inferiors meant to serve Mechanics. They didn't matter.

Except that they did.

Rubbing the back of his neck, Mage Alain squinted into the distance. "It should not matter...they do not matter," he said, as if trying to convince himself, unknowingly using the same phrase which had come to Mari as she thought of her training.

Mari grimaced. "Can you think of any reason we shouldn't start walking west right now instead of waiting for nightfall?"

"No. We will not overtake mounted bandits unless they stop to watch for us, and if they do lie in wait, perhaps I can avenge those who died here." The lack of emotion in his voice matched that in his face.

But Mari thought she could see the anger smoldering deep in the Mage's eyes. She could have pointed out to Mage Alain that his desire for vengeance meant he did care about what had happened here, but she simply nodded and said nothing, feeling reassured that this Mage, at least, did think the fates of others mattered.

They walked westward until close to sunset, taking full advantage of any shade cast by the heights around the pass. Just before sunset they cleared the pass, coming to a point where the road zigzagged down a fairly steep slope before continuing in a long curve toward the northwest across desert flatlands which ran all the way to the horizon. Mari, wishing she had brought a far seer, gazed out over the panorama for any sign of the bandits, but except for a tiny cloud of dust far down the road saw nothing.

After eating a small amount of the trail rations and drinking as little water as they dared, they started down the slope, cutting across the back-and-forth twists of the road designed to accommodate wagons. That sped them up enough that they reached the bottomland before moonrise.

The road proved easy enough to follow in the moonlight. Mari tried to maintain a steady pace as they strode through the desert waste, the only sounds the soft crunch of their feet on the sand drifted across the road, their breathing, and the occasional faint sigh of a breeze that seemed as exhausted as the two humans trudging along the apparently endless road. She saw nothing moving, no living thing except her companion, but did hear the occasional rustle of some small creature nearby.

The stars were more brilliant than she had ever seen them, but Mari didn't dare look upward as she walked for fear of tripping and falling. Mechanics didn't look at the stars much, anyway, any such study being strongly discouraged even though officially the Mechanics were a separate and superior group who had come from those stars. No matter their origin—and most of the Mechanics Mari knew considered the story to be just a grandiose myth—Mechanics were taught to keep their eyes on the ground and their minds firmly focused on the only world there was: Dematr.

Mari was staggering with weariness by the time she noticed the sky to the east beginning to pale.

Mage Alain spoke with a voice deadened even more by fatigue. "We should rest during the day," he said. "We will not be able to keep moving like this in the sun's heat."

"I can't keep moving even if I wanted to," Mari said. "Do you see anything that might offer us any shade or protection?"

The Mage shook his head. They went on a bit longer, until the sun poked its head above the horizon. As their shadows stretched far off to the side, Mari spotted a slight depression a little ways off the road that offered the only trace of cover and waved Mage Alain toward it. "I will take the first watch," the Mage offered after they had drunk a little more of the water.

Mari nodded glumly. She shrugged off her pack, letting it fall with a sense of immense relief, then rolled onto her side to lie exhausted.

"You should remove your jacket," the Mage said. "Use it to shade your head."

She didn't want to remove her one sign of authority, her one piece of armor, though in both respects the jacket offered little right now. "I'm a Mechanic."

"I know that. Is there anyone around that you need to impress?"

Blasted Mage. Was she teaching him sarcasm? Rather than answer, she rolled to face the other way. The jacket felt like an already-warm burden, making it difficult to breathe. Mari counted to ten slowly, then without saying a word to the Mage awkwardly pulled off her jacket and tented it over her head, sighing involuntarily with relief.

Mage Alain wisely refrained from making any comment, and she fell asleep quickly, overcome with fatigue.

Mari awoke feeling dizzy and disoriented from the heat. Pushing the jacket off her head, she managed to sit up, blinking against the glare of the sun. The Mage had collapsed on the other side of the depression, his face hidden by the cowl of his robes. Mari plucked at her shirt, which was once again plastered to her skin by sweat. *I'll have to put my jacket back on when Mage Alain wakes up. I don't want him seeing as much of me as he could with my shirt this wet. A Mage leering at me...that's just too disgusting to think about.*

That's not fair. This Mage has been perfectly decent with me.

But sorry, Mage Alain. Even you don't get to check me out with my shirt stuck to me like this.

She took a small drink, then lay down again, her back to the Mage and her jacket spread over her head and upper body.

✳   ✳   ✳

Mage Alain roused her again at sunset. She stared up at him, thinking that she ought to be panicking at having a Mage looming over her like that while she was lying down, but she couldn't hold to any thought except for wondering why his face kept swimming in and out of focus.

"Drink," Mage Alain ordered. She drank one mouthful. "More. The whole bottle."

The small amount of water she had drunk had revived her enough to think again. "We need that water."

"We will not survive the night unless we drink more."

She wanted to argue that but felt the truth of the statement in her body's weakness. Reluctantly, Mari drank the bottle down. The Mage discarded it, then examined their remaining supply and shook his head. "Can you walk now?"

"Give me a little while." Mari wondered if he would wait, or head off to take his own chances alone.

But Mage Alain sat down a lance-length from her. "You waited for me to rest when we escaped the ambush," he said, as if knowing her thoughts.

"I'd never been told that Mages believe in paying back debts."

"Mages do not believe in that. Mages believe in—"

"Nothing. I know. Thanks anyway." After resting some more, Mari stood carefully. "All right. I can move."

"We have three bottles of water left."

Mari felt fear as a far-off thing now, dulled by pain and tiredness and a thirst that the bottle she had drunk had done too little to satisfy. "How long can we make it last?"

"I think we should each drink another bottle tonight, then split the remaining one tomorrow."

At least Mage Alain had stopped asking why she wanted his opinion. "And if we don't reach a well or some help by tomorrow night?"

The Mage stared stoically at the ground. "I do not think we have any choice but to risk it."

Mari rubbed her eyes, wishing they didn't feel so dry and gritty. "I never expected to agree with a Mage on anything, but it's been happening a lot lately. Let's do what you suggested." She struggled to her feet, then barely managed to get her pack up and onto her back, the Mage watching impassively until she was done.

They started walking, saying nothing more. Mari wondered if their mutual silence was just to conserve energy or if the half-companionship of their ordeal was finally coming to its inevitable end. Mages and Mechanics didn't mix any more than oil and water did. Everybody said that. And yet she knew so little about Mages. Where did they come from? "Mage Alain."

"Yes, Master Mechanic Mari."

"Were you always a Mage?"

His reply took a moment. "I served as an acolyte before becoming a Mage."

"What I mean is, were you born in a Mage Guild Hall? Were your parents Mages?"

"No."

The single word came out like a slamming door, carrying more emotional force than anything Mari had heard from the Mage before this. "Sorry." He obviously didn't want to talk about his parents, and she certainly didn't want to talk about hers. But something else had been bothering her. "You know what people say about Mages, right? That Mages will do or say anything they want and not care who they hurt?"

His reply was as impassive as ever. "There is no truth, there are no others to hurt, and pain itself is an illusion."

"And you really do believe that?"

"Yes."

"Then why didn't you walk off while I was asleep, taking all the water? Why didn't you attack me while I was asleep?"

The Mage took a long time to reply. "I do not know."

"I assume both of those options occurred to you," Mari pressed.

In the darkness, she could barely make out the glance he gave her. "I know I could have tried taking the water. I did not consider it a choice I would make. As for the other..." His voice trailed off, then the Mage simply said one word more. "No."

"Well, thank you." That seemed an odd thing to say to someone who had just denied having any thought of physical assault on her, but no other words occurred to Mari. "Were you taught not to do things like that?"

"I was taught that such actions would have been acceptable."

Mari stared at the desert passing beneath her feet. "To be perfectly honest, Sir Mage, so was I. If I came back to my Guild and reported that I had shot a Mage and taken his water so I could survive in the waste, no one would criticize me at all."

"My Guild would do the same if I reported having killed you," Alain replied. After another moment, he spoke slowly. "I was taught that others do not matter and do not exist, but no elder ever told me that Mechanics were taught the same."

"In some ways." It hurt to admit that, but Mari felt she owed it to the Mage to be honest with him. "Other Mechanics count, but common folk and Mages don't matter. Even though Mechanics think those people are real like us, we're not supposed to care about their feelings or anything else. They're just here to do whatever we tell them to do."

"But you do not follow your Guild's teachings? And your Guild accepts this?"

Mari snorted a sad laugh. "Let's just say that my Guild and I haven't always seen eye to eye on things. How does your Guild feel about Mages who don't follow Guild teachings?"

He took a moment to reply. "Mages must follow the dictates of our elders."

"I'm glad you didn't follow their dictates concerning me," Mari remarked. "I promise not to tell your elders."

Mage Alain gave her one of the those looks, not revealing much but conveying confusion nonetheless. "My elders would not speak with you."

"I know. I was just... Never mind. I'm glad that I didn't do what Senior Mechanics in my Guild would have expected me to do when I met you. Just because you're taught something doesn't mean you have to accept every word of it. Unless it's technical stuff, like operating instructions. Those you have to follow very closely. But that's different."

He didn't answer, and she wondered if the Mage were ignoring her, or if he was thinking about what she had said. But she was too tired to try to draw him out again, so Mari focused on putting one foot in front of the other.

The night wore on, her pack seeming to be getting heavier with every step, and Mari began feeling an irrational resentment of the much lighter load of their remaining food and water that the Mage was carrying. She knew it was irrational: no Mechanic would entrust her tools to a Mage, and Mages were as notorious for their pride as Mechanics were. She couldn't ask him to carry her pack, and he would never agree to even if she did.

But she was also feeling a gradual building of fear again as the stars wheeled overhead in the slow ballet they had followed for countless years. Being eighteen allowed her to recover relatively quickly from tiredness, but even a young body had only so much to give. Mari could sense her final reserves of endurance draining down to exhaustion. The night still stretched unrelieved by signs of human presence in any direction. The sky remained clear, bringing a desert chill at night but promising another brutal day of sun hammering at them.

I'll carry your pack, Calu offered.

Mari shook her head, not looking to the side where Calu's image paced her. *I can handle it.*

You never let anyone help, Mari, Calu scolded her. Even though he was wearing a Mechanic's jacket, he seemed perfectly comfortable. *You were always like that when we were apprentices. You don't have to do everything yourself.*

Then why do people keep asking me what to do? Why, whenever there's a problem, do lots of apprentices and Mechanics look to me? I'm going to die out here, and there's no one I can ask what to do.

You've got that Mage, Calu suggested. *You can't trust him, though.*

I know! We had our last full bottles around midnight, and now there's only one left to split between us. What if the Mage lied to me? What if there's more than one bottle? What if he's been sneaking extra drinks from that bottle all along? What if this Mage is just planning on walking me to death and then continuing on with all his hidden bottles of water until he reaches safety?

She was on the verge of spinning around to confront the Mage with her suspicions when Mari caught herself. Calu wasn't walking beside her. No one was. *I'm getting delirious.* "We'd better have another drink of water," she croaked.

"That is probably necessary." Mage Alain sounded as weary and dry as she felt. But he pulled out the last bottle and offered it to her. "Take it."

She drank slowly, hoping the moisture would soak into the lining of her throat on the way down, but stopped herself when the bottle was still about half full. "Here. The rest is yours."

"No. You have the rest."

Her suspicions flared again, then Mari took a close look at the Mage's face and the obviously empty pack in which the water bottles had been carried. "You're in as bad a shape as I am. Take your share."

"There is not enough for two. It does not matter. This is just a dream."

"No!" Mari shoved the bottle into his hands, anger and frustration giving her a little extra strength. "I already told you that I'm not going to abandon anyone if I can help it. There's no way I'll let you die for me!"

"I will do what I will," he responded with a deathly calm.

"Drink it!"

"No Mechanic can give me orders."

"Do what you want, then, but I won't drink that water!" She turned to walk onward, torn between anger at his stubbornness and distress at the Mage's inexplicable willingness to sacrifice for someone else. "Just drink your share and let's go." Not waiting for him to answer, Mari took a step.

Then paused.

The Mage took a couple of steps to stand beside her. "What is wrong?"

"Listen." They did, and the sound she had heard gradually became clearer. The clop of shod horse hooves on the packed surface of the road they were following, coming slowly closer from behind. "Is it the bandits?" Mari whispered.

Mage Alain reached out to grab her arm and push her into motion. Mari followed him off the road a short distance, where they lay down to watch. She yanked her pistol from its shoulder holster, checked the clip of ammunition, pulled back the slide to load a round and clicked off the safety. She noticed that the Mage watched her actions with uncomprehending eyes.

As the sound of hooves grew closer it became apparent that there were a lot of horses approaching, moving at a slow and steady pace that could be maintained for hours. It took a long time for the horses trudging along the road to reach them, a long time spent staring into the darkness and wondering if the end would come quickly after all at the hands of bandits instead of gradually as her body failed in the heat. But if they avoided being spotted by the riders on the road, then they would be overcome by the heat before the next day ended.

We'll die either way. Those people on the road are our only chance to live, if they're not bandits. She made a decision, and as the riders came near, their shapes hard to see clearly in the dark, Mari stood up and took a few wobbly steps forward, leveling her pistol at the figures on horseback. "On the road!" Mari called in a dried-out voice that nonetheless seemed to echo across the silent land. Worried that she might sound like an exhausted and frightened girl, Mari put every ounce of Mechanic command that she could muster into the words she spoke. "Halt in the name of the Mechanics Guild!"

CHAPTER FIVE

Alain did not know whether Master Mechanic Mari had made a conscious decision to die quickly or had simply begun hallucinating. He had noticed a couple of times when she seemed to be carrying on conversations with others who were not present, but given his own experiences with physical stress Alain did not hold that against her.

However, this time when she acted he had no choice but to rise and stand near her. If he still allowed himself emotions, Alain would be very unhappy with this Mechanic. Even though he had been surprised that she had kept asking his opinion, he had already become used to it, making her sudden action doubly annoying. As worn out as he was, Alain had no idea what kind of spells he could manage right now, but he felt certain they would not be sufficient to deal with the number of riders he could see. If Mechanic Mari valued his opinion so much, why had she decided to enter into a fight to the death without at least saying something to him beforehand?

She was a Mechanic, so it been foolish of him to expect her to act wisely. But she had seemed to be wiser than to confront so large a threat with her one weapon.

The riders had come to a halt, faces turned toward Alain and the Mechanic. For a moment, the only sound came from the small movements of the horses shifting restlessly on the road. Alain noticed

Mechanic Mari's extended arm wavered noticeably, but her weapon stayed aimed toward the road.

One of the riders dismounted, using slow, cautious motions, and came toward them, his hands held out in the universal symbol of parley.

The rider stopped a few paces from them, staring at the Mechanic. "What do you wish with us, Lady Mechanic?" His robes were well suited to the waste, similar to those the bandits had worn, but this man was unarmed except for a knife at his belt. The man looked over at Alain and jerked in surprise. "And...a Mage?"

Alain took a careful step forward, determined not to reveal his own weakened state. "I am a Mage."

The riders on the road began muttering among themselves, plainly startled to find such a pair confronting them. The Mechanic made a sweeping gesture with the hand that wasn't holding her weapon. "I... we require transport to Ringhmon, or to a place where such transport can be found."

The man before them raised one hand to stroke his beard. "Lady Mechanic, how came you to be here?"

"That is none of your business," she responded.

The riders would not have heard the fear under her authoritative words, but Alain did. Mechanic Mari was creating an illusion of her own, acting like any other arrogant and high-handed Mechanic. Why had she adopted that illusion?

He understood almost as soon the question formed. Facing these numbers, isolated from the support of her Guild, she sought to dominate these riders to ensure her safety. Seen in that light, the tactic had merit.

But it would be to their own benefit if these riders were alerted to the danger from the bandits. Alain spoke up, keeping any feeling from his voice as he recited events which threatened to bring emotions back to life within him. "The caravan we were traveling in was attacked and destroyed at Throat Cut Pass ."

His emotionless tone of voice made the disaster sound no more consequential than a stop to repair a broken wheel, but the words were clear enough. More murmuring came from the riders, this time sounding alarmed. "Destroyed? Did the caravan have no guards, Sir Mage?" the man in front of them asked.

"It had a complement of guards," Alain replied. "The bandits who attacked were numerous and had many powerful weapons. Only the Mechanic and I escaped."

The man's voice sounded troubled. "We are traders, heading to Ringhmon ourselves from the salt fields which lie near the mountains to the south. We want no part of bandits, yet we cannot afford to return home to avoid them."

Alain deigned to gesture with one hand. "Give us the transport we require to Ringhmon, and the Mechanic and I will be with you to give you protection. She has her weapon, and I have my spells." Taking a deliberate risk, he caused heat to form above his hand, the air glowing there in the dark, then cut the spell before the effort could stagger him.

"I mean no disrespect, but I am responsible for the safety of all who follow me, and you ask me to risk them on the word of a Mage?" the man asked, his voice doubtful but also tremulous at having to ask.

"You have the word of a *Mechanic*," Mari snapped, her own voice still domineering. "Does that suit you, trader?"

Alain was surprised to see how good the Mechanic was at intimidating people when she tried, and wondered why she had never tried to do that with him. Perhaps she had thought it would not work on a Mage, or perhaps just not on him in particular. But then, he still knew very little about her, and her current behavior revealed that Mechanic Mari could present different fronts to the world. Had he seen the true version these last few days, or an image meant to mislead him? Now that they were once again among others, even though these others were just commons, Alain felt his training about Mechanics, their deceit and the danger they posed, coming once more to the forefront.

The trader bowed deeply toward them. "I am honored to accept the gracious offer of the Lady Mechanic and the Sir Mage. Please, Sir Mage and Lady Mechanic," he quickly added, changing the precedence in which he mentioned them this time so that each had shared first billing, "be so kind as to allow me to give you transportation to either Ringhmon or such other place short of Ringhmon as you desire." In the dark, his face couldn't be seen, but his voice was humble enough.

"We—" Mechanic Mari bit off the words, then spoke again with more deliberation. "I accept your offer."

"I will accompany you," Alain said.

There it was. Had she realized it first, or had he? They were no longer "we." Once again they were separate from each other.

Alain and Mechanic Mari followed the trader as he led them back to the road. Two of the riders dismounted, one giving his horse to Alain and the other to the Mechanic before walking back to hoist themselves onto spare horses without saddles. The Mechanic, her pack weighing her down, eyed the saddle grimly, then heaved herself up and managed to settle herself. Alain, impressed by her obstinate resolve, mounted his own steed. Her determination reflected that of the shadow he had accompanied to this point, so perhaps he had indeed seen her as she was during their time together. Mechanic Mari's refusal to give in or admit to personal weakness had a Magelike quality to it that he could recognize and accept. Did Mechanics during their training endure the same sort of ordeals that Mages did?

Earlier in the night he could have asked her that, even though such curiosity would have been frowned upon by his elders. But not now. Alain did not think he would speak to any Mechanic ever again.

Even through his fatigue, he felt an odd sense of disappointment as that realization struck home.

The leader of the traders waited until sure they were settled, then urged the column back into motion. Alain's mount did not need guidance, staying with the group as it plodded along under the night sky. He felt an overwhelming urge to sleep but fought it off, knowing he might fall out of the saddle since he was not accustomed to riding. Alain could see the Mechanic's head drooping and then jerking up repeatedly as she fought the same battle.

He could endure, though. Alain did not feel pride in that. As with so much else, it simply was what it was, the product of the merciless training he had survived.

The road continued to arrow through the night, the desert beyond still and empty, but Alain could see in his mind's eye a clear vision of the courtyard at the Mage Guild Hall where he had first been taken to be an acolyte. Children stood in ranks that first day, young Alain among them, shivering in the cold, eyes on the blank wall of one side of the court as the sun rose, peaked, then fell. One by one the children fell, too, dropping from exhaustion as Mages walked among them reciting wisdom. *The pain is not real. The cold is not real. You feel nothing. There is nothing but you, and you must overcome and control the illusion which surrounds you.*

The young girl Asha had been near him, and when she sagged to the ground he had caught her without thinking. He had "helped" her. The elders had been unhappy. *She does not matter. You have erred. She is nothing.* The punishment had been bad enough that Alain and everyone else had learned not to "help" others. Over time they had learned never to use the word at all, to forget the very idea.

Those experiences and many other lessons had given him the ability to change the world illusion, to be a Mage. He had stopped questioning that a long time ago. Of course the powers of a Mage were worth any sacrifice. The elders had drilled that into them all.

But a chink had developed in that armor because of the words and actions of the Mechanic. If he had been with another Mage, he would not have spoken to the Mechanic Mari. He would not have remembered what "help" meant.

Surely the helping he had done was wrong, even though right and wrong did not exist. Then why, even now, did helping the Mechanic not feel wrong?

The last time he had seen Asha, as he left the Guild Hall a full Mage, they had gazed at each other without feeling and said nothing. That was right, how things should be. And yet...

Why did wrong now seem right, and right seem wrong?

The Mechanic had done this to him somehow. That must be the true threat that Mechanics represented. Why had the elders not been clearer about that danger?

As the sun rose again, the leader finally called a halt. Alain dismounted stiffly, then noticed the Mechanic still in her saddle, her face drawn with exhaustion, and guessed she was afraid to dismount because of the likelihood her pack would cause her to fall. Her pride mattered a great deal to her. She did not wish to appear weak, or too young, in front of these common people.

Alain realized that he knew exactly how she felt. Not only did he know a feeling, but he knew that a shadow was experiencing the same feeling. It was a strange moment, a strange sense of connection which he tried to suppress.

Lost in that internal struggle, he did not realize that he was walking toward the Mechanic's horse until he came to a stop beside it. She looked down at him, her face slack with weariness, her eyes desperate but determined as well. Nothing lay hidden there. This was her. She knew what she faced but she would not surrender to it.

Leave her. She is nothing. But as if it were acting on its own, Alain's hand rose to grasp the horse's bridle. Then his other hand reached up and stopped at shoulder height, open before the Mechanic.

Staring at him, she swung one leg over the saddle, gripped his offered hand and almost fell anyway as she dismounted.

The Mechanic managed to keep her feet, releasing his hand the instant she could stand without the support.

They looked at each other, Alain very aware of the commons about them. He suspected the Mechanic also felt that. After a long, silent moment, she nodded wordlessly to him, then turned away.

The traders were setting up small triangles of cloth to serve as individual sun screens through the day. As the sky brightened, Alain saw them herding the horses into one area and hobbling them, then herding together the mules from the back of the column, removing from each mule the pack frames carrying slabs of salt. Within a very short time camp had been made.

The lead trader came over to Alain and indicated one of the sun shields. "For you, Sir Mage." He then offered Alain water, salt and bread. "It is all we have."

"It is enough," Alain answered, then watched as the trader went to the Mechanic and showed her to a sun shield on the other side of the camp. The trader had assumed they would not want to be anywhere near each other, and that was indeed how it should be.

How had she made him help her to dismount? Did Mechanics have other powers that did not involve their weapons?

The one great art that escaped Mages was the ability to do something directly to another person. Even though others were shadows, mere illusions, no Mage could change anything in someone else. Alain could heat the air about someone and burn them that way, but he could not heat that person's body until it exploded. The elders had told him that this was because no Mage had yet achieved a perfect state of understanding that all else was false.

Could the Mechanics do such a thing? Had this Mechanic reached into him and changed him somehow? Surely he would have been warned if Mechanics could do that. Unless this one Mechanic was somehow special...

If she meant him ill, why had she saved his life? Even if Mechanic Mari had been a Mage, Alain was sure he would have been able to detect some measure of deceit in the times they had spoken. Instead, her feelings were always clear to read, even if sometimes impossible to understand. There had been no lies there. Was even she unaware of the powers she possessed to manipulate others?

Nothing could be certain except the need to avoid her from now on. Mechanic Mari...no, he must think of her as just the Mechanic from now on...and they must once again behave as strangers. He must refocus on his training and forget her strange influence.

But as the Mechanic lay down under her sun screen, separated slightly from those of the traders as well as that of the Mage, Alain's gaze lingered on her for a moment. It was then that he saw something else, a strange image floating directly over the Mechanic so that she seemed a part of the vision. A second sun glowed in the sky there, storm clouds raging against it, seeking to block its rays. The storm surged against the second sun, trying to eclipse it with darkness, the roiling clouds taking the form of armies and mobs of unarmed people clashing, the dead falling in huge numbers. He felt a terrible sense of urgency, as if the vision were calling him to action, but as Alain gazed in disbelief the image faded, leaving only normal sky unmarked by visions and the Mechanic. But an echo of the urgent summons remained.

More foresight? Three times now I have experienced foresight, and each time differently. What does it mean? This time the Mechanic was clearly involved.

The second time, when I heard a warning of danger waiting for her in Ringhmon, she recognized the threat though she would not admit that to me.

At least the first time, my foresight warned of danger to me, not to her.

Except that we were together then. The warning might have been for either of us. But this...this spoke of some greater danger. Something far beyond either her or me.

Why? Who is this girl, this Mechanic? If she is a threat to my powers, then why does my foresight keep speaking for her? Why does it not warn me of her? She saved me, yes, but I am a Mage: her actions mean nothing, she is nothing, she is a shadow. What is this vision calling me to do? Once we reach Ringhmon I will surely never see the Mechanic again.

That thought brought a strange pang to Alain. He did not

understand it. All he could do was fall back on his Mage training, to deny anything that might deceive him.

Foresight will lead me astray. This Mechanic will lead me astray. I must reject both.

But he could not shake thoughts of that awful storm from his mind, the sense that it loomed near and held great peril.

Four days later the horses and mules of the salt traders finally trudged through the gates of Ringhmon. Alain watched listless crowds of people entering and leaving the city, their faces somehow as faded as the colors of their clothes. The only individuals who appeared fully alive were the gate guards, who stood watch in numbers large enough to protect the grandiose entry from the advance elements of an Imperial legion. Even more unusual, one of them openly displayed a Mechanic weapon, as if that extra intimidation were needed. Alain, who before the attack on the caravan probably would not have noticed the odd weapon, now gave it a side glance, unable to tell if it was the same as the bandit weapon the Mechanic had shown him.

He looked over, seeing the Mechanic dismounting clumsily. She looked his way, their eyes meeting for a moment. They hadn't exchanged any words since joining the traders, which was how it should be between Mechanic and Mage, and had not even exchanged glances since that first morning. But now, despite his resolve to be quit of her, Alain nodded a wordless farewell, keeping his face blank of emotion as a Mage should, and she nodded back with a similar lack of expression. Then she was turning away and he did the same.

The Mage Guild Hall of Ringhmon lay a fair distance from the caravansary, but after days of riding and being given adequate food and water by the traders, Alain was grateful for the chance to stretch his legs. He walked steadily through Ringhmon, the commons shying away from him to leave a clear path. The commons feared Mages.

None of them would knowingly block the progress of any Mage. They averted their faces as well, fearing what a Mage might do to them if eye contact was made. He might now be walking down a crowded street, but he was still alone.

A few times Alain noticed girls on the street ahead being hastily shoved through doorways or otherwise removed from where he might see them. He knew the reason for that. The elders had advised him and the other acolytes to satisfy their physical needs on commons, who would not dare to resist. He had never done that and never would, because any thought of it brought to mind the mother he could no longer admit any feelings for.

She would not have approved. Though he could remember little of her, that impression remained strong. *And I remain her son, though I can never admit that to any other Mage. I could not admit to the Mechanic my reason for not assaulting her. I cannot even admit it to myself.*

Finally the blank, windowless face of the Mage Hall loomed before him. Only a doorway marred that façade, the one begrudging acknowledgement that a world did exist outside. The massive hall occupied the center of a large lot, wide expanses of gravel separating it from any other structure on all sides.

Alain knew there would be no lock on the doorway, for who would dare to enter a Mage Hall except a Mage or someone needing their services? Inside, an acolyte sat in meditative stance but yanked herself awake at Alain's arrival. "Sir Mage." Her eyes went from his robes to his young face, and it was obvious her training at not showing emotions was being stressed.

"I am Mage Alain of Ihris," he said, sensing a dark burden inside now that he had to report his failure. "I have just arrived in Ringhmon. I must report to the elders on the outcome of my contract."

"Yes, Sir Mage." She led the way deeper into the Hall, through dim passages whose coolness was a welcome relief after the bright, scorching heat of the lands around Ringhmon. Bowing him into a room almost bare of furnishings, as were most rooms in the Hall, she left to return to the entrance.

Despite his well-buried worries about the way his report would be received, still Alain welcomed being safe inside the walls of Ringhmon after spending days on constant lookout for bandits. A middle-aged Mage assigned to receive new arrivals greeted Alain without any meaningless courtesy or trace of suppressed surprise at his youth, and then took down his report. Alain, reciting without outward feeling the destruction of the caravan he had been contracted to protect, found himself grateful that the other Mage did not display any emotion.

But even the experienced Mage facing him had trouble keeping his expression controlled when Alain laid out his escape with the Mechanic and their journey together through the waste.

By the time Alain's report had been completed to the satisfaction of the record keeper, the sun was setting over Ringhmon. Alain picked out a small guest room to sleep in, cleaned up quickly in the cold water offered at the rudimentary bath facilities, then got some food. Unseasoned boiled meat. Plain boiled grain. Bread. A mash of fruits and vegetables using whatever was available. Watered wine. A meal designed to feed the body but not to distract the senses, just like every other meal in a Mage Guild Hall.

No other Mages took notice of him, but that was to be expected. For any other Mage to greet him without purpose would have been a shocking act. Returning to his room after a silent meal, Alain found that acolytes had already cleaned his robes. Feeling physically drained and disturbed by the tugging of emotions once safely buried deep within him, Alain lay down to his first decent sleep in too many days.

But though he closed his eyes, his mind stayed awake, perversely dredging up memories long suppressed. He would not think on the separation from his parents, but the first night at the Mage Guild Hall stood out clearly. So many things had changed after that. He had clung to the details until realizing how they were misleading him, but now they were with him again.

A room full of young children, many of them with eyes red from crying, their clothing replaced by the thin, unadorned robes of acolytes. The children, Alain among them, shivered in the cold room, not yet having learned to ignore physical discomfort. Each child sat or lay on a sleeping pallet which was little more than a threadbare blanket on the stone floor. Next to each pallet rested a loaf of stale bread and a cup of water.

A very pretty girl on the next pallet looked at Alain, trying to force a smile despite the tear-stains on her face. Her blond hair was tangled and uncombed. *"At least we know they don't want us to die,"* she had said in a hoarse voice as she picked up her bread. She had brushed some strands of hair from her face, looking very weary. *"Did you want to be a Mage?"*

"No. Did you?"

"No. We don't have any choice, though. I have an uncle who is already a Mage. If he could survive this, I can."

"I'm not sure I will." Even across the years, Alain could remember the despair which had filled him then.

The girl had forced another smile. *"You'll make it."*

"Thanks." That was when he had last said that word. *"You'll make it, too."*

"I'm Asha."

"I'm Alain."

Two Mages had entered the room then, watching everyone, their presence making every child fall silent even before one of them spoke. *"You are alone. Do not speak to shadows."*

The Mages had still been there, watching the shivering, silent acolytes, when Alain finally fell asleep that night.

He and Asha had spoken only a few times after that, growing distant first from fear of the Mage elders and later from knowledge that neither mattered, that nothing was real.

Now Alain kept his eyes closed, but he could still see the acolytes' room, still recall something of what he had felt that night. The long suppressed memories were troubling him again.

This, too, must be the work of the Mechanic. What had she done to him?

✳   ✳   ✳

As their horses plodded into Ringhmon, Mari studied the Mechanic weapon openly carried by one of the guards they passed, seeing that it was another standard model repeating rifle. The arms workshops in Danalee had found more than one customer in the area of Ringhmon, it seemed. It was unusual for such a valuable weapon to be entrusted to gate guards, leaving Mari wondering who Ringhmon was trying to overawe. From the subdued behavior of the commons using the gate, she guessed they might be the targets of that threatening display.

Mari searched the crowd around the caravansary, hoping to find a representative of the Mechanics Guild Hall of Ringhmon awaiting her. She saw no one, though. She had not had any privacy once they got close to Ringhmon and so had not been able to call ahead using her far talker. Still, she was overdue. Why hadn't the Guild Hall tried to call her? Why hadn't they posted anyone here, even an apprentice, to watch incoming travelers and demand any news of the late caravan?

The group of traders clattered to a halt and Mari dismounted, wincing as her muscles protested. Her horse had been docile enough, but days of riding had left Mari wondering if her thighs would ever stop aching. *Give me a seat in a locomotive any day.*

She glanced across the caravansary and her eyes met those of the Mage. What was he thinking now? No telling. Not her problem, she told herself. But he had saved her life, and even helped her dismount the first morning as if he had known how important it was to her dignity not to fall, so Mari wished him well. She gave the Mage a brief nod, then turned away.

She took leave of the head of the traders, getting his name so that she could arrange payment for him, and received in return directions to the Mechanics Guild Hall. Hoisting her pack into a slightly more comfortable position, she started walking, her Mechanics jacket earning her easy progress through the streets. Citizens of Ringhmon stepped aside to give her room, eyeing Mari nervously and bowing as she passed, radiating resentment yet also acting more servile than commons usually did even in the Empire.

The buildings around her appeared grand enough, if you didn't look too closely beyond the façades. Mari's engineering specialty wasn't architecture or construction, but she knew enough of both fields to judge the buildings around her. All of them boasted features intended to make them look grander, such as dozens of roof angles on a single structure, but the work was shoddy, with cracks and sagging easily visible. Mari wondered why the local Guild Hall hadn't contracted the design and building of some truly impressive structures. That would have cost Ringhmon more money than these false fronts, though, and that might be all the answer she needed.

The crowds got thicker, so Mari set her jaw and plowed through them, the commons hastily clearing the way and keeping their grumbling just low enough that she couldn't decipher it. She was used to that. Imperial citizens were particularly good at acting respectfully to the face of the Mechanics, who dictated even to the Emperor. But a quick enough turn would reveal the citizens at your back showing their true feelings.

Mari kept her face impassive so no trace of her own unhappiness could be seen. Mechanics were superior, they could fix and design and build things that the commons couldn't. They used that power to dominate the commons everywhere. The commons helped, naturally. Whenever one group tried to rise up, another group could always be found willing to fight against them in exchange for some brief advantage. Hand out fifty rifles or so and enough ammunition, let the commons kill each other, and the Mechanics Guild remained in control. Since the Mechanics Guild liked that arrangement, it did everything it could to make sure nothing changed.

Century after century, the world kept unchanging.

If you were a Mechanic, if you were a cynic, if you liked that power, it was a great system.

Sweating in the heat, Mari paused at the top of a hill to catch her breath and gazed backwards to see the view. The afternoon was well along, the sun sinking toward a dust-hazed horizon that brought out a glory of red hues in the sky. Under that display, the "great" city of Ringhmon didn't look quite as seedy. Far off, Mari could just make out the shape of a Mechanic locomotive belching smoke as it pulled into the city, coming from the west along the ancient rail line running to the Bakre Confederation. For a moment she wished she was on that locomotive, that she had never gone to the Guild academy but had just become a regular Mechanic on steam powered equipment. That she never noticed the looks on the faces of the commons when they didn't think a Mechanic could see them. That she didn't question the way things were and had always been.

That would have meant giving up, though, settling for less than her heart told her she should aim for.

Turning to continue on toward the Guild Hall, Mari froze in her tracks. A small group of riders wearing frighteningly familiar garments was riding up the street, their horses and clothes coated with dust. One of the riders carried a repeating rifle. Another was in the act of turning to look her way.

CHAPTER SIX

Her heart pounding, Mari spun on one heel and dodged into the nearest shop. A few citizens of Ringhmon browsing among the racks of clothing pretended to be engrossed in their shopping as the owner came bustling up and bowed. "How may I help you, honored Lady Mechanic?"

Mari calmed herself before answering. "I just came in for a moment to get out of the sun."

The owner backed away, head down to hide his expression. Mari turned and gazed out the small front window of the shop, searching for the bandits in the crowded street. Seeing nothing, she reached under her jacket toward her pistol, then cautiously edged to the door again.

The street held no sign of dusty riders now. Mari scowled around her while the passing commons tried to ignore a plainly unhappy Mechanic. Turning, Mari walked back into the shop. "Do you have a private room in the back?" she demanded as the owner hastened up again.

"Yes, Lady Mechanic."

"I need it."

A few moments later, Mari shut the door firmly, then went to stand near the small window of the back room and dug into her pack until she surfaced with the far-talker. She eyed the large, heavy thing, thinking of how many times she had fantasized about dumping it in the desert in order to lighten her pack. But Mechanics didn't dump equipment.

It just didn't happen. Especially not something as important as a far-talker.

She flicked a switch to power it up, extended the antenna, and held it near the window. "Mechanics Guild Hall of Ringhmon, this is Master Mechanic Mari of Caer Lyn. I have arrived in the city." She released the button and waited.

And waited. Muttering angrily, she broadcast her message again.

The third time she called a reply finally came, weak and laden with static. "This is Senior Mechanic Stimon, Guild Hall Supervisor in Ringhmon. You are late arriving in this city."

Mari stared at the speaker of her far-talker. Since when did Senior Mechanics monitor incoming calls to Guild Halls? And not just any Senior Mechanic, but the one in charge of the entire Guild Hall. Answering far-talker calls was a job for an apprentice. "The caravan bringing me to Ringhmon was attacked by bandits and destroyed," she said. "I barely made it to the city alive."

Stimon's response took a moment longer than it should have, then held no sympathy. "Bandits? Enough to overcome the guards of a caravan? I hope you are prepared to provide a detailed report."

A detailed report? That was his reaction to the news? "Yes. I can provide a detailed report," Mari said, trying to keep her voice level. "Especially since I just saw some of the bandits inside the city. I need an escort to the Guild Hall. An armed escort."

"An armed escort? You're safe in Ringhmon now."

"I don't think so. The bandits knew I was with the caravan and were after me. They were armed with at least two dozen rifles. Do you copy that? Two dozen rifles."

Stimon's reply once again took a little longer than it should. "You're certain of that?"

"There's no other way to explain the number of bullets fired. I personally saw one rifle in the hands of a dead bandit, but was unable to recover it. I also saw a rifle being carried by the bandits just now."

"How did these bandits know you were in the caravan when your presence was supposed to be a secret?" Stimon's voice sounded accusing now.

Mari glared at the far-talker as if it were Stimon himself. "I have no idea how they knew. The Guild Hall here arranged my contract. At the moment, I'm more concerned about my own safety."

"Mechanic Mari, there's no reason to think you are unsafe in Ringhmon. There is no need for an escort."

Mari had to pause to count to five before speaking so that her voice wouldn't sound too upset. "That's Master Mechanic Mari," she corrected him, "and I repeat that I just saw some of the bandits in the city."

"Master Mechanic Mari," Stimon repeated, somehow giving the title a very subtle and mocking twist. "I'm sure you are mistaken."

"Senior Mechanic Stimon, perhaps I didn't make clear that the caravan was wiped out except for myself and one other person!" She tried to put a lid on her temper, not wanting to fly off the handle and give anyone grounds for questioning her professionalism. "We barely survived."

After a long pause, Stimon's voice came back on, so little emotion apparent in it that for a moment it reminded her of the Mage. "A Mechanic shouldn't be so easily frightened by the sight of a few commons. It seems you lack the experience for dealing with routine situations."

Experience. She had already figured out that was the Senior Mechanic code word for "age." "Fine," Mari replied in as icy a voice as she could manage. "I will walk the rest of the way to the Mechanics Guild Hall and I will provide a full report of this to Guild Headquarters. I'm sure *they* will be concerned at a threat to a Mechanic from commons, as well as by a lack of concern for the safety of Guild members."

Stimon didn't seem fazed by Mari's reply. "Good. You were expected two days ago. Report to me as soon as you arrive at the Guild Hall."

Mari didn't trust herself to say anything in response to that last. She shut off power to the far-talker, taking a few moments to stew in anger. *I've earned my status as a Master Mechanic, and that means I've earned the right to expect respect from Senior Mechanics. Just because they run the Guild and handle all of the administrative tasks doesn't mean they can treat a working Mechanic like this.*

Does he want *me to get killed?*

That thought was so outrageous that it at least cooled her temper a bit. The smart thing to do now would be to find a spot to lie low until dark, then sneak into the Guild Hall. But there was no way she would give Stimon the satisfaction of being able to talk about the frightened little girl who thought she was a Master Mechanic. Checking her pistol again, Mari stuck her far-talker back into her pack, set the pack on her shoulders, and strode out of the back room.

The owner stood to one side, watching her with worried eyes.

"Thanks for the use of the room," Mari said, trying not to let her anger at Stimon color her words to the owner.

The owner didn't reply, only bowing in farewell as Mari left the shop.

Once outside, where danger could be anywhere, Mari felt her mood darken again. The unusually rapid way commons shrank away as she stalked down the street told her just how ominous her expression must be. She searched the streets for any more signs of the bandits, on or off their horses, almost wishing some would show up so she could have a nice, noisy gunfight with them in the middle of the city. That would show Stimon. But no more of the dusty riders appeared.

The Mechanics Guild Hall sat near one edge of the city and had been here as long as Ringhmon, just like Mechanics Guild Halls in many other places. The aqueduct carrying water to Ringhmon from the mountains to the north ran right through the Guild Hall before continuing on toward the center of Ringhmon. Commons thought this reflected some Mechanic conspiracy to control the water supply. Mari and other Mechanics knew the water actually ran through hydroelectric generators inside the Guild Hall, which powered not only the hall itself but Mechanic workshops and those common places in Ringhmon willing to pay for the wires and electricity.

Of course, that arrangement gave the Mechanics control over the city power supply as well as its water supply.

The sun was setting by the time Mari reached the large open area fronting on the fortresslike Guild Hall, her temper not mollified by the long walk in the heat of Ringhmon. She almost stomped across the plaza, then up the broad stairs to the heavy doors.

An apprentice was on duty at the entrance, studying a text as most apprentices did when they weren't dealing with visitors, so he didn't see her until she was up close. Then his eyes went directly to her face and he grinned. "Hey, princess. What's the matter?"

Mari stopped dead, her momentary outrage subsiding as she realized the apprentice had automatically assumed someone her age had to be another apprentice.

An instant later the apprentice's face reflected horror as his eyes dropped slightly and he realized she was wearing a full Mechanic's jacket. "L-lady Mechanic. Forgive me. I—I didn't—"

"Obviously," Mari agreed. The apprentice's natural mistake and quaking fear helped draw off her anger. "I'm Master Mechanic Mari of—"

"M-master Mechanic?" The apprentice stared at her helplessly. "Lady, please, I didn't know."

His fear was so real that Mari stared back at him. "Yes. You didn't know. Now you do know. Relax."

The apprentice stayed pale, bowing his head toward her. "I beg your forgiveness, Lady Master Mechanic."

Mari gazed back, feeling her aggravation evaporate as concern rose for the apprentice and his fellows in Ringhmon. If Senior Mechanic Stimon had been so unpleasant to her, what must apprentices in this Guild Hall endure? Any apprentice anywhere was subject to harassment from full Mechanics, but Mari had heard that some Guild Halls were worse than others. "Apprentice," she said firmly. "You are forgiven. Understand? No further apology is necessary."

He raised his head to stare at her again, then nodded. "Yes, Lady. Thank you. I'll report this incident to my shift leader so he can—"

"You'll do nothing of the kind! I've accepted your apology and that's all there is to it. It's now forgotten."

The apprentice blinked in surprise. "But, Lady—"

"That's an order from a Master Mechanic. All right?"

"Yes, Lady. You have my thanks." The apprentice sounded almost breathless with relief. "If I'd known you were coming—"

"You weren't told I was coming?" Stimon hadn't even done her that small courtesy.

"No, Lady," the apprentice stammered as Mari's expression hardened again.

She relaxed with an effort. "That's not your fault, either. I need a room."

"Of course, Lady Master Mechanic!"

The apprentice almost fell over himself summoning another apprentice to carry her pack and escort her to a room.

Mari sighed and just stood for a moment after the door closed, trying to calm herself, then glared at the air cooling unit. The breeze coming out of it was barely moving. Mari rapped the unit irritably, causing the fan to stutter. *Ha! Think you can mess with me, you worthless piece of junk? I've fixed more complicated things than you in my sleep.* She dug in her bag, pulled out her tool kit, popped off the front panel and peered in at the fan. As she had suspected, the screw holding one wire to the fan motor was loose, causing a weak connection. Mari got out a screwdriver, tightened the screw, causing the fan to roar fully to life, then put the panel back on, rapping it home with the handle of her tool.

The simple repair brought a feeling of satisfaction. She thought of the task she would tackle tomorrow and felt another lift to her spirits. *I'm one of the only Mechanics in the world who can do that job. Girl, am I? Wait until they see me at work. Then they'll call me Lady and mean it.*

She thought about cleaning herself off. Thought for several seconds about doing the quiet thing, the expected thing, the typical thing. She had spent years thinking about those sorts of things, really, years of staying relatively quiet and trying not to raise a fuss, though rarely with complete success. She always asked too many questions, always chafed at rules that didn't seem to make sense, and other apprentices and later on Mechanics had for some reason looked to her for ideas. It had gained her Master Mechanic status, a recent, close brush with death, and nasty attitudes from Senior Mechanics.

Mari settled her dusty jacket on her shoulders, ran one hand through her matted hair, set her jaw and went looking for Senior Mechanic Stimon.

Since dinner hour had sounded, Mari headed for the dining hall. She found Stimon where the Senior Mechanics were dining, seated at the head of the table as befitted the Guild Hall Supervisor. Mari walked briskly across the floor, knowing her boots were leaving dusty footprints, knowing every other Mechanic in the dining hall was watching her. She halted before Stimon's table. "Master Mechanic Mari reporting in."

The Senior Mechanics all looked back at her with disapproval, then Stimon stood up. He had a shaven head, a broad stomach, and a truly impressive frown. All other conversation in the dining hall had stopped, so Stimon's voice had no trouble carrying clearly. "What is the explanation for your appearance?"

"I informed you earlier that my caravan had been attacked and almost wiped out, and that I had been forced to make my way to this city by my own means across the desert waste," Mari said. "What little water I had went to narrowly avoiding dying of thirst, so I was regrettably unable to use it for washing up each evening. However, you instructed me to report to you as soon as I arrived, and I am following your instructions." Mari jerked her head to get some hair out of her eyes and a fine cloud of dust arose from her, drifting toward the Senior Mechanics' table.

"Mechanic Mari—"

"*Master* Mechanic Mari."

Stimon sat down again, drumming the fingers of one hand on the table. "It appears the stresses of your journey were too much for you."

Mari smiled. "Not at all, Guild Hall Supervisor."

"I decide whether or not Mechanics are prepared for contract work."

"You intend defaulting on the contract with Ringhmon, then?" Mari asked. "I'm the only Mechanic within a few hundred thousand lances who can do the job. I assume you don't want to discuss that here, though."

"No, I don't," Stimon said, his face reddening. "You are dismissed. I will see you in the morning, after you have returned your appearance to that expected of a Mechanic."

"Thank you, Guild Hall Supervisor Stimon." Mari pivoted like an apprentice, then walked to a table with a few other Mechanics seated at it. As an apprentice hastened up with a plate of food and a drink, Mari nodded in greetings to the others.

One of the Mechanics pretended she didn't see Mari. The other two, a man and woman, smiled in greeting.

"You really survived the Waste?" the male Mechanic asked, his voice pitched low as conversations began around the dining hall again.

Mari rubbed her forehead, then looked at the dirt on her hand. "I think I did. I won't be sure until I get all of this dust off me."

The Mechanic who had been ignoring Mari shook her head. "This is what comes of making a child a Mechanic."

Mari smiled at her. "A Master Mechanic. I made Mechanic at sixteen."

The woman glared at Mari before getting up and walking to sit at another table.

The face of the female Mechanic who had stayed lit up in recognition. "You must be Mari. A friend of mine at the academy mentioned you in his letters to me. I'm Cara."

The man nodded again. "And I'm Trux. The Senior Mechanics are glaring at us."

"I get that a lot," Mari said, digging into the food.

"They're on edge more than usual lately, what with the rioting in Julesport."

"Rioting?" Mari took a drink to clear her throat. "I've been out of touch for weeks now. What happened?"

Cara answered. "It started out with the usual protests against the Mechanics Guild, but when the Guild Hall at Julesport told the local authorities to shut down the protests the people went crazy and raised blazes for a few days before Confederation troops restored order. Typical. They say they want to rule themselves and then they prove they're incapable of it."

"Not too typical," Trux commented. "I mean the rioting. It was pretty strange for the commons to explode like that. Like they were primed to blow."

"But no one has identified anything unusual going on," Cara said. "Things are just like they've always been. Except that the commons went berserk."

"It's a good thing all of that fury was unfocused," Trux added. "The commons need a leader, and they'll never get one that they'll all follow. That's why they cling to that daughter of Jules nonsense."

"What is that all about?" Mari asked. "I've heard that expression a few times."

Cara laughed mockingly. "The commons think there was a Mage prophecy a long time ago that a daughter of Jules would someday overthrow the Mechanics Guild. Can you imagine being desperate enough to believe something a Mage said?"

Mari took another drink to avoid answering, hoping that she wasn't revealing her reaction to the last statement.

"The commons think she'll overthrow the Mage Guild, too," Trux pointed out. "Jules hasn't risen from the dead, so the commons have to hope some descendant of hers can do the job."

"If any common could have, it might have been Jules," Cara said. "Not that even Jules could have overthrown the Guild, right?"

Mari made an uncertain gesture. "I don't really know anything about Jules." She saw the surprise on the others' faces. "History wasn't my strongest subject."

Trux laughed this time. "If you made Mechanic at sixteen, you wouldn't have had time for much besides technical subjects. Jules was an officer in the Imperial fleet a long time back, when only the east side of the Sea of Bakre had been settled. She left Imperial service, got her own ship and headed west, exploring and engaging in piracy. She was the first one through the Strait of Gulls into the Jules Sea and the first to sail the Umbari Ocean. Jules helped found a couple of the cities in the Confederation, and when the Empire tried to move in she organized the cities in the west to fight back and keep Imperial control confined to the east."

"She must have been an undiscovered Mechanic," Cara added. "No one who was really a common could have done all of that."

"Wow," Mari commented. "But why did the unrest at Julesport throw off the Senior Mechanics out here? Even if the rioting was unusual, Julesport is a long ways off, and it's not like there's never been commons rioting or even attacking the Guild."

"Because of Tiae," Cara said. "How long has it been since the kingdom fell apart? Something like fifteen years, and it just keeps getting worse. I hear it's complete anarchy there now."

Trux nodded. "The Guild pulled the last Mechanic out of there about ten years ago. Too dangerous. Since then the Guild has been trying to hold the line at the border between the Confederation and what used to be Tiae. We think that's what has the Senior Mechanics spooked, the worry that the unrest in Julesport was the first sign that the problems in Tiae might spread north. If we lose the Confederation like we did Tiae, well, that's a big chunk of Dematr."

"But that won't make the Guild change the way it does anything," Mari grumbled, then instantly regretted saying that aloud.

The other two nodded, though. "Something has to be done," Trux agreed, his eyes on Mari. "I've heard..." He glanced quickly toward the table where the Senior Mechanics sat. "Maybe Cara and I should let you eat."

Both Trux and Cara had grown nervous enough that Mari didn't debate the point. Besides, she didn't want them asking her what everyone should do. Just because she thought Mechanics should offer solutions rather than sticking to the past, and just because she had said that more than once, and just because she was willing to stomp in here covered with dust, other Mechanics thought she was crazy enough to...

To what?

She didn't know the answer to that, but she did know what could happen to Mechanics who complained too loudly and too often.

Mari ate quickly, apprentices refilling her glass several times as she tried to make up for the dehydration of the desert journey. As she tipped back the last glass, Mari caught a whiff of something that didn't smell very good. "Is that me?" she asked Cara.

"Uh, yeah. Understandable, though, if you walked here through the Waste."

"Understandable or not, I appreciate you putting up with it. I'd better get cleaned up."

She felt the eyes of everyone in the dining hall upon her as she left, then a rising roar of conversation behind her.

Back in her room, Mari had to let the water out of the bath and refill it after the dirt on her made the first tubful too filthy to get clean in. After getting her hair clean and combed, then putting on fresh clothes, Mari held her breath as she rolled up her old clothes before setting them outside to be laundered. She couldn't launder the jacket, but she did clean it as well as possible.

She put her jacket back on and checked her reflection in the mirror. *No wonder that Mage never hit on me.* A couple of weeks confined in a stifling hot wagon, followed by a week out in the open desert, had not done her complexion any favors, but at least she was clean now. Mari flipped her hair lightly, causing the tips to brush her shoulders, and not for the first time thought about cutting it shorter. Some days her hair was just a pain. Other days she liked it, though, so she might as well keep it at this length.

Tired but restless, Mari carefully drew her pistol from the holster draped over the room's chair. After all her time in the desert, the dust-covered pistol needed cleaning, too. Sitting down, Mari got out the oil and wire brushes and worked away, finding comfort in the simple task. Once she had finished, she reassembled it, pulled back the slide to check the mechanism, clicked off a dry shot on the empty chamber, then reinserted an ammunition clip, set the safety, and returned the pistol to its holster.

Only to yank it out again when a knock sounded on her door. "Who's there?" Mari called, wishing that she could control her voice as well as that Mage had.

"Mechanic Pradar. I was wondering if you could tell me anything about my uncle. He was at the Guild Hall in Caer Lyn."

Angered at herself for panicking, and surprised that she would react that way inside a Guild Hall, Mari shoved her pistol back into the holster. She paused to control her breathing before opening the door.

The Mechanic there looked to be in his mid-twenties, and seemed as nervous as Mari had been. "Master Mechanic Mari of Caer Lyn?" Pradar asked.

"Yes. Though it's been a couple of years since I left. Do you want to come in and—"

"No!" Pradar smiled anxiously. "Better we just talk here."

"All right. What's your uncle's name?"

"Rindal. Mechanic Rindal." Pradar must have seen her reaction. "Do you know anything?" His voice had taken on a pleading quality.

Mari hesitated, thinking that she was in enough trouble already. But if Rindal was this guy's uncle... "Yes. What do you know?"

Pradar made a helpless gesture. "He just disappeared. Uncle Rindal stopped sending letters, and my father's letters to him were never answered. We checked with other Mechanics we knew at Caer Lyn and they said he was gone. Nobody knew where or how."

"I know how," Mari said, her voice barely above a whisper. "I don't know where. Not for sure."

"What do you know?" Pradar asked, his eyes lit with hope and dread intermingled. "Please. My father...it's been years."

"Four years," Mari said. She had never forgotten that night, because nightmares weren't supposed to happen while you were awake. "I was on night internal security watch in the Guild Hall. You know how boring that is. Nothing ever happens. Except this night, a little after midnight, I got a call to come to the entrance guard post. There were Mechanics there, ones that I'd never seen before. They were all armed, all of them had pistols and rifles, and they seemed...dangerous. The Guild Hall Supervisor was there, too. He told me to do whatever these other Mechanics said, then he left."

Pradar nodded, his eyes locked on hers. "Dangerous Mechanics?"

"Yes. Like they were soldiers or something instead of Mechanics. But they were Mechanics. I can't explain it. Their leader told me to take them to Mechanic Rindal's room. So I did." Mari clenched her teeth at the memory, old guilt flooding through her.

"You didn't have any choice," Pradar said. "You were just an apprentice given direct orders by a Guild Hall Supervisor and some full Mechanic."

"Thanks. I thought, stars above, Rindal's finally going to get it. Because we'd all heard him arguing with Senior Mechanics, saying things like 'we need to do this differently' and 'it's wrong.' "

Pradar nodded with a pained look. "Father said that Uncle Rindal had a big mouth. I remember he was...sort of opinionated."

"I took them through the Guild Hall to Mechanic Rindal's room," Mari said, reliving memories of that night. The strangely menacing Mechanics walked in a tight group, saying nothing, Mari in the lead terrified of doing something wrong, whatever "wrong" was to those people. The normally busy halls had been otherwise empty and silent as they always were at that late hour, dimly lit at intervals by night security lighting. Mari had kept hoping that someone else, anyone else, would come by, but she saw no one. Finally reaching Rindal's room, she had pointed it out to the strange Mechanics. "The leader told me to walk away and not look back, told me that I hadn't seen anybody or anything, and that I was never to talk about it to anyone by order of the Guild Master. But I did look back as I was rounding the corner and partly in a deeper shadow. I saw them pulling Mechanic Rindal out of his room, and his arms were already locked behind his back, and there was a hood over his head."

Mari shook her head, the old helpless feeling returned. "And in the morning, all anyone knew was that Mechanic Rindal was gone."

"That's...what we've feared," Pradar whispered back to her in anguish. "You never told anyone?"

"I told a couple of my friends. They told me to keep quiet, that I couldn't do anything but...but I might end up just like Mechanic Rindal if I didn't keep my mouth shut. Because...everybody already thought that I had a big mouth, too."

"That was good advice," Pradar said. "You couldn't have done anything. My father told me he thought Uncle Rindal had been sent to the Guild prison at Longfalls, but we could never turn up any evidence of that. I'll tell him what you said, though I won't tell him who told me, and maybe he can finally find out what happened to Uncle Rindal. Maybe he's still..."

Still alive? Mari's thoughts had never gone there. Imprisoning a dissident Mechanic was one thing, but executing him? "Be careful," Mari said. "If your father raises too much fuss—"

"He'll end up disappearing like Uncle Rindal. I know. You probably thought Uncle Rindal was a lot more than a big mouth, right?" Pradar asked. "That he was a traitor or something?"

"Yeah," Mari admitted. "Just arguing shouldn't have—"

"Made him disappear. Yeah. But he wasn't a traitor, Mari. My father said Uncle Rindal wanted only the best for the Guild. He was loyal. But he wanted to fix things."

"I can understand that."

"It's what Mechanics do, right? What we're supposed to do." Pradar glanced up and down the hallway, his nervousness returned stronger than ever. "Thank you. I really mean that. Keep your head down. The Senior Mechanics here are as touchy as old explosives."

"I heard about Julesport—"

"It's not just that. It seems to have something to do with you. If I can do anything—"

Mari shook her head. "No. You keep your head down, too. I'll do my job and I'll get out of here. Analyze, repair, test, and gone."

"Good idea." Pradar nodded in farewell, then walked away quickly.

Mari shut the door, ensuring the lock was set, then leaned back against the wall. *Great. I had trouble sleeping for weeks after that incident, and now the memory's come back full force.*

I never really believed that Rindal was a traitor. Why keep it secret, if he was?

Why would me being here upset the Senior Mechanics so much? Pradar must be reading too much into that.

Trying to relax by sheer force of will, Mari lay down on the bed, staring up at the ceiling and wishing she could gain access to the long-distance far-talker in this Guild Hall so she could speak to someone at the Guild Headquarters in Palandur. No, even if the opportunity arose she wouldn't request access to long-distance communications, even though that was her right as a Master Mechanic. Her first job, and the first thing she did was run crying back to someone like Professor S'san? That would just convince everyone that Mari really was too young to be a Master Mechanic.

And what would she say? That Senior Mechanics were acting unhappy with her? That wasn't exactly a new development. The Senior Mechanics had to abide by the rules they had written for advancement to Mechanic and Master Mechanic status, but one of the last things Mari had heard before leaving Palandur was that those rules had been changed to establish requirements for longevity as an apprentice and Mechanic rather than just using tests of expertise. Change was not permitted. Except apparently change was permitted if it meant that someone like Mari could be blocked from promotion in the future. It seemed her records for reaching Mechanic and Master Mechanic status would stand forever, since no one else would be allowed to move up as fast as she had.

It couldn't be more obvious that the rule change was aimed at me, but it didn't go through in time to block my promotion to Master Mechanic. That was thanks to Professor S'san. I didn't know why was she pushing me so hard those last six months at the academy, but now I know she must have been tipped off about the rule changes wending their way through the Senior Mechanic bureaucracy. She wanted me to qualify before they took effect.

And what have I done to repay her? Things like my little show with Guild Hall Supervisor Stimon in the dining hall. S'san would probably rip my ears off for that. "Unprofessional, Mari." Which it was, I guess. But it felt good.

I could try talking to Trux and Cara again. But I don't really know them, not well enough to confide in, and if I do seek them out, and if the Senior Mechanics have marked me somehow, then I'd just be causing trouble for Trux and Cara.

There's no one else in this city I know.

A memory of Mage Alain arose unbidden. It wasn't that they had talked a whole lot, but rather a feeling that despite their differences they could have talked more. Was it his youth, so close to her own that made him somehow seem sympathetic to her despite his disreputable status as a Mage? Was she feeling pity for a boy who hadn't remembered what to do when someone said thank you? Or had she actually found something to like in him in their time together in the desert?

Unthinkable. Yet as Mari lay in the dark, listening to stray sounds within the Guild Hall that should have been comforting in their familiarity, she found herself wishing the Mage were here to keep an eye out while she slept, just as he had in the desert. *You're crazy,*

Mari. *Wishing a Mage was in your room with you? You were out in that desert sun too long.*

And I can take care of myself. I've known I was on my own for a long time now, ever since—

No. I will not think of my...parents. They abandoned me, but they cannot hurt me anymore.

Think about the job, Mari.

But that attempt ended up looping back to thoughts of the Mage. *How did Mage Alain know about my job here? I can't talk to anyone about that. I can't even admit I know the name of a Mage. If anyone in the Guild even suspected I had divulged Guild secrets to a Mage I'd be busted back to apprentice and shipped off to...well, actually, there isn't anyplace worse than Ringhmon, I guess.*

Except Longfalls.

I am not a traitor. I'm totally loyal to the Guild. They wouldn't send me there.

They sent Rindal.

The job, Mari. Focus on the job. It has to be tough or they wouldn't have sent for you to do the repairs.

"Beware that which thinks but does not live." What about my job tomorrow worried Mage Alain?

CHAPTER SEVEN

The next morning, Alain had barely finished his filling but tasteless breakfast when an acolyte informed him that his presence was required in another part of the Hall. Alain followed the acolyte, not looking forward to explaining the fate of the caravan.

Alain found himself led into a darkened room. The acolyte bowed his way out, shutting the door and leaving Alain alone to face the vague shapes of Mages seated before him. He could not see their faces, but they could see him clearly thanks to a shaft of light coming from a lamp positioned near his face. Alain had never experienced an Inquiry before, but clearly his elders were now calling him to account for his failure.

A woman's voice spoke without feeling. "We are told you were in the company of a Mechanic for days."

"A Mechanic escaped the destruction of the caravan with me," Alain confirmed, surprised that the Inquiry had led off with that question.

"Why?"

"She sought safety from the bandits."

"Do not mock us, youthful Mage!" The emotionless voice managed to hold a harsh edge. "Why did this Mechanic accompany you? Why did she seek safety with *you*?"

"She—" *Ordered me to accompany her? No. I should not say that.* "We were the only two survivors. She said that she believed we had a higher chance of surviving together."

"You spoke with her." The flat words nonetheless carried a surprising amount of force and condemnation.

"Yes. She is a shadow. Whether I speak with her or not does not matter, for she is nothing." Let them condemn that.

The following pause might have meant they were searching for grounds to deny his reasoning, but if so could not come up with any. "The Mechanic gave no other cause for attaching herself to you?"

Thinking up a lie would require a delay which the elders would spot. Alain answered immediately and tonelessly. "She said that she did not want me to die."

"An obvious lie," a man's voice declared. "No Mechanic would care about the fate of a Mage. Could you not tell it was a lie?"

The less said this time the better. He did not want to betray to these elders how the Mechanic had affected him. "No. I did not see deception in her when the Mechanic said that."

"Too young," one of the elders grumbled tonelessly. "A capable Mage would have seen the lie. The Mechanic must have wanted something. What did she ask of you?"

Alain had to think this time before answering. The Mechanic had actually asked very little of him that he could recall. "She asked me how I created fire. She did not understand how I could do it. I did not tell her."

The third shadowy figure spoke, his voice that of an old man. "Of course she could not understand. Surely you had at least enough sense to not waste your time trying to explain wisdom to a Mechanic? What else did you tell her? What did she want?" the old Mage continued, his voice becoming accusatory enough for the emotion to be obvious.

"She wanted to survive," Alain repeated, unable to think what else his elders expected him to say. *She would not drink the last of the water and leave me.* He did not understand that himself. How could he explain it to these elders?

The woman spoke again, suspicion shading the blandness of her tone. "This Mechanic was a female? A young one?"

"Yes, elder."

"You are young as well."

"Yes, elder."

"What did she attempt with you? Did she ensnare you?"

"Ensnare me?" Alain asked, not sure what that meant.

"Did she seduce you, fool, while you were alone together?"

Alain could not remember the last time he had laughed. It had been a very long time ago. The absurdity of this question almost caused him to gasp with something that might have sounded a bit like laughter, though, which would have angered his elders beyond measure. It took all of Alain's training to snuff out that sound before it reached his lips. "No, elder. The Mechanic never approached me in any way."

"She never touched you?"

"Once. She touched me once." As far as Alain could recall, there had been only one time when the Mechanic had initiated a touch, and he would be a fool indeed to volunteer that he had one time extended a hand to her.

"Once?" The elder pounced on that.

"I was weak from casting spells to kill bandits. She took my arm and helped me stand."

The silence was longer this time. Then one of the elders said a single word. "Helped?"

Alain hoped desperately that no emotion was showing on his face. "That is what she called it." Not a lie. No. He had told these elders exactly what had happened. Would they press him on whether he understood what the word meant?

Another pause, then the elders apparently decided not to pursue an issue that might awaken the wrong memories in Alain. "She teased you with her touch, then withheld her gifts," the woman elder said. "Did she display herself, offer the promise of her gifts in the future?"

"Display herself?" What could that mean?

"Did she flaunt her body before you?" the elder demanded.

Alain could not think of anything which the Mechanic had done which qualified as flaunting. He was not certain exactly what "flaunting" meant. He had been around only female Mages or acolytes since he was very young, and all of them followed Mage teachings to take little notice of physical appearance or physical desires. That certainly was not flaunting.

The Mechanic had not seemed all that different. She clearly kept herself clean when not fleeing bandits in the desert, but she also had not worn the heavy make-up that Alain had noticed on some common women. *Common attempts to create their own illusions of beauty,* another elder had said contemptuously to Alain before he left the Guild Hall in Ihris.

But none of those women, who had displayed much more flesh than he had ever seen of the Mechanic, had seemed so...interesting. Why had they settled into a barely recalled blur while she remained clear in his memory?

He had been aware of the Mechanic's body. He had sometimes found himself watching her walk when he was behind her, and even though she had kept her jacket on almost all of the time, Alain had caught glimpses of her wet shirt clinging to her. The memories of those sights had been troubling his nights since then. "She wore a shirt which was sometimes soaked with sweat—"

"Ah." That answer had pleased the elders into showing their feelings. "And tight trousers, no doubt."

"She wore trousers, elder," Alain confirmed.

They had not been tight trousers.

Though where those trousers had been tightest across the back...

No. No. No. Do not think on it.

Some trace of his own discomfort must have been noticeable, because satisfaction could still be heard in the voice of the elder who asked the next question. "How did she act toward you, young Mage?"

What answers did they seek? He knew that, and so he gave his own answers in a form that was accurate and yet matched the expectations of the elders. "She tried to give orders to me. She made decisions on her own. She was stubborn."

"Of course."

She was intelligent, resourceful, and steadfast...she saved my life. She asked my advice and listened to it. Somehow she has caused me to remember things that I should not. But Alain left all of those words unspoken. Why should he say them? These elders would be the first to tell him that nothing was real. Why invite their displeasure by saying things they certainly did not want to hear?

Especially when he could not explain any of it. The Mechanic, her actions, did not match all that he had been taught about Mechanics. *But if I tell the elders that, they will accuse me of failing to show wisdom, even if they also cannot explain it.*

And so I will say nothing of such things. For that is wisdom here.

"Even one so young as you should know that Mechanics do nothing without purpose, Mage Alain," said the oldest of the elders, "and those purposes are always contrary to the welfare of the Mage Guild. You traveled with this Mechanic in the same caravan before it was attacked. Did she seek you out before then?"

"No," Alain answered, certain his voice was betraying no emotion this time. "She spent the entire journey before the attack in her wagon. I was not even aware of the presence of a Mechanic until during the attack."

The woman asked the next question, her voice still frigid despite its detachment. "Why did you allow her to accompany you? Why did you not leave her to her fate?"

"I was contracted to protect the caravan. Since the Mechanic was a member of the caravan, and the Mage Guild had contracted my protection for all in the caravan, I felt required to protect her as well."

"That is a lawyer's argument, Mage. Wisdom born of more experience would have told you that your services were to the caravan master, not to some Mechanic who will surely continue to work against the welfare of your Guild."

Alain inclined his head toward the dim figures, even though he thought their arguments had more of the lawyer to them than had Alain's own statement. "This one understands."

"You should have refused to speak with this Mechanic," the first elder insisted. "You should have left her to her own devices in the Waste. A more experienced Mage would have known this."

The other two elders sitting in the room made noises of agreement. Alain almost frowned at the thought of leaving Mechanic Mari to die in the Waste before he remembered to block any show of emotion. These three had already sent barbs about his youth his way. He might as well ask a question suited for an acolyte, since they apparently expected nothing more. "This one has questions."

There was a noticeable pause before one of the male elders answered. "This one listens."

"The caravan I was to protect was attacked by bandits armed with Mechanic weapons. I saw one of these Mechanic weapons closely, though of course I did not touch it. I have been told that Mechanic weapons are elaborate fakes of limited use. Yet the weapons I faced were deadly beyond anything I have heard of."

"We are aware you reported this," the woman noted in a dismissive voice. "You are young. The Mechanics are clever enough in their own way. Their tricks are complicated and difficult for one unskilled to see through. Did these weapons slay you? No. Your skills, limited though they are in one so young, were enough to overcome the Mechanic weapons."

"But the caravan was destroyed."

"That is no matter to us. You said that only you and this Mechanic survived. You will tell no one of the fate of the caravan, and no one will believe a Mechanic's tale. Some shadows are gone, but the illusion remains."

Alain stood silently, trying to accept the words of his elders, knowing that they were right, that the fates of shadows and illusions didn't matter. But he had been personally responsible for protecting the caravan. He remembered the faces of the caravan master and the guard commander. Nothing but shadows. But they had expected him to protect them.

Shadows. His parents had been shadows. They had died at the hands of raiders perhaps not much different from the bandits of the Waste. He had not been able to save them, either. Alain felt a sudden certainty that he would never be able to disregard the fates of shadows. Perhaps that was the reason he had stayed with the Mechanic. It was a terrible error, a failure of wisdom, a betrayal of what he had been taught. *In that, my elders are right. I have failed my Guild. I will never be a great Mage.*

"Do you have anything else to report?" one of the elders asked. "Your spells worked properly? There were no changes in your skills?"

He could mislead them about that, too, but Alain decided not to. The odd sense of urgency generated by his last vision prodded him to say more. "I experienced foresight. It is one of my skills now."

"Foresight," the oldest muttered. "Of all Mage arts, the most useless and the most dangerous. Paying attention to foresight is a certain way to cripple your Mage skills by making the world illusion seem too real. You should know that. What do they teach acolytes these days?"

"I was so taught, elder," Alain replied. "I did not seek foresight."

"Finally, some sign of wisdom in you."

"Elder," Alain said in the most emotionless voice that he could manage, "I saw a vision which seemed to warn of great danger."

"To you?" the elder asked.

"I do not know, elder. I saw a threatening storm, and—"

"Enough," the elder cut off Alain abruptly. "What you saw was simply the illusion of danger created by your mind after the attack on the caravan. It was an echo. Nothing more. A wise Mage would say nothing more of this."

Alain did not say anything else, wondering why, despite the elder's attempt to sound completely uninterested, an undercurrent of tension had been apparent in his voice. And he had cut off Alain's description of the vision. It was as if Alain's words, or the vision itself, had actually upset him.

The woman addressed him again, her voice stern in its indifference. "You have much to learn. That is obvious. Even an acolyte should know not to speak of meaningless visions born of the misleading art of foresight. I do not understand how the Guild could have given you full Mage status at your age."

"The Guild did not give me Mage status," Alain said. "I earned my status by demonstrating my skills to the satisfaction of the elders of the Mage Guild Hall in Ihris." To the satisfaction of most of those elders, anyway. They had known him and judged him based on his skills, not his age.

"We must accept the decisions of those elders even if we do not approve of them," the woman said in a way that made it clear she did not actually accept what the elders of Ihris had done. "Here you are subject to the elders of this Guild Hall. Learn from their experience. The ability to work spells does not mean a Mage has the wisdom to act as one should."

"This one understands," Alain replied, a formal acceptance of the elders' words that should have ended the discussion. He had no interest in hearing more declarations of his inadequacy.

But the elders were not going to let him go yet. "You must practice your basic skills. Focus your mind away from the falsehoods of foresight and unto the wisdom your elders have given you. Your inability to defeat a small gang of bandits shows that you lack confidence in your powers."

Alain tensed, fighting not to reveal any anger. "This one understands."

"If this Mechanic attempts to approach you again, you must not speak to her. You must have no more contact with any Mechanic. You will report any such attempts at contact to the elders here."

"This one understands."

"Then this may end." Alain saw one of the shadowy figures raise a hand. The shutters blocking high windows fell open and light entered.

The woman and two men came forward, their impassive faces a bit jarring after the bland hostility of the Inquiry. "How long will you stay in Ringhmon, Mage Alain?" the woman asked.

"I have not decided," Alain answered. "I must see what employment opportunities exist here."

"There are few," the oldest Mage grumbled. "Very few. Ringhmon squanders too much of its treasure on Mechanic toys. Vain fools."

Alain nodded respectfully. "Then perhaps I shall see the city and learn more of it."

"Why?" the third Mage asked. "It is all false. Seeing the false brings you nothing."

"I do not know if my services will ever bring me to Ringhmon again," Alain said. "I should become familiar with even the false image of the city, enough to be able to serve as my Guild requires. After all, I am young and have much to learn."

Yet another thing that the Mechanic had done to him. What had she called such speech? Sarcasm? When was the last time he had spoken in such a way, knowing that he was mocking the words he said?

But he hid the mockery very well, or else the elders did not recognize it, because the three Mage elders nodded in approval. "A few days, then," the woman said as if Alain had already agreed to the time frame. "No one will learn the fate of the last caravan you protected, so any other caravan leaving the city will be glad to have you since you do not command the same price as more experienced Mages."

Marveling at the elders' abilities to get in digs aimed at his capabilities and youth, Alain nodded again. "Then, if there is nothing else, I will take leave of the Guild Hall so that I may see what there is to be learned in the city of Ringhmon."

The woman shook her head. "Go if you will, but keep your nose close. Do not stick it in places where it might get cut off, young Mage."

The oldest almost grimaced. "Dark Mages. An ugly thing, but you know of them. They are here in some numbers, drawn by offers of employment from the city. Oh, the city denies it, but we know they hire Dark Mages. You do not want to encounter one of them, young Mage."

Wishing they would stop commenting on his youth, Alain began backing toward the door. "I shall remain alert and wary."

Once outside the chamber where the Inquiry had been held, safely alone in an otherwise empty hallway, Alain stopped for a moment to think and recover his full composure. *A small gang of bandits. They give me no credit at all. They did not accept my words. What would they have said had I died there? It would have been my fault, my own failure due to youth and lack of experience, and none would have ever blamed Mechanic weapons, which are deadlier than any crossbow.*

They said I should have left the Mechanic and let her die. Perhaps I should have, before she twisted my own thoughts. But twice she would not leave me to die. Am I to be less than a Mechanic?

They asked if she had "displayed her gifts." Alain thought of the Mechanic's dusty, sweat streaked face and the drab jacket she insisted upon wearing even in the worst heat. *The gifts she displayed were those of who she was. Shadow she may be, but I...liked the person I saw there. I had forgotten how it felt, to be in the company of another and to wish it to continue. What fate made her a Mechanic and me a Mage?*

Startled that such a thought had even come to him, Alain tried to banish his memories of the Mechanic. *Like? She has made me remember "like"? I must not let her lead me farther astray. But I also must not let the elders here disorder my thoughts. If I dwell on their criticisms it will make it hard to concentrate on my spells, maybe even weaken them so that my abilities as a Mage could be called into question.*

Perhaps that is what they intend.

This Mechanic...is different. I have felt a strange restlessness since my last vision. A vision centered on her.

Why did the elders react the way they did to my report of that vision?

Feeling tired and irritable after a bad night's sleep, Mari got breakfast amid the other Mechanics, all of whom appeared standoffish now. She was used to that attitude from Senior Mechanics, but not from others. It was almost as if they had been warned not to speak with her.

Cara caught her eye long enough to deliver a cautionary look, then glanced away.

Apparently they *had* been told not to speak with her.

A female Senior Mechanic came up to the table where Mari was eating alone and glowered down at her. "You're to see Guild Hall Supervisor Stimon immediately."

"As soon as I'm done eating—"

"Immediately."

Mari nodded slowly, then got up with equal slowness and walked unhurriedly from the room. *Childish,* she reproached herself. *Keep acting like a child and you'll be giving them ammunition against you.* But she sped up only a little after that.

Mari accompanied the woman through the Guild Hall, along corridors which reeked of age and were familiar even though she had never walked them. Every Guild Hall was built to the same floor plan. Only furnishings and art differed from Hall to Hall, except in the Imperial capital of Palandur, of course, where the basic plan had been repeated twice to accommodate the demands of the Guild headquarters building.

Stimon's office was very large, as in every Guild Hall, and very well appointed, which wasn't always the case. Senior Mechanic Stimon sat behind a huge desk made of highly polished wood from the far southern tropics, the sort of wood that had become much harder to get since the Kingdom of Tiae had fallen apart. The female Senior Mechanic directed Mari to enter, then closed the door, staying outside.

Stimon waved Mari to the plain seat before his desk. She noted he hadn't risen from his own comfortable chair to greet her.

He nodded at her as if they were meeting for the first time. "Welcome to Ringhmon. I trust you enjoyed the courtesy of this hall last night, after you arrived *safely.*"

Mari's temper flared but she managed to keep her voice calm. *Needle me, will you? Let's see how you like it.* "The accommodations were adequate, but the air cooling unit was malfunctioning."

Stimon froze for a moment at the implied criticism of his Guild Hall, then nodded. "I'll look into that. Some apprentice doing substandard work, no doubt."

"Surely your apprentices are supervised by full Mechanics when working?"

This time Stimon's smile was strained. "That's usually the case. I'll make sure someone repairs the unit."

Mari shook her head. "I already fixed it. It only took a moment."

The smile vanished. "Mechanics are required to do work only within their area of specialty unless otherwise directed. Surely even someone of your limited experience is aware of that."

Mari met Stimon's angry gaze, keeping her own face calm despite another direct jab at her youth. "Surely a Senior Mechanic is aware that Mechanics of Master rank are allowed to direct their own work. Guild regulations are clear on that point."

Stimon's face darkened, but he quickly changed the subject. "The Guild wanted your presence in the caravan to remain unknown so as to ensure the contract with Ringhmon remained confidential. Your presence has in fact been made public."

"Yes. You told me to report as soon as possible. That meant walking openly through the town."

The Guild Hall Supervisor gave her an appraising look that quickly hardened. "You compromised your presence before that."

Mari took a long, slow breath before replying. "As I told you, the caravan was attacked by a heavily armed force. I had to escape, which meant leaving the wagon in which I'd been confined."

"So you say. But you said the caravan was wiped out. Did anyone else see you or these bandits you say attacked?"

Mari took a moment to answer. A lie would keep her out of trouble now, but could too easily be found out. Too many people had seen her arriving in the city, and the salt traders knew who her brief traveling companion had been. "One other person."

"A common? Who?"

"He wasn't a common."

"There were no other Mechanics with that caravan," Stimon said. "Your story isn't holding up."

She glowered at the implication that her report had been false. "He was a Mage."

At least she had finally managed to rattle Stimon's composure. "A Mage?"

"Yes. He'd been hired by the caravan to help protect it."

Stimon stared at her. "How do you know that?"

Blast it. She still hadn't learned to think before talking. That had probably been why Stimon had angered her, to get her to say something without thinking. But now she had no choice but to say the simple truth. "He told me."

"He. Told. You." Stimon leaned back, looking stunned. "You spoke with a Mage?"

"Yes." Leave it at that. See if Stimon would drop it.

Stimon didn't drop it. "How long were you in a position to *speak* with this *Mage*?"

Mari sighed. *Just get it over with.* "About three days. Alone, that is. Then we met up with some salt traders heading for Ringhmon and traveled with them. I didn't have any further contact with the Mage after that."

"After that? You didn't have any *further* contact with the Mage after that?" Stimon shook his head in disbelief. "You spent three days *alone* with a Mage?"

"He and I escaped together. The bandits were chasing me. It seemed preferable to dying," Mari said.

"Some would prefer death to the sort of things a Mage would do to an unaccompanied girl!"

"What?"

"Don't pretend ignorance! No wonder your clothes needed laundering so badly! They probably carried his stench from all the times that Mage forced himself on you!"

Mari's face became very hot as she sprang to her feet. "How dare you? The Mage never touched me! If he'd tried I would've blown his head off!"

Stimon glared back. "Are you saying the threat of a weapon kept him from assaulting you?"

"Yes! No! I didn't have to threaten him! He didn't try anything! I deeply resent the implication that I would invite or allow any physical contact with a Mage!"

"What did the Mage want, then?" Stimon demanded.

The question hadn't even occurred to Mari before this because the answer seemed so obvious. "What did he want? To get away from the bandits."

"He could have done that alone."

True enough. Mari knew she had to tell the full truth again. "He felt obligated to protect me."

"A Mage. Felt obligated."

It did sound absurd, even to her, and she had been there. "He had a contract to protect the caravan, and I was part of the caravan. I don't know why a Mage cared about that, but he did."

"You believed that?" Stimon leaned back again, shaking his head. "He must have wanted to spy. What did he find out about Mechanic arts? What did you tell him?"

The Mage's warning about her job in Ringhmon rose in her mind again, but she hadn't said anything to him to prompt that. However the Mage might have learned something about her contract, it hadn't come from her. "I didn't tell him anything! We just escaped the attack together and then sought safety together."

Stimon regarded her silently for a moment. "Did you see any of his tricks?"

Mari hesitated. Tricks. That's all Mages were supposed to be able to do. But that superheat thing had been one amazing trick.

This time she thought before speaking, though. Something about the way Stimon had asked felt wrong. Tricks. A trick question? To get her to admit to what?

To having witnessed something that the Mechanics Guild said did not exist?

Yeah. I really want to admit to that to this guy. Had she actually *seen* anything when the Mage did that superheat bit? "No."

Senior Mechanic Stimon's jaw tightened. He didn't say anything for some time, then spoke with deceptive quietness. "Alone, with a Mage, for days. Do you have any idea what a gross breach of Guild rules that is?"

Mari felt herself getting angry again. *Don't act like a child. That's what he wants. How would Professor S'san handle this?* The answer came to her. Mari sat down again and assumed a questioning look. "Exactly which rules did I break, Guild Hall Supervisor?"

Stimon glared at her. "Are you actually claiming that you were never told not to associate with Mages?"

"No, Guild Hall Supervisor. I am asking you which Guild rules address conduct toward Mages. I am unaware of any written policy or formal standing orders. I am, however, aware that according to Guild rules I am under an obligation to protect my tools and to carry out my contracts. If I had died in the Waste, my tools would have been lost and my contract would have been forfeited." Mari gave Stimon her best obedient underling look. "I was following the Guild's rules in order to serve the Guild's interests."

The Senior Mechanic just stared at her, disbelief shading into impotent anger. Then he unexpectedly smiled. "I will, of course, have to ask for proof of the attack on the caravan. Please do not insult both of us by invoking the Mage as a witness. What can you tell me about these bandits? Did you see any faces? Hear anything which would identify them?"

Mari shook her head, wondering what Stimon was up to now. "They were in full desert robes, including coverings for their lower faces, not that I saw many close up. The only detail I know is that they were armed with standard model repeating rifles out of the workshops at Danalee."

"You're certain of that?" Stimon asked sharply.

"Yes. I examined one closely."

"You claim you had one in your possession and you didn't bring it with you?" the Senior Mechanic asked.

"I was being pursued by the other bandits at the time, and the weapon was broken!" Mari tried again to keep her temper in check. "As it was, I had so much to carry that I barely made it to safety."

Stimon grimaced, shaking his head. "I suppose I shouldn't have expected anything more from a..."

"A what? I'm a Master Mechanic and insist that I be treated as such."

Mari's words hung in the air for a moment, then Stimon smiled again. "Of course. It's a pity that a Master Mechanic observed no useful details of these bandits. Nothing which we could use to verify her story."

"Do you think I took a walk in the desert voluntarily?" Mari demanded. "You know the caravan did not arrive on time. Send someone to the pass and they'll find a very big crater and a lot of dead bodies."

"Caravans are often late, and sometimes never appear for reasons which have nothing to do with bandits. I do not have the luxury of sending Mechanics off on long journeys to investigate stories that have no other evidence to support them." Stimon made a regretful gesture. "Due to the lack of proof, I have to register you as late for contract work without authorization."

"You—" Mari really had to struggle this time to keep from yelling at Stimon. "I insist on the right to enter a protest and an explanation."

"That is your right," Stimon agreed readily.

He knows other Senior Mechanics will pay no attention to what I say. A black mark. He's giving me a black mark on my first contract, because I almost got killed trying to get to it. Mari gave him an angry glare. "The word of a Master Mechanic would not be questioned in Palandur."

"This isn't Palandur. It's Ringhmon. I run this Guild Hall. And even in Palandur the Guild is run by Senior Mechanics. You had best keep that in mind." Stimon drummed his fingers on the surface of his desk for a moment, seeming very pleased with himself. "You may now proceed to the Ringhmon Hall of City Government to carry out your contract."

Mari sat for a moment, trying to calm herself down. "Who's escorting me to the contract site? Where do I meet them?"

Stimon frowned at her. "Escorting? No one. You're a Master Mechanic," he added with a thin smile.

After ten years of the Guild trying to supervise her every move, why was it that now so many Senior Mechanics wanted her wandering around alone? "The Mechanic who normally works on that equipment—"

"Master Mechanic Xian has no interest in acting as your apprentice. He feels he could have fixed the problem himself, given more time."

Fat chance. It's about getting the job done, Xian, not your pride. Mari tried again. "I don't know the city. I assume the Hall of City Government is some ways away. Guild policy—"

"Policy regarding multiple Mechanics on the same job is often waived. Experienced Mechanics know that. Do you need directions to the Hall of City Government?"

Directions. Not an escort. Not transportation. Directions. "No. I'll find my way there."

"I should not have to say this, but you are ordered not to allow further contact between yourself and any Mage. I will put that in writing." Stimon smiled, but it was a smile without any pretense of humor.

Mari bared her teeth back at him, stood up and left.

She barely kept from slamming the door of Stimon's office, then stood a moment in the hallway trying to control her temper.

Fortunately, the female Senior Mechanic had vanished. Mari wasn't sure how she would have handled additional unpleasant treatment.

This wasn't anything like what Mari had anticipated when she had left Palandur. She could handle being alone, feeling alone. Getting to the academy at sixteen had meant she was years younger than the other students, a kid out of place among her older colleagues. She had earned respect among those peers there for her abilities, but here in Ringhmon for the first time she felt unable to control her fate at all, no matter how well she did her job. *My first independent job and it's turning into a total disaster. It's like I'm fighting my own Guild. I can't ask anyone like Cara or Trux or Pradar to help me when it's obvious the Guild Hall Supervisor wants to trip me up and will hammer anyone who gets in his way. But if even one person would volunteer to help me, it would make this so much easier to handle.*

One person had helped her without thought of the cost, Mari realized. *The Mage. A blasted Mage, who was willing to die protecting me. He was willing to cut his own chances to nothing in order to give me that last bit of water. Why couldn't Alain have been a Mechanic? I could use a friend like that right now.*

Stars above, did I actually just wish a Mage could be my friend? Wake up, Mari. Focus on the job. You are going to get to the Hall of City Government and do the best job anyone in the Mechanics Guild has ever seen. And if anyone else tries to get in your way, they're going to regret it.

She reached into her jacket to check her pistol, then walked through the hallways rapidly, willing to face whatever threats waited outside as soon as possible rather than spend any more time here.

CHAPTER EIGHT

Ringhmon in the morning seemed to be just as hot as Ringhmon in the afternoon, though the yellowish cast to the sky appeared to be a little less prominent. Mari had left her pack at the Guild Hall, but even the smaller tool kit seemed to weigh more with every step. She singled out one of the commons on the street. "Where is the Hall of Government?"

The common lowered his head and tried to keep walking.

Amazed, Mari stepped in front of him. "I'm talking to you!"

The common jerked to a halt, pretending to have just noticed her. "Yes, Lady Mechanic?"

"Where is the Hall of Government?" she repeated.

"It lies on the Square of Heroes, Lady Mechanic," the common answered, then tried to dart around her.

Mari flung out one arm to block him. "How do I get there?" she demanded.

The common scowled, looking around as if seeking a way past her. "I don't know."

Commons never liked talking to Mechanics, but Mari was startled by this level of hostility and unhelpfulness. Disconcerted, she put on the full Mechanic attitude, letting her tone become menacing. "I'll give you one chance to rethink that answer, and if I'm not satisfied with what I hear you're going to be very, very unhappy. Do you understand?"

The display of confidence worked. The common nodded rapidly, his face still averted. "The blue markers, Lady Mechanic. On the road. The trolley which stops at them goes to the Hall of Government." His voice held fear but also resentment.

Mari just looked at the common for a long moment, trying to figure out how to handle him. According to all she had been taught, she should unleash a series of threats and put the common in his place, but even if that worked she would hate herself afterwards. "That's all." She walked onward, looking for the blue markers.

The trolley proved to be a horse-drawn wagon moving at glacial speed. The operator at least knew better than to ask a Mechanic for a fare, though he did betray the same fear and resentment as the earlier common had. Bad attitudes from commons weren't unusual, but this intensity of them, the openness of them, was abnormal. Was it just Ringhmon? Or was this part of the problem which had erupted at Julesport? Surely the commons here knew that if they created a big enough problem for the Mechanics Guild, the Guild elders could simply provide the Empire with the assistance to reach their city in overwhelming force and turn Ringhmon into a conquered outpost.

Mari sat glumly watching the glorious and grimy city of Ringhmon roll past at the slow clip the single horse pulling the trolley could manage. The city appeared to be overrun with guards and police as well as negative behaviors.

At least the presence of all of those guards was reassuring. Mari wondered if the riders she had seen yesterday actually had been unrelated to the bandits. Everything she had seen of Ringhmon so far made it seem unlikely that people could ride freely through the place brandishing weapons. Unfortunately, that was the only thing she had seen about Ringhmon so far that wasn't unpleasant.

Thoughts of the bandits led her back to thoughts of the Mage. *I wouldn't have made it here without his help. At least he knows what help means now. I hope his Guild Hall in Ringhmon treated him better than mine has so far.*

✳   ✳   ✳

Alain traded the dim passages of the Mage Guild Hall for the bright sunlight of the streets outside. A night of meditation and a morning of darkly suspicious Inquiry had become a day of more light but no further enlightenment. *I will not allow the insults of elders who do not know me to affect me. I will not allow a brief encounter with a Mechanic to destroy my future as a Mage. The elders cannot change me, and the Mechanic cannot control me. And I will not allow foresight I do not understand to continue to unsettle me.* His thoughts going around in circles, Alain sought release in movement and the distraction of a strange city.

On a whim, as he left the Guild Hall Alain wrapped himself inside the spell which bent light and made him virtually impossible to see. Even another Mage could only sense his presence and location. The spell took effort, but he maintained it for a while, strolling along invisible to the commons and the occasional pair of Mechanics he spotted, just like an acolyte hiding from other acolytes who had not developed their skills enough to sense him. The Mage elders would have been annoyed to observe him playing with that spell. Perhaps that was why he was doing it.

As he crossed a street, Alain could see that the stone edgings were cracked and chipped, and in some cases well out of line with their neighboring stones. The buildings revealed the same sort of evidence of long decline. What commons and Mechanics called reality was only an illusion, but it took careful study of the illusion to know what to change, so Alain took in every flaw, every variation in the buildings.

He walked down a street lined with what at first glance were grand mansions with fronts of fitted stone. But the "stone" was another attempt at illusion by commons, just wood planks beveled at intervals to look like stone blocks and then covered with paint mixed with stone dust.

Alain found himself wondering what the Mechanic would have thought of these attempts to mimic other substances. *What would she say? Something I could not understand, probably. The words she used did not seem to mean the same things as the words I use. If I could ask—*

No. Stop thinking about her.

Still unseen inside his spell, Alain glanced at the commons who unknowingly shared the street with him, all of them plodding along with expressions that seemed to combine stubbornness and weariness. The pride of the city of Ringhmon appeared to exist mainly in the minds of its leaders.

As Alain went deeper into the city he could see that many of the street intersections were guarded by tough-looking individuals whose leather armor marked them as some sort of local militia. They all wore short swords and carried wooden clubs about as long as Alain's forearm. The citizens kept well away from the toughs, averting their eyes. Sensitive to the emotions which shadows displayed, Alain felt as if he were drowning in a sea of despair and oppression.

Alain finally dropped his concealment spell, getting a little perverse satisfaction from the panicky way nearby commons reacted to the sudden appearance of a Mage among them. He strolled over to examine a monument commemorating some great event, but when Alain got close enough to read the inscription he found that the "victory" involved one of the failed Imperial expeditions through the desert waste. Alain studied the images of larger-than-life warriors carrying banners from the city of Ringhmon as they trampled Imperial legionaries. In a corner of one "gold" panel, he saw where the thin layer of gilt had been worn away, exposing a dull gray metal beneath. Another illusion of wealth, this one within an illusion of victory. Layers of falseness. Did the commons here believe any of it?

Shaking his head, he turned away to see several citizens of Ringhmon standing close and watching him with wary eyes. They appeared abnormally bold in their attitudes, so Alain gave them the dead, emotionless look of a Mage and they scattered hastily. He had been told that commons believed Mages could use spells on them, changing their shape and nature, turning them into animals or insects, or overturning their reason. Alain knew this was false, that no Mage could harm or change a shadow directly, yet the Mage Guild had encouraged such superstitions, seeing them as a good way of keeping the commons properly subdued and fearful. He probably should have simply ignored the commons, though. If the elders at the Guild Hall could see him playing such tricks on shadows they would call him young indeed.

Alain squinted upward, seeing that the morning had advanced. The day was already once again hot and unpleasant, and the cool, dark rooms of the Guild Hall were beginning to seem a lot more attractive. The Hall would have a records section, a place holding the words of others in which he could find relief from the emptiness of the world.

Alain started back the way he had come, crossing a large street. A trolley had just passed, moving slowly away under the pull of a large draft horse which seemed either old or simply as dispirited as the people of this city. Alain felt a sensation as if he were being watched by sightless eyes, or as if his name had been silently called. He looked toward the trolley. Most of the seats were packed with commons sitting with their backs to him, but one bench held only a single individual, someone wearing the short, dark jacket of a Mechanic. Just as unmistakable as the jacket was the shoulder-length, raven-black hair of the Mechanic wearing it.

Master Mechanic Mari.

Alain came to a halt, oblivious to the carts and wagons which had to veer around him. *Mechanics are shadows. None of them matter. She does not matter. I should walk on and return to my Guild Hall.*

Yet, how odd that in this city our paths crossed in this time and place. Some of the elders at Ihris told me that the illusion which is this world guides us in certain ways, sometimes toward wisdom, sometimes toward error. What led me to this street at this time? What led that Mechanic to be on that particular trolley?

How did she make me look toward her?

Did she cause that? She has not looked back. Why attract my attention in such a subtle manner and then avoid even meeting my eyes?

I am on this road for a reason. I feel that. But is this the road to wisdom or error? Is it a road the Mechanic chose for both of us? Or did something else place us both on it, both unwitting?

He knew what the elders here in Ringhmon would say. Alain considered that, thinking of the difficulty those elders would have controlling their outrage, thinking of their dismissive words toward him. *If nothing matters, then nothing matters. Why not see where this road leads?*

Still, the consequences if he were seen near this Mechanic again...

Uncertain, Alain took another look at the back of Master Mechanic Mari. His expression did not change, but his breath hissed in between his teeth in a momentary reaction that he could not suppress. The foresight had come to him again, once more centered on this Mechanic, and the dark mist was more ominous than what he had seen in the waste. Black as the darkest night and shot with red veins, the mist foretold danger and violence in terms he needed no elder to interpret. Oddly, once again he sensed the storm clouds from his earlier vision, pressing in toward the Mechanic from the fringes of the dark mist. *The Mechanic is in peril still. Does it have something to do with this thing which thinks but does not live? What is such a thing? The Mechanic knew when I spoke of it, though she tried to hide it.*

Is it some form of Mechanic troll? Trolls do not truly think or live, and Mechanics are not supposed to be able to make such things. Do I not have an obligation to learn if Mechanics can do this, so as to warn my Guild?

And if this Mechanic can control the actions of a Mage such as I, make me think certain thoughts and react to calls which were not made, then that too the Mage Guild must know.

This is not about the Mechanic. She is nothing. I have already given her warning of danger here, a warning she seems not to have heeded. I am doing this for my Guild. He repeated that to himself, but wondered how much of an illusion his rationale really was. At least it served to justify his actions while he decided what to do next.

Why hadn't the Mechanic taken his warning? Alain felt rising irritation and ruthlessly restrained the emotion. And why, when the other Mechanics he had seen this morning had all been in pairs, did she travel alone? Was she so careless?

She had not acted careless in the waste. Desperate, certainly, especially when she risked them both to confront what proved to be the salt caravan.

What were the Mechanic's elders like? She had said they were like his own, strange though that sounded. Did they listen to her? Had she passed on the warning, only to have her elders dismiss her words as Alain's elders had dismissed his?

He suddenly felt certain that this Mechanic had no choice but to go onward to danger. Once again, he knew how she must feel. A strange sensation, worrisome. How to make it go away? How to release the hold she had placed upon him?

She had saved his life. Alain almost smiled before he caught himself. That was it. Several times she had "helped" him. The Mechanic had used that to influence him. No wonder the elders warned against helping.

How to cancel it out? Like canceled like. Power could defeat power. She had saved him, she had helped him. He would help her, perhaps even save her life. That would cancel whatever the Mechanic had done to him. He would be free of her.

The logic had no flaws. This must be wisdom. Alain began walking behind the trolley, staying close enough to keep it in sight, which was easy enough to do given its slow pace. The way out of error led through this Mechanic. He had gotten into it by associating with her, and now he had to get out of it the same way.

Mari reflected glumly that the only good thing about this journey was the fact that no one dared share a bench with a Mechanic, so that no matter how crowded the trolley got, Mari still had plenty of room to herself. Unfortunately she also had plenty of time to think: about Senior Mechanics who seemed determined to trip her up, about Mages who didn't act like Mages were supposed to act and gave warnings about things they weren't supposed to know, and about a city full of hostile commons who seemed ready to blow like a boiler under too much pressure.

She felt some sympathy for the Senior Mechanics concerned that Ringhmon could erupt like Julesport had, but only a little. Senior Mechanics insisted on the policies which kept the commons not only under control but resenting their inferior status. As an apprentice, Mari had gotten into more than one heated argument with other apprentices over her belief that the commons could be controlled without rubbing their noses in it. She had been gaining converts to her point of view when those arguments were abruptly halted. She was called in for some extremely serious questioning by the Guild Hall Supervisor at Caer Lyn, ending in a very clear order. *We know what we're doing. We have centuries of experience. A few years ago you were living in a hovel among the commons, thinking you were no better than them. You were wrong then and you're wrong now. Listen, learn and obey.*

She had shut up like a good little apprentice, because she wasn't stupid. But she hadn't understood then and still didn't understand why the Senior Mechanics refused to consider a different approach. It wasn't as though the superiority of the Mechanics was artificial, something made up. The commons couldn't do the things that Mechanics could. They needed Mechanics. That reality couldn't be altered by treating the commons with a little dignity.

Nothing is real.

Blasted Mage. He believed some really strange things, and she would do best to forget them as soon as possible. She knew what was real and what wasn't.

It wasn't until she had spent a few moments studying the distant shape of a Mage crossing the road ahead of them, easy to make out because of the way the commons left a wide berth around him, that Mari realized she had been looking for a glimpse of one particular Mage. That one ahead couldn't be him. Too short and too wide.

Why was she looking? He was in the past. Gone. Stop thinking about him. The job was ahead of her. Eyes front. Focus.

Eventually the trolley dragged its weary way to the Hall of City Government. The vast structure looming up across a broad expanse of courtyard was, outwardly at least, the grandest Mari had seen in Ringhmon, with a profusion of columns, balustrades, roof angles and balconies. The courtyard itself was sprinkled with larger-than-life statues of noble-looking individuals who literally looked down from their pedestals on those citizens who were trudging across the open area toward the big building.

Mari slung the strap of her tool kit over her shoulder and joined the stream of humanity. She glanced at some of the pedestals as she passed them, reading inscriptions which praised the persons whose statues surmounted them as "servants of the people." If there had been another Mechanic with her, Mari would have made some comment about servants looking down on those they were supposed to be serving.

There were plenty of guards standing around, looking brutally alert. Mari paused to consider whether she wanted to worry about carrying a concealed weapon into the city hall. The pistol could be awkward if she needed to squeeze around equipment or take off her jacket to do anything. She didn't want anyone in Ringhmon knowing she had a weapon if she could help it. Mari knelt down, pretending to adjust the lace of her boot. Bent down like that, Mari could slip her hand inside her jacket and reach her pistol without being seen. She opened a compartment on the outside of her tool kit and stuffed the pistol in, then resealed the compartment. It wasn't a great hiding place, but no citizen of Ringhmon was going to be looking in there.

Finally reaching the steps, Mari saw her path blocked by a long line of citizens waiting to be passed by the guards. That was fine for commons. Mechanics lived by other rules, and this was one time she wasn't the least bit unhappy about that. Mari went to one side and walked up past the entire line until she reached the entry where two soldiers in highly polished breastplates were using their authority to give randomly chosen citizens a hard time.

One of the soldiers caught sight of her out of the corner of his eye and swung her way, one hand going to the elaborate hilt of his short sword. "Hold on— " Then he caught sight of her jacket. "Uh, yeah?"

That was the limit. These goons might be able to abuse the common folk of Ringhmon, but they wouldn't get to play that game with her. Mari glared at the man. "Did you address me?" she asked.

He got the hint. "Yes, Lady Mechanic?"

"I have a contract with the City Fathers of Ringhmon."

The guard turned to his companion, who made a baffled gesture. Mari tried to keep her temper at yet another set of people expressing surprise at her presence. The second guard called to someone inside the building. "Gerd, there's a Mechanic here, says she's got a contract."

Gerd came out, his breastplate just as bright as the others, but carrying a Mechanic rifle as his weapon. Mari glanced at it, confirming that it was another repeating rifle. *I don't care what Guild policy is. If I ever get to Danalee I'm going to have a long talk with the Mechanics there about their choice of customers.*

How many rifles has the Guild let Ringhmon buy? A city this size shouldn't have more than a dozen.

I guess that's where the money went that could have paid for truly impressive buildings in this city.

Gerd eyed Mari doubtfully. "A contract, you say, Lady?"

"That's correct," Mari said, annoyed by his skepticism. "Master Mechanic Mari of Caer Lyn."

"Master Mechanic?" Gerd took one look at Mari's hardening expression and apparently decided not to pursue that question. "What's the contract for, Lady?"

"That's between me and the City Fathers. I'm not permitted to discuss it with anyone else."

Gerd thought about that for a moment, his brows lowered. Mari imagined she could almost see rusty wheels turning slowly inside his head. "Then it's a matter for City Manager Polder, Lady. I'll take you to him. But first we need to search that, Lady." The guard pointed at her tool bag.

"This is my equipment. My tools. You don't search it." Everybody knew that. Commons weren't allowed access to Mechanic tools, and commons weren't allowed to search Mechanics.

"I'm sorry, Lady, but there are no exceptions." Gerd puffed himself up in a routine which he must have pulled on countless common folk. "Those are the rules. No exceptions."

Unbelievable. That attitude hadn't developed overnight. Why had Guild Hall Supervisor Stimon, who had seemed to enjoy slapping her down, let the commons in Ringhmon develop that kind of behavior? Did he want to force a Guild intervention here? "You can make any rule you want, but I don't have to pay any attention to it," Mari said. "I don't know why your city is so afraid of its own citizens, but I am a Mechanic. Has Ringhmon totally forgotten the treatment expected by members of the Mechanics Guild? Does Ringhmon wish to offend the Mechanics Guild? Shall I walk back down those steps this moment and return to my Guild Hall along with every other Mechanic in this city to await a formal apology from the City Fathers, and the payment of a large fine, for their actions toward our Guild?" Surely even Guild

Hall Supervisor Stimon would back her up on this. No city could be allowed to treat Mechanics that way.

Mari was certain that she hadn't yelled, just spoken very clearly, yet the two lesser guards and Gerd leaned back as if being subjected to a gale. Gerd, considerably paler now, nodded several times. Even a low-ranking guard supervisor had to realize what would happen to any city put under a Mechanics Guild interdict. It would forbid any repair of existing equipment, prohibit sales of new equipment, halt train shipments, and cut off all electrical power coming from the Mechanics Guild Hall. "Yes, Lady. I'll take you and your bag to City Manager Polder."

Mari, having made her point, nodded in agreement. Polder's name was on her contract, so she knew he was an acceptable person to speak with. "All right."

Out of the corner of her eye she could see the commons waiting in line doing a poor job of hiding their glee at seeing the guards dressed down. Some even seemed to be directing looks of approval at her. *Master Mechanic Mari, champion of the common folk*, she thought. *Yeah. That's me.* The guards had deserved to get chewed out, but throwing her weight around had always left Mari with a bad taste in her mouth. She also knew that even though Gerd and his pals couldn't touch her, after she left they could and would take out their public embarrassment on those commons. *"There's nothing you can do about that, Mari. You can't fix everything."* How many times had Alli said those words to her?

Gerd whispered some instructions to his subordinates, emphasizing his words with angry gestures, then with a bow waved Mari into the building. She followed, trying to walk in a confident and competent manner. Most Mechanics adopted a swagger to their walk, a special way of emphasizing their superiority, but Mari had never been able to do it right. When she tried to swagger, it usually looked as if she were swinging her hips in an awkward attempt to look seductive. That wasn't quite the professional image that she wanted to cultivate, so Mari had eventually decided to leave the swaggering to others.

Secretly, she had always thought the swagger looked a little silly, anyway, so she stuck to her decision even after some other Mechanics mocked her for walking like a common. They weren't the sort of Mechanics whose opinions she cared a great deal about anyway.

Gerd led the way to an unadorned doorway and, gulping nervously, announced their presence to those inside.

City Manager Polder proved to be a small, balding man with a sharp face and a sharper smile. Mari wondered why Polder reminded her of the taller and heavier set Guild Hall Supervisor Stimon, then realized Polder's smile was just as false as the one Stimon had sometimes worn. *Twins under the skin, those two.*

Mari noticed that Polder dismissed guard leader Gerd with the casual ease of someone used to exercising power. She noticed as well that Polder's garments were very nice but not ostentatious. The man appeared to have so much power he didn't worry about trying to impress people. That also echoed a Mechanic's attitude in a disquieting way.

Polder led the way deeper into the building. "How was your journey to Ringhmon, Lady Mechanic?"

In no mood to be reminded of the misery she had endured, Mari responded frostily. "I've had better. My caravan was destroyed by bandits."

Polder's false smile didn't waver in the slightest. "The Waste is a forbidding place. The Empire does a very poor job of policing its side, and the brigands there too often harass those on Ringhmon's territory, fleeing before Ringhmon's forces can call them to account. It is fortunate that you were rescued by a band of salt traders."

It wasn't surprising that Polder had learned that a Mechanic had entered the city with that group of traders. But why had he made a point of telling her that he knew it?

"You were not the only survivor so rescued, I understand," Polder continued.

So that was it. He wanted to know more about the Mage who the traders would have said had been with her. Mari made a gesture of indifference. "There was some Mage also from the caravan. He showed up when I found the salt traders."

"You were not traveling together?"

Mari turned a frown on Polder. No need to lie on this one. Just say what anyone would expect to hear. "A Mechanic traveling with a Mage? Are you seriously asking that?"

"No, Lady Mechanic, of course not." Polder cleared his throat. "I must admit to some surprise, Lady Mechanic. Our contract with your Guild specified that we needed someone extremely well qualified for the task. The best to be found in the eastern lands. Your Guild offices in Palandur insisted that you were that person."

"My Guild had good grounds for saying I met the contract's requirements."

Somewhere along the way, two more guards joined them. Mari tried not to look wary as she took in their plain but very good armor and alert movements. No shiny flashiness like the gate guards. These were the sort of guards she had seen clustered around the Emperor in Palandur, guards who were chosen not for looks but for ruthless efficiency. Yet Polder, officially just the City Manager, somehow merited such wolflike guardians.

Mari started to wonder who really ran Ringhmon. The City Fathers might think they did, but Polder seemed more and more like the one in charge.

After passing through several more guarded entries and along narrow hallways lined with identical doors bearing cryptic designations, the small group halted at a wooden door reinforced by bands of high-quality metal. Polder produced a large key and unlocked the door, then rapped several times before entering.

Once inside, Mari could see the reason for knocking on the door. Three more guards were in the room, one positioned behind the door, and all watching them alertly. But then she caught sight of the machine she had come to fix, and her breath caught.

"Impressive, is it not?" Polder asked.

"Very impressive," Mari admitted. She stepped closer, taking in the size and complexity of the device that dominated the room. She felt her spirits rising, a rush of anticipation at being able to work on this machine and prove her ability to fix it.

"A Model Six out of the Mechanics Guild calculating and analysis device workshops of Alfarin," Polder stated, his voice smug.

"I know," Mari replied. "It's actually a Form Three of the Model Six, with additional data storage and analysis capability added." She glanced at Polder, who let himself look mildly impressed.

"Then you know this device well?" he inquired.

"As well as anyone but the Mechanic who builds them, and that Mechanic was among my instructors for a while." He had overseen the construction of only one of the Form Threes, as far as Mari knew. Someone had wanted to spare no expense to get the best calculating and analysis device that could be built, and the Mechanics Guild had been happy to comply.

But, according to the records she had been shown in Palandur before she left, Ringhmon had purchased only a Form One of the Model Six, and that several decades ago. The Mechanics Guild Hall here had an ongoing contract to keep it operating. The average city had only one calculating and analysis device, because the Guild kept them very expensive and the supply extremely limited. They were all Model Sixes, of course. The Guild built only one design, though it allowed buyers to add a few extras to the basic Model Six, which had been around for a very long time. Mari had never met anyone who had seen a Model Five, and when the Fives were pulled from service however many decades ago, every one of the operating and repair manuals had either been destroyed or consigned to the no access permitted vaults at Mechanics Guild headquarters in Palandur.

She had asked questions about that, too, until the uncomfortably paternal Professor T'mos had warned her about it. *The Guild will tell you what you need to know, Mari. If something is locked away, there's a good reason. You obviously don't need to know whatever it is if it's locked away.*

No wonder history hadn't interested her. Too much of it was hidden.

Mari glanced around at the three room guards, City Manager Polder, and his two other guards. "I can't work with this crowd in here. I don't need the distractions and I don't need to be stepping over them to get to things." She wasn't worried about them watching her work, since calculating and analysis thinking ciphers were far too complex for commons to figure out. Even the great majority of Mechanics couldn't grasp them, but the Guild didn't worry about that because only a few calculating and analysis devices existed.

Polder nodded without argument, then gestured to the three room guards to leave.

Mari evaluated the size of the room again and glanced at him. "It's still too crowded."

The City Manager regarded her, then pointed at his two guards and with two quick flicks of his finger indicated that his two guards should also go into the hallway. Both men went, standing out in the hall so they could look inside from slightly different angles, their hands resting near their sword hilts. Polder himself stepped back, flat against the wall, and folded his arms. He obviously intended to stay.

Fine. He would be standing there for hours while she went about the tedious work of getting this machine working properly again. Polder would not be enjoying himself, and he would get a ringside seat to see how well Mari knew her job. Yes. That was fine with her.

She opened her tool kit, pulling out the necessary equipment, then went to the Model Six's main control panel and begin entering some test requests. Instead of issuing the proper response on a punched stream of paper, the Model Six did an advanced-mechanical version of gagging.

Mari smiled, the forebodings of the morning lost in the joy of doing something she could handle very well. Her first job would be easier than many of the tests she had passed to earn her Master Mechanic rating. She could fix this. Uncertainties disappearing like dissipating steam, Mari got other material to print out on the paper stream, examining the thinking ciphers for errors. They weren't hard to spot, though surprising in a Model Six whose design had been around for so long. Getting happily into her work, Mari painstakingly put together a cipher fix, loaded it into the calculating and analysis device and then repeated her tests.

Then she frowned. The Model Six gagged again, but in a different way. That shouldn't happen. She knew the Model Six cipher very well, and her fix should not have caused that. Mari developed a new fix, loading it in, ran the tests again...and found that some of the original problems had reappeared.

Mari rubbed her chin, studying the large, hand-crafted metal boxes that sat before her. There was one possible explanation for what was happening. It was an explanation that wasn't supposed to be possible, involving something that wasn't supposed to exist, but she had been taught about it anyway at Professor S'san's insistence. Taking a deep breath, Mari started putting together a new set of tests. Lost in the challenge of her work, Mari was oblivious by now to the passage of time and the silent form of City Manager Polder standing against the wall. Mari didn't even notice when electric lights were switched on to brighten a room going dim as the sun sank low in the sky.

The tests ran. Mari stared at the long, long strip printing out. *There it is. No doubt. This isn't an error in cipher code. It's a contagion. Someone infected this Model Six with another cipher designed to keep it from working right. No wonder Master Mechanic Xian couldn't fix this. The fact that such contagions could be created was so secret that few Mechanics knew about it, and even fewer had any training in dealing with them.* Mari was one of that last tiny group, which explained exactly why she had been needed here.

If someone knew or suspected this was the problem, why didn't they tell me? And who created this? I don't recognize the hand that crafted this contagion, and I know just about everyone who can build ciphers like this. And creating a contagion is strictly banned. Anyone caught creating one would lose their heads. Literally.

Fixing this is half the problem. The other half is figuring out who did it. Mari looked over at the City Manager. "The contract I have stated that you had no idea of the origin of the problem with this machine. Have you learned anything since then?"

Polder shook his head very deliberately. "No. Nothing. Are you saying you cannot fix it?"

He had to be lying. All of the security, all of the guards, all of the Mechanic weapons argued that Ringhmon considered itself surrounded by enemies. Why wouldn't Ringhmon suspect those enemies? And if the contagion had been installed for blackmail, the city would have surely received a demand for payment in exchange for a fix. Instead, Ringhmon had come to the Mechanics Guild and claimed ignorance. "I can fix it. I'll have to wipe the existing thinking cipher and reload it, but your information and calculations should be fine since they're stored outside the analysis components." She pointed at the spools of wire on which the machine kept the results of its work.

"You are certain we will lose nothing?" Polder demanded.

Mari shook her head, wondering why that particular concern had finally rattled Polder's composure. "You'll lose nothing."

An extra Model Six, and the effective ruler of this city worried about what was stored on it. Mari tried to keep a calm appearance as she resolved to find out more about that before she left here.

❈   ❈   ❈

By the time Mari finished purging all trace of the contagion and reloading the thinking cipher, the sky outside the windows set high up on one wall was completely dark. Suppressing a yawn, Mari ran her tests again and was rewarded with perfect results. It felt very good, bringing a warm sense of accomplishment. *Who else could've fixed this? Maybe a total of two other Mechanics, one of whom rarely leaves Alfarin and the other rarely leaves Palandur. Hooray for me. First contract successfully completed. Good job, Master Mechanic Mari, and to blazes with Senior Mechanic Stimon's black mark. I might as well praise myself, since I'm not sure anyone else will.*

Now for the rest of the job. She called up another readout, which should give line headers for the information stored on the Model Six. Neither Polder nor any other common would be able to know that was what she was looking at, so there shouldn't be any risk in it. But Mari still had to work to keep from showing any nervousness as she called up that data.

The coded printout scrolled past as she scanned it. Not the usual listing of financial information, payrolls, inventories and such. No. Mari had to take a second look to be sure what it was. Measurements. Length, width, thickness. Shapes. Materials. Specifications.

In a crude way, it was a description of a disassembled Mechanic device.

A repeating rifle.

This could only have come from someone trying to reverse-engineer a Mechanic rifle, taking it apart piece by piece to discover how to build a copy. Who would do such a thing? And why? Only Mechanics can do that kind of work. The Guild strictly prohibits commons from trying to learn any Mechanic secrets, and regularly tells the commons about the severe penalties for anyone caught trying. Why hasn't Master Mechanic Xian already spotted what these commons are doing? He can't be that incompetent! What the blazes is going on in this city?

A contagion of unknown origin. Hostile, arrogant commons. Somebody playing around with Mechanic secrets. Mari felt like she had when the bandits attacked the caravan. *I don't know what's going on, but I've got to get out of here.* "That's it," she stated in what she hoped was a calm voice. "It's done."

Polder's face lit with eagerness. "The Model Six works as it should again?"

"Exactly as it should." Mari slowly stretched, feeling the strain of the day's work and tense with what she had learned. *Take it easy. You're tired, ready to leave, work's done. Be like that Mage. Don't show anything else.*

"Excellent." Polder gave her a look of polite interest, waving his guards back into the room. "What was the nature of the problem?"

I have a nasty suspicion that you already know, and if you don't know, I'm not telling you. "The exact cause is a Guild matter, not to be discussed with outsiders."

Instead of bridling at her words, or even showing the usual resentment commons couldn't hide when Mechanics declined to share their secrets, Polder nodded in a humble way that seemed very out of character. "Naturally. But can you tell me how to ensure the problem is not repeated? Is it anything we're doing on the Model Six?"

Mari shook her head. "No."

Polder looked regretful. "You saw nothing out of the ordinary? Are you asking me to believe that you do not understand the problem you claim to have fixed?"

Polder's attitude set off alarms inside Mari. She had been assuming that no common would dare do anything, not when it was known that she had come here. It was only at this moment that Mari realized how late it was, how dark outside. Polder and his guards could swear that she had left this building before mysteriously vanishing. She was abruptly aware of the fact that she was alone, inside a building owned by commons, surrounded by commons, some of whom were clearly dangerous. *They wouldn't— Would they? This isn't supposed to happen.*

With the pistol hidden in her tool kit, Mari had no weapon within easy reach. No weapon except her status as a Mechanic. She tried to reassert her authority fast. "I'm a Mechanic with the full power of my Guild behind me. I don't *ask* commons to do anything, I *tell* them. I am done here, and I am leaving. My Guild Hall will send you the bill for my services."

Instead of moving out of her way or getting angry, Polder gave a small, humorless smile. "I see. Perhaps it's time that your Guild learns that the people of Ringhmon don't want to stay any longer in the box the Mechanics have made to confine this world."

"I have no idea what you're talking about, nor do I care," Mari said with what she hoped was the right mix of anger and authority. "I've finished my job and I'm leaving," she repeated more forcefully.

"As you wish." Polder made a small gesture, looking somewhere behind Mari where his two guards were standing.

Mari started to turn, then something hard slammed against the back of her head. Her last sight before darkness came was of Polder still watching her with that grim smile.

CHAPTER NINE

Alain had watched from a distance as the Mechanic left the trolley and entered the very large building which served as the center of Ringhmon government. Already the subject of curious and worried glances from passerby, the Mage began walking around the outside of the area bounded by the great building. As he had expected, there were numerous small and large restaurants dedicated to feeding those who labored inside the building. He also located a store which sold written items, and found a large volume dedicated to the history of Ringhmon. The bookseller he selected reacted to Alain's presence in his store with ill-concealed unease, but Alain gave no sign that he noticed.

He carried the book out of the store, past the payment desk where the clerk pretended not to see Alain. Commons paid elders for the services of Mages, but Mages did not "pay" for anything, Alain had been told. They took what they wanted or needed from whichever common had those things, and the commons, who did not matter anyway because they did not even exist, should be grateful that the Mage had not chosen to take more. If a Mage needed shelter, he walked into a room and any commons there left. If he needed food, he took it from a roadside stall or entered a place where commons ate and was fed. No one would dare deny a Mage.

Except a Mechanic. He had been warned that Mechanics would resist, and so should be ignored. *Do not walk into a room with them or take their food. Just realize that the Mechanics do not exist and are not worthy of your attention.*

Unless they threaten you, and then you must kill them, Mage Alain. Mechanics are as merciless as they are mercenary. If any appear dangerous, kill them.

"How can I ever repay you?" Master Mechanic Mari had asked him.

Alain stood on the street for a moment, looking at the book he had taken. He could not do what commons did even if he chose to. "Pay" had something to do with money. He knew that much, but he had no money. Why would a Mage carry money when he or she never needed it?

Unless they threaten you, and then you must kill them.

What if he had remembered that advice during the bandit attack, when the Mechanic had pointed her weapon at his face? He could have killed her then. He could have tried, at least. Then, when she was dead, the bandits would have found Alain and killed him, too.

Clearly the advice of his elders was lacking in some respects.

On his journey from Ihris to the Imperial port of Landfall, Alain had taken rooms and food just as he had been told to do, but not without noticing the fear and resentment on the faces of the commons who provided those things. They tried their best to hide it, worried that he would do something terrible to them, but it was always apparent to a Mage.

It had bothered him. Despite all of his training within the Mage Guild Hall, once out among the commons again, whenever he saw a man and a woman he thought of his parents. When around Mages, Alain had acted as they had, oblivious to the cowering commons. Now, alone among commons, he could choose how to act.

Perhaps he would take back the book when he was done with it.

He had to eat, however. Alain chose a restaurant with a window seat which gave a good view of the entrance to the government building and settled down to watch for the Mechanic's reappearance. He still had no clear idea of what he was doing or what he would do next. If this course of action was a road, he should reach a point where it offered a choice, to go onward or back, or to turn off onto another road.

A trembling server came to stand near him, afraid to speak. Alain gave her a dispassionate glance, then pointed to another table where a common was eating and drinking. The server went to grab the food and drink from the common, paused as if realizing that might not be the best course of action, and looked back at Alain, who shook his head and pointed to the kitchen.

Within a very short time Alain had his own meal set before him, after which the commons pretended he wasn't there while they discreetly watched for any sign that he wanted anything.

Yes. It did bother him. He wasn't certain why the faded memories of his parents came at such times.

It did not seem like the sort of question that he should ask an elder, though.

He ate without tasting, in the Mage way. Food was another illusion, of course, and while it was necessary, too much focus on it would distract a Mage. Or so he had been taught, and acolytes did not vary from or question the wisdom they were told. Finishing, Alain settled into meditation, outwardly unmoving, barely aware of the commons avoiding coming near him, the book showing the alleged, officially approved history of Ringhmon open before him but unread.

The sun sank through the sky until darkness began creeping across the courtyard, and large numbers of citizens who either worked in the city hall or had business there filed out and dispersed into the city. Alain blinked his way back to alertness, certain that the Mechanic had not yet left the building. How much time had passed? He had reached here before noon, and now sunset was passing. He was hungry again.

Alain looked toward a server, who jerked with fear at his glance. Pointing toward the kitchen once more, Alain soon had dinner before him. He ate it just as heedlessly as he had the earlier meal, paying no attention to the food, thinking that this road he had taken appeared to be leading nowhere. What did Mechanics do, anyway? It had never concerned him, but now Alain thought that whatever it was, it took awhile. Perhaps it took days. He almost got up to leave, but decided that if nothing mattered, then waiting here also did not matter. Besides, he had no wish to encounter the impassively hostile Mage elders of Ringhmon any sooner than he had to.

It was fully dark outside the restaurant when Alain's road finally took a turn. A deeper darkness flashed before his eyes and sudden pain filled his head, before both vanished without a trace as quickly as they had come. *What did that mean? Pain that was not my own? How could— ?*

Alain looked down at his hands, trying to apply what he knew to what had happened. *Foresight? Of something due to happen soon? Yes, very soon. Not a vision or something heard, but a physical sensation felt. I felt someone else's pain. How is that possible? Others do not exist. Their pain is not real. How can I feel it even through foresight?*

If only I knew more of foresight.

What he had experienced had felt real enough for that moment, though. *I did share feelings once, with Master Mechanic Mari, when I knew that she too did not want to appear too young or too weak. That was very different, and yet...* He tried to recall what he had just experienced, to recreate the moment of darkness and pain, in hopes of gaining more understanding. Instead, Alain felt something like a thread, thin and insubstantial. The thread wasn't real, either, but it ran from him, going out into the night, toward the looming, silent bulk of the Ringhmon Hall of City Government. He studied the thread that wasn't there, and somehow knew that it did not go somewhere, but to someone. He was linked to a shadow in some mysterious way.

As he examined the thread that wasn't there, Alain realized that in an indefinable way it felt like the Mechanic.

This was worse than he had thought.

Was the thread the means by which she had kept his thoughts on her, and caused him to act in ways contrary to his training? But he could feel no power running through the thread. It simply was. Without power there could be no spells.

A strange road this offers, indeed. No elder ever spoke of such a thing as a thread between a Mage and another. Mages can feel each other's presence at a distance. Not like this, not in any way like this, but perhaps the things are related. Alain hesitated, torn between his training, his curiosity, and that strange thread leading into the night. Up until this moment he could observe, seeing where the road led, putting off any decision. Now he saw two roads, one leading back to the Mage Hall and away from the thread, and the other following the thread. Would the thread break with increasing distance? How to judge the strength of something that was not there?

One road to safety, to the certainty of the wisdom his elders taught, and the other road into the dark, in every sense of the word.

The Mechanic was surely in trouble.

That did not matter at all. She did not matter at all.

If she died, would the thread break?

Alain felt a strange sensation as he thought about that. He had felt her pain. If she died, would he feel...?

His eyes stung in a strange way. Alain lowered his head and raised the cowl of his robes to shadow his face. He blinked several times, unable to understand why his eyes were watering. It had started when he thought of feeling the Mechanic die—

There it went again. The two things were somehow related.

Memory. Little girl Asha looking at little boy Alain on the first night after they had been brought to be acolytes. Her face streaked with... tears.

Crying. They had learned not to cry, to deny anything that might bring betraying tears and the punishments that came with them. They had striven to forget everything about tears.

The Mechanic had made him remember this, too.

He did not want her to die.

I could not save my parents. I could not save the commons with the caravan, the master or the commander of the guards or any of the others. I can save the Mechanic. I can try. Perhaps when I do so her spell on me will be lifted, the thread will break, and I can seek wisdom anew. If her uncanny influence has not already crippled my ability to work spells.

He should ask advice on this. Ask older and wiser Mages what the thread might mean, whether the Mechanic's effects on him could be reversed. But it would take a long time to return to the Mage Guild Hall, ask of the elders, and return. What if the Mechanic died in that time?

What if the elders would not let him return? What if they were watching when he felt the Mechanic die?

I must act. I must do what I think should be done. My elders already believe me to be a fool, too young to be a Mage, too young to follow wisdom. Alain stood up, looking into the darkness where the thread ran invisibly. *Perhaps they are right. The only way I will know, the only way I will learn, is by following this new road. I am young, but I know this.*

She may be only a shadow, but I will not leave her to the dark. I will not feel her die if I can prevent that, even though I do not understand why I am so resolved.

❀　　❀　　❀

Something very large seemed to be trying to beat its way out of Mari's head. She clenched her eyes tightly against the pain, slowly becoming aware that she was lying on something rough. Forcing herself to open her eyes, Mari waited until they could focus on her surroundings, gradually making out stone walls decorated only by strong metal rings set into them at various heights, and a ceiling made of heavy wooden beams. Weak light which flickered like that from an oil lamp filtered into the room through a small grating in a hefty wooden door which was reinforced by metal bands and bore an impressively large lock mechanism.

Wincing at the pounding in her head, Mari used one elbow to lever herself carefully to a sitting position. She had been lying on a wooden cot covered only by a thin mattress made of coarse fabric that had apparently been stuffed with straw a long time ago and never refreshed. She was still wearing everything she had before, including her Mechanics jacket and her empty shoulder holster under it, but her tool kit was nowhere to be seen. Reaching up, Mari gingerly felt the back of her head, her fingers encountering a lump surrounded by hair matted with what she assumed was blood.

A fresh wave of agony in her head made Mari decide to lie down again, staring at the heavy door across from her. She didn't see any sense in trying the door, since it was surely locked. As far as she could tell, that door marked the only entrance or exit from the room.

She rubbed one hand across the front of her Mechanics jacket. *I thought this jacket was the sort of armor no sane common would dare try to challenge. That's what the Guild always told me. "The Guild is your family. We'll always protect you." But here I am. At least I'm not dead. Why not?*

Think it through, Professor S'san always said. They still need me. If that Model Six breaks again they want me handy to fix it. What makes them think I'd help?

Mari thought of the torture methods she had heard about, things that rulers inflicted on commons, things she had never expected to worry about being done to her. Maybe she would be able to hold out. Hold out until they killed her, anyway. *I'm still supposed to be planning everything I'll do in my life, not trying to imagine how soon it'll come to an ugly end.*

Would Stimon bring the resources of the Mechanics Guild to bear on her behalf? If he did, she would be free before morning. But would he? What if Polder and his allies swore that Mari had left? A too-young Master Mechanic, wandering alone through a strange city after dark— and never mind that Stimon had set that up—he would accept that her disappearance was her fault.

No one here would want to rock the boat for Mari. Ringhmon was clearly spending a lot of money on Mechanic devices, everything from rifles to what must be a huge contract for that secret Model Six. How much profit would the Guild Hall here in Ringhmon, and the Guild as a whole, sacrifice in the name of questioning a perfectly reasonable story told by the oh-so-respectable rulers of Ringhmon?

Why hadn't any other Mechanics already noticed how Ringhmon was using that Model Six? If they had, why hadn't Mari been told? Why hadn't something been done? Commons couldn't do the work of Mechanics, but still it was forbidden for them to try.

As she lay there, Mari remembered whispers in the dark. She, Alli and Calu, sneaking out of the apprentice barracks in the middle of the night and climbing up onto the roof to share a few moments of pretend freedom from the oversight of older apprentices, Mechanics, and most of all Senior Mechanics. Calu, frowning up at the stars as he spoke in a voice so low only Mari and Alli could possibly hear. *If commons can't do Mechanic work, why is Mechanic work secret? It's like forbidding horses to learn algebra. What's the point? They can't. You only need to keep secrets from someone who can use those secrets. So why do we have to prevent commons from learning Mechanic secrets?*

Alli had punched him in the side. *Shut up, you idiot! Are you planning on asking some Senior Mechanic that question?*

No! But what do you think the answer is?

And, as Mari had already become used to, both Ali and Calu looked at her for an answer. She had pretended indifference. *I bet the answer is that if you ask the question you end up catching blazes and getting demoted back to entry-level apprentice. You guys want to bet on another answer?*

They hadn't, going on to other topics, like who was the stupidest Senior Mechanic, or who Mari should try dating *because you really are hopeless with boys, Mari.* But she had remembered Calu's question. It had nagged at her, even as she accepted what the Mechanics Guild told her about commons.

She lay there, her head pounding with pain, thoughts bleak, for how long she didn't know. The pain gradually lessened, and a stubborn flame of determination grew. *I am a Master Mechanic. I'm Master Mechanic Mari of Caer Lyn. I'm the youngest person ever to qualify as a Mechanic and the youngest ever to qualify as a Master Mechanic. I won't let anyone do this to me. Not Stimon and not Polder. Not anyone. I won't just lie here helpless until somebody comes for me. I'm going to get out of here and get some answers.*

She managed to sit up again, finding the hammering in her head stayed manageable this time. Moving very cautiously, Mari stood up, her feet a bit unsteady. Taking each step carefully, she crossed to the door, confirming that it was indeed locked. She knelt to examine the lock, discovering that it was tightly sealed behind a heavy armor plate so she couldn't have accessed its workings even if she had possessed her tools. *Odd. Why so much trouble when commons couldn't crack a lock? Am I not the first Mechanic who's disappeared in Ringhmon? But how could they hope to get away with having more than one Mechanic vanish after coming to the city hall? Surely they would have been smart enough to plan on a kidnapping that couldn't possibly be tied to them.*

That ambush. Mari, you idiot! The so called bandits equipped with lots of expensive rifles. The same type of rifles that Ringhmon has bought for its army. You fool. Why did it take you so long to figure out that connection? Who else even knew a Mechanic would be coming in on that caravan? They planned to kill everyone but me and probably bring me into the city with a hood over my head and a gag in my mouth, just one more anonymous prisoner. My Guild would've searched the Waste in vain for any trace of me. No wonder I saw some of those 'bandits' in the city. They were probably soldiers of Ringhmon, back from trying to find me, and once I made it to the city I bet they had orders to let Polder's guards handle it.

She had figured it out too late, though Mari suspected that even if she had realized the truth sooner no one would have listened to her.

Just a nervous girl, promoted too quickly, not really ready to do her job, and finding excuses to avoid it. Right. Well, water under the bridge. Now the problem is how to get out of here. She stood up again, going over the door and walls in search of any feature that might offer something she could use.

There was nothing. Just that extremely solid door and walls made of closely fitted blocks of extremely solid stone. Mari looked upward, staring at the ceiling. The beams of wood offered no signs of help, either. Hardwood, thick and massive. Even an axe would have trouble biting into them, and she didn't have an axe.

Mari squinted, spotting what seemed to be a large knothole in one beam. Something about it didn't look right. Grabbing the cot, she pulled it under the knothole, cautiously stood on the cot, and raised her hand to probe inside.

Something metal rested in the hole, concealed from sight in its shadow. Mari got her fingers around it, blessing the fact that her hands were small enough to allow that purchase, and twisted the object free. She started to pull it out, finding it resisting like something attached to wires. Yanking viciously, Mari pulled the object out, hearing and feeling wires snap. Then she stared down at what she had found.

A far-listener. Someone had installed a device in this cell that would detect any sounds made and send them along the wires to a place where someone else would hear them. She knew Mechanics produced such things. She had never imagined a common cell apparently designed to hold a Mechanic would include such a device.

Mari examined the far-listener closely, seeking clues to where it had been made. To her bafflement, she couldn't find any of the telltale makers' signs that should have provided a guide to which workshop in which city had crafted the thing. *It's as if this were made by Mechanics who aren't in the Guild. But that's impossible. All Mechanics are in the Guild. All Mechanics are trained by the Guild. No one is allowed to work outside the Guild. Someone trained by the Guild who tried freelancing would face death, and those who hired them would be banned from receiving Mechanic services.*

The far-listener couldn't exist. But it did.

Mari stuffed the broken far-listener into a pocket and sat down on the cot, staring at the stones of the wall. First she'd seen a Mage do things which Mages weren't supposed to be able to really do, then commons attacked her and imprisoned her, and now she had evidence that unauthorized Mechanic work was being done. Three "impossible" things. *My education wasn't nearly as thorough as I thought it was. I can't be the first Mechanic to experience this stuff. What the blazes is going on? If Professor S'san suspected enough to insist on giving me a pistol as a graduation gift, why didn't she tell me more?*

What else haven't I been told?

The light changed slightly. Mari looked up and over at one wall. There was now a narrow, roughly door-shaped hole in it. Standing in that hole was Mage Alain.

Mari stood up, realizing that her mouth was hanging open. *That wall was solid. I felt it. There wasn't any opening.* She watched as the Mage took two shaky steps into the cell, then paused, some of the strain leaving his face. She blinked, wondering what she had just seen, as the hole in the wall vanished as if it had never been. One moment it was there, the next it was gone.

Mari walked rapidly past the Mage and slammed her hand against the wall where the hole had been. The stone stung her palm, as hard and unyielding as it had been when she had checked it earlier.

Mari whirled back to face the Mage, the sudden motion making her still-throbbing head dizzy. "How did you do that?" she demanded, pointing at the wall, shocked by how ragged and hoarse her voice sounded.

The Mage looked at her with that unrevealing face. "I have come to...help," he said in an impassive voice tinged with weariness.

"Help? You've come to help me?" Mari felt a wave of weakness and leaned back against the solid stone for support. "A Mage has walked through a wall into my cell to help a Mechanic." She couldn't suppress a shudder. "My head. They hit me and now I'm seeing and hearing things."

The Mage came closer, peering at her. "You are hurt, Mechanic Mari?"

"Master Mechanic Mari," she muttered automatically, then reached out and grabbed his arm. "I'm not imagining this. You're real."

"Nothing is real. All is illusion. But I stand here," the Mage agreed.

"Don't confuse me. I can't handle it right now." Mari worked to control her breathing and to calm her nerves. Realizing she was still holding Mage Alain's arm in a tight grip, she let go. *"Never touch a Mage." "Why would I want to?"* "How did you get in here?"

"I learned that something ill had befallen you," he explained without apparent feeling. "I felt your pain."

"You felt my pain? You're not talking empathy, are you?"

"Empathy?" Mage Alain shook his head. "I do not know that word. No. It hurt. In this place." He reached up to touch the back of his head.

Mari staggered back to the cot and sat down. *All right. Stop and think. A Mage felt me get hit on the head. Then he walked through a wall to find me. But either I'm crazy, or it happened. If it happened, then I can analyze it, figure it out.* "Let's take this one step at a time. How did you know where I was?"

"I could sense your location," the Mage said dispassionately. "A thread connects us."

She looked down at herself. "A thread?"

"That is...a metaphor. I sense it as a thread. It is not real, but it is. I do not know why it exists, or its purpose." Something about the way the Mage said that made it sound...accusing? She must be imagining that.

I don't think I'm ready to examine the question of why there's a metaphorical thread connecting me to this Mage. Or why he thinks there's some thread. "I'm sorry, but I know nothing about Mage stuff."

"The thread is not the work of a Mage," Alain said.

"Then who—?" Her head pounded again. "Never mind. Next topic. Where are we? Still in the city hall?"

"Yes," Alain confirmed. "A city hall with a dungeon. It is what would be expected in Ringhmon."

"You've noticed that about them, too, huh?" Mari swallowed and pointed to the wall. "How did you do that?"

"I cannot tell you."

"Mage secret?"

"Yes."

Mari took a long, slow breath. *"They use smoke and mirrors and other 'magic' to make commons think they can create temporary holes in walls and things like that. It's all nonsense."* "Mages actually can make real holes in walls."

"No."

Her head hurting with increased intensity, Mari glowered at the Mage. "You *didn't* make a hole in the wall?"

"I made the illusion of a hole in the illusion of the wall."

Mari looked at Mage Alain for what felt like a long time, trying to detect any sign of mockery or lying. But he seemed perfectly sincere. And unless she had completely lost her mind, he had just walked through that solid wall. "If the wall is an illusion, why can't anybody walk through it?"

"It is a very powerful illusion," Alain explained.

"But you made it go away, so you must be more powerful than that illusion."

"No," Mage Alain said, shaking his head. "Even a Mage cannot negate the illusions we see. What a Mage does is overlay another illusion on top of the illusion everyone sees."

In a very strange way, what he was saying seemed to make sense, or at least seemed to sustain a consistent logic, if logic was the right term for something that involved walking through walls. "We can get out the same way that you got in?" Mari asked. "Through imaginary holes in the imaginary wall?" She wondered how her Guild would feel about seeing that in her report. Actually, she didn't have to wonder, but she also wasn't about to turn down a chance to escape.

The Mage took a deep breath and swayed on his feet. "No."

"No?"

"Unfortunately—" Alain collapsed into a seated position on the cot next to her—"the effort of finding you has exhausted me. There were several walls to get through. I can do no more for some time. I am probably incapable of any major effort until morning." He shook his head. "I did not plan this well. Maybe the elders are right and seventeen is simply too young to be a Mage."

Mari stared at him. "Are you telling me that you came to rescue me, following a metaphorical thread through imaginary holes, but now that you're in the same cell with me you can't get us out?"

"Yes, that is correct. This one erred."

"That one sure did. Now instead of one of us being stuck in here, we're both stuck in here."

The Mage gave her a look which actually betrayed a trace of irritation. He must have really been exhausted for such a feeling to show. "I do not have much experience with rescues. Are you always so difficult?"

Mari felt a sudden urge to laugh, but cut it off when the laughter made her head throb painfully. "To be perfectly honest, yes. You're not the first guy to ask me that, by the way. Thank you for coming. Thank you for getting this far. At least I have company. Unless I'm insane or drugged and imagining all of this, of course. Maybe you're not real."

"I am real," Mage Alain said. "You are not."

"You know, that's really not helping." Mari spread her hands. "I have no way of getting out of here. You don't have any more tricks?"

"Tricks?"

"Sorry. What do you call...?"

"Spells." Alain shook his head, his weariness again obvious to Mari. "Small ones. I cannot open a hole large enough for either of us to pass through. Not for some time. The effort required grows rapidly as the size of the opening increases."

"Well, sure, that makes sense. Does it increase by the square like an area measurement or a cube for volume or is it some exponential progression?"

It was his turn to look at her, saying nothing, for a long moment. "I do not know," Alain finally answered. "Do those words have meaning?"

"Yeah. I guess Mages don't spend much time on math, huh?"

"Math?"

"Never mind." It was as if she and Mage Alain occupied two entirely different worlds even though they were sitting side by side on the cot in this cell.

"Do you have any Mechanic...tricks?" Alain asked her.

"I haven't come up with any yet that can get us out of here." Mari looked glumly toward the door of the cell, then her eyes fixed on the lock. "You can't make another big imaginary hole for a while, you said. Can you make a little imaginary hole right now?"

He followed her gaze. "Yes. It will be very tiring, but I feel certain I can do that. Where do you need it?"

She stood up carefully to prevent another bout of dizziness, then walked over to the door and pointed at the armor plate protecting the lock. "Right here. About this big," Mari added, outlining an area with her cupped fingers. She didn't stop to think about how much sense any of this made. As long as it worked, it could be pure crazy. If she could get at the back of the lock, maybe she would be able to jimmy it open before the Mage's imaginary hole disappeared.

"If you believe this to be important, I shall do so." Mari watched nervously as the Mage narrowed his eyes and seemed to concentrate, then opened his eyes wide. "Hurry with what you wish to do. I cannot hold it long."

She turned back to the door, and stopped, aghast. There was a hole there, a little bigger than she had asked for. But there wasn't simply a hole in the armor plate. There was a hole right through the plate and the back of the lock and the lock itself and out the other side of the door. She could look through into the passageway.

Mari just gazed blankly for a second, unable to accept what she was seeing, then abruptly remembered that she needed to do something. Reaching into the hole with a fear that it would vanish and leave her hand embedded in steel, Mari fumbled for the lock bolt, which now hung in the door jamb unsupported by anything where the lock mechanism had been. She pulled out the heavy bolt, hastily looked for anything else protruding into the frame from the door, then yanked her hand free and dropped the bolt as if it were on fire. "Done."

The Mage sighed and relaxed. The hole vanished at the same moment the sheared off bolt hit the floor inside the cell with a muffled thud. Mari studied the door, which once again looked and felt completely solid. But the end of the bolt still lay on the floor where Mari had dropped it. She pushed against the door and felt it begin to swing open. *I am insane. I have to be. This can't be happening.* She pushed at the door again and it scraped open a little more. *But if I'm going to imagine I'm escaping, I might as well go through with it.*

She pushed open the door far enough to be able to stick her head out, searching quickly to confirm no guards were in sight, then looked back at the Mage, who was still sitting slumped on the cot. "Don't you want to come along?"

The Mage eyed her. "You want me to accompany you."

"Yes, I want you to accompany me! Do you think that I'd leave you in this cell? Blazes, Mage, I'm not *that* difficult! Come on!" He rose and walked after her as Mari slid out through the partially opened door. She paused, looking and listening for any sign of guards, but could detect nothing. "Shouldn't they have someone watching the cells?"

Mage Alain stopped beside her. "Perhaps they do not want underlings in a position to hear things their prisoners may say. This is not a large dungeon, and seems to have had only you as a prisoner, so perhaps it is reserved for certain special needs."

"That makes sense." Mari took a couple of cautious steps, glancing through the grate in the door of the cell next to hers. She froze. No other prisoners were there, but carefully placed in the center of the cell floor was her tool kit. She pulled at the door, finding it locked securely, then looked around for a key. "I don't believe it. We found my tools and we can't get to them."

"Your tools?" Mage Alain asked.

"They're important! I need that tool kit." She turned to the Mage, her hands upraised in a pleading position. "Those tools are...they're my spells. And my...elders will give me a very hard time if I lose them. Please, Mage Alain, can you make a hole in that door's lock as well? Just for a few seconds? Please?"

Mage Alain eyed her. "You need these things to cast your spells?"

"Yes!"

"And to undo spells?"

"Undo spells?" What did that mean? "Um, yes. I mean, unscrewing stuff and disassembly and disconnecting—"

"Disconnecting?" Mage Alain faced the door. "Then I must do this." He stared at the lock, sweat appearing on his brow. "Quickly," he whispered.

Mari tore her eyes from the Mage and saw a hole in the lock, though smaller than the one he had created before. Reaching in, she found enough of the lock mechanism remained to hold the bolt, but could turn the mechanism by hand to withdraw the bolt. Shoving the door to make sure it was unlocked, she pulled her hand free. "Done."

The Mage nodded, the hole vanished without a trace, then he fell against the nearby wall, his body limp with exhaustion.

Mari grabbed him to keep him from falling to the floor, guilt surging within her. She had touched him before, but this was the first time she had held him, and his slimness made it all the more clear that the Mage was but a boy close to her in age. That was fortunate, because she might have had trouble holding up a bigger man, but it also drove home to her that she had been pushing him hard and somewhat selfishly. "Forgive me," she said formally, "and thank you."

Settling the Mage into a resting position, Mari darted into the cell, hoisting her tool kit with a feeling of joy. Most of what it held were just simple tools like screwdrivers, pliers, and wrenches, but with those tools she felt more confident and complete. She ripped open the compartment on the side, finding her pistol still there. Holding the weapon, she chambered a round and released the safety, then keeping the pistol in one hand and carrying her tool kit with the other she left the cell, shoving the door shut again with her hip.

Mage Alain struggled to his feet, fending off her offered help. "I should be stronger," he mumbled. "I can walk."

Mari stepped back, recognizing that in this at least the Mage was like any other young man. She had stung his pride by pushing him into revealing just how weak he was. "As you will, Mage Alain."

She walked in the lead, keeping her pace slow enough to accommodate his exhaustion even though Mari's nerves were screaming for her to run, run, run, until they got out of here. For a brief time after leaving her cell she had been in an almost dreamlike state, half convinced this was all unreal, but now she had fully accepted it and was increasingly worried about some pack of guards showing up to overwhelm them. She could use her pistol if necessary, but as when they were watching the bandits, she knew that the sound of a single shot would bring an avalanche of enemies upon her.

Together they moved down the passageway, dimly lit by oil lamps set at wide intervals. After passing several more cells, all empty, the passage took a turn and ran past a few additional cells. At the end of the hall, a door blocked further progress. Mari approached the door, her weapon poised, then halted in mid step as Mage Alain hissed a warning. "Stop. No farther."

CHAPTER TEN

Mari held herself absolutely still, looking around. "What is it?"

"An alarm spell, set on the area near the door. If someone not wearing the right charm passes through it, it will alert its master or masters."

Mari gave the Mage a level look. A big part of her wanted to just keep walking, because that sounded ridiculous. Another part of her pointed out that she wouldn't be standing here unless something even weirder had already happened. She stood still. "Mages? Like you?"

"Not like me," Alain denied. "This feels like the work of Dark Mages."

"Dark Mages? What are Dark Mages?"

Alain gave her a look in which surprise could actually be seen. "You have not heard of Dark Mages?"

Mari shook her head. "I'm beginning to understand that there's a whole lot of things I haven't heard of."

"Dark Mages use the same methods as the Mages of the Guild," he explained, "but they apply their skills in different ways and undertake tasks which the Mage Guild will not. They are unsanctioned by the Guild, their works often the sort of thing no one wishes to openly admit. They do not wear robes or other distinctive garb, instead hiding among the common folk."

"Are you saying that there are things Mages won't do?" That was certainly contrary to the stories that Mari had heard.

Alain nodded almost absentmindedly, his attention focused mainly on the area just in front of her. "There are things which diminish wisdom, which harm a Mage's ability to gain power and learn new spells." He paused, giving her a sidelong look which seemed...worried?

"All right." Mari nodded back to him, wondering why any Mage's worries would be aimed at her. She must have misinterpreted that.

But as she stood still, her mind raced. If there were Dark Mages hidden among the commons, could there also be Dark Mechanics? Unsanctioned Mechanics didn't exist, her Guild claimed. But then who was responsible for what she had found here? Commons, who were supposed to lack the necessary special talent to do Mechanic work? That thought was a lot scarier than the idea of Dark Mechanics. She had to ask some pointed questions. She wasn't an apprentice now. If she demanded answers, even Guild Hall Supervisor Stimon would have to provide something in return.

But that could only happen after they got out of here. "Can we do anything about this alarm?"

Mage Alain stood silent for so long without answering that Mari started to worry. Then he shook his head. "Not yet. I need to rest, then perhaps I can get us through it without alerting its master."

"Any idea how long you'll need to rest?"

Mage Alain twitched his shoulders in the most minimal of shrugs. "A while."

"Five minutes a while, half an hour a while, an hour a while?" Mari pressed.

He finally looked at her again. "Minutes? Hour?"

"Got it. A while," Mari agreed, thinking guiltily that if she hadn't insisted that the Mage create the hole to let her get her tool kit, he might already be able to handle this. Unfortunately, along with not learning math, Mages didn't seem to worry about measuring time in anything more precise than morning and afternoon. She pointed to the nearest cell. "That door's ajar. Let's wait in there where we'll be hidden if anyone comes along."

"That is acceptable." Once inside, the young Mage sat down against one wall, breathing slowly and deeply.

Mari checked for any sign of a far-listener in this cell, didn't find any, then sat near the door, her hand holding the pistol ready, pointed at the ceiling. The throbbing in her head had faded to a continuous dull ache.

Mage Alain sat silently until she had settled. He was looking not at her, but between them, his expression revealing nothing.

What was he looking at? Oh. "Is it still there?" Mari asked.

Alain's gaze rose to meet hers. "No."

"That's a relief."

"It was never there. It does not exist. But it does remain." His eyes stayed on hers. "Your...tools. You said you can disconnect."

"You mean the thread? The metaphorical thread that isn't there but is?" Mari asked. "Unfortunately, all of my tools only work on stuff that's really there."

"Nothing is really there," Alain insisted.

"Blazes! I...my tools only work on the strong illusions. I can't unscrew an allegory or disconnect a metaphor, Mage Alain!"

"You cannot?" He definitely appeared disappointed.

Absurdly, she felt bad that she couldn't do it. "I'm sorry. Honest. But neither my tools or my training can do that. I'm sorry if I gave you the impression that I could."

His eyes were on hers again. "You gave me the impression that you could do many things and do them well."

Flattery? From a Mage? "I wish you were a Senior Mechanic. None of them feel that way." Mari shook her head, feeling overwhelmed as the reality of their circumstances still trapped in the dungeon overcame the last traces of euphoria after the escape from her cell. "I'm not experienced enough even though I'm well-trained. This is my first job outside a Guild Hall, the first time I've really been outside a Guild Hall without a lot of other Mechanics around." Life in a Guild Hall, life at the academy in Palandur, safe and simple and predictable, seemed like one of the Mage's illusions now. "I don't know what the blazes I'm doing."

"You are certainly good at creating the illusion of competence, then."

Mari stared at the Mage, who showed no signs that his comment was meant anything but seriously. He seemed to think that he had paid her a great compliment. She started giggling, fighting to stay quiet. "I'm going to have to make sure that's in my next performance evaluation. 'Master Mechanic Mari is good at creating the illusion of competence.'" Her sides shaking with suppressed laughter only a few steps removed from hysteria born of injury and stress, Mari slumped against the wall.

The Mage watched her intently. "Are you well?"

She managed to get her laughter under control with the help of some renewed throbs in her head and sat straighter, wiping her eyes. "Oh, just great. I've got a lump on my head, I'm in a dungeon with a Mage, and if I'm honest with my Guild about what's happened down here I'll be locked away forever. Couldn't be better." Mari paused to look at the Mage's face, no sign of emotion on it. "Do you ever laugh?"

"No. It is not permitted."

There was that sense of pity filling her again. Mari looked away. *He's not a lost puppy. He's a young man. He chose this life. He's not my responsibility.* "Why did you come after me?"

"There is a thread—"

"The one that's not there but is. Yeah. But I asked why. *Why* did you follow that thread, assuming there is a thread?"

The Mage looked at her, and for a moment she could see the concern in his eyes. "I felt that I needed to...help you."

Mari smiled at him. "Well, thanks."

"Because," Mage Alain continued, "I thought that might be the only way to break the spell you have placed upon me."

Her smile vanished. "Spell?"

"The thread may have something to do with it. It holds us together.

That is why I wanted you to disconnect it, to remove what you have done to me."

"I—" Mari paused to try to reason out what the Mage was saying. "You think I'm doing something to you? Using that metaphorical thread? You think that I made that thread that isn't there?"

He nodded. "It must be so. I keep thinking of you. You make me remember things that I should not. I do things when you are involved that I would not ever considering doing otherwise." The Mage's otherwise blank expression contained just the tiniest hint of accusation. "I do not know how you have done this to me. I thought that if I returned the help you had given me that I would be free of the inexplicable influence you have over me. But it does not seem to be working, and you say you cannot break the thread."

Mari realized that her mouth had fallen open as she stared at Mage Alain. "Are you serious?"

"What would I be if I was not serious?"

"You're saying that I put a spell on you that controls your thoughts and actions?"

"Why else am I here?" the Mage asked.

"Because it was the right thing to do!"

"The...what? I am still uncertain about what right thing means— " The trace of puzzlement had returned to him.

"Listen...*Mage Alain*! I don't...*put spells* on boys! Or men! Or anybody! I have no idea why you think that you are thinking about me, but I assure you that it has nothing to do with me thinking about you or making you think that you want to think about me!"

Mage Alain looked back at her for a while before speaking. "I could not follow all of that."

She gazed at him, feeling helpless. "All right. In short, whatever you are thinking or doing is all from you. I have nothing to do with it."

"Then why does the thread link us? Why is it you I think about? Why is it you I want to help? This does not happen with others. Only with you."

Oh, no. A Mage was crushing on her. What had she ever done to deserve ending up in a dungeon with a Mage who was crushing on her? Why couldn't Alli be here to help her explain things? Alli understood boys and men. Better than Mari did, anyway. What would Alli say to Mage Alain? "It's not anything that I did. All right, maybe what I did were things you liked. But I didn't do them to make you think about me or to make you do things."

"Liked?" Alain asked. "I am also still unsure as to what that means."

Stars above. Better make this as simple as possible. "It's because... you're a boy." Mari chose her words carefully. "And sometimes boys get...interested in a particular girl, and maybe, for some totally inexplicable reason that completely escapes me, you...got interested in me."

The Mage actually frowned as he thought about what she had said. Then his expression cleared. "Love."

She stared at him, amazed and appalled. "*What?*"

"We were warned about love by the elders," Alain explained without any feeling in his voice. "It is a very serious error."

"Yes," Mari quickly agreed. "They were right. You don't even want to think about...about *that*."

"But what is it?" Mage Alain asked. "Is thinking about someone love?"

"No! Whatever you're thinking, it isn't that."

"Why are you concerned? You are much more alarmed. Do you sense that enemies are near?"

"Yes," Mari said. "That must be it. But I don't hear anything now, so I can relax. Let's both relax. Hey, I know. Let's talk about something else."

Alain sat, his eyes hooded in thought. "You are difficult."

"Yes. We already established that."

"Do you experience love with other Mechanics?" Alain asked the question in the same way someone else would have asked whether it was going to rain today.

Mari took a deep breath. "No. Not that it's any of your business. But, no."

"Because you are difficult," he deduced.

"That probably has something to do with it, yes. Is there a point to this?"

"You are a challenge," Alain concluded triumphantly. "Something I must overcome."

"Uh...that's not exactly the greatest compliment that I've ever received, but if it helps you figure out that you're not in...love... then great." How could she get him off this entire line of thought? While also hopefully making it clear that she wasn't interested in that kind of thing with a Mage, even if that Mage was Alain? That they had no possible future together? "Um, I don't know what your marching orders are, but I was told not to have any more contact with you."

Alain nodded dispassionately. "I was told not to have any more contact with you, as well."

"That's a...a real shame. I mean, that we won't see each other again after we get out of here," Mari said, trying to sound regretful rather than grateful. To her own surprise, she didn't have to try very hard. In fact, she sort of did feel regretful and not at all grateful. What was that about?

"I have already acted against my instructions," Mage Alain said. "By being here."

"I can't say that I'm sorry you came here," Mari admitted. She felt bad now. Bad about maybe somehow leading on Alain, bad about rebuffing him after he had just gotten her out of a cell, and bad thinking about what his upbringing in a Mage Guild Hall must have been like for so many things to be unfamiliar to him. "And I doubt that I'll admit to my Guild Hall Supervisor that I was in contact with you again. I guess neither one of us is very good at following orders."

He nodded in solemn agreement. "No, Master Mechanic Mari, we are not good at following orders."

Mari couldn't help grinning at him. If only Alain wasn't a Mage. The more she learned about him, the more she liked him. But she really still knew very little. "You haven't lied to me, have you?"

"Not to my knowledge."

"Why not? Everybody knows how Mages are. You've been honest with me about...well, about what you're thinking." That was what had made his statements to her so disconcerting, she realized. This wasn't some smooth-talking Mechanic looking to score another notch in his belt and willing to say anything that would further that. No. Alain just said things, speaking his mind rather than hiding behind politeness or social games. *He doesn't seem to understand, or has never been taught, all of the ways people use to avoid saying what they really think. Not that I want to pursue whatever he's thinking or feeling... Feeling. He never talks about feeling anything. That's what he hides. He doesn't hide thoughts. He hides feelings the way the rest of us hide our thoughts.* "Um...anyway, I haven't caught you in a lie yet. You do things I can't explain with the science I know. I have an irrational inclination to believe you. Why?"

She could have sworn that the Mage almost smiled. "Perhaps you are a good judge of character."

For somebody who never showed emotion, he could be really charming. "Oh, yeah, that's it."

"But," Alain continued, "truth and falsehood do not mean the same thing to one trained in the Mage arts. If all we see is false, where is truth to be found? If the people we think we see are but shadows of the world illusion, what matter what we tell them? It becomes not a matter of truth and lies, but a question of whether either matters. The choice of what to do is mine."

Mari watched the Mage, but he seemed to be perfectly serious again. "That sounds like a good excuse for doing whatever you want to do."

"It can easily become exactly that," the Mage agreed. "But..." He seemed to be struggling for words. "I do not follow that road."

That was a relief to hear. No wonder other Mages were infamous for just grabbing any woman who took their momentary fancy.

With all that she had been taught about Mages, all of the stories she had heard, why hadn't she felt revulsion at the idea that Alain was attracted to her? Because he was Alain, Mari realized. He had stopped being just a Mage. He was a person to her. A wounded person. And she really did like that person.

Maybe to such a person, taught to hide feelings, the mildest forms of companionship, of liking, would seem overwhelming. Maybe all he needed, all he wanted, was a friend.

She could do that.

"Good for you, Mage Alain," Mari finally said. "Truth matters to me. So does being willing to stick your neck out for someone else, and you've certainly done that for me. But if you're going to be my friend you'll have to make sure you don't tell me any lies. We have to be honest with each other."

Alain frowned very slightly. "I do not know how to do that. I can only be what I am."

"That's good. That's fine. If that's who you've been up until now, just keep being you. How's the resting coming?"

❊   ❊   ❊

"I am recovering." Alain shrugged, wondering why this conversation with the Mechanic had become complicated at times. "If I were older I would be stronger, but I would also take longer to recover. Under these circumstances, I guess it is lucky I am who I am."

His words made her smile slightly. "I'd say we're both lucky you're who you are." She settled back again, holding her strange hand weapon pointed upward, closing her eyes and letting her face settle into lines of pain and fatigue. Alain was not surprised by the pain she showed. He had seen the back of her head and the blood matted into the hair there. Unfortunately, he had no training in the healers' arts. But if he ever encountered the person who had struck Mechanic Mari like that, Alain knew he would use the skills he did have to even the score. He did not know why he resolved to do that, but he did.

At least he was fairly sure that his reason was not love. Whatever love was, other than something to be avoided. Master Mechanic Mari had shown clear signs of being concerned when Alain spoke of it, and had denied experiencing love with other Mechanics, so perhaps Mechanics also were warned to avoid love. It must be a very dangerous thing.

She had mentioned something else, though. He watched her as he sat, trying to rebuild his strength, thinking about her words. "Master Mechanic Mari, could you..."

"What? Are you all right?" She opened her eyes, concern there again. It was so easy to see her feelings, yet something always remained unseen. Alain could not understand that, either.

"Yes. You said I could be...friend?"

"Sure. It's a little weird. Maybe a lot weird. But you're all right, Mage Alain."

"What is being your friend?"

She showed that expression again, the one that seemed sad but also something else, the one that always made her look somewhere else for a moment. This time she blinked her eyes rapidly, too. "Why are you a Mage?" Mari asked abruptly. "Did you go volunteer or something?"

"Mages came to my home, when I was much younger. I was taken by them to the Guild Hall."

"Oh." The Mechanic looked at the floor this time. "Not your choice, then."

"No. It was what had to be, because I had the talent."

"Yeah," she whispered, seeming distressed about something else for a moment, then took a deep breath and smiled at him again, though Alain could still see a hurt behind the smile. "All right. Uh, a friend is someone who did what you did, coming to help me, and don't think I'm not very grateful for that, whether we manage to get out of here or not. A friend helps you, hangs around with you, not because they have to do that, but because they want to do that. A friend is someone you think about sometimes and want to do things for." She added the last with a smile that seemed oddly strained.

Alain thought carefully. Did that violate the teachings of the Mage Guild? Yes. But maybe not. It depended on why he did those things. As long as he continued to know this girl was a shadow, what difference did it make if he chose to help her? To think of her? If you helped a shadow, someone who did not exist, the act itself must be an illusion as well. "I can do that."

"Well, good." She was doing that other thing now, as if he had said something intended to evoke humor in her. "You sound real enthusiastic about it."

"I always sound the same."

"I had noticed that," the Mechanic replied with another smile, one which grew anxious as she watched him. "What?"

"There is something wrong?"

"You were looking at me like...I don't know." Mari firmed her smile. "When we get a chance, we ought to talk more about what friends are. And what they aren't."

Perhaps he thought about her so much because the things she said were often so hard to comprehend. "Why do I need to know what something is not?"

"Because...you wouldn't want to believe that something that wasn't real actually *was* real, would you?"

Alain gazed at Mari, thinking that perhaps his surprise had shown. "That is an argument worthy of a Mage. It shows wisdom. I knew you were not like other Mechanics."

Mari appeared to be at a loss for words. "I meant...maybe I shouldn't say anything else."

Something occurred to him, an explanation for the inexplicable. "The thread. Is that because you are friend? I have never heard of such a thing as the thread, but I know of no other Mage with friend."

"Maybe... Maybe that is it," she said, considering the idea. "Maybe when Mages make friends they see it as something like that. Like a connection to someone else."

A soft noise came from outside the room. Both froze, then Mari cautiously looked around the door, her weapon held ready. "Probably just a rat," she finally whispered. She gave him another look, a question in her eyes.

Every moment they waited was necessary to regain his strength, but every moment also increased the risk to them. He came slowly to his feet, testing his strength as he did so. There was plenty of power in this area to draw on, which would make his task a little easier. Was it enough? He looked toward Mechanic Mari, watching him with worry and hope easy to see in her expression, and suddenly he felt enough strength, almost as if it had come to him along that thread between them even though it had not. But this surge of strength did seem to be related to the thread in some strange way. "I am ready to attempt the alarm. We must go. I do not know how close to morning it now is."

The Mechanic gave him another concerned look. "Are you sure you're ready?"

She had been extra careful with him ever since he had almost fallen. That bothered Alain, although he tried not to show it. It was oddly as if Mechanic Mari were an elder whom he did not want to disappoint. "I do not need more rest."

"All right." She stood up, wincing at what must be renewed pain in her head.

He did not feel it as he had when his foresight worked, but still Alain felt a strange urge to wince himself. "I must lead the way through the alarm."

"Have I been leading?" she asked. "I'm sorry. I do that. I don't mean to."

"It is not a difficult thing about you," Alain told her, and to his surprise was rewarded by another of her smiles. "You lead well."

Was that a friend thing, to want to see her smile?

Her smile was distracting, though, and he needed to concentrate. Alain led the way back toward the door with the Mage alarm, Mechanic Mari staying close behind him. Focusing his Mage senses, Alain could see the alarm as fine strands of suspended power drifting across the hallway like filaments of spider web. Touch one and the power in it would be released, creating a change that would be felt by a Dark Mage somewhere. An alarm spell, like all spells, was temporary, though the drain on the power locked in it was so small that it could last for a month before dissipating. This one felt a couple of weeks old and still strong enough to be a worry.

Alain drew upon the power here, channeling it with his own energy, using that power to gently push away the strands to either side so that a path lay clear down the middle. That temporary minor alteration in the alarm spell should be invisible to the Dark Mage who had placed it. "Follow closely and directly behind me," Alain instructed, stepping forward. He walked steadily down the open path, watching for any strands that threatened to drift back in front of them. "We are past it."

The Mechanic stared back along the way they had come, her expression baffled. Then she shook her head and knelt down at the door barring their way. Alain braced himself, wondering if he could find the resources inside to open a hole in this door. But instead of asking for his assistance, Mechanic Mari pulled open her bag and began to extract strange items which she started using on the door near what she called the lock. Alain watched her work, trying to grasp what she was doing and not understanding any of it.

Somehow she easily loosened pieces from the apparently solid block of metal and began piling them on the floor. Finally there came a metallic click and a pleased exclamation from the Mechanic. "It's open." Then she began picking up the loose pieces and returning them to the lock, where by mysterious means she fastened them into place again, forming it back into a single piece of metal. "Good as new, but unlocked now."

"How did you do that?" Alain asked. "It held the illusion of being whole, then it was in pieces, then you made it appear whole again, but I felt no power being employed."

She looked up at him with another smile. "Guild secret. And elbow grease."

"You used those weapons."

Mari frowned in puzzlement, then glanced down at what she still held, something that looked like a knife with a round blade and a point that had notches in it. "This is a screwdriver. Those are wrenches. They..." She paused, her eyes growing shadowed. "They're tools. They could be used as weapons, I guess. Mage Alain, tools can build things, and help people. Or they can destroy things, and hurt people. It's my responsibility to use my tools wisely."

"Do all Mechanics believe that?" Alain asked.

Another pause, then Mari sighed. "I had instructors who told me the importance of using my tools wisely, and others who said it didn't matter. I think it matters."

Alain thought about that, trying to understand. "Then your tools are so important to you because of the things you choose to do with them?"

She gave him a startled look. "Yes. That's exactly right." Mari finished putting away the objects she had been using. "Let's see what's on the other side of this door."

The door swung open under the Mechanic's push, she edging through with the hand weapon pointed forward. They found themselves in a short hallway ending in another locked door, with rooms on either side. Mari glanced back at him questioningly. "Are there any of those alarms here?"

Alain studied the hall, walking slowly down it. "I see none."

"Good." She pointed upward, at a small metal object on the ceiling. "That's a Mechanic device, but it's just a smoke-sniffer. It sounds an alert if there's a fire. Not exactly cheap, but with everything Ringhmon has in this building, they sure wouldn't want an uncontrolled fire starting down here." Mari grimaced. "I hate to think what they do with fire down in this dungeon that they are worried about it spreading. Probably something involving hot metal applied to human skin."

"Does that cause harm?" Alain asked.

"Oh, yeah." Mari said it in the manner of someone recalling an event. "Believe me, you only put your hand on a non-insulated steam pipe once. Anybody who doesn't learn their lesson from that is too dumb to be a Mechanic."

He nodded in understanding, remembering his own training. "The Mechanics teach lessons to their acolytes by using physical punishment just as Mages do."

Instead of nodding back, she stared at him. Then Mari swallowed and spoke in a strained voice. "It wasn't— I'm sorry. You were— No. I can't go there. Let's get out of here."

She hastened forward, kneeling again by the new door, frowning as she examined it with unusual intensity.

He watched her, trying to understand what had caused her distress this time and curious about these strange Mechanic arts. Alain had been satisfied briefly by his conclusion that the thread and his thoughts of Mari were part of a test, a challenge on his path to greater wisdom. But once she had mentioned her orders not to contact him again, Alain had realized that he did not want the thread to break. If the thread meant friend, though, it could remain, though he was still hazy on just what friend was.

He had feared thinking of Mari would weaken him, lead him astray, but Alain had been surprised to be able to walk after getting past the alarm. He should have been worn out from his exertions. Instead, Mechanic Mari's presence, or perhaps the thread he saw between them, had pushed him to be able to do more than he ever had before. His conclusions had been right. The challenge she represented would make him stronger.

Would other Mages be able to detect the thread? That would create difficulties. He would have to explain it, not as what he believed it to be, but as something the elders could accept. *They have taught me that there is no truth and no lie, so I will hold to their teachings and say what will serve my purposes.*

Mechanic Mari had said that truth mattered to her, but surely she would not object to Alain misleading his elders in that fashion.

Mari gave a small cry of dismay that cut off Alain's thoughts. "I don't believe it," she complained. "There's three—no, four—bolts or hasps holding this door shut, and they're locked from the outside. I can't get us through this." She slumped, sitting on the step before the door and rubbing her head with both hands, then looked up at him. "Can you do it? We'd need a hole this big." The Mechanic outlined a large section of one side of the door. "And you'd need to hold it longer because I'd need to disable or open all four locks."

Alain evaluated his overtaxed strength, felt the power here, then shook his head. "I cannot get us through the door, either. Not for some time. Only the guards could open it for us. They will surely not come before full day without good reason, and then they will come in force, and we will have to fight our way out."

"If we *could* fight our way out of here. What could make the guards come earlier...distract them...?" Mari looked up at him, her eyes still holding a stricken quality but lit with inspiration. "A good reason. Mage Alain, you're a genius." She jumped up and made a fist, but before he could react to the shocking attack Mari had merely lightly bumped the fist against his shoulder. She turned, but then spun back to face him. "I don't know what they did to you. I don't *want* to know. But something good survived that. He's still in there. I can tell. I'm difficult. I can be very difficult and hard on my friends. But I'm always there for them and I never let them down. All right?"

He gazed back at her, mystified anew by her words. "This is part of friend?"

"Yeah." She forced a smile, then pivoted and ran toward one of the side rooms. Mari looked inside, then beckoned to him. "Just what we needed," she remarked.

The room held a number of the thin mattresses like that which had been in her cell. "It's a storeroom," she explained. "With lots of flammable material." Shoving some of the dry mattresses together, she pulled another Mechanic thing out of her tool kit and clicked it with her thumb, making sparks fly. The bright spots landed on the fabric of the mattresses and began to send up thin trails of smoke from where they lay. "If we need to, we can go back and try to pry free one of the oil lamps, but that would mean getting past that alarm thing again. I think this will do the job."

"What are you doing?" Alain asked.

"Starting a fire, of course." Mari held up the thing in her hand. "It's a fire-starter. A really simple device. Haven't you ever seen one?"

Alain shook his head. "Never. That thing seems very complicated. I do not understand how it can work."

"How do you start fires?"

That was a Guild secret. Or was it? The elders had told him that no Mechanic could understand how it worked. What would this Mechanic say if he told her? "I use my mind to channel power to create a place where it is hot, altering the nature of the illusion there," Alain explained, "and then use my mind to put that heat on what I want to burn."

"Oh," Mechanic Mari said. "Is that actually how you visualize the process?"

"That is how it is done," Alain said.

"That's...interesting." She grinned. "So, instead of making a fire by doing something complicated or hard to understand like striking a flint, you just alter the nature of reality. That *is* a lot simpler."

"Your tone of voice," Alain said. "You are saying sarcasm."

"I do that too much," Mari said apologetically. Her smile this time seemed more natural, though it was still stiff with some strain as she nursed the small spots of flame into larger blazes. "Sometimes denying reality is all that keeps a person going, isn't it?"

"Reality? Do you mean the illusion?"

"Right. You have no idea how many people superior to me in rank and age have insisted on trying to explain reality to me over the years." Mari gasped a short laugh. "That's the one area I'm a slow learner in, I guess."

Alain studied her. "You are speaking quickly. You are frightened."

She met his eyes. "No. I'm nervous. About getting out of here, and about the risk of what I'm doing right now, and about...about talking to you. I start to think maybe I understand who you are and what you've been through and then...stars above. I'll get over it. Let me explain what's going on, because I just realized that I was assuming you know, but we don't operate on the same wavelength at all."

"Wave length? We are nowhere near an ocean."

"Um..." Mechanic Mari paused. "Never mind that. Listen. When this fire gets bad enough, the smoke-sniffer will set off an alarm and the guards will come charging in through that door to put out the fire. While they do that, we'll go charging *out* the door under the cover of all the smoke and confusion and stuff." She sat back, eyeing the flames now leaping upward to lick at the wooden beams of the ceiling. "If this fire gets out of hand, or if the guards take too long to come, you and I may be in a lot of trouble."

"We are already in a lot of trouble."

"That was my reasoning, too. Of course, if that happens and the fire gets too big before the mighty citizens of Ringhmon stop it, it'll also gut this little palace and destroy everything inside it. Including the enormously expensive Model Six that I just fixed, which they'll be responsible for paying for, and probably the other Model Six that they openly own." She shrugged, trying to appear unworried. "That'll teach them to kidnap me. But that won't happen. We'll be fine."

"You say that and yet you are frightened."

"Yes, I'm frightened! I admit it! Happy? No, wait, Mages are never happy. Just try not to die, all right? I don't want that to be my fault."

Alain thought through her words. "I will attempt not to die. Your plan appears to be sound, as well as potentially very destructive. I see that it is a mistake to offend you."

"Yes, yes, it is," Mari agreed, a smile flickering briefly to life. "Stay on my good side and you won't have to worry about it." She backed away from the fire, which was now burning brightly, sending up flames and sending out heat. "Let's toss some more mattresses on it to get some good smoke."

He assisted her as they mounded a couple of more mattresses on the burning one, producing billowing clouds of smoke which stung Alain's eyes and throat as he backed out of the storeroom after her. Fire had sprung to life on the beams of the ceiling in the room, illuminating the smoke from above. "Over here," Mechanic Mari called, coughing as the smoke began filling the hallway as well. He followed her again, to the room on the opposite side. A harsh sound began blaring around them, echoing off the walls. "That's the smoke-sniffer."

As they waited, the Mechanic coughed again, her eyes watering. "Mage Alain? There's something I forgot to take into account."

Alain squeezed his eyes to try to clear them, but the irritation from the smoke kept blurring his vision. "How so?" he asked, coughing as well.

"The smoke. It's spreading faster than the flames right now. We have less time than I thought. If those guards don't get down here soon, the smoke will kill us."

"That would be unfortunate," Alain admitted. "So you have erred as well?"

"Yes. I have erred. Let's hope it wasn't a fatal error. I hate it when that happens."

She had attempted more of her sarcasm, but Mari's fear stood out clearly despite the front of bravery she was attempting, the feelings radiating from the Mechanic like the heat from the fire. As Alain used his training to keep his own fears deeply buried, he wondered about her. "Master Mechanic Mari, is this a time when a friend would help?"

"If they could, yes," she gasped.

"Death is just a passing from one dream into another. It is nothing but another journey."

She blinked at him with eyes watering because of the smoke. "Thanks. That doesn't really help, but thanks for trying. I—" Whatever else the Mechanic might have said was forestalled by shouts from the other side of the barred door, accompanied by a metallic rattle and clicking. "They're unlocking the door," Mari whispered. Moments later the door slammed open and a group of guards carrying pails of water surged into the hall. The heat and smoke from the fire met them and threw the group back as it billowed into the new space the open door now offered.

Alain felt a hand grab his arm and followed its tug downward toward the floor. The smoke wasn't as thick down here. Mechanic Mari moved in a low crouch toward the door, still holding onto him and trying to avoid the guards, who were milling about in confusion while someone shouted orders. They bumped into the legs of several guards, all of whom were so disoriented they didn't react, then reached the door, where another wedge of guards was being urged forward into the hall. For now, that wedge completely sealed the doorway against them. Alain let Mari lead him to crouch to one side, tears streaming down her face as the smoke irritated her eyes, holding her hand over her mouth as the roar of the fire grew behind them. He was having a lot of trouble breathing himself, and wondered how long they could last here.

The plug of guards burst out of the doorway under the urging of their leader, hurling their buckets of water randomly in all directions before stampeding back to the doorway. Alain once again let Mari lead as she merged with the tangle of guards, who were fleeing up a long flight of stairs. He caught a brief glimpse of a guard commander howling curses, then a gust of smoke roiled up the stairway and blotted out his sight.

Pounding up the stairs in Mari's wake, Alain's breathing grew more labored by the moment. Coming on top of the weakness he still felt from his earlier efforts, it left his head spinning. He had thought her lost in the smoke ahead, but suddenly Mechanic Mari appeared before him, reaching back to pull Alain onward. The knowledge that she had backtracked into danger to ensure his survival kept him going as much as the tug of her hand.

Just when he feared he would collapse, they came to a small landing, then out the door at the head of the stairs and around a corner, where the air near the floor was almost completely clear of the smoke fountaining from the doorway and along the ceiling above them. Alain struggled for breath, coughing as he did so. He noticed Mechanic Mari lying on her side nearby, curled up and coughing constantly. Acting on a vague memory, Alain crawled to her and began thumping her back hard with his palm.

The Mechanic's coughing broke and she started breathing. Mari grabbed his hand to stop him. "That's enough. Thanks."

He peered at her, blurry through the water filling his eyes from the irritation of the smoke. "You came back for me on the stairs."

"Didn't you believe me? I don't leave anyone behind, Alain."

She had simply used his name, not the title of Mage. He should have objected, but instead felt a desire to do the same with her. "I will believe you next time...Mari."

"Good. You're a quick learner." She looked both ways along the hall, where individual commons were running about in panic, none of them seeming to take note of the Mechanic and the Mage on the floor. The night shift in this building must be substantial, though nowhere near as large as the number of day workers. "Do you know how to get out of this building?" Mari asked.

"I came in through walls."

"Then the answer is no," Mari gasped, pushing herself to her hands and knees. "Let's just get away from the fire before any of those commons starts thinking and wondering what the blazes we're doing here. This way looks as good as any."

They crawled away, trying to avoid any other occupants of the building as those rushed by. The smoke gradually diminished as they turned corners, but the roar of activity behind them didn't relent. Mari got to her feet, helping him rise as well, and they both staggered along. Some of the commons stopped to stare at them but Mari's glare got them moving again quickly.

Something crashed somewhere, causing the entire building to shudder. Moments later a huge cloud of smoke came billowing along the hall. Alain could not help thinking that the smoke seemed to be pursuing them, as if the fire did not want them to escape its grasp.

Mari stared at the oncoming wave of smoke, but instead of fleeing immediately knelt to press one hand against the floor. She straightened quickly, shaking her head. "The floor is hot. That means the fire is spreading rapidly beneath us. We have to get out of this building. Fast. This way."

They managed a stumbling trot, trying to reach the end of the long hallway. Alain realized that the smoke was coming not just from behind them, but also shooting up in geysers through tiny cracks in the flooring. "Your plan is working," Alain said to Mari as he struggled for breath. "This building will be destroyed."

"My plan didn't involve us being inside when that happened! Just keep your head and keep moving. Look! A window!" Mari called, tugging at his robes again. The window, a large one divided into several panes and almost floor to ceiling, the night sky visible through it just beginning to pale with the dawn, sat at the end of the wide corridor they had just turned onto. Alain yielded to Mari's pull, scrambling along with her toward the promise of safety.

The thud of feet startled him, then several soldiers of Ringhmon came charging around the corner near the window. They stared down the hall at the smoke billowing in their direction, then at the Mechanic and Mage coming toward them in front of the cloud. Faces stark with panic, four of the soldiers leveled crossbows. One brought a Mechanic weapon to his shoulder.

Mari began to skid to a halt, her face a mask of despair, her hand weapon looking far too small compared to the weapons carried by the soldiers. But she was leveling her weapon, ready to fight rather than try running back into the smoke chasing them down the hallway.

Alain grabbed her jacket and pulled her forward. "Keep going," he ordered, then called on everything he had for one more effort. The world illusion said the air in this hallway was clear. It let light pass. But the air could be dark. It could stop light. Change the illusion. Reverse it.

He did not have the strength to do this. He knew that. But it came to him in a sudden release and the power flowed through him as he pushed the Mechanic.

The air around them went pitch black.

Through a haze of total exhaustion, Alain could hear shouts of alarm and terror from in front of them. A familiar thunder boomed in the hallway and things whipped past him with angry cracking sounds. The Mechanic weapon must be launching its projectiles, but with no way to see his targets the chances of the soldier getting a hit must be very small. Alain stumbled, falling, his strength almost totally gone, but a firm grip caught him and propelled him forward. He realized that Mechanic Mari must almost be carrying him, despite his weight and her own tiredness. She was again risking her own life to save him.

Mechanics were not supposed to do that sort of thing. But this was not a Mechanic. This was Mari. Where was she getting the strength to carry him along? His fatigue-addled mind dredged up an answer: that it must come from the same place he had found the means to cast this last spell, a place where strength could be found when none remained. She had shown him how to find such a place, and now she was using it as well to save them both. The thread and its odd effects ran both ways.

They crashed into a tangle of bodies, broke through in the confusion, and moments later hit something hard that shattered under the impact. Their rush carried them through the broken window and there was nothing under their feet.

His strength completely failed, the spell broke and sight returned. Pieces of glass were flying through the air all around, rotating and spinning away with what seemed to his overstressed mind to be dreamlike slowness. Next to him, one arm wrapped about his arm, Mari rolled in midair with her head tucked into her elbow for protection. As his own body spun in the predawn dimness, Alain saw bushes rushing up to meet him. Or perhaps he was falling onto them. Both were only illusions of his mind, so he surrendered to weariness and waited for his body and the bushes to rush together.

CHAPTER ELEVEN

Guild Hall Supervisor Senior Mechanic Stimon didn't look happy. Mari gazed back at him, her own face carefully showing nothing. She was surprised to realize she had learned a little more of that useful trick from watching Alain. She felt triumphant inside, though. Triumphant and in high spirits. She was free, and she had gotten some serious revenge last night, all with the help of Mage Alain.

Stimon's nose kept wrinkling, so Mari guessed that she and her clothing must reek of smoke even though she couldn't smell it any more herself. "The Hall of City Government in Ringhmon has been totally consumed by fire," Stimon growled. "The fires still rage amid the shell of the structure. The city is in an uproar. And you come here covered with ashes and trailing the scent of burning."

Mari nodded. "I was close to the fire. I had a contract at the city hall, as you recall."

"You went to that contract yesterday! What were you still doing there in the early hours of this morning?"

"It was a very complex job," Mari said earnestly. *If you know more, tell me. If you suspected I might have been in danger, I want to hear it from you.*

Stimon's face reddened. "The City Manager told us you had completed the job and left the building."

"Obviously, he was mistaken." Mari locked her eyes on Stimon, daring him to take the word of a common against that of a fellow Mechanic. "Though I certainly appreciate your concern for my welfare, Senior Mechanic Stimon. You'll be happy to know that the healer in the Guild Hall has seen to the injuries I acquired...while escaping the fire."

"How fortunate that you were able to escape...the fire."

Glowering at Stimon, Mari leaned forward. "Shall we dispense with the lies? As you should've already been told, I've reported that I was knocked out, kidnapped by the City Manager of this stinking pestilence of a city, and managed to escape only by great luck." It had been hard to explain how she had done so without mentioning the Mage, but Mari had kept the details fuzzy, claiming lingering effects from the blow to her head.

Stimon sat, glaring at her. "Is there anything else?"

"Does there have to be? A common person assaulting and kidnapping a Mechanic? You should be calling for the man's head," Mari snapped. "And it's certain that the attack on my caravan was also an attempt by Ringhmon to kidnap me before I even reached the city."

"Do you have any proof of that?"

"The bandits used the same rifles—" She broke off as Stimon shook his head.

"Proof," Stimon repeated.

"I saw some of them in Ringhmon!"

Stimon's voice remained implacable as he slammed his hand on the desk. "Proof!"

"You want proof of something?" She dug in one pocket and tossed what she found onto Stimon's big desk. "I found that inside the cell where they'd locked me." Stimon just looked at it, his face revealing nothing of his thoughts. "It's a far-listener, one apparently not made in any Mechanics Guild workshop. And the problem with the Model Six that used to be in the city hall? The secretly contracted Model Six Form Three, that is, and thank you so much for informing me of that before I went there. The problem was a contagion, Senior Mechanic Stimon. Do you know what a contagion is? A banned piece of thinking cipher. One that bore no hallmarks of anyone I have ever encountered in the Guild who knows thinking ciphers."

Stimon finally pursed his lips, his face intent. "We shall have to look into this."

"Pardon me, but you really don't seem to be as alarmed as you should be. I'd appreciate knowing why."

"This is a very serious matter." Stimon looked at her steadily, his own face now as unrevealing as that of a Mage. "I will look into this," he repeated. "I will send a full report to Guild headquarters. Did you find anything on the Model Six aside from the contagion that should not have been there?"

"Yes. I found evidence that Ringhmon was trying to figure out how to make rifles." It was this news that finally made Stimon's eyes widen and his jaw clench. "But that doesn't matter, does it?" Mari demanded. "Because no matter what they learn, commons can't do that kind of thing. Right?"

"Of course," Stimon said in a tight voice.

"Because I also found a contagion of murky origin on a calculating and analysis device, and a far-listener apparently not made in any Mechanics Guild workshop. Guild Hall Supervisor, as a loyal member of the Mechanics Guild, I am concerned about the implications."

"The implications?" Senior Mechanic Stimon had gone cold and still. "What are you implying? That commons can do the work of Mechanics? Are you saying that the justification for the Guild's existence is a lie?"

Her confidence unraveled as the leading questions came at her. Mari tensed. Here, inside the hall of her own Guild, she felt as frightened as she had inside the dungeon of Ringhmon. "No. I want to know the real reasons so I can act in accordance with the needs of the Guild and in its best interests." She hoped her voice had sounded calm and not as shaky as she felt inside.

Senior Mechanic Stimon watched her, his eyes narrow. "Do you believe that your interpretations of recent events are accurate?"

"I—" Mari had been taught to respect her Guild and her superiors in the Guild. Fear had played a role in that teaching—fear of failure, fear of administrative punishment and demotions—but she had never been truly afraid of her Guild. The Guild was her family. The only family she had left. How could her family threaten her? She wasn't a common. "No. They were possible explanations and I want to know the real ones."

Stimon smiled thinly. "Mechanic Mari, before you arrived, this Guild Hall was told that you were extremely good at your work, but weak in the areas of discretion and experience. You have proven the first part of that to be true by accomplishing what Master Mechanic Xian could not. It would be in everyone's best interests if the second part proved to be false and you displayed much more discretion than is to be expected from your past behavior."

She let the deliberate dropping of Master from her title pass this time. *"Think, Mari,"* Professor S'san's voice sounded in her memory. *"Think before you decide what to do."* "I understand."

"Do you? The Guild takes care of its own, so your word will be accepted," Stimon declared, as if believing her was a great concession rather than simply what should be expected. "The Guild will deal with Ringhmon," Stimon added, in a voice that sent a shiver up Mari's back. "There will be an example made. If revenge is what you desire, then you need not worry on that count."

Mari simply nodded, not trusting her voice.

"Now, as to you." Stimon leaned back, keeping his eyes on her. "Your information is placed under Guild interdict. Do you understand? Everything that happened here. Everything you found. You are to mention nothing of this to anyone while the Guild investigates."

Mari stared for a moment, jarred out of her apprehension. "Guild interdict? A Guild Hall Supervisor can't order a Guild interdict on his own."

"You're not very good at following Guild rules, but you seem to have memorized them all. I'm not ordering the interdict on my own." Stimon shoved a piece of paper toward her. Mari reached for it, saw the ornate letterhead and read: *Any Mechanic reading this is advised that the things he or she has learned must not be divulged to anyone. Matters of Guild security and Guild interest are involved. Only a Guild Master may lift the restriction. Signed, Baltha of Centin, Grand Master of the Mechanics Guild.*

She looked up and saw Stimon watching her. Mari read the letter again, trying to understand why the Guild would give Stimon open-ended power to apply an interdict. Stimon must have the backing of powerful Mechanics elsewhere. This wasn't an isolated operation, whatever was going on. Her tentative ideas of reporting Stimon to Palandur crumbled half formed. "How will I know the progress and outcome of the investigation?" she finally asked.

"If you are meant to know, you'll be told," Stimon informed her. He opened a drawer, pulled out a document and shoved it toward her. "By happy coincidence, the weekly train to Dorcastle departs at noon. You're to be on it."

"Dorcastle? I thought I was supposed to return to Palandur when my work was done here."

"Dorcastle," Stimon repeated, his voice hardening. "The Guild is ordering you to Dorcastle. You will find out why when you get there."

A new contract already? Why would Dorcastle need her skills? But it was obvious that Stimon was not going to provide any more information. Mari picked up the ticket, reading it with a growing sense of disorientation. "At noon? Today?"

Stimon steepled his fingertips and nodded. "Today. You're to be on that train without fail, Mechanic Mari. Do I need to put that in writing?"

"No." She looked back at Stimon's smug expression, her sense of right and wrong warring with her common sense. Provoking Stimon now, challenging Stimon now, would be foolish no matter how he baited her.

As too often happened, common sense lost. "It's Master Mechanic Mari," she corrected him.

Stimon curled his lips in a false smile. "Master Mechanic Mari."

"Will I have an escort to the train station?" She already knew the answer, but wanted to hear it from him.

"No. You can make your own way there." Stimon's smile stayed fixed.

"Even with recent events in Ringhmon? You still don't think I'm in any danger?"

"You have your orders. For the good of the Guild," Stimon stated calmly.

How can he do this? There shouldn't be any doubt in his mind that I'm really in danger here. I could so easily be waylaid on my way to that train station. It's like Stimon doesn't just want me out of here, but that he wants me...dead? No. That's impossible.

Isn't it?

The Guild would never—

The Guild lied to me about Mages.

How many other lies have there been?

Stimon let impatience show. "Is there anything else?"

She shook her head, worried that anything else she said might condemn her.

Stimon nodded. "Good. But there's one more question the Guild has for you. You were seen dragging someone away from the building during the fire. You did not mention that person in your report. Who was it?"

Mari wondered how Stimon knew that. At the least it implied that Stimon had spies keeping an eye on the city hall. Spies who should have been able to tell him that she hadn't left the building last night. Even if she hadn't been increasingly worried, Mari wasn't about to be truthful about who she had been with.

She shrugged as casually as she could. "A young man. He jumped from a window and landed in some bushes. Since he needed help, I dragged him to safety."

"Where is this young man now?"

"I don't know. After he recovered he went his own way, and I had to return to this Guild Hall. He wasn't my responsibility." She met Stimon's gaze as coolly as she could. Mari had lied to Guild superiors before, about things like sneaking out of the apprentice barracks at night, but never about anything like this.

"All right. Go." Stimon waved her out. "I don't want to see you again."

Mari, feeling dazed, left the Supervisor's office and found the female Senior Mechanic with the apparently permanent sour expression awaiting her again. Once more Mari was escorted through the Guild Hall, down to the service areas where she was allowed a few moments of privacy to change clothes and have her old clothing cleaned of the smoke smell and ashes, the Senior Mechanic invoking the Guild Hall Supervisor's authority to obtain a rush job. "I need something to eat," Mari insisted while they waited for the clothing to be cleaned. She was led to the dining area and grabbed a late breakfast, sitting eating alone while the Senior Mechanic took care of some paperwork at another table and the other Mechanics in the room avoided eye contact with her.

But as she looked up one time, she saw Cara and Trux watching her anxiously. Trux made a thumbs up and an encouraging grin while Cara and the other Mechanics at that table nodded. Then they all looked away quickly, before their actions could be noticed by any Senior Mechanic. *I guess I'm not completely alone, but everyone else is too scared to act. Maybe they've got more common sense than I do. Maybe? Admit it, Mari, there's no "maybe" about it.*

An apprentice entered, carrying her cleaned clothes, followed by a male Senior Mechanic who seemed upset. Mari was used to that by now, but instead of focusing on her the Senior Mechanic went to the woman who had been herding Mari along and began speaking in a low voice that sounded unhappy. She recognized him as the Senior Mechanic who had taken her report when she got back from the fire, and who had roused the healer to ensure Mari's head injury was treated. Now that Senior Mechanic gestured toward Mari more than once, and Mari caught fragments of his sentences as he spoke to the female Senior Mechanic. "No way to treat... rules do not permit...safety of a Mechanic...I protest..."

But the female Senior Mechanic glowered back at him, her own words barely audible to Mari. "The good of the Guild...orders of the Guild Hall Supervisor..."

While the two Senior Mechanics were arguing, the apprentice set down Mari's bundle of clothing, giving a nervous glance at the Senior Mechanics. "Lady," he whispered.

Mari finally took a good look at the apprentice. He was the one she had met at the entry to the Guild Hall...yesterday? No, the day before.

"Lady," the apprentice murmured while pretending to fuss with the bundle of clothes. "You leave on the train this afternoon?" Mari nodded minutely. "Mechanic Pradar asked me to tell you that the Guild Hall Supervisor has canceled a shipment of Guild materials due to go on that train."

Mari licked her lips nervously, flicking a worried glance at the quarrelling Senior Mechanics. "What does that mean?" she murmured.

"I don't know. Mechanic Pradar said it would be too dangerous to speak to you himself, but he wanted me to thank you on his behalf again. Take care, Lady."

As the apprentice backed away, the male Senior Mechanic frowned down at his female counterpart, his last sentence clear to Mari. "This is the breaking point. I will file a formal protest."

"If you wish to live with the consequences of that," the female Senior Mechanic replied coldly.

"I'm more concerned about being able to live with myself," he retorted, then spun on his heel, stopping as he faced Mari. The Senior Mechanic hesitated, then spoke even louder. "Thank you for your service to the Guild, Master Mechanic."

A ripple of applause broke out from some of the Mechanics as the Senior Mechanic walked quickly from the dining hall, but died out abruptly as the female Senior Mechanic pivoted to see who was clapping. Mari knew the applause wasn't about her, since none of the other Mechanics in this room were likely to know exactly what she had done here for the Guild, but was rather a small mark of support for a Senior Mechanic who had dared to stand up for regular Mechanics.

Mari looked down at the table, thinking about the apprentice who had taken the risk of passing on an admittedly ambiguous warning to her, about the Senior Mechanic who might well just have crippled his own career out of a dedication to doing his job right when it came to how Mechanics were treated, and about the Mechanics who were scared but knew she was on their side. About Mechanic Rindal, Pradar's uncle, who had disappeared because he was unhappy with Guild policies. *Yes, there's a lot I have to learn, but how can those things be right? How can those things be in the interests of the Guild? Why not tell me the real reasons? Why not let those who care about the Guild do what they can to help it?*

No longer able to stomach food, Mari wrapped up the remains of her meal and added it to her pack.

The female Senior Mechanic led Mari through the Guild Hall again, but not to the front entrance, instead stopping at a side door. "For your security," the Senior Mechanic advised with obvious insincerity as she waved Mari out.

The door closed behind her, followed by an audible thunk as the heavy bars inside which normally kept it closed were relocked by the Senior Mechanic. Mari stood outside of the Guild Hall, breathing slowly and trying to think.

Get a grip on yourself, Mari. You've been under a tremendous amount of stress ever since the attack on the caravan. You've taken a nasty blow to the head. Now you're letting all of that get to you, letting your imagination conjure up ridiculous ideas. Senior Mechanic Stimon is obviously a rotten Guild Hall Supervisor, but it's a long step from that to the sorts of things you're afraid of. Commons able to do the work of Mechanics? A Guild Hall supervisor who's actually a threat to the lives of other Mechanics? It's all impossible. Tell yourself it's all impossible. Because it has to be.

Just like making a hole in solid metal or walking through a solid wall. What's going on?

Stars above, I'm scared of my own Guild and not sure where to turn. The Guild's been my entire life since I was taken to the schools as a little girl. The Guild is all I've got.

I'm going to get to that train station, I'm going to get to Dorcastle and rest and talk to some other Mechanics and try to forget all of this craziness. I'm sure once I've rested and gotten away from Ringhmon all of these fears will seem as ridiculous as they surely are. And if they don't... I'm going to start looking for more answers.

Mari hefted her pack, thinking of the distance to the train station, and groaned inside. The painkillers the Guild Hall healer had given her had reduced the ache in her head to a mild throb, but after all the exertions of last night she had no desire to lug her pack across half the city. She started across the wide plaza that surrounded the Mechanics Guild Hall.

"Are you well this morning?"

The voice was familiar and totally emotionless, but Mari looked in vain for the robes of a Mage. Then she focused on a young man standing nearby, wearing nondescript clothing like that of common folk. "Mage Alain? Where's— ?"

"My robes?" He made a dismissive gesture. "I decided it would be wise to be invisible when moving about the city today, but am still too weak from my efforts to be certain of maintaining that spell long enough. Then I realized that there was another way to be invisible, for who looks at commons?"

Mari felt a smile forming, her fears receding into the background to be replaced by relief at seeing him. "Are you all right? Last night you didn't think you had been hurt by the fall, but I was worried."

"I was exhausted from my spells and stunned when I hit the ground," Alain said. "But other than some bruises I took no harm. I know you had much to do with that."

"Well, yeah," Mari admitted, feeling self-conscious. "I also had much to do with you getting into that mess in the first place. Did you get in trouble with your elders?"

"Yes," Mage Alain said without feeling. "I got in trouble. I was asked to explain my actions. I provided various reasons consistent with Mage wisdom, but the elders did not accept them."

"I guess you couldn't say that you were my friend," Mari said.

"No. I eventually admitted that I had followed you to spy upon you."

"You...what?"

Was there humor showing in the Mage's eyes? "That is what I told them. There is no truth, so one story was as good as another. The elders were willing to accept that I was motivated by a desire to learn more about a possible threat to the Mage Guild."

Mari felt herself smiling widely. Being able to lie with a clean conscience probably had its advantages. *I really like the guy hidden inside him. That good person I keep getting glimpses of. I think I'd like him even if he hadn't saved me at least twice.* "What did you find out while you were spying on me?"

"Not to start fires inside buildings unless I am already near a window." He waited while Mari winced. "Otherwise I could tell them little, since I explained I often could not understand your words or actions."

"Yeah," Mari said. "A lot of people have that problem with me, and to be perfectly honest I'm having a little trouble figuring them out myself right now. Look, I've got some issues I need to work out with my Guild. I don't know exactly what's going on. Anyway, there's no sense in you getting in more trouble with your Guild, too. Hanging with me isn't doing you any good, and might get you in trouble."

"But you are a friend." His voice remained impassive, his face unrevealing. "You also saved my life, carrying me to the window. How did you create the strength to do that? It was an impressive manipulation of the illusion."

Mari shrugged and looked down, feeling the heat of embarrassment in her face. "I have no idea how I did that. I guess I was highly motivated. I wasn't going to leave you behind, not after you got me out of that cell."

"You never leave anyone behind," Alain recited as if it were a lesson. "No. I don't."

The Mage's mouth worked, then he spoke hesitantly. "Thank...you."

They had been walking, but now Mari stumbled to a halt, staring at him. What had it taken for a Mage to say those words? She had heard him say them before, but only repeating her own words back to her. He hadn't actually said thank you to anyone, to her. But now he had. *Say something to him, you fool. Anything.* "You're thanking me for throwing you out a window?"

"Yes, if you wish to say it that way, using your sarcasm." Mage Alain twisted his face slightly. "I am uncertain about the right things to say. As an acolyte, the use of those words would bring punishment."

You poor— "Well, uh, that's...I mean...I'm really glad...you're...all right."

"A friend wants to help," Mage Alain said. "Because it is the right thing," he added, quoting her.

"Uh...yeah...that's...right." He had paid that much attention to what she said? And he really liked her? Or whatever Mages used in place of "like," anyway. He had saved her life, he had gone into a dungeon to get her out, he had listened to her. He had that thread thing between them that wasn't there but was.

He hadn't left her when that would have been the easiest, most acceptable thing to do. Instead, he had taken the hardest road he could, because he wanted to help her.

Mari stared at Alain, wondering why she was suddenly having so much trouble talking, why she couldn't seem to string two words together without fumbling, why she felt so awkward, why she couldn't take her eyes off of Alain's expressionless face and his firm jaw and his soulful eyes—

Soulful eyes?

Oh, no, Mari. No no no no no no no. You are not going there. That is so crazy it's off the scale. He's a Mage. You're a Mechanic. Yes, he's damaged, and yes, it would be oh-so-romantic to try to fix him, but that is not the sort of repair job any rational woman would undertake, and it is certainly not the sort of job you should even be considering. He doesn't even know what love is. He doesn't know what like is. He has only the vaguest idea what a friend is.

You told him it wasn't love. You told him not to think about love. That was smart. You're smart, Mari. You won't get involved with some badly damaged guy who thinks nothing is real just because he's more real than any other guy you've ever met. You will...you will...

I felt safe when he showed up here.

Why is he looking at me? He's waiting for something. Did he ask me a question? Oh, right. "Where am I going? Uh...I'm...uh...I... Dorcastle. I...I'm going to...Dorcastle." *Stars above, help me, I sound like I'm six years old.*

But Alain didn't show any sign that he had noticed her discomfort, even though he must have. "I also must go to Dorcastle. My elders insist that I leave this city."

"Oh...um...good. Are you...taking...the train?"

"Train?" Alain asked.

"Yes." She pointed in the direction of the yard. "Train."

"This is like a caravan?"

"No...yes. I mean, it takes people, but...faster. Much faster." She took a deep breath, trying to collect herself. "Mages never use trains, but if you are wearing that—those clothes—you could ride it."

Alain considered that. "How would I do this?"

"It's easy." *So easy a Mage could do it. I have to stop using that expression.* "You...you go...there. That way. There's a...a sign. Train Station. You can read? Sorry. Of course you can read. And there's another sign. Passengers. I can...get you a ticket. You go to...to that window...and you say, 'will call ticket for Alain of Ihris.' Don't...*please* don't...say the Mage part. You're not wearing those robes so...no one will know you're a Mage." *Unless they look at your face.* "And...and they'll give you a ticket. That's a piece of paper with writing on it. And...you follow the other passengers...and the train takes you to...

to Dorcastle." She wanted to bury her face in her hands out of sheer embarrassment. *Please, please, let this end.*

"Is there something wrong?" Alain asked. "You are distressed."

"No. Nothing. Nothing at all. Do not, do *not*, tell anyone that you're a Mage. Some of my fellow Mechanics might...do the wrong thing. But I...I have to go. Myself." What had happened to her? An awful suspicion occurred to Mari as she looked at the Mage. She had never believed the stories about Mage spells, but look what he had done last night. Maybe some of the other stories were true, about the ability of Mages to make people act in strange ways. "Alain...tell me the truth."

"There is no truth."

"*Try anyway!* Would you...would you do anything to me...without me knowing?"

The Mage looked at her silently for a while.

Stars above. There's hurt in his eyes. I can see it way back there, almost completely hidden, but I hurt him with that question. I hurt the feelings of a Mage. They don't even have feelings, but I hurt them. Way to achieve the impossible, Mari.

Finally, Alain shook his head. "I would not do anything like that."

Could she believe him?

But as if sensing the question, Alain added more. "There is no truth, but I will not mislead you. A friend would not mislead."

"Thank you." Mari tried to gather up the shattered shards of her dignity. "I'm sorry. I really have to go. Um...thank you. Thank you for everything. Goodbye." *Forever. Absolutely, positively forever, before I make the biggest mistake of my life.* She hoisted her pack and almost ran down the road, away from the Mage Alain.

❋   ❋   ❋

Leaving the Mage Guild Hall was the work of a moment, informing the acolyte at the door that he would not be returning, but would be heading for Dorcastle as instructed by the elders. Alain suspected those elders, who had regarded him with ill-concealed suspicion at a second Inquiry this morning, would be grateful enough for his departure not to worry about how he was leaving. No one had ever told him specifically that Mechanic "trains" were off limits to Mages, and asking permission seemed a needless complication, so he did not bother about that. Alain had brought no baggage from the ruin of the caravan, and Mages had few possessions in any event. He had acquired a small bag to hold his robes hidden, and now walked toward the Mechanic place which Mari had told him to look for. The common clothes he wore still felt very odd, but he would grow used to them.

Following some commons, Alain carried his bag inside the Mechanic station, looking around and absorbing the noises, smells and vapors that swirled through the station. Some of those noises and smells always seemed to go with Mechanics and their doings. Sharp bangs and sudden, loud crashing sounds. The tang of things heated too hot, overlaid by something like rancid cooking oil left too long on a fire. Metal grinding against metal. What purpose did such things serve?

Not long ago he would not have come this far, avoiding anything with the taint of Mechanics about it. But he could still sense the thread. Mechanic Mari was here, and she would not have sent him into danger.

The window was not hard to find, and when Alain gave his name a boy who must be a Mechanic acolyte shoved a piece of paper forward without even looking at Alain. Mechanics must also teach their acolytes to ignore others. Alain took the paper and followed commons again. They walked to a series of identical, long, narrow buildings next to a platform. The sides of each of the buildings were lined with windows. At the very end of the line stood a building which appeared grander than the others, and had some of the Mechanic acolytes standing as if guarding it. Alain guessed that one would be for the Mechanics themselves. In front of the windowed buildings were a number of similarly shaped buildings with no windows, but rather large doors through which boxes and other objects were being brought inside.

It all seemed incomprehensible, but the commons ahead of Alain walked into the nearest building and he followed, finding the single room inside filled with benches along each side and an aisle down the middle. Seating himself as the commons did, Alain waited, wondering what to do.

Alain could wait. He gazed out of the window impassively as the room gradually filled with commons, taking many of the seats, some of them giving him curious looks. Someone might have said something to him, but he ignored them, and they went away.

He heard a rumbling sound, felt vibrations, then a sudden shock rocked the building he was in. None of the commons appeared alarmed, and Alain of course hid his own reaction, but he had more trouble remaining impassive when the building slid backwards a bit, then forwards, with its own rumbling vibration.

Very odd. Then he saw one of the buildings being rolled by on a nearby set of metal lines and realized the buildings had wheels on them. Clever. They were wagons, not buildings, linked together into a single long caravan. But what kind of creature could pull so many?

Up ahead, somewhere past the wagons which carried boxes, Alain heard a deafening, wild screech, as if a huge creature had been stricken. Once again, he barely kept from showing any reaction. Mechanics were shouting orders, then with a lurch the wagons surged into motion.

Mechanic Mari had said she would be on this train as well. Alain wondered whether she would be in the last car with the Mechanics. But the thread led forward, not back. Mari was up front, perhaps near the beast that pulled this strange Mechanic caravan.

The train kept going faster and faster, the outlying buildings of Ringhmon whipping by quicker than a galloping horse could manage. Alain stared out the window, remembering how Mechanic Mari had looked when he had walked into her cell through the hole he had imagined in the wall. He suspected she had felt then as he did now, astonished at something which should not have been possible, according to what he had been taught. What he had been taught instead was to pay no attention to the works of Mechanics, not even to look upon them. Tricks deserved no attention, required no attention.

This was not a trick. He had been trained to see through illusions, and this was a very good one. How did the Mechanics do this?

In the sky above, Alain noticed a trail of smoke which appeared to come from the front of the train. Whatever was pulling all of these wagons, whatever had screamed, must also be producing the smoke. A dragon? A troll? No, neither created smoke, nor could a troll move fast.

But the Mechanics had made something, using their own arts, just as Mages could create creatures. What would Mage Guild elders say if Alain asked about this? *They would tell me I was fooled, being young. They would accuse me of having strayed from wisdom, of having been overcome by the illusions of the Mechanics.*

They would ask me why I chose to ride what Mari called a train.

I will stay silent on this while I try to learn why my Guild is so much in error when it comes to Mechanics.

The wheels of the wagons clicked in a rhythmic way as the train rolled along, the wagons swaying back and forth slightly. The gentle motion brought back memories of long ago, before he had been taken by the Guild. Being gently rocked, a soft voice singing.

Alain focused tightly on his training, unwilling to give in to that memory. It lay behind a locked door in his mind, and somehow he knew that if he opened that door it would bring more buried emotion than his training could deal with.

The seat was far from comfortable, with cushions as thin as those in the dungeon of Ringhmon, but Mages were taught to disregard physical discomfort. He fell asleep watching the land roll past, the accumulated fatigue of the last several days catching up with him, only to awaken when the train slowed to a halt. Outside, low vegetation and an occasional tree could be seen, but no sign of the ocean. This was not Dorcastle.

"They're feeding the Mechanic engine," he heard one of the commons say to another. "Water and that liquid like lamp oil they make that burns really well."

The Mechanic creature ate and drank. Interesting. He could feel no drain on power in the area as the Mechanic train moved, so the Mechanic creature did not draw on that as a Mage spell would. The creature must rely on the aid of power provided in another form.

Alain fell asleep again after the train began moving once more. He woke as the Mechanic train finished skirting the rugged mountains which blocked access to Ringhmon from the western side and turned west toward Dorcastle. The air took on the bracing scent of salt water, and before long Alain could spot the lowering sun glittering on the surface of the Sea of Bakre. The wide coastal marshes he could see soon gave way to rocks on which waves beat unceasingly.

He had never seen that sea until recently, when he had ridden a ship south to find employment far from Ihris. Alain watched it, thinking of his time with the Mechanic. Thinking of Mari. So many changes, so many challenges to the wisdom he had been taught. Yet his foresight had not warned him of her. If she were a danger, if she were leading him astray from wisdom, such a warning would surely have come or would come.

He thought again about the vision involving Mari. A second sun, and a terrible storm that threatened it, and perhaps more. What could that mean?

Had the vision regarding Mari come to him for the same reason the thread had appeared? Did being a friend have something to do with it? Or was it simply because of Mari herself? Alain recalled Mari's own warnings that other Mechanics were likely a danger to him, and wondered what would have happened if there had been another Mechanic traveling with the destroyed caravan. Would any other Mechanic have done what Mari did, forcing their alliance and thereby saving them both?

Friend. He remembered more now. Asha would have been a friend. He felt sure of that from the brief time before the elders had taught acolytes to avoid even mentioning such things. What would that have been like? Not like being a friend with Mechanic Mari. But it had not happened, it could not happen. If Asha was not already a Mage, she surely would be one soon. The biggest thing holding her back was the natural beauty that no amount of neglect could diminish and which created deep suspicion among elders. But she felt nothing, just as he felt nothing.

Those memories roused something inside him that Alain did not understand but wanted to avoid. He tried to concentrate on Mari again. That was not too hard.

She had acted oddly when last they met. He had wondered if she would greet him here. But she had never said "we" would travel on this Mechanic caravan. She had spoken of them being separate once again. Had Mechanic Mari developed second thoughts about being a friend? They had been thrown together twice, but each time she had needed him as he had needed her. Now, neither needed the other.

Surely friend meant more than that.

The way she had looked at him before parting in Ringhmon...what did that mean? He could not sort out the emotions he had seen in her. But her eyes had been wide as she looked at him and...and...

Those thoughts were disturbing, too.

As long as light lasted, he watched as the Mechanic caravan climbed ever higher along the steep cliffs which marked the southern shore of the Sea of Bakre. Inland from the cliffs were even higher mountains, forming barriers so rugged to travel that they were almost impassable. There were no lights within the caravan, at least not this part of it, but the moonlight shone brightly. Alain could easily see the moon and the smaller twins that forever chased it across the night sky. At last, even the spectacular view could not overcome the tempo of the clicking wheels, and Alain fell asleep again, thinking that this Mechanic way of travel was indeed superior to anything commons offered. The Mage Guild had its own means, of course, faster than this Mechanic device.

Had Mari ever flown on a Roc? It seemed unlikely.

Alain dreamed of flying above the clouds, looking down on toylike cities, Mari by his side. He felt...what was this? Like when he had qualified to be a Mage, passing all tests. Better than that, though. Much better.

But the clouds darkened, forming into the storm of his vision, towering thunderheads filled with rage rising higher to threaten Alain and Mari.

The Roc screamed and they fell...

Alain woke to hear the screaming still in his ears as a huge, invisible hand grasped Alain and hurled him against the seat in front of him. It held him there while the shrieking of tortured metal continued and the view of a rock wall outside the windows on one side showed the wagon was slowing rapidly. The sense of great danger, of something being very wrong, was so strong that Alain felt a momentary sting of panic despite his training.

CHAPTER TWELVE

The screaming of metal came to an end, and the mysterious force holding Alain against the seat before him released its grip, allowing him to fall to the floor.

Alain blinked in the darkness, wondering what could have happened. All around, the shocked silence was starting to give way to cries of alarm and, in some cases, cries of pain.

Still bemused by the sudden waking from his dream, Alain sought to feel for the presence of Mages and the drain on the power in this area as they cast spells. He felt nothing, though. Whatever had caused the Mechanic train to screech to a halt, it had not been the work of Mages.

If it had been bandits again, they were now silent. No crashes of Mechanic weapons broke the night, no thump of crossbow bolts striking home, no shouts of battle. All that Alain could hear outside were the voices of a few commons who had already spilled out of the wagons and were loudly speculating on what had happened.

Checking himself for injury and finding none, Alain followed the rest of the travelers as they filed out of the wagon. The Mechanic train had stopped along the face of a high cliff, with only a small shelf of land to stand on next to the metal lines the wagons ran along. A three-quarter moon cast an icy light across the area, revealing a view of remarkable but cold beauty as it sparked silver from froth thrown by angry waves crashing in endless array against the cliff face below.

Unfazed by the sheer drop, Alain looked down on those cliffs forever standing sentinel before the waters of the Sea of Bakre.

He was still taking in his surroundings when there came a rumbling sound from the rear of the train. Alain looked back that way, seeing that the last and grandest wagon had been separated at some point. Mechanics were now rolling it back into contact with the rest of the train. The Mechanic wagon struck with a crash that bounced from wagon to wagon past Alain, then the Mechanics began walking forward, the commons scattering hastily to clear a path. Alain watched the Mechanics approach, not even realizing he was acting like a Mage in robes, before he recalled in the nick of time that he was dressed as a common person and had to likewise get out of the way. He hastily stepped back against the wagon he had ridden in, just in time to avoid being shouldered aside.

Alain fought down a wave of un-Magelike emotion, of irritation, gazing after the Mechanics. *Arrogant,* the elders had said. *They think they rule the world.* He had forgotten that advice, which seemed accurate enough in the case of these Mechanics. Mari did not show that arrogance.– But these Mechanics even walked differently than she did.

He heard the word "accident" being repeated as the commons around him talked. They seemed content to wait on whatever the Mechanics decided. Those who had received broken or sprained arms and legs in the sudden stop were being tended to by other commons, the Mechanics ignoring them.

I can wait as well, thought Alain. *But if I go ahead after those Mechanics, I will see whatever creature pulled this train and learn more of it. Did it die, or did it rebel against the lash of the Mechanics? Trolls and dragons can slip their control if the creating Mage loses his concentration. Is that what happened here?*

And Mari was up there, the thread told him.

Why not see? Alain began working his way forward through the crowd, finding himself disconcerted by the need to avoid commons who did not shrink away from him as usual. Appearing to be a common was not without its disadvantages, but at least he had some practice with threading through crowds because of his occasional use of the concealment spell.

When he finally got close enough to the front, Alain could see the groups of common travelers came to an end at the last wagon, leaving a good-sized gap before the group of Mechanics standing near a hulking shape from which smoke rose into the sky. Alain could not make out details in the moonlight, but he could feel the heat radiating from the creature, and hear a low, steady rumble which might be its breathing. None of the Mechanics appeared worried at being close to the creature, which sat unmoving before the wagons. If it had slipped its bonds before, the creature was surely under control now. Why had not the train begun moving again?

A hand fell on his shoulder, surprising him doubly: no one touched a Mage, and he had grown unused to unexpected physical contact. "Praise the stars we stopped in time, eh, lad?" a bluff voice remarked.

Alain looked back at a large, older man as the common pointed forward past the Mechanic creature. "That's what you're looking for, isn't it? See? The rails just stop at the edge there." Following the man's gesture, Alain could see that the metal lines indeed seemed to vanish as they reached a place where the strip of land on the cliff came to an end. "If those Mechanics hadn't gotten this thing stopped in time we'd all be at the bottom of the cliff right now," the common continued.

Another man spoke, his voice harsh but low to keep it from carrying to the Mechanics. "It's their bridge! Why did it fail? We pay a lot to use their trains, and a safe journey is the least we expect for that."

"It's not the Mechanics' fault," a third man interjected. "Not this time, anyway. It's the dragons. We're near enough Dorcastle. It's got to be them."

The first man nodded in agreement. "Like as not. Them blasted Mages— "

"The Mages claim the dragons aren't under their control," the second man insisted.

"And what's the word of a Mage worth?"

Murmurs of agreement came from those around Alain. "There are dragons near Dorcastle?" Alain asked, realizing too late that while it was too dark for the commons to see his Magelike impassivity, they would be able to hear the lack of emotion in his voice.

But the commons assumed there was another reason for his stiffness. "Relax, lad, you're fine now," the first common said. "And the dragons haven't killed anyone yet. That we've heard of."

The third man nodded. "Aye, boy. Dragons. They've been threatening the city and doing harm to force Dorcastle to pay enough to get them to leave. But Dorcastle won't pay."

"It can't," a woman protested. "Those dragons want enough to beggar a city twice Dorcastle's size."

"Dragons are greedy, they say," another added.

Alain listened, his puzzlement growing. Dragons wanting money? How could that be possible? "Are the Mages in Dorcastle doing nothing to stop these dragons?"

"*Relax*, buddy. The Mages *say* they are," the first man replied. "And maybe they are, because it's bringing them no profit. Dorcastle's been screaming to the Mage Guild leaders and threatening to sanction every Mage and break every contract. They're trying to get the rest of the Bakre Confederation to back them up, and I hear the Confederation's likely to do so for fear another city will be targeted by these dragons next, or by the Mages controlling them, more likely."

The travelers began arguing among themselves about who or what was responsible for their near disaster. Alain stared forward again, thinking.

A smaller figure walking with a familiar gait came back from the ranks of the Mechanics. One hand reached toward the train creature as if running a calming touch down its flank. Was Mari its creator and controller?

She paused at the end of the creature, speaking, and Alain saw another Mechanic leaning out from what he had thought the back of the beast. Her conversation done, Mari turned back, but then halted again. As if sensing his gaze, she turned and stared toward him.

He inclined his head toward her. She stood silent, then walked quickly up to him, he walking forward a couple of steps too so that they could converse quietly without either Mechanics or commons overhearing. "Are you all right?" she asked. "I need to know."

"I am not injured. Are you well?"

"I'm fine." Mari shuddered visibly. "I was riding in the locomotive. We came very close to going over the break."

"Locomotive? That is the creature's name?"

"Creature?" She hesitated. "It's not alive."

Alain nodded. "Like a troll."

"A what? No."

"Did you create it?"

"Me?" Mari shook her head. "This locomotive is well over a century old. It's been around a lot longer than me. I just know how to run them, to operate them. Do you understand?"

"No. Whoever creates the creature is the only one who can control it."

"I can't explain now. It doesn't follow Ma— your rules." She looked forward past the locomotive. "The Mechanic who runs the engine on this shift told me he usually gets bored along this stretch and has trouble staying awake. But I was assigned to ride with him because of my specialty in steam. I was nervous and looking forward, and thank the stars above I saw the break just in time. Otherwise we'd all be dead."

"Perhaps you have foresight," Alain remarked. "But not all would have died. Your fellow Mechanics in the last wagon would have survived."

She looked startled. "What do you mean? Not about that foresight thing. The bit about the last wagon."

"The last wagon was separated from the rest of the train. I saw it being brought up to rejoin the other wagons."

"You saw that?" Mari paused. "Did you see or hear anything else?"

"The commons say this was caused by dragons."

Mari stared at him. "Dragons?" she finally asked.

"Yes. Everyone thought so. It surprised me to hear it."

"You don't sound surprised. But then you never sound like anything. It's kind of creepy." The Mechanic glanced back at her fellows, who were still conversing among themselves. "I'm sorry. I shouldn't have said that. My nerves are still shot. I shouldn't be talking to you. But— We were heading for the edge, and slowing down, and I couldn't tell if we would stop in time, and it wasn't that long but it also seemed that time was moving very slowly, and—" she looked at him, "and I was less worried about dying myself than I was about you dying."

"Why?" Alain asked. "Because you are a friend?"

"Yes. No. Maybe. Maybe because I had suggested that you take this train and I had bought the ticket. If you had died or been hurt, it would have been my fault."

Alain considered that, then shook his head. "My decisions were my own."

"That's very sweet of you to say in that emotionless voice of yours, but I'd feel guilty." Mari hesitated. "It really focused my mind, watching the edge getting closer and closer, thinking about you the whole time. And I realized something else, that running away from something was wrong. That's not how you solve a problem."

"What were you running from?"

She stared at him before answering. "A problem. A really big problem. Something that needs to be fixed. But if you stay with a problem long enough, instead of running from it, you'll learn more about it, and then you'll realize its, uh, flaws, that it's really not all that...wonderful a problem. And then it won't be a problem, because once you understand what is wrong, you can fix it. I hope."

Alain looked back at her, trying to comprehend her words. "Which problem is this? The dragons?"

"Right. The dragons. Of course." Mari turned quickly to point toward the chasm ahead. "We were thinking maybe a washout of some kind caused this, though that doesn't seem likely. This is a very old line, but the engineer told me that trestle was replaced only a few years ago. No one mentioned dragons," Mari continued. "Dragons? Do those really exist?"

"Nothing really exists."

He heard a strangled sound come from her, then Mari spoke heavily. "Just tell me about dragons."

"You know nothing? They are created, which requires a Mage of great strength and an area with substantial power to feed the spell. The more power that can be put into the spell, the more skilled the Mage who creates it, the larger the dragon. But like all other spells, they fade. I do not know how Mechanics could keep this locomotive creature in existence for so long."

"It takes a lot of work," Mari whispered. "What else?"

"Dragons are not very intelligent. Like trolls, they exist only to destroy, and like trolls they must obey the commands of the Mage who created them. This is what I do not understand. These travelers all spoke of dragons acting on their own, outside the control of the Mages in Dorcastle."

"Why are they destroying train trestles?" Mari asked.

"There is some sort of ransom being demanded. A very large sum. The city will not pay, and the Mage Guild Hall in Dorcastle is attempting to deal with the problem and failing. All this according to my fellow travelers. I have not heard of this from Mages."

Mari nodded. "How strong are they? Could a dragon have pulled out the supports from a trestle like this? Wooden supports bigger around than I am?"

"It depends on the dragon. But, yes, they can be very large and very strong."

"I'm asking about dragons. This is crazy," she muttered, just loud enough for Alain to hear.

"They do not act like the dragons I know of," Alain repeated. "Could they be Mechanic dragons?"

"Mechanics don't have dragons. I need to check on this and why the last wagon was detached from the train before we stopped. Wait here. Please," she added hastily, then walked back to talk to her fellow Mechanics.

Alain waited, aware that he was standing out from everyone else and thus the object of attention from both the Mechanics ahead and the commons behind. That felt odd, too. Normally everyone tried not to look at a Mage. Now everyone seemed to be looking at him.

The voice of the large man who had first talked to him came from the commons. "Hey! You know one of the Mechanics? On speaking terms?"

Alain considered the best way to answer. He needed to maintain the proper illusion. "I was able to do some services for her in Ringhmon."

"You're not free and easy with them, that's for sure," the man commented. "Don't worry, we don't think you're one of them. Try to calm down. You still sound like you're in shock."

"Maybe he's really a Mage," another common joked, and several other commons laughed.

Mari came back, her face troubled, and the commons hastily backed away again. "We've contacted the Guild in Dorcastle to come get us, but it'll take until morning for a train to get here." Almost immediately she flinched enough for it to be visible in the dark. "I shouldn't have told you that."

"Why not? Do Mechanics not have something like message Mages?"

"Message Mages?" Mari blew out an angry breath. "One more thing my Guild claimed wasn't real. For now, just don't mention what I said to anyone." She looked at the other Mechanics. "They said the two Senior Mechanics in the last wagon were able to open the coupling to the train and set the brake when we started the emergency stop. One single wagon was able to stop a lot faster than the entire train could."

"I understand very little of what you said, except that it seems fortunate these Senior Mechanics were where they needed to be."

Mari looked at him. "What do you mean by that?"

"When your train began stopping," Alain explained, "some force held me in place. Are Mechanics not affected by it?"

"Yes, of course they are. It's called momentum. It—" Mari stopped speaking. "They had to be exactly where they needed to be when we hit the brakes on the train. One at the coupling and one at the brake. Those are real close to each other, but..."

Alain studied her expression. "You are concerned."

She took a deep breath. "Is that what it seems? It's just...the last car would've survived even if the rest of the train had gone over, and if we had seen the break just a little later the locomotive would have gone over even if the wagons were able to be saved."

"You said you were in the locomotive."

"Yeah."

He saw her emotions change, fear shifting to anger, then to resolve. "I need some answers. Some of the Mechanics are going to go down and look at the wreckage of the trestle to see what we can discover. I've been trying to decide whether or not to go with them."

"Why would you not go?" Alain asked.

"If it's dragons, what could I learn? I'm an engineer. I work with facts."

Alain pondered that. "Then why do you not seek facts about dragons?"

She did not answer for a moment. "Very good point. All right. I'll go, too. Now, this is going to sound weird. I can't believe that I'm saying it. But...you're the only person on this train that I trust."

Alain felt his lips twitching, as if the sides wanted to curl upwards. But that would form a...smile? Unthinkable. He had to work to avoid showing his reaction. "You trust me?"

"I told you it was weird. I don't know any of these other Mechanics. That shouldn't matter, but there's been some strange stuff happening."

"It is not weird," Alain objected. "You do not know the Mechanics. I am a friend."

"Yeah." He could see the flash of teeth in her smile. "Would you come along? Down to the wreckage?" Mari added quickly.

"Me?"

"Yes. Because I trust you, and because you actually know stuff about dragons, and, heavens above, if you'd told me a month ago that I'd be saying this I would have— Well, I wouldn't have answered, because I wouldn't have talked to you."

"Nor would I have talked to you." Alain looked toward the Mechanics, considering what Mari had said. The elders would have warned him not to trust her, that she was planning some trick, perhaps to get him alone among the Mechanics and then strike. Long years of training, of being told wisdom, warred with the experiences of the last few weeks. "Master Mechanic Mari, you are a friend, and you ask for help. I will do this."

"Thanks. You're a *good* friend." She hesitated again. "You do understand, I'm *only* a friend. Nothing more."

"More?"

"*Nothing* more. Just remember that. Now, don't use my name around anyone else. Just call me Lady Mechanic. Would you be willing to carry my tool kit down?"

It was Alain's turn to hesitate. "Mechanic tools? I have been told many warnings about those. I was told they were dangerous. You said they could be weapons."

"If you misuse them, they can be dangerous," Mari admitted. "And they can be deliberately used as weapons in an emergency. But they are perfectly safe to carry. I swear it. I need to have a reason for you to be with me. I'll tell them that I got injured in Ringhmon and need someone to carry my bag down the cliff for me. The other Mechanics know I was at the City Hall fire, so they'll believe me. I'll say that I'm paying a common to haul my stuff. Mechanics do that when we need manual laborers. Understand?"

"You were not really hurt in the fire?"

"No." She sounded pleased. "It's nice of you to ask again, though."

"Your fellow Mechanics will not think it odd that you would not just leave your tools near what you call the locomotive?"

Mari paused before answering. "It's hard to explain. It's not just that the tools are really expensive because so few are made, or that apprentices get it drilled into them that losing a tool is a sign of incompetence. Those tools represent who we are in the same way that your...skills...represent you."

Alain nodded. "I understand the importance that shadows can attach to illusions, but wisdom would say that what represents a Mechanic, or any other shadow, is what is found within them."

"Um, yeah," Mari admitted. "Maybe we're not all that wise in wanting our tools close at hand. But a tool you don't have is a tool you can't use, so it's more complicated than a matter of self-image. Anyway, that means everyone will think it's perfectly normal for me to want my tools with me."

"Then I will do this."

For the second time that night, he saw her smile. "Thanks."

A few minutes later a group of the Mechanics detached themselves and headed for the cliff edge. Mari followed, beckoning to Alain. By the time they reached the edge, the other Mechanics were already climbing down toward the patch of beach dimly visible below, now choked with tangled wreckage. Mari offered him the bag she had been carrying, and Alain, after a moment's hesitation, took it. She smiled encouragingly at him, an expression which almost immediately changed to intent worry as she turned away. Then Mari started down, moving cautiously from rock to rock.

Alain looked downward to the barely seen jumble of broken wood. Then he gazed out to sea along the dark lines of waves rolling toward the shore. If a dragon had done this it might still be lurking nearby, in water shallow enough to stand in. It might attack again, this time rending not wood but anything else it encountered. Alain tried to judge his strength and the power to be found in the area around them. *I probably could not defeat a dragon big enough to do that kind of damage, even at my best.*

But Mari has asked for my help. She seems confused and uncertain.

I want to help her. I had thought that helping her would remove my need to help her again, but the more I help Mari, the more I want to help her. I erred a great deal in my assumption. But that error is not of importance. My road leads down this cliff tonight. I do not care if it is wisdom or not.

He took another look at Mechanic Mari, clambering stubbornly downward, and began climbing down after her.

✳   ✳   ✳

Mari started to wonder if she was actually having another kind of nightmare. As she went farther down the cliff, the rocks kept getting looser and harder to get good hold on. Lower still her hands and feet started slipping where spray flung up from the sea had wetted the rocks. Beyond that, she started to get into the tangle of fallen pieces of trestle, mighty pillars of wood which had been twisted and splintered into jagged spears. Worse yet, thoughts about the Mage kept distracting her. A near-death experience had led her to do what she had absolutely, positively vowed not to do: reach out to Alain as a companion again.

Just a trusted companion. I'm a big girl. I'm not a slave to emotions. My feelings caught me by surprise, that's all. I was scared. I was vulnerable. I felt sorry for him. He had saved me. So it wasn't really real feelings, just gratitude and stress and all. I can handle this, get to know him and find out everything that's wrong with him. He may be a Mage, but he's also a guy, so he has to have plenty of stuff wrong with him. I'll learn what his flaws are, and then I can put him in perspective.

Unless he turns out to be as good as he seems. Then I'm in trouble.

At last she ruthlessly blocked out all thoughts of anything but the climb down, until Mari found herself taking a final step down onto a small area on the beach where she could stand.

As beaches went, it wasn't anything to inspire songs. Small and covered with pebbles instead of sand, the only truly good thing was that it offered decent footing in the areas not covered by wreckage or by large rocks which had fallen from above.

The other Mechanics were already clambering over the wreckage, muttering to each other. One pulled out a knife and thrust it into a broken piece of wood. "Solid here, too. No rot," he called.

"The foundations are still firm," another announced.

"No fire damage visible," a third declared.

Mari watched for a moment, waiting for Alain. None of the other Mechanics took notice of her. They all seemed to know each other, and most seemed to be from Ringhmon. The only Mechanic on the train with whom Mari had gotten on halfway familiar terms was the engineer, who had stayed up on top of the cliff with his locomotive.

"Obvious sabotage," a Senior Mechanic was concluding, his voice angry. He kicked at a shattered pole. "These were broken not far above ground by something pulling at them from seaward."

"By what?" a woman Senior Mechanic demanded. "This has to be the work of Mages. No one else has the resources and the cold blooded deceit to carry it off. But how did they do it?"

Mari spoke finally, her voice carrying over the group. "Wouldn't it have been easier for Mages simply to set fire to the trestle?"

The Senior Mechanic gave her a disdainful look. "How would they have built a fire down here with that salt spray wetting everything?"

"They're supposed to be able to produce heat by some means," Mari said. She couldn't have been the only Mechanic present who had seen the results of that, and she wanted to see how these Mechanics reacted to her carefully phrased suggestion.

The woman Senior Mechanic shook her head, the gesture aimed as much at Mari as at her statement. "No, child. That's just a parlor trick. It has no practical use. You're that sixteen-year-old, aren't you?"

"*Eighteen*-year-old," Mari corrected, realizing that the correction didn't sound as impressive as she would have hoped.

"Of course," the woman Senior Mechanic said. Turning away

from Mari, she began conferring with the male Senior Mechanic and some others in a low voice.

Mari, trying to control her anger at being so summarily put down, noticed a couple of the other Mechanics frowning toward the group including the two Senior Mechanics. Another one gave Mari a what-can-you-do sort of look before going back to examining the wreckage.

"Your elders?" someone murmured very softly near her in an emotionless voice.

Mari turned to see that Mage Alain had reached the beach and was eyeing her with his usual dispassionate expression. "My superiors, yes. How could you tell?" she added dryly before pointing toward the wreckage. "Well?" she whispered. "Give me some facts to work with."

The Mage ran his eyes over the mess. "If it were a dragon, it would need to use its hind legs to do the heaviest work. Those are much stronger than its forelegs."

"Really?" Mari nodded, trying not to think about the absurdity of seriously considering facts about dragons. "Then do you think it would have had to brace itself, maybe with its front limbs, and push back against the bases of the poles? Wouldn't that have buried it when the wreckage fell?"

"Dragons can be very swift, and they are very tough."

"I don't think I want to meet one. Have you?"

"Yes. In my training. It was..." Alain paused. "Interesting."

"I bet it was." Mari beckoned him to follow and led the way through an ugly mess of splintered wood and bent metal until they found a sort of open area framed by wreckage. Here they could view the cliff face as long as they didn't try to stand up. She pulled out a hand light and clicked it on, causing the Mage to utter a sudden low gasp. Smiling to herself at having impressed someone who could walk through imaginary holes in walls, Mari ran the light across the rock. "Look. These abrasions." She pointed at scars on the rock.

"Those could be claw marks," the Mage agreed cautiously.

Another voice intruded. "Did you find something?" It was one of the sympathetic Mechanics. He gave both Mari and Alain curious looks.

Mari nodded, then gestured toward Alain. "A common I hired to carry my tools down here. I got hurt at Ringhmon."

"Oh, yeah, I heard about that. So what's back here?"

Mari pointed to the rock face. "This."

The other Mechanic, ignoring Alain now, crouched to look. "Those are fresh." He looked up and around at nearby wreckage. "And they weren't caused by any of the wreckage hitting the cliff. Good job, Mechanic."

Mari smiled at him. "Master Mechanic, actually."

"Right, right. Sorry."

"Not a problem. Do you mind me asking how you guys managed to get your car uncoupled from the train and stopped?"

The other Mechanic blew out a gust of air with a relieved expression. "Dumb luck, I guess. Our two Senior Mechanics happened to be out on that little shelf between cars, so when they felt the train stopping they figured they'd better plan for the worst and make sure we stayed safe."

Mari's eyes rested on the cliff face. "Amazing luck. Of course, the engineer and I might well have been dead."

"Yeah. I didn't mean to minimize that."

"Why would they have been out there this late?"

He shrugged. "Maybe they like each other and needed some privacy."

"That's a scary thought." The other Mechanic grinned as Mari jerked a thumb in the direction of the group still conferring together. "Should we tell them about these abrasions, or do they already know everything that needs to be known?"

The other Mechanic rolled his eyes. "You know the type, I guess. Go through the motions of researching the problem when they've already decided what the problem is and what they're going to do."

"I usually end up having problems with Mechanics like that."

"Don't we all." He gave her a searching look. "It sounds like you've heard what we were told about you."

"No, but I've got some pretty good guesses. Unprofessional? Inexperienced? Out of her depth?"

"Loose cannon," the other Mechanic added. He looked unhappy this time. "Not very professional of them to attack your qualifications that way, if you ask me. The academy wouldn't have certified you if you hadn't passed the exams. Who was your primary instructor at the academy?"

"Professor S'san," Mari said.

"S'san?" The Mechanic's eyes widened. "If you got her approval, you're one of the best. Don't worry about those Senior Mechanics. We think they got sent to Ringhmon because no one else would have them. I'll tell them what you found. My name's Talis, by the way." He scrambled off through the wreckage.

Mari became aware that the Mage was watching her. "What?"

"He seemed like...a friend toward you," the Mage said in a voice that as usual didn't reveal much.

"I suppose. Nothing like you, though." Mari rubbed her forehead, wondering when her head would stop aching. Was it her imagination that her last statement had caused the Mage to relax a bit? "But he acted like you weren't even there. Like you didn't exist."

"He believes me to be one of the commons," the Mage pointed out.

Mari stared into space. "So he ignored you. Because commons don't count to Mechanics."

"Or to Mages."

"I do that, too."

"Not to me."

She glared at him. "You know what I mean!"

The Mage regarded her. "I have been thinking on this. You and I have been taught to think in a certain way of those who do not belong to our Guilds. I know you to be a shadow, one with no significance. You know me to be a Mage, which you were told are but frauds and liars."

Mari looked out to sea, through the tangle of wreckage. "And if what we were taught about each other is wrong, maybe what we were taught about commons is wrong. Or do you think what we were taught is wrong?"

He stayed silent for a moment. "I think that there are questions which what I was taught do not answer. I did not even know some of these questions existed until I met you."

"That's funny. Pretty much the same thing happened to me. And now that I have those questions, you're the only person I can talk to about them."

"Would another Mechanic have done what you did at the caravan?" Alain asked abruptly. "Insisted I come with them?"

"No," Mari said, reluctant to admit that but not wanting to lie to Alain. "Even if they hadn't shot you, they would have just run off in another direction and left you. Would another Mage have reacted the way you did?"

"I do not know. Some other Mages might have. If it was you. You... are different."

"I hope that's a compliment," she said dryly. "There's nothing all that special about me." Mari closed her eyes, feeling a sudden urge to admit something she had not been able to talk about for years. "My parents were commons. Both of them."

"Were?" the Mage asked. His voice actually seemed to hold a little sympathy. "I am..." Alain struggled, as if trying to say *sorry* but the effort was too much for him.

"That's all right. I know what you mean. Thank you for trying to say it. But they're not dead." She turned her head and studied the marks on the cliff face as if something new could be seen there. "Might as well be. After I tested as having the skills and was taken to the Mechanics Guild for schooling, I never heard from them again. After awhile I stopped writing, too." *And it doesn't hurt anymore, it doesn't hurt anymore, it doesn't hurt anymore.*

Silence stretched, punctuated by vague sounds from the other Mechanics discussing the wreckage and the low, constant boom of the surf against the rocky shore. Finally she heard the Mage speak again, his voice clearly revealing emotion this time. "My own parents are truly dead. They were commons who lived on a ranch near the southern edge of the Bright Sea, north of Ihris. Raiders killed them after I had gone to study at the Mage Guild Hall in Ihris. They were shadows, but...I cannot stop believing they mattered."

"I'm very sorry," Mari said. She looked at Alain. "I don't know just how we ended up becoming friends, but I'm glad for it, and I'm glad you think of me as a friend you can say things to. You've never been able to tell anyone that, have you? I know that feeling."

"I have been taught that loneliness is all there is. That each of us is alone. Perhaps that is wrong as well." The Mage couldn't bow in the midst of the wreckage, but he inclined his head toward her. "I am also...glad, Lady Mechanic."

She smiled. "You might try sounding like you're glad."

"I thought I was."

"Not even close," Mari said.

A scuffing sound marked the return of Mechanic Talis. He gave Mari a rueful look. "They don't think it's worth looking at."

"Did they ask you who found it?"

Talis made a face. "Yes."

"I'm sure that helped them decide it wasn't worth looking at." Mari thought a few dark thoughts aimed at superiors with brains of clay, then tilted her head outward. "Fine. Let's go."

But as she started to climb out of the wreckage near the cliff, Mari saw the Senior Mechanic who had disdained her suggestion about Mage abilities standing near the edge of the water with a far-talker. Mari motioned Alain to stay out of sight, not wanting to be accused of letting a common see a far-talker in action even though she was far enough away that whatever the other Mechanic was saying couldn't be made out over the sound of the surf.

Then the Senior Mechanic lowered the far-talker, her voice ringing out in disgust loud enough for Mari to hear clearly. "Not a thing! This piece of junk can't get any signal through at all from down here."

"It's too new," one of the other Mechanics noted. "If we used one twenty or thirty years older, maybe— "

"Fifty years older would be more like it! Do we have any working older far-talkers down here? Anybody? No. Isn't that great! I'll just have to try again once we get up the cliff." She went to the rocks they had come down and started climbing.

Mari looked over at Mechanic Talis, who had paused next to her. "In another few decades, portable far-talkers will be too heavy to lift and they won't work at all," Mari observed.

"I worry that's the trend," Talis replied.

"It *is* the trend." Mari gestured toward the east. "A few months before I graduated from the academy, Professor S'san took me to a sealed storeroom." S'san had refused to say where they were going or why, and Mari strongly suspected that what she was doing wasn't permitted, based on the number of locks on the nondescript door keeping that room secure. "Inside I was shown a shelf of far-talkers. On the right end was a far-talker like we use today, about as long and thick as a lower arm, with an extendable antenna. On the left end..." She paused at the memory. "A far-talker that seemed to have been machined or molded from one piece of material. I'm not sure what. It was the size of my palm. It weighed less than a deck of cards. And according to the specifications listed below it, it had several times the range of our current far-talkers and battery life good for days of continuous use."

Talis stared at her. "That sounds impossible. That small, that light, and that kind of performance? How could you even build that?"

"I don't know. It didn't look like you could take it apart, so I don't know how it was built. And between that ancient one on the left and a current far-talker on the right were a series of far-talkers, each model larger and heavier than the one that came before, and each one with worse performance."

"Mari, blazes, you know what that has to mean?"

"Yes. And it's not just far-talkers. Complicated devices like electronics are regressing, getting less sophisticated and less reliable.

Most Mechanics don't realize it, because it's happening too slowly, but seeing all of those together brought it home."

"Like we're forgetting how to build certain things, or losing the ability to build them," Talis whispered, his eyes on the Senior Mechanics climbing the cliff. "The rugged, simple things like locomotives are still working well, but we've all seen the problems with complex stuff. And those problems feel like they're getting worse at an accelerating rate, as if it's all falling off a cliff." He turned to stare at her. "The Guild has to be working on it. Our leaders can't be ignoring whatever's causing the problem. The Senior Mechanics can be hidebound and stupid, but this is too important to ignore. How old was that first far-talker model?"

Mari shook her head. "There weren't any dates on any of them. I recognized the current one, and the one before that because I've seen a couple of those that are somehow still working, but there's no telling how old that first one was."

"Something's broken," Talis whispered. "What do we do?"

And he looked at Mari.

"I...don't know yet," she said. What was the matter with people? Talis had a couple of decades of experience on her, and he was looking to her for an answer to this? *Why did you show me that display, Professor S'san? You wouldn't tell me. "Draw your own conclusions, Mari." For once couldn't you feed me one blasted answer, so I'd know what to tell people like Talis?*

"Keep me in mind," Talis said, then headed toward the cliff.

Mari waved to Alain to let him know he could come on, then started ahead herself. By the time she and Alain had worked clear of the wreckage near the cliff, most of the other Mechanics had already started the steep climb. Mari felt a light touch as she stared at the pile of rocks she would have to climb up and looked over to see Alain pointing at the places where the timbers anchoring the trestle had been broken. Mari bent to look closely. The impressions forced deeply into the wood weren't of rope or wire. They seemed to have been made by gigantic claws. *How did the other Mechanics miss this? Or maybe they didn't. Maybe they chose to miss it. Maybe they didn't see anything that didn't match their own predetermined theories.* "I guess we can't rule out anything at this point, can we?"

Alain looked thoughtful. "One possibility can be eliminated. The rulers of Ringhmon could not have done it in revenge for what happened to their Hall of City Government. They would not have had time to get here before the Mechanic train."

"True." Mari felt a tightness in her chest. *Unless somebody helping the rulers of Ringhmon had far-talkers. Unless the wreck had been set up by some of the people on the train with me, in the last car. Was that why the Guild cargo shipment from Ringhmon was canceled? Too valuable to lose while disposing of an inconvenient Master Mechanic with a big mouth and too much knowledge of things people weren't supposed to know? I need to ask some questions where no one else can hear.*

She nodded to Alain. "Give me a good head start up the cliff," she whispered.

He nodded back, not asking the question in his eyes.

Mari walked to stand beside Talis, the only other Mechanic still on the beach, and waved upward. "Shall we?"

Talis didn't appear thrilled at the prospect. "It didn't look as bad coming down, did it? Maybe because we couldn't see the bottom too well. But that moon's lighting up the top just fine."

They started up, climbing close to each other. Mari tried to think through what to ask, wishing she hadn't already been ordered to say nothing about possible non Guild Mechanics. She couldn't mention that unless she already knew someone would be willing to talk to her. But that left a big topic available for opening a conversation. "Talis, have you ever seen a Mage do something that you couldn't explain? Something real?"

The other Mechanic stopped moving for a moment, his face gone to stone, then did a search of the immediate surroundings to make sure they wouldn't be overheard. "Put it out of your mind, Master Mechanic Mari. It didn't happen."

"But if I saw— "

"No. I told you. You saw nothing."

Mari felt her temper rising. "Facts cannot be ignored."

Talis shook his head. "There are facts and there are facts. There is truth and then there's truth. As far as the Guild is concerned, whatever you thought you saw, you didn't see. No one ever sees a Mage actually do something. That's all there is to it."

She stared at him. "How can we follow such a policy?"

"I don't know what the Guild's thinking is, but you and I don't have any alternative! Do you want to be kicked out of the Guild and imprisoned at Longfalls? That's your choice. Beat your head against a wall and accomplish nothing, or keep your head down and continue doing good work as a Mechanic."

Mari looked at the rocks before her, silently absorbing the information. "Do all Mechanics know this?" *All but me, anyway.*

Talis shrugged as best he could while climbing. "Not until they get out in the field. After that, most know something to a greater or lesser extent, depending on experience. Some are so diligent about avoiding Mages that they never learn anything to shake their confidence that Mages are total frauds. Then you've got the old-timers like Saco up there," he pointed up at one of the Senior Mechanics far above them, "who I think have honestly convinced themselves that they've never seen anything. Their brains are like lance-thick armor plate. Totally impervious to anything they don't want to see."

"Why wasn't I told?"

"How do you tell somebody something that no one's supposed to know? Something that isn't even supposed to be real? Besides, I think most Mechanics learn like I did, by running into something we couldn't explain and then when we asked, being firmly told to forget about it." Talis paused, then spoke forcefully. "And like you're learning about it. For your own sake, Master Mechanic, *forget about it.*"

"Thanks. I do appreciate the advice." Mari stopped short of saying she would follow it. There was so much to take in, so many things that clashed with what she had been taught. *Did you set me up, Professor S'san? Trained me not to settle for easy answers, insisted on the importance of truth in our work and our actions, and then sent me off to tangle with a system which denies truth?*

I can't blame her for who I am, though. If Professor S'san helped make me who I am, all she did was sand off the rough edges. I was already me when I got to the academy.

Me. I'm one girl. What can I do alone? Maybe everyone looks to me for answers, but if it were a matter of going against the Guild, no one would follow me.

A rock rolled behind her and she looked to see Alain laboring up the slope beneath them. *One might.*

How can I do that to the first friend I've found since leaving Caer Lyn? A guy who might even be...no, no, no. That's not going to happen.

Especially since I don't know what might take place in Dorcastle if I do make it there. Is whoever did this planning something else?

Is whoever did this after me for things I haven't even done yet?

CHAPTER THIRTEEN

Alain could see the sky brightening in the east by the time another Mechanic train arrived from Dorcastle, its locomotive creature chugging gingerly along the metal lines while extra look-outs watched for more of the dangerous gaps. Alain gazed at the strange device, wondering how the Mechanics had created such a creature. Mari had told him that Mechanics did not use spells, but how else could something like that, or a dragon, be brought into being?

The Mechanics from the old caravan, and then the commons, inched their way across the gap where the trestle had been, using a narrow trail against the cliff just wide enough to walk single file. Most did their best not to look down into the depths where the trestle had fallen.

The last of the commons, a man who had hung back until everyone else had gone, balked halfway across, frozen with fear, eyes shut and clinging to the rock wall behind him. Alain could see the Mechanics laughing, and some of the other commons did, too. Most of the commons didn't laugh, but were arguing among themselves. It did not occur to Alain to do anything, but he did wonder if the common would be abandoned there.

Mari swung down from the locomotive and walked onto the narrow strip, looking stubborn and ignoring comments yelled by some of the Mechanics. She said something to the commons watching as she passed them, and some of those sheepishly fell in behind her. Stepping onto the narrow area, Mari made her way to the common paralyzed with fear and put a hand on his arm, speaking in a low voice.

Everyone watched as she gently tugged the man into motion, getting him step by step across the remaining distance until the commons waiting at the end could grab him and pull him onto the wider area. Mari walked back to the locomotive as the commons called out thanks to her, watching her with different expressions than they turned on other Mechanics.

Only a few Mechanics remained behind with the original train, and Alain saw them begin backing it up as soon as the last commons were clear. He wondered if they would back up all the way to Ringhmon.

After that it was simply a matter of loading everyone aboard the new train. Alain overheard some of the commons grumbling about the freight belonging to them which remained on the stranded Mechanic train, which now would have to either await repair of the trestle or be transported overland by caravan southwest out of Ringhmon to the Silver River, where barges could carry it on to Dorcastle. The additional time involved, Alain gathered, would be substantial, and that would cost the Mechanics Guild a lot of the fees it would otherwise have earned. "At least we know the Mechanics aren't behind this," one of the commons muttered in a low voice, afraid of being overheard. "It's costing them money."

The other commons laughed harshly in agreement. "It's costing the Mages money, too," another suggested. "Maybe they really are innocent." Then he laughed harder at his joke and everyone joined in, though Alain ducked his head to avoid letting the others see his lack of reaction.

He thought on that later. *To Mages, the Mechanics are not only shadows but also false, being nothing like us. Mari says the Mechanics see the Mages the same way. Yet to the commons, the Mages and the Mechanics are much the same thing. I did nothing for that common who was scared to move, and neither did any of the Mechanics except Mari. Had I been wearing my robes, and Mari not been here, the actions of Mage and Mechanic would have been identical. I understand now why the commons speak of the Great Guilds as if we were one.*

As everyone got aboard the new train, Mari stopped on her way back to the locomotive to tell him where she would be the second evening after they arrived in Dorcastle. "It's a restaurant," she explained after giving the address. "One of the other Mechanics told me about it. If you want to meet again, I'll be there."

Something about the way she said those words, something about the way she avoided his gaze, made him ask a question. "Do you want to meet again?"

She had looked at him, her expression uncertain, then nodded. "Yes."

"Then I will be there. Why did you help that common?"

"He needed to be helped, and no one else was doing anything." Mari gave him an angry look. "You could have helped. You understand what that it is now."

"He is not a friend."

"That's not the point. Some of the other Mechanics are giving me a hard time about him being a common, and that's not the point, either."

"What is the point?"

"Don't let people suffer! Don't let anyone be hurt! If you can help, then help! What about that is complicated?" Mari demanded.

Alain thought about her words. "It is not complicated, but doing it might be..." What was the right word? "Difficult."

"Yeah, well, that's me in a nutshell, isn't it?" She had gazed at him defiantly, as if waiting for something.

He had nodded to her. "It is."

Whatever she had been expecting, that wasn't it. Mari looked startled, then grinned. "I hope I see you in Dorcastle. But it really is up to you."

She had entered into the back of the great locomotive beast, and he had entered the part of the train where the commons sat. Everyone was tired, so no one bothered Alain as they all tried to catch up on their sleep.

He could not sleep, though.

He knew that he should not go to that restaurant. He should not meet Mari again. Somewhere in the night, Alain had felt emotions boiling beneath the seals he had placed upon his feelings for so many years. He thought of tears, and help, and friend. Memories once safely buried haunted the darkness.

What manner of challenge was this, that threatened to devastate him as a Mage? All that he had done, all that he had endured, might be destroyed within a short time by his association with Mari. Once again he wondered at the power she had to influence him. To change him. Perhaps to ruin him.

He knew what the teachings of the elders called for when the world illusion pressed too forcefully. A Mage must retire to an empty chamber, devoid of anything but blank walls, and there work to rebuild his certainty of truth: that nothing else existed but him, that feelings and emotions were barriers to wisdom and power, that everything and anything that might connect him to the shadows which were only illusions of other people must be denied and locked away beyond retrieval. Alain had seen Mages do just that a few times while he was still at Ihris, emerging from their voluntary isolation after days or weeks with the total disinterest in the world that marked wisdom.

He should do that when he reached Dorcastle. Deny these memories, deny helping, deny friend, and especially deny Mari. That was the road back to the certainties he knew.

He recalled a lesson taught by an elder who rarely punished the acolytes, but rather enforced his will by the strength of his words. The elder had stood before them and spoken of a creature of legend, something whose hands held greater power than those of any Mage. In one hand was the power to create, and in the other the power to destroy. When he had finished, the elder held out both of his hands. *"Choose one,"* he had called to the acolytes.

"Which hand is which?" one of the wiser acolytes had asked.

"You will know that when you have chosen," the elder replied.

None of them would choose, and the elder finally lowered his arms and nodded. *"You see. We give you wisdom. We give the knowledge that has been gained by Mages and elders before you. If you stray from that knowledge, then in your ignorance of consequences you are standing before that creature. It will offer its hands, and you will have to choose one of them, not knowing whether your choice will destroy you. That is the price of walking an unknown path."*

He had never thought the creature would be in the form of Master Mechanic Mari. Everything he had learned told him that she was dangerous to him, that what she offered was surely the hand of destruction. But as Alain looked out the window, he realized something that had never occurred to him before. That elder had not told him and the other acolytes never to stray from the path they were taught, had not told them never face the choice in the hands of the creature. The elder had instead warned them to consider the consequences. Perhaps destruction. Perhaps something long sought.

Other elders had been much more direct in their warnings. *"Male acolytes, beware of the females you will see outside of Guild Halls. They seek your undoing, to take your wisdom from you and lure you into becoming shadows just as they are."*

Mari is taking me from the path of wisdom. I see her and feel... happy. Admit it. I will connect to the false world and to the shadows again, and my spells will dwindle to nothing.

And yet...the thread is still there. I can sense where she is, ahead of me in the Mechanic locomotive. What is that thread? What does it represent?

Do I want a wisdom which would make me cut that thread?

I have not yet been weakened. I have withstood any loss of power. What if it becomes clear that my choice is my powers—my hard-won standing as a Mage—or Mari? Which would I choose then? How could I give up being a Mage?

How could I give up Mari?

As he thought that, Alain realized that his choice had already been made.

If the elders at the Mage Guild Hall in Dorcastle sensed his decision, then Mari would not have a chance to destroy him. His own elders would take care of that very quickly.

The morning was well advanced when the train rounded a bend in the coast and Dorcastle finally came into view. The city occupied the slopes of a river valley rising above the harbor, a valley which was the first real break in the cliffs blocking the southern coast of the Sea of Bakre after the salt marshes north of Ringhmon. Dorcastle rose up from the water in a series of defensive walls which looked impressive even from a distance.

Soon enough they were passing the outer defenses of the city, sentries standing on ballista towers gazing down at the Mechanic train. They arrived surprisingly quickly at the Mechanics' station in Dorcastle, and the train groaned to a stop, this time with only a faint echo of the screaming of metal on metal.

None of the commons went in the direction of the locomotive, instead heading along a plainly marked route into the city. Alain stayed with them, walking steadily away from the Mechanic train. The thread stayed with him, offering an illicit sense of comfort as it pointed back toward the locomotive. The elders at Ringhmon had not sensed the thread, but that was no guarantee the elders here would not. If they did, he had a series of outwardly accurate but misleading answers for them. Not every lesson an acolyte learned was one intended by the elders.

As the crowd broke apart and dwindled, Alain found an isolated spot and pulled on his Mage robes, not trying to suppress the feeling of calm brought by the familiarity of the robes. It had been surprisingly hard to pretend to be a common. After so much training in hiding his feelings, the need to avoid showing that he was avoiding showing emotions had been amazingly tiring. He spotted another Mage, got directions to the Guild Hall and before the sun had sunk much past noon had reached the place that would hopefully prove a more welcoming sanctuary than the Mage Guild Hall in Ringhmon had been.

The acolyte at the entrance bowed Alain inside. "This one will perform any tasks needed by the Mage."

Alain paused to look at the acolyte, memories of his own time as an acolyte filling him. *How long did it take for them to make you forget what a friend was? Did you ever try to help another acolyte? Do you find comfort only in the wisdom of the Guild, because there is none in the presence of the shadows and illusion which surrounds you? These are not the questions your elders will ever pose, but now they cannot be banished from my mind.*

By the time Alain had dumped his now-empty bag in one of the rooms set aside for Mages traveling through the city, he had already received a message to report to the elders of this Hall. Ushered into a small office, Alain could not help feeling relieved that this time he was not being subjected to an Inquiry right off.

The old Mage seated behind her desk waved Alain to a seat with unusual informality. "Greetings, Mage Alain.—Your age has been a source of astonishment to our acolytes. They have been forced to work harder to conceal their emotions." She showed open amusement for a moment, a Mage's smile which barely moved the mouth and then vanished, but still it startled Alain. "Mage Alain, have you heard of the troubles our Guild faces in this city?"

"I have heard of dragons," Alain admitted.

"Yes! Dragons! Behaving as they should not. As they cannot. But if all the world is false, why should not our understanding of our spells prove false on occasion as well?" The old Mage sighed, once again showing emotion. "You will find few Mages here. Except for a few kept on hand in case they are needed to defend the Hall, the rest are scouring likely dragon lairs in the area. Do you know of the means by which Mages can search? Good, good. One so young, I can take nothing for granted. You understand. But so far, all our efforts have been in vain." She sighed again. "It is frustrating."

Alain tried not to stare at the old Mage. To speak of feelings like frustration? This elder's failings must be tolerated because of her experience and past contributions to the Guild. "My understanding is that the search methods should easily find a spell creature as large as a dragon, let alone more than one."

"Should, yes," the elder agreed. "Yet we find nothing. No Mage sensed the creation of the dragons, even though such spells should have been apparent to our senses. There is something else at work. We have not discovered what it is, but suspicions are that Dark Mages have foolishly tampered with the wisdom that guides the nature of dragon spells."

"I did not know that was possible," Alain said.

"It is not possible. The illusion is perceived to be the same by all, and all must follow the same patterns in working their spells or the spells fail. A dragon can only be a dragon. I have reminded the other elders of this, but still they seek the kind of dragon that cannot be created by any spell. Little wonder they fail," she grumbled. The old Mage stood and walked with difficulty to a shelf. "If you wish to study, Mage Alain, I have some texts."

"I have already studied those," Alain said.

"Have you? Well, one so young." She stood irresolute for a moment, then came back to her chair and sat down. "There is nothing in those texts to help with this. I know that. Now, as to you."

It had not occurred to him that he might have immediate obligations to his Guild which would prevent him from meeting Mari tomorrow evening. But Mari would surely understand if that happened. "I will join whichever search party you think I can best serve."

The old Mage blinked, then actually smiled reassuringly for an instant. "No. Dragons are a threat for the most experienced to face. As for other service, I cannot offer you chance of employment soon, because all in and around the city blame our Guild for this plague of dragons and are refusing us contracts until we halt the predations of the spell creatures."

"Lady Mage," Alain said in his most formal voice, "honored elder, allow me to serve with the other qualified Mages."

"No, Mage Alain."

"I do not need protecting. I can protect the interests of the Guild."

"Yes, yes." The old Mage tapped her desk with the fingers of one hand. "I have seen the report of your attempt to defend the caravan. You did not know it had been sent to us? But of course the Guild Hall in Ringhmon wanted us to know what you have done. It is well you have not been discouraged by that failure, but still you must redouble your efforts to master wisdom and our arts." She gave him a searching look. "And this female Mechanic who stalked you in that city. Strange business. Be satisfied that you are away from that one. Whatever hoax the deceitful little minx was planning, you are safely clear of it and the other temptations Ringhmon offers."

So the Guild Hall in Ringhmon had used a message Mage to send a report on Alain to the hall in Dorcastle even before Alain arrived. He ought to feel flattered that they had gone to that much effort, except that even this old Mage with her very un-Magelike sympathy had obviously read things in it which cast Alain as not ready for full Mage duties. She also clearly shared the opinion of the elders in Ringhmon as to the threat to him posed by a female Mechanic. "Elder, I am capable of assisting the Guild in this matter."

She shook her head. "Mage Alain, rest, study and be ready if this Hall should be attacked by these dragons. Then we shall need everyone who can work spells."

"Will you inform the other elders that I am ready to assist them?"

This time the old Mage nodded. "Very well, Mage Alain. Your dedication to the interests of the Guild will be noted."

He felt like a fraud for a moment, a vision of the "deceitful little minx" Mari filling his memory, but the Guild had taught him to hide even the worst emotions, and the elder did not seem to be paying too much attention to his reactions anyway.

Alain started to rise, then sat back down. This elder was not like others he had encountered. Perhaps she would answer queries which would be dismissed by other elders. "This one has questions."

A flash of pleasure showed on the elder's face. Alain imagined that she was rarely called on to teach anymore. More likely, she was the one greeting him only because the other elders were off searching for the dragons. "This one listens."

"Elder, do you have any knowledge of foresight?"

"Foresight?" The old Mage perked up even more. "Why do you ask? Have you that gift as well?"

"Only recently, honored elder. It gave me a vision not so long ago, something I cannot understand."

"Ah." The old Mage nodded. "A vision. And you have asked other elders about foresight and they have told you that foreseeing was not a fit art for a Mage, did they not?"

"They did. I was told it would imperil my pursuit of wisdom and I should not speak of what I had seen."

"Pah! I have pursued my knowledge of foresight, young Mage. Despite the words of others. I am not as strong as I once was, but I still have wisdom and my spells still work." She gave Alain a questioning look. "Did you see yourself in this vision? No? That is important. When you see yourself, alone or with shadows, that means you are seeing what *may* be, a chance of what *might* come to pass if you do everything that leads you to that future. In such a case, you may not even actually survive to fulfill the vision if you should make the wrong choices. But other elders said you should not even speak of what you saw? What did you see in this vision?"

Alain took a moment to call up the memory, focusing on the details. "A second sun in the sky, against which a violent storm raged, trying to extinguish the sun."

The elder looked at him for a moment before saying anything else. "A second sun? And a violent storm? Did this vision carry any sense of urgency, young Mage?"

He barely managed to hide his surprise at the question. "Yes. The storm moved swiftly. I felt a need to act, though I do not know what I was supposed to do."

The elder nodded, her expression shadowed. "And this vision was alone? Nothing was near it?" she asked as if certain he would agree.

But Alain shook his head. "A shadow was near it. It appeared over her."

This time the elder took a longer while to respond. "A shadow. The vision was close to this shadow?"

He hesitated, remembering. "Yes. Just above her. It was focused upon the shadow. I have no doubt of that."

"Her." The old Mage chewed her lip, looking down, her feelings impossible to spot. "The vision was focused upon her? A female shadow? You are certain?"

"Yes, Elder."

The elder took so long to speak again that Alain wondered if she would say anything else, but finally she surprised him with another question. "Young Mage, have you heard of a prophecy the shadows speak of? About one they call the daughter?"

"No," Alain said.

"The prophecy was made long ago, and somehow the shadows learned of it." The elder sat back, her eyes distant as if gazing into the past. "They speak of a daughter of the shadow once known as Jules of Julesport. They believe that this daughter will overthrow the Mage Guild and the Mechanics Guild. They believe in that prophecy, but they do not know all of it."

Another pause, then the elder focused her gaze on Alain. "Others will not tell you this, but the prophecy was real. It said that this woman would unite Mages, Mechanics, and those known as commons into a single force that would change the world. And so the Mage Guild has always considered the prophecy to be a fantasy. How could anyone do such a thing? Mages working with Mechanics? It could never be. Commons joining their efforts? Nonsense. No one could do such a thing."

Alain nodded as if in agreement, but he was thinking of himself and Mari escaping from the dungeon in Ringhmon, and of the way Mari had gotten commons to aid her in helping another on the cliff. "Do you believe my vision has some connection to that prophecy?" Alain asked, making his strongest effort to hide any feeling from the words.

The elder leaned forward, tapping one finger on the desk to emphasize her words. "Other Mages have seen visions, young Mage. More and more in recent years. Visions of armies battling, and mobs of shadows tearing down all that is and will be, and even visions of Mage Guild Halls and the halls of the Mechanics being overrun and destroyed. And with each year the sense of urgency in these visions has grown, young Mage. The sense that this storm comes closer, that it sweeps toward us more swiftly than any can see, that it will wrap us in its chaos and destroy everything, leaving only ruin in its wake."

She gazed intently at Alain. "Against this storm many have seen a sun, a promise of a new day, a promise of what may defeat that storm, but always that vision floated without reference to anyone or anything. But you, young Mage, you say you have seen that vision of a sun and a storm focused on a shadow. You have seen the battling images of a new tomorrow and a tomorrow filled with death all centered on *one shadow*. It must be her, the one the old prophecy spoke of. The one who can bring a new day to this world. And these visions make it clear that if she fails, if this shadow ceases, then the storm racing toward us will triumph."

Alain wondered how he managed to keep his expression emotionless. "How can a shadow be so important?"

"A reasonable question, given the training that acolytes receive. I will explain," the Elder said, frustration once more apparent. "Normally foresight tells a Mage what will or might happen to someone. Some specific event. Some specific danger. Yes? They did not tell you that, either, did they? But it is so. You see an image of a Mage or a shadow somewhere, doing something, and so you see what will someday happen to that shadow. Understanding what you see is far more difficult than the seeing, young Mage, for the vision cannot tell you why anything came to pass or what led to it. All you see is an event, with no way of seeing the occurrences or decisions which created it. But in this case you did not see the shadow in the vision, but rather a vision focused on the shadow. What you saw in this vision, then, was not the shadow's future, but the future that shadow will decide."

"You are certain?" Alain did not know how to take what the old Mage was telling him. "This shadow is that important?" he asked again.

"Important? Yes. All are shadows, yet shadows can cast their shade widely on the illusion of the world, and Mages do not exist independent of that illusion. This shadow, the one you saw, is the only one who can stop the storm which threatens the entire illusion which we call this world."

"The Mage Guild—" Alain began, overwhelmed by what he was hearing.

The elder stopped his words with a sharp gesture and an actual frown. "There are two sides to the visions and the prophecy, young Mage. This shadow can stop the storm, but she is also foretold to overthrow the Mage Guild. Many elders do not wish to acknowledge the visions which warn of the coming storm. They mistrust foresight, and they mistrust anything which might lessen their own power." She looked toward the door, as if ensuring no one was close enough to hear, and lowered her voice. "For that illusion, young Mage—the power many elders wield—is of great value to them. I have heard them talking.—They say that if this one the commons call the daughter should appear, she must be destroyed. For the Guild must be preserved, even if such an attempt only leaves it exposed to the storm that will follow."

"Destroyed?" Alain said.

The elder gave him a sharp look, causing Alain to wonder if that single word had betrayed his feelings. "They wish to protect what they have, young Mage. They will destroy anything that threatens their authority. You already know this."

"What should I do?" Alain asked.

"Walk carefully, young Mage. Decide what is important to you."

"Nothing is real, nothing is important," Alain recited the lesson automatically.

"That is not so," the elder whispered. "I sense you have already learned that. Do you wish to try to stop the storm—for nothing is certain and no outcome guaranteed—or do you wish above all to try to preserve the current form of the Mage Guild?"

"Elder, if what you say is accurate, then the current form of the Mage Guild is doomed."

"Exactly, young Mage." The elder looked into his eyes. "The question is how it will fall. The storm threatens this world, and it threatens that shadow. I do not know what path that shadow must walk to become the sun that will light the new day and hold back the storm. But if I knew who that shadow was, I would do what I could to protect and aid her. The storm the Mage Guild, the Mechanics, shadows of every kind will aim at her. Only she can stop the storm. If her image vanishes from this world, the storm will triumph, perhaps within only a few more years, and then those who destroyed that shadow will themselves be consumed, along with all else. The daughter must live, or all else dies."

"I understand, honored Elder," Alain said.

"Do you? Then do not speak of this again. Any mention of that vision could bring the storm's wrath upon that shadow, who must depend upon remaining hidden and unknown until she has the means to stand against the storm. Tell no one. We have not spoken of this. Do you understand that?"

"Yes, Elder." Alain rose, bowing, emotions churning inside him. "This one has listened, honored elder. Your wisdom has given me much to think about."

She waved off his words. "We have talked only of small matters," she said loudly enough for the words to carry into the hallway beyond. "But remember this, young Mage," the elder added in lower tones. "Do not let others tell you that wisdom decrees a Mage must see the false world in only one way."

Alain had been about to leave, but he paused. "Honored elder, if all is false, as we are taught, how can wisdom exist as a single path? How can there be but one proper road for all of us?"

The old Mage smiled once more for an instant. "You have gotten there, have you? Well done, young Mage. Many Mages never reach that place, to question the wisdom of that which is wisdom."

"But, what is the answer, honored elder?"

"The answer? There is no answer. Only choices which can have many outcomes, some expected, and some unforeseen. Perhaps that is the only wisdom there really is, young Mage: that our choices matter. As your choices matter, perhaps more than those of anyone else at this time."

Alain bowed his way out and walked back toward the room he had been given, aware of little outside himself as the elder's words kept running through his mind. One who would unite Mages and Mechanics. One who the commons would also follow.

One who could stop the storm.

He felt as if a cold wind were blowing hard upon his mind. What should he do? The elder said he must protect Mari, but how best to protect her when his presence might endanger her? She had also said that Mari's best protection was anonymity, to be but one more shadow among the others, lest the storm know exactly where to bend its efforts.

He sat in his room as if meditating, but his thoughts were centered not on wisdom but on Mari. She would seek to learn more about the dragons imperiling Dorcastle. Amid all of his uncertainties, Alain felt sure of that. Mari would seek to find the answers, the way to "fix" the dragon problem. And that in turn would very likely lead her into danger.

He did not know exactly what to do, but if Mari would be facing danger then he needed to be close to her. He needed to "help" her, by learning what he could.

His plan for the immediate future decided, Alain went to the dining rooms and ate a quick meal, barely aware of the food and drink, then sought out the other Mages the elder had said were still at the hall.

By nightfall he had been able to talk to them about the predations of the dragons and what the Guild had been doing to try to stop the spell creatures. The latest attempt involved trying to use spells to trace the common people the dragons claimed to be holding prisoner. Those people were being forced to write out the dragons' ransom demands. In theory, some connection to the persons might be discovered using the ransom documents which had mysteriously appeared in the city from time to time. Alain nodded with understanding, thinking of his thread to Mari, though of course he was not so foolish as to mention that. But he was not surprised to hear that the Mages undertaking this effort, having no ties to the shadows they sought to trace, had seen no success.

Later Alain lay in bed in a small room with bare, white walls, staring at the ceiling and trying to think through what he had learned. Worrying about Mari, about what he should do, only led his thoughts in circles, so he tried to concentrate on the problem posed by the dragons. *They do not act like dragons, yet the destruction they have wrought seems the work of dragons. They are here, but cannot be found. As the elder said, even this false world is supposed to maintain its illusion in a predictable way.*

My training told me that I must obey my elders and deny this world. I have already chosen a different path than I was instructed to seek, but I would not have found it alone. Acolytes are not taught that any other way exists. Is this why some Mages become Dark Mages, because they decide to cease obedience but can see no other road, no purpose for their powers beyond personal gain?

Mari would not lead me down such a path. If I know anything now, it is that. She believes that wisdom lies in helping.

Is that what will enable her to defeat the storm?

If the storm does not destroy her. I must tell Mari about that vision. I must protect her.

At that thought, he could feel that insubstantial thread leading to Mari strengthen. He despaired inside, wondering how he could protect Mari if his emotions caused him to lose the ability to cast Mage spells.

Oddly, though, he felt no weakness. Instead, a strength filled him. In some way Alain could not understand, that strength did not come through the thread, but owed its existence to the existence of a thread that was not there. And there was no one he could ask about that.

✳   ✳   ✳

He learned little more the next day. For dragons, the creatures terrorizing Dorcastle had left few signs of themselves aside from the occasional act of destruction. Down at the harbor he heard sailors gloomily discussing the lack of trade. Ships would not sail for fear of being set upon once away from Dorcastle's defenses, and so the cargo coming down the Silver River by barge from the inner lands of the Bakre Confederation piled up in warehouses and sailors went unpaid.

His mind preoccupied with thoughts of a storm of ghostly armies and mobs, Alain could not help noticing and marveling at Dorcastle's stout defenses. They brought a sense of reassurance and solidity against the urgent warning of the vision he had experienced in the desert.

Alain stopped at two of the monuments to past battles, finding them as true to history as Ringhmon's had been false. Dorcastle wore its glory lightly, honoring past triumphs without exalting them and memorializing past sacrifices. There was as well a grimness to Dorcastle's monuments, a sense that the costs had been necessary but must be remembered in any celebration of victory. It was hard to imagine a greater contrast with Ringhmon.

As the sun sank behind the cliffs to the west of the city, Alain finally made his way to the eating place where Mechanic Mari had said she would be. The thread, sometimes so thin with distance that it had grown weak, was now strong enough to tell him that she was there well before he reached the restaurant.–Just short of the place Alain went into an alley and pulled off his Mage robes, folding them into his bag again. He could not help imagining how the commons in this city would react to seeing a Mechanic and a Mage sitting at the same table in conversation.

A Mechanic and a Mage working together. If the commons saw that...

Low clouds had been closing in as the day ended, and before he reached the restaurant a thin rain had begun to fall, pattering off the gray stone streets and gray stone walls of Dorcastle, pooling in the indentations left by ancient weaponry in the many sieges which Dorcastle had endured.

Mari was not wearing her Mechanics jacket. She must have followed the same plan as he, trying to avoid attention. Alain came to the table where she sat, back in a corner by itself away from any windows, and bowed slightly. "My friend."

Mari glanced up, her expression sharp and worried, one hand jerking toward her own bag in what Alain recognized as an abortive grab toward her concealed weapon. Then she grinned with relief. "I really am on edge. You'd think I'd recognize an unemotional voice calling me a friend. But I've been fending off the occasional romantic male citizen of Dorcastle. I'd never realized how much my jacket keeps commons from even thinking about approaching me."

"You are not used to being approached by men?" Alain asked as he sat down opposite her.

Her expression turned rueful. "No. I'm not exactly a raving beauty, and I've always been more comfortable with machines than I have with males. And I'm a...you know. That sort of narrows the field of men who'd even think about coming on to me."

"What is a raving beauty?"

"You know, some woman who's so attractive that men can't take their eyes off of her. I know Mage women don't go in for, uh, cosmetics, so maybe you haven't seen much of that." Mari blushed slightly with embarrassment, as if concerned she had offended Alain. "I'm not saying Mage women aren't worth looking at, though I never really have."

Alain nodded, remembering Asha. "I know such a woman. A raving beauty."

"Give me a break."

"I did not mean you."

Mari's mouth hung open for a moment, then she blushed a deeper shade. "All right. Let's pretend I never said that."

"Why?" Alain asked.

"Because. The point is, the, uh, jacket tends to drive off men like the ones who have come on to me so far tonight."

"But it must have been more than the jacket," Alain said. "You are intimidating whether you wear it or not."

She laughed. "All right, this time I have every right to say give me a break."

"It is so."

Mari laughed again. "I'm not intimidating compared to you."

He shook his head. "My elders do not agree. Those here also see me as too young to be capable."

"There's something we still have in common." Mari twisted her mouth in a half smile, an expression that Alain found fascinating. She had never mentioned her appearance before, but now that she had, he realized how much he wanted to watch her.

"I'm certain the Guild Hall Supervisor in Ringhmon sent a message about me here on the train," Mari continued, oblivious to Alain's thoughts, "or by...the arts of my Guild. It didn't take long after I arrived for many of the other members of my Guild here to start treating me like I had some serious, communicable disease. It really does feel like the Senior Mechanics think other Mechanics will catch something from me. But enough of that. Let's get some food and then we can talk."

He stole glances at Mari as she ate, amazed at the play of emotions and feelings as she tasted, as she talked, as she looked out the nearest window at the city. "This food is good," she commented.

Alain looked down at his own meal. "What is good when speaking of food?"

That earned a look of surprise followed by sadness. "They kept that from you, too? It's taste, texture, everything. You don't notice that?"

"We are taught to eat quickly and take no notice of taste," Alain explained. "It could be a distraction."

Mari rubbed her forehead, her head lowered so he couldn't see her expression, then looked back up at him. "It doesn't matter. If that's important to you, I mean."

He examined his own food, trying to pay attention to how it looked. "It cannot be a greater distraction than you are."

"What?"

"I meant that if you have not already harmed me, then tasting my food should have no impact."

She eyed him, her expressions shifting too fast to follow. "I am really going to have to think about that before I can figure out whether it was a compliment or a cut down."

Alain began trying to savor his own food, cautiously paying attention to taste and texture, and found some sense of forbidden pleasure returning to the act of eating. Or maybe he was just seeking to distract himself from thinking about Mari, and about his vision and the words and advice of the elder.

Some time later Mari sat back with a contented sigh, drinking her wine slowly, her gaze on the raindrops pattering on the window and the street beyond. "This city really is a fortress. No wonder it's got "castle" in its name."

"You did not know that?"

"No. I'm really not up on history. Why is this place so fortified?"

"Dorcastle is the first good harbor on the south coast of the sea west of the Imperial lands," Alain explained. "From Ringhmon's marshes to here are cliffs, and for some ways past Dorcastle are more cliffs and rugged coast. For anyone seeking to strike inland, this is the place from which such a strike must be made. The river valley beyond Dorcastle gives good access to the heart of the Bakre Confederation, and has little in the way of natural defenses. As a result, Dorcastle's defenses have always been critically important to the Bakre Confederation. They have been tested many times by Imperial legions."

"Really?" Mari looked at him curiously. "You know a lot of history? I thought Ma—your kind of person didn't care about the world."

"As a rule, they do not. I know some of this from the military knowledge I was given in anticipation of fulfilling contracts with military forces of the commons. But the Mage Guild does have records of what has happened in the world illusion. Most of my Guild members do not bother to study much of the history of that illusion." Alain shrugged. "But I am a little different."

"I've noticed." She smiled at him again. Something else in her face caused Alain to look down in confusion at how it made feelings want to boil up inside him, but when he looked at her again Mari was also looking away, seeming worried.

"Is something amiss?" he asked.

"No. Nothing is wrong," she said firmly. "I can control this. Myself, that is."

"Control?"

"I'm not going to make the most important decision of my life until I know more about...this problem I have to deal with. Never mind. You were talking about history."

Mari was eager to change the subject, so Alain did not object. "I have always been interested in history, and even my training could not quench my interest. Since my Guild says the study of the illusion aids in altering it, I was able to pursue this with the agreement of my elders."

"That's nice." She was still looking away from him, focusing on the outside. "So, that's the story with Dorcastle? People keep attacking it?"

"The Empire keeps attacking it. For centuries, Dorcastle has held against the best that the rulers of the Empire could throw at it." He pointed out into the street. "There is a monument out there, at the end of the street. It marks the high point of the last Imperial advance. The legions got this far and were broken, hurled back to their ships."

Mari stared out the nearest window at the rain-wet street. "It's odd to think this street must've once run with blood as it now runs with water." She shuddered.

He blinked, seeing the shapes of phantom soldiers running past through the street. Behind the soldiers came a few ghostly cavalry who must be a rear guard, one carrying a broken lance, their horses stumbling with weariness. Before any vision of the enemy pursuing them could be seen the images disappeared, leaving only rain pelting down through the night. Had he simply imagined it? Had it been, somehow, a vision of past events which had occurred on that street? Or had it been a touch of foresight again, a vision of a future battle?

A future battle. Armies clashing. "There is something we must discuss," Alain said.

"I know," Mari said. "We should get down to business. Are you free to tell me whether your Guild is really innocent in this dragon stuff?"

"It is not about the dragons. It is something that...must not be shared. This must be between only you and I."

She eyed him, a different kind of alarm showing. "Alain, I don't need...we don't need...any private talks about anything about us."

"But there is something that you must know. It is very important, about the future."

"Alain," Mari said, holding out both palms in a warding gesture, "I know what you want to talk about, and I don't think we should."

She was fearful. Alain could see that. Not afraid of him, but worried about something else. "You know?" Alain asked.

"Yeah, Alain. I know. I'm trying to deal with what I know. Let's not talk about it. All right? I know everything that I need to know, and what I don't know, I'm learning. If...if there is anything that we need to talk about regarding...you and me and the future, I'll bring it up. Can you agree to that?"

Alain nodded. He had no idea how Mari had learned about her role in the future, but perhaps she had experienced some visions as well. "Yes."

"Good." Mari exhaled with relief. "Now, the dragons. What have you learned?"

"There is no doubt in my mind that my Guild is baffled by these events," Alain said. "Baffled and frustrated, since they should have been able to find and defeat the creatures by now. Finding a way to stop the attacks would be a service to my Guild."

Mari's eyes regarded him over the rim of her glass. "Your Guild is really trying to stop whatever's going on?"

"Yes, though they believe my own skills would not contribute to that effort."

"Jerks," Mari muttered, draining the last of her wine.

"One elder was actually pleasant about it," Alain added. "Pleasant for an elder, that is. She told me many things, including explaining about the thing you wish us not to speak of."

"Oh, the elder explained that, did she?" Mari laughed, the sound sending a nice sensation through Alain even though he could not understand why she would react that way to his words. "I guess that saved me the trouble of having to do it. All right, then." Leaning back again, Mari stared over Alain's head. "I can't believe I'm doing something which goes against all I was told, but I'm approaching this dragon thing as if it were a scientific problem." She lowered her eyes to his. "You shamed me into that, you know. I was just going to discount anything about dragons without even thinking about it, but thanks to you I realized that I need to follow the same rules in evaluating information about dragons that I use in evaluating things I already believe in. So, you told me before that these dragons weren't acting in a way dragons should act. Is that still what you think?"

Alain nodded. "Yes. All of the members of my Guild who I have talked to agreed. This is one of the causes of the frustration."

"And from what you've told me, if dragons were terrorizing Dorcastle then your Guild should have been able to deal with the problem by now."

"That too is so. It is a contradiction, an inconsistency."

She spread her hands on the table surface, gazing at it as if an answer was written there. "Then the source of these events doesn't act like dragons and hasn't been stopped by people who can stop dragons. That has to mean one thing. Whoever or whatever's causing this, it isn't dragons."

Alain stared at her. "How do you know that?"

"If it doesn't act like a dragon and can't be found by people who can find dragons, why should anyone think it *is* a dragon?"

"Because..." He scratched his head. "That had not even occurred to me. According to my training, anything we see is false, so any inconsistency means nothing. It is just an inconsistency born of my own perceptions. The patterns that govern the illusion remain unchanged."

"It hasn't occurred to any members of my Guild here, either." Mari made an angry gesture. "Plenty of people in my Guild prefer to disregard inconvenient inconsistencies, too, even though they don't have the excuse of being trained to ignore facts. Not officially, anyway. They're fixated on the idea that the Mages are doing this, and so they're trying to find out how the Mages are doing it and any evidence that ties the Mages to it."

"But," Alain said slowly, "as with the Mages searching for dragons, if the Mechanics are looking for things that do not exist, they will not find them no matter how hard they try."

"Right." She smiled broadly at him. "Stars above, you're listening to me."

"Of course I am listening to you. Your words, your ideas, are always of interest to me."

"They are?" Mari's expression changed, her eyes widening, then she looked down hastily, covering her face with one hand. "There have to be some flaws," he heard her barely whisper.

"Something is wrong again?" Alain asked.

She kept her gaze averted. "Only with my head. I've been called crazy by people before this, but now I'm beginning to wonder if all of those people were right. I'm...feeling...thinking...something that no rational Mechanic should feel or think. And the more I think about it, the more I know how impossible it is, but I keep thinking about it.

And even though I told you that I don't want to talk about it, here I am talking about it. Maybe I am crazy."

"You do not seem stranger to me than any other member of your Guild."

Alain waited as Mechanic Mari went into another of her muffled laughter episodes. When she recovered enough to talk again, Mari tried to bend a stern look at him. "We have to do something about the way you talk. Get some feeling back into it."

"Around Mages, I cannot speak differently than I have been trained. That I cannot agree to try. But it would be interesting to see if I could speak in a manner which displayed some emotions when around others, if I could manipulate the illusion in that way. I am willing to attempt that, if that is your wish."

"If that's what I wish?" She stared out the window. "I want you to do things, and then you want to do them, but you're also strong enough that you're setting limits and obviously not just bending to whatever breeze I blow your way. Are you for real?"

"Nothing is—"

"I know. You don't have to say it anymore. What were we talking about?"

"What you wish?" Alain ventured. "And something about me that I did not understand."

"No," Mari said. "That has to do with the stuff we do not need to discuss. Before that."

"People believe you are crazy?"

"Before that, too."

He thought. "Your ideas. Listening to them."

"Right." Mari was once more looking at the street outside. "The Mechanics who will listen to me say I need to convince the Senior Mechanics. But the Senior Mechanics all say they're too busy to talk with me. I've managed to corner a few of them long enough to outline my idea, but they've listened with these blasted indulgent expressions and then given me a metaphorical pat on the head and essentially told me to go off, play like a good little girl, and leave them alone. Or I get a verbal slap across the face and am essentially told to shut up and leave them alone. I was supposedly sent to Dorcastle in a rush to fulfill some contract, but there's no work for me here. I need to do *something*, though."

Alain watched the rain, too, for a little while. "My Guild elders will not listen to me. Yours will not listen to you. Neither of us can tell our elders that we have learned something important from a member of the other Guild. What are we going to do? Is there a way we can act on this idea of yours?"

Her eyes lit up. "We? You'll help me?"

"Why do you think you have to ask? Friends help. You have said help should always be given, even if someone is not a friend, but we are friends." He did not mention the other reason why she would need protection, but Alain did not see any need to do so since Mari had said she knew all about it, and the elder had cautioned against speaking of it.

"Yeah. You listened to that, too." Mari stopped speaking and just gazed at him for a long moment. "I was just remembering the desert waste, when even saying 'we' sounded weird. That was you, and yet you're different now."

"I am," Alain agreed. "You are not quite the Mechanic I met then, either."

"Really? What's different?"

He paused to think. "Then, your worry was turned toward me and the bandits. Now, your worries face elsewhere."

Mari bit her lower lip as she looked at him, then finally nodded. "You're right. But I think if we can solve this dragon thing, maybe things will start getting back to what they're supposed to be." Her voice carried more worry than conviction when she said that, though. "Assume that what we've seen and heard about isn't related to dragons at all. Is there any other, uh, what do you call them?"

"Spell creature?"

"Yes. Any other spell creature that could be doing it?"

Alain pondered the question. "Do you mean one which inflicts major destruction, demands ransom, acts on its own, and cannot be found or dealt with by the resources of the Mage Guild within this city?"

She nodded. "Exactly."

"No."

"Can you think of any Mage explanation for what's going on?"

He thought again. "Dark Mages? No. My Guild suspects them, but as a wise elder reminded me that the spells of Dark Mages can be detected just like those of Guild Mages. Their dragons do not and cannot differ. If any kind of Mage were involved, my Guild would have already solved the problem."

Mari laughed briefly, the sound carrying no humor. "You'd think that would make them wonder after a while if they were barking up the wrong tree." Her mouth twisted once more, this time in thought, and Alain thought she had never looked more fascinating. "If we assume it really isn't dragons, that means we have to figure out what else could be doing this. Or who else." She shook her head in frustration. "There are too many secrets, and I keep getting the feeling that some of those secrets are really dangerous."

"There are many dangers," Alain agreed, certain that she was speaking of the storm visions that threatened. "But, at this moment, I see no specific danger aimed at you."

"Well, neither do I. At this moment," Mari replied, looking around.

"No, I mean my foresight."

"Your—? Oh, yeah." She looked very uncertain. "I have a lot of trouble accepting that. Other things you can do, I can see counterparts to in Mechanic work. But seeing the future? That's real?"

"Nothing is—"

"*Don't say that.* I mean, it actually warns of danger?"

"Sometimes," Alain explained. "It is unreliable. A wise member of my Guild does not depend upon it. My Guild elders discourage any use of it, but it comes and goes by its own rules and not by being summoned as other spells are. Other elders have told me that it can be very important." He looked at her. "Visions of what may come can be very important. You know this."

"I...what?" Mari shook her head. "Do you mean like estimates? Forecasts?"

"What is a forecast?"

"For weather, mostly," Mari said. "To predict when a storm is coming. That's what you are talking about?"

"Yes," Alain said, now absolutely certain that Mari knew of the prophecy and her role in it.

"I don't know enough," Mari said. Her mouth set in a stubborn and defiant expression. "But with your help, I'll learn what I need to know." Mari stood up suddenly, tossing a coin on the table as she did so. "That should cover the meal, as long as you don't mind me paying."

"You pay?"

She gave him another look. "I'd heard that Mages—Alain, when you're with me, we pay for things. All right?"

"All right."

"Right now I need more data to solve this problem. Come on. We need to look at as many places as we can where these supposed dragons have torn things up."

Alain got up more slowly. "In the rain? And the dark? Those will not hinder your work?"

Mari gave him a startled look, then glanced out the window again. "Oh. Yeah. Maybe we ought to wait until morning. Are you free?"

"Unfortunately, yes, since my Guild elders believe I am not yet suited for anything but studying."

Mari gave him a sympathetic look, then unexpectedly reached out and gave his wrist a squeeze. Instead of letting go after that, Mari kept her hand on his wrist, and Alain realized after a moment that both of them were looking at where her hand rested.

She pulled it back slowly, her expression worried. "Alain...no. This isn't working the way I thought it would. Are you sure you want to do this together?"

He could not tell from her tone of voice or her expression what answer she wanted, so he simply replied with what he felt. "Yes."

Mari took a long time to answer. "Me, too. All right, then. Tomorrow we'll set about proving your and my 'elders' wrong."

They paused in the doorway, looking out at the rain. "I don't suppose," Mari asked, "that there's some, uh, spell that keeps someone dry in the rain?"

The question surprised him. But then, how could she know? "No. A Mage has to concentrate on the piece of the world illusion he or she wishes to change." Alain waved at the rainfall. "That would mean concentrating on each individual raindrop as it falls toward you. It is possible but very difficult."

"And I thought advanced calculus was hard. So you couldn't stop a storm?"

It was not surprising that Mari would ask for reassurance on that count. "I said it would be difficult," Alain said. "Not impossible. It must be possible."

She gave him an appraising look. "Difficult isn't the same as impossible. That's true. Mages are supposed to be able to call up storms like this, though."

"That is not so. I have never known a Mage to create a storm such as this. And I do not know of any Mage who has tried to stop rain or snow. Why would a Mage do so?" Alain added. "We are not supposed to worry about rain, or cold, or other hardship. It is all illusion."

"I would have made a lousy Mage. See you tomorrow. Where do you want to meet?"

"I can find you wherever you are."

"You can?" He could see her thinking. "That thread thing? It's still there?"

"Yes. And no."

She was looking down at herself, her face troubled. "Am I doing that?"

"The thread? I do not know. It is and it is not, and it remains."

"Sort of an imaginary number. No, an irrational number. That's more appropriate, I guess." Mari seemed to be talking to herself, not to him. "Is it not affected by distance? I mean, is it always the same no matter how far apart we are?"

Alain shook his head. "When enough distance separates us, it grows weaker. I suspect that if we were far enough apart it would grow so weak I could no longer sense it."

Mari gazed at him. "But it would still be there?"

"I believe so," Alain said slowly. "I do not know if too much distance would break the thread. It is possible. Can something that does not exist be able to break? It is an interesting question."

"More like the sort of question that drives an engineer crazy." Mari looked troubled, then shook her head and gave him a quick glance, her eyes locking on his for a moment. "Well...good night. Be careful." The worry in her voice was now not about herself, but clearly directed at him. With a wave she dashed out into the storm, pulling her Mechanics jacket out and donning it as she ran. Alain watched until she disappeared from sight, but the thread remained, invisibly revealing the way to her.

CHAPTER FOURTEEN

Mari had spent a good part of the night tossing and turning, trying to decide whether she should get on the next train out of the city.

What are you doing, girl?

You need to stop seeing that guy, for his sake and for yours. He's a Mage. Remember? If any other Mechanic knew that I'd been seeing him, I'd be dead. Not literally dead, I think, but something close. If other Mechanics knew how I keep feeling about him...what's worse than death? There's got to be something. I'm sure the Senior Mechanics have figured something out, and they'll do it to me if they find out about Alain.

What does he see in me? Why do I like him so much? It doesn't make sense. Nothing makes sense. That doesn't seem to bother Alain. Nothing seems to bother him because he never shows any feelings. But I'm used to equations that balance and things that work in predictable ways. Not threads that aren't there even though they are. He said if I went far enough from him the thread would get too weak and he wouldn't able to find me again. Maybe. Wouldn't I be doing him a favor if I did that?

He wanted to talk about it last night. About him and me and the future. How awkward would that have been? Even I could see how tense he was when he brought it up. At least he listened when I told him it wasn't the right time. I mean, it's not easy to tell what Alain is thinking, but he must have wanted to talk about us getting serious. Why did he mention me to some elder? I'm sure he didn't say I was a Mechanic, but still...

What will happen to Alain if his other elders learn that he's been seeing me? That's even more scary. Those elders torture their apprentices, or acolytes I guess Alain calls them. What would they do to a Mage who is... how does he feel about me? He talked about love once, but he has no idea what it is. How can I talk to him about his feelings, how can I explain that... stars above, I do care about him. No. Don't even think it. I do not want to see him hurt because of me. I don't want to see anyone hurt because of me, but especially not him.

Everything is upside down. I can't trust any of my fellow Mechanics here since Talis was sent back to Dorcastle. And that just leaves me Alain to trust. If only some of the Mechanics here were people I had apprenticed with. Like Alli. It's been years. Why did she stop writing to me? Is Alli still my friend? I know what she would tell me about Alain. "Run away, Mari! Run as fast as you can! You promised me that you'd only get with the right guy!" But Alli, he feels so right.

Focus, Mari. There's only one way out of this with my fellow Mechanics. If I can solve this dragon problem, I'll prove my competence and my loyalty, and then the Mechanics here will listen to me. There have got to be plenty of decent Mechanics here, decent people like Talis. Maybe they'll explain things once they trust me. Even the Senior Mechanics will have to listen to me if I help the Guild with this. And the only person who will help me solve the dragon thing is Alain. I'll get my fellow Mechanics to trust me by working with a Mage.

That sounds crazy even to me.

What are you doing, girl?

You need to stop seeing that guy, for his sake and for yours...

Now Mari sat near the base of one of the walls of Dorcastle, the rising sun shining down through the ragged remnants of morning mist.

She knew she looked haggard from lack of sleep, and her breakfast formed a hard lump in her gut. Her Mechanics jacket and her pistol were hidden in her bag. She had decided that investigating this openly would only produce orders from the Senior Mechanics to butt out, so she would do the thing undercover, just one more common to whom no Mechanic would pay any attention.

Alain said he could find her. This would help prove whether or not that was true. Her common sense, which seemed to have almost deserted her, kept telling Mari that it would be far better if the Mage never showed up. Better for her, and certainly better for him.

But when he did appear, she couldn't help smiling happily at seeing him. The Mage was also dressed as a common, and also carrying a bag which doubtless contained his Mage robes. "Good morning," she said, feeling better.

He nodded back, one corner of his mouth twitching.

Had that been an answering smile? "I guess the thread didn't break," Mari added.

"No. It is a remarkable thing," Alain agreed tonelessly, then he paused and tried to put more emphasis in his voice. "No, it did not break."

"Great." Mari held up a piece of paper. "I've got a list of places we need to look at. It'll be a walk to get to the right parts of the city, but at least it'll be downhill." Mari pointed ahead, where the city of Dorcastle sloped down to the water in successive terraces of streets and defensive walls. "All of the places are located around the harbor."

They walked through the crowded streets, having to deal with the unusual problem of commons who always made way for either a Mechanic or a Mage. But no one cleared a pathway for two more commons. Wagons and carriages rattled by, the horses or mules pulling them one more type of obstacle to progress, and street merchants called out offers to them with an aggressiveness that Mari wasn't accustomed to. She ignored them, since she wasn't certain how a common would respond and didn't want to give herself away as a Mechanic. For the same reason, Mari didn't talk at all with Alain for fear his emotionless voice would give him away as a Mage. But as they passed commons she started noticing some of the commons giving her and Alain knowing or sympathetic looks. What was that about?

Mari stole a glance at Alain's totally impassive face as he walked next to her. She knew she looked worn out and probably worried and— *Stars above. The commons think Alain and I are a couple who have had a big fight.* She felt her face warming with embarrassment. *I need to work on that guy's face. Not just his voice, the face, too. Both projects at once.*

Planning that out at least kept her distracted until they reached the harbor.

Mari consulted her map, then led Alain along the waterfront to a section of piers screened by warehouses from the main harbor. They paused, looking at a large section of wooden pier which had been torn and buckled. Harbor workers and sailors passed the wreckage with curious or worried glances. Standing near the wreckage was a middle aged common wearing an old but serviceable chain-mail shirt that strained around a belly which reflected too many meals enjoyed too well. A small dagger and a wooden club hung from the guard's belt, both as dilapidated as the mail shirt. Mari walked up to the guard with her most winning smile, trying to pretend that the guard was another Mechanic so she wouldn't start ordering him around. "Is it all right if we look at this?"

The guard waved them toward the wreckage. "Look all you want. I'm just here to make sure no lackwit with his head in the clouds walks into the holes in the pier. Not much to see, though. There's no dragons around. If there was, I wouldn't be!" The common chuckled at his own joke.

Mari smiled obligingly and nodded in thanks. She and Alain went closer to the wrecked area. "Something definitely used a lot of strength here."

The Mage bent down, gazing at the torn wood. "As we saw at the beach. Something has pulled these timbers out and broken them." He pointed to the indentations of what seemed to be huge claws.

"Wouldn't something capable of doing this be really large?" Mari asked. "Do you think someone saw it?"

"No one saw it," the guard remarked. He had come to stand near them.

The familiarity startled Mari, who was used to the deference and distance commons always gave Mechanics. But she managed to cover up her reaction and look interested in the guard's words.

"The warehouses block the view," he continued, waving around to indicate the structure.—"But they heard it all right, over the sound of breaking wood. Hissing and moaning like the monster it was."

"Hissing?" Alain asked.

"Yeah. You feeling all right, fella? Nothing to be scared of here now. Anyway, lots of hissing. These dragons are like big snakes, right?"

Alain made a gesture of ignorance. "Is that what they are?"

"Well, I'm no Mage, but that's what I hear." The guard grinned. "Of course, if I was a Mage you couldn't believe what I was telling you, could you?"

"No, I could not," Alain agreed, absolutely serious.

"Excuse me," Mari interjected, trying to break up the conversation before the common figured out why Alain was so unexpressive. "Have you seen any Mechanics down here?"

The guard thought, scratching his head. "A couple, I suppose. Soon after it happened. They just looked around a little and then left. Like it wasn't their business, you know?"

"They didn't say anything? Ask any questions?"

"Mechanics? Say anything to the likes of me or you?" The guard laughed.

She hoped she didn't look too uncomfortable at the guard's blunt words. "They might've given some orders."

"Orders? Nah." The guard shook his head. "Like I said, they acted like it wasn't no affair of theirs. I expect they're happy seeing the

Mages get raked over the coals about this. Why would they worry about whether you or me runs into a dragon or loses their job because the harbor's closed?"

Mari kept her voice composed. "The Mechanics make a lot of money off the trade through Dorcastle. I understand they're not happy about the harbor being closed."

"Is that so? Hard to tell, since whenever one looks at me they're always looking down, and I don't figure they care about me any more than a Mage does. You know what I mean?"

"Yes," Mari said after a moment. "I know exactly how it feels to be looked down upon. Thanks for your information."

"No problem. Helps pass the time," the guard replied with another smile.

As they turned to go, Alain faced the guard again. "Hissing? You are certain there was hissing?"

"Clear as could be, son," the guard assured him. "Maybe you ought to lie down somewhere for a while. You might be sick. You look as blank as a Mage."

"Come on," Mari said, grabbing Alain's arm and pulling him away from the guard. "What was that about?" she asked in a low voice as they walked away. "The hissing stuff?"

"Dragons do not hiss."

"What do you mean, they don't hiss?"

"They do not hiss." The Mage spread his hands as if trying to pantomime something huge. "They are not like snakes at all. They have scales, but otherwise— "

"Hissing," Mari broke in. "What about the hissing?"

"They do not. I have been near two dragons, and the breathing sound they make is what you would expect from any very large creature. A big rumbling noise and the sound of the wind rushing in and out of their throats."

Mari frowned. "Would a dragon hiss if it was working hard at something? Really exerting itself?"

"No. They need even more air when working hard. I know your locomotive creatures hiss at times, but do you know of any other creature which breathes through its teeth when it is in need of more air?"

"How do you know stuff about animals?" Mari asked.

The Mage lowered his gaze to the cobblestones of the street. "The farm I lived on as a young boy. The memories have been coming back to me in the last couple of weeks."

"They have? Why do you think—"

He was very obviously not looking at her now.

"Oh." *Ever since he met me. Change the subject, Mari.* "Let's take a look at some of the other sites."

She led the way toward another place where dragons had caused damage, trying to think of something else to talk about, something to distract Alain. "Um, you know, if I had worn my jacket, that guard wouldn't have spoken to us unless I asked him stuff, and he probably wouldn't have told us about the hissing."

Alain nodded. "We were taught as acolytes that instilling fear has its purposes, but it can also create problems."

"I wonder just how many problems."

"You can work with commons," Alain said.

"I guess," Mari admitted.

"And Mages."

"One Mage. That is unusual, I know, but if I can make it work, why not?" Mari grimaced. "I want to be in control of what I do. The hardest part of being in my Guild is having so many rules and restrictions and people telling me what to do. Some of the rules make sense. You can see why they're necessary. But a lot of other rules feel like they're just there because someone wanted to control Mechanics who were lower in rank. And yet that is so much easier than the life of commons. What it would have been like growing up as a common, with no power at all, no control at all, just a pawn in the games of the Great Guilds?"

"I do not think you would do well under those conditions," Alain said.

"I don't think so, either." The next words came out before she quite realized what she was saying. "Why am I helping to force other people to live in a way I couldn't stand to live?"

The Mage didn't answer, seeming to be sunk in thought, but she didn't know what the answer was, either, and was horrified at having said such a thing. If the Guild ever found out that she had said that...

Mari had regained her composure by the time they reached another secluded area, where a section of unloading dock had been reduced to splinters. At yet another place, a small coastal freighter, the sort whose crew normally slept ashore, had been holed and left lying on the bottom of the harbor next to the pier where it had been tied up. Asking around, Mari learned that most of the small ship's side opposite the pier had been ripped open. Farther along, a warehouse fronting on the harbor had seen half of its seaward wall stove in, the bricks forming piles of rubble.

By the time they had finished looking over the wrecked warehouse, the sun was past noon. They stopped to grab some hand food from a small cart catering to the waterfront workers, finding seats on bollards at the edge of the pier. Below them, the waters of the harbor surged gently back and forth, some trash on the surface bumping against the piles holding up the pier. Looking down, Mari could see only a little way beneath the surface, the water so clouded that within a short distance all was hidden.

She ate slowly, trying to grasp something that was bothering her. Something that tied together all the sites they had viewed. But what? She looked around, trying to spot anything that might help her figure out what it was. Around at the water, up the long slope through the city... "That's it."

"What?" Alain followed her gaze. "Something is up there?"

"No. That's the point. Nothing's up there." Mari could see the Mage's eyes reflecting confusion, and felt a sense of satisfaction that she was getting better at spotting his thoughts and emotions despite his efforts to hide them. "Can dragons fly?"

The apparent change of subject didn't seem to startle the Mage. "No. Not at all. They do not have wings, but even if they did I do not see how they could fly. Their large muscles, their heavy bones, their armored scales, it all ties them to the ground.–Although by using their hind legs, the largest can jump impressive distances," he added. "If you want a flying spell creature, you need a Roc."

"A what?"

"A Roc. It is a giant bird," Alain explained.

Mari shook her head. "A giant bird. I'm crazy to be listening to this, you know that?"

"I have thought..." He fumbled for words, for a moment looking just like any other seventeen-year-old young man. Was that actually embarrassment showing? "You might...be interested...someday...in flying...on a Roc. I mean...with me."

"Are you asking me on a date?" Mari tried desperately not to laugh at his discomfort. "A date on a giant bird?"

"Um...I do not know...just something to do...together. That is not dangerous," Alain added hastily.

"Doing something together that isn't dangerous?" Mari asked. "That would be a change of pace for us, wouldn't it? Maybe that would be fun, someday." She wanted to let him down easy, even though the idea of flying on some giant bird felt not just impossible but also far from safe. "Have you ever gone...flying...with a girl before?"

Was he blushing? Just the faintest hint of it, but— Stars above. She had made a Mage blush.

"No," Alain said.

From what she had seen and heard of Mages and their acolytes, from what she had learned of Alain, that wasn't surprising. A Mage social probably consisted of everyone standing in the same room and ignoring each other. "Sure, Alain. Let's do that someday." *I really hope I don't end up regretting that.* "For now, never mind the giant birds. Could dragons get up there?" She pointed up toward the city.

"Of course." Alain regained his composure quickly. "The wide streets would make their passage easy."

She smiled with satisfaction. "Then can you think of any reason why everything these dragons have done is close to the water? Even the train trestle was destroyed down at ground level, right at the shore."

Alain stayed silent as he thought. "No. Now that you mention it, it is very unlike them. Dragons do not like water all that much, especially deep water."

"They don't swim well?"

"Not at all. They are heavy, as I said." The Mage rubbed his chin, clearly thinking. "I have thought you were right about this not really being the work of dragons, but now I am certain. Only a leviathan would be tied to the water, and a leviathan would not cause the kinds of damage we have seen."

"Leviathan." Mari tried not to wince. "Giant fish?"

"Not exactly. Squid? Whale? It is a bit like both. But much larger."

"Fine." Hopefully he wouldn't ask her out for a ride on a leviathan. "All I need to know is that we're not dealing with one." She started walking along the pier, Alain falling in beside her. "Just out of curiosity, and not that I ever expected to be asking someone this, but can you make a dragon?"

Alain shook his head. "No. To be able to create a spell creature you need different training, different ways of knowing how to change the world illusion. It is not something I ever sought."

Mari nodded back. "Then it's a specialty. That's what Mechanics call that sort of thing."

"Do we need a dragon?" Alain asked.

"No!" She fought down the image of a monster adding to the problems of Dorcastle. They came to some more bollards and Mari sat down on one, staring across the harbor. "If it's not some spell creature doing this, then it's got to be some Mechanic device. Nothing else could generate that kind of power without taking a lot of time or being so big it would be obvious. But my Guild's not behind this. It's costing us a lot of money."

"It is also causing the Mage Guild a lot of trouble," Alain pointed out, sitting down on an adjacent bollard. "That could be seen as worth the lost money for your Guild."

"Well, yeah. But I don't think so. That's just a guess, of course, but the Senior Mechanics in Dorcastle are all acting very unhappy. I think I'd have spotted some signs of smugness if this was a plot cooked up by my Guild. And," she continued, "that train accident we almost had. I don't see how the Guild would have approved the possible destruction of the train and all its passengers. Whoever set it up might be a Mechanic." Was she really telling a Mage this, even if that Mage was Alain? "But I don't see how that Mechanic could be following Guild orders."

"Could the accident have been an illusion?' Alain asked.

"An illusion? Oh, you mean a staged accident? No. I was in the cabin of that locomotive, and the driver of that train was scared witless that we'd go over the edge. He would've had to be part of a staged accident, and I'm positive he was just as shocked and frightened as I was."

Alain nodded. "Then a Mechanic thing, but not controlled by your Guild? There are Dark Mechanics?"

Mari grimaced. The Mage had quickly reached the same possible conclusion she had, and she couldn't discuss it with him. "No comment. I can't say a word on that subject."

"I do not understand."

"I can't say anything on that subject. By order of my Guild."

"Ah." Alain didn't seem to find arbitrary orders from a Guild anything remarkable. He looked out over the water, where sea gulls were swooping down to pick at the contents of a passing garbage scow. "What if I imagine a world illusion that includes a creature such as Mechanics use? Like your locomotive, but a creature which could cause the destruction we have seen? What would it be like?"

Mari smiled at him, amused and impressed that Alain had quickly figured out how to work around the restriction on her. "Something that could generate a lot of power. Hydraulics? No. That would leak fluid sooner or later. We would have seen the stains."

"Fluid?"

"Sort of, uh, blood for the hydraulic machinery."

"I see. Trolls and dragons also bleed, though it is not actually blood."

"That's...interesting." Mari frowned, looking down at the low swells lapping against the quay. "Anyway, not hydraulics. That leaves steam. A steam engine of some kind. With something to multiply the force. A steam engine would need the boiler, the fuel, water, and pipes. And, unlike a dragon, a steam engine *would* hiss. Put it on the water and it's mobile, but also confined to the water." She shook her head. "There's one big problem with that theory. Keeping it hidden. It wouldn't need a ship, but you couldn't fit one in a boat."

Alain pointed. "What about a large boat such as that?"

She studied the barge that Alain had indicated. Even empty, the barge sat fairly low in the water, yet she knew barges had shallow drafts since they were designed to navigate rivers. That and its blunt ends and almost vertical sides would let a barge come close to shore from any angle, and a large wooden structure for protecting cargo covered most of the deck area. "Yeah. That big enclosed area. You could put a steam engine and all its stuff in there. It would look like just a typical barge."

"There are many barges in Dorcastle now. I have heard the sailors talking about it. Because cargoes are not coming in or going out of the harbor, the barges which come downstream have nothing to take upstream. They just wait at the increasingly crowded barge docks."

"Which are near the warehouses, right?"

"I believe so. Will you tell your Guild what you have learned?"

She made an exasperated noise. "We haven't learned anything! We've made what I think are some excellent guesses, because we looked at what was going on before we made up our minds what was causing it. But that's not going to impress my Guild leaders."

"If you tell them what you have learned about dragons—"

Mari put her hands over her mouth, trying to control her laughter. "Oh, right. That'll work. I tell my Senior Mechanics that I talked to a Mage about what dragons are really like—"

"They are not real."

"Will you stop that? The point is, I can't explain my logic because I can't tell them what I've learned because they won't accept the source of that information."

"I do not understand," the Mage said. "You are a Mechanic—"

"Shhh. Somebody might hear."

"And I have seen that you always look at things. You look at them and then you decide what to do. This is not how others in your Guild work?"

"It's how they're supposed to work. A lot of them do. But there are a lot who don't." Mari scowled, still staring out over the water. "I had a professor in Palandur that I really admired. An elder, I guess you would call her. Her name is S'san," Mari continued. "One time we started talking about what people do when they see danger coming, and Professor S'san said that a lot of times when people or organizations see danger coming, they just keep doing what they were doing and hope everything will work out fine. And I said that was crazy, that it was like being on a mountain path and seeing a boulder rolling toward you and all you do is close your eyes and stand there instead of keeping your eyes open and stepping to one side." The rush of words halted for a moment as Mari pondered the memory.

"Did she agree?" Alain finally asked.

"Sort of." Mari sighed. "She agreed it wasn't smart or rational, but she said that's what people often do, unless someone gets their attention and convinces them to get off the path before the boulder hits them." She shook her head. "I didn't understand her. Now I'm beginning to. She was telling me something important. Whatever's going on with my Guild has been happening for a long time. I still don't know exactly what's wrong, but I'm beginning to think there's some kind of boulder rolling toward my Guild—maybe more than one boulder. I think it's already doing damage to the Guild and has been for a long time, that the rate of damage might be increasing like the speed of a boulder rolling downhill. And the Guild leadership is closing its eyes and hoping for the best."

Alain looked straight at her. "I have been told that most Mage elders are doing the same."

"Your elders should be worried, too?"

"A storm strikes all in its path."

As metaphors for trouble went, Mari thought, that wasn't bad at all. "My Guild likes things the way they are. We control how many of our devices are available and how much they cost, we're the only ones who can fix them, and the commons do what we say because they can't afford to offend the Mechanics and get cut off from our devices. I think that's what City Manager Polder was talking about back in Ringhmon when he told me the commons were tired of being in the box the Mechanics Guild had made to keep the world in. The commons are unhappy, but the Mechanics don't want anything to change." Mari shook her head. "And things in this world don't change, do they? You know history. Has there been change?"

"Not for a long time," Alain replied. "The only change in recent history has been the sundering of the Kingdom of Tiae as it fell apart in a succession of civil wars. The parts of the former kingdom remain in anarchy. For centuries the Empire has dominated the east, trying to expand into the lands along the northern or southern coasts of the Sea of Bakre, only to be stymied time and again. The Bakre Confederation, the Western Alliance and the Free Cities are almost as old. There have been no great changes since the days when Jules led the founding of the Confederation in the west."

"What if things are starting to change?" Mari said. "What if what happened in Tiae is a warning that our world is going to see major changes? That the system under which the Great Guilds control the world is accumulating stresses that will cause it to crack like old metal?"

"When metal cracks," Alain asked, "does it happen slowly or quickly?"

"Quickly," Mari explained. "The weaknesses build up gradually, but the warning signs aren't always easy to spot. One moment everything seems fine, and the next it comes apart."

"But someone who sees the metal weakening can do things to save it? To keep it from coming apart?"

"Well...yes," Mari said. "But it can be hard, especially if the damage has accumulated for a long time. It can reach the point where saving the metal is extremely hard and you're better off replacing it."

Alain nodded. "And if our world was this metal?"

"If our world— ?" Mari let that sink in. "That's scary. Why would the rest of the world crack like Tiae?"

"I have a memory," Alain said. "From before the Mages took me for training. A pen had been made for the animals on my parents' land. They had been placed within it, many of them in a small space, and something caused them to begin to rush about. Some panic or pain." He paused, recalling the terror with which a little boy had watched the scene. "There was no room, but still the animals tried to rush from side to side, trampling those who fell. The fallen...screamed as the others crushed them. But still the panic grew, and my father, I think it was, broke open the pen and let them run, because otherwise they would have killed themselves."

Mari stared at him, saddened. "That must have been awful to watch. An animal pen. A cage. A box. Like that man in Ringhmon talked about. Is that what you think might be happening? The commons have been penned in for so long and..."

She shook her head, frightened by the visions that idea had created. "Alain, I haven't been able to figure out why the leaders of Ringhmon kidnapped me and did some things on . . . a Mechanic device, things that they knew were absolutely forbidden by my Guild. The risks were insane. And suppose someone did try to destroy that locomotive to get rid of me? Overkill. That's what Mechanics would call that. Using far more force than made sense. It's as if people are starting to act that way, like those animals you remember, panicked and pushing against the walls confining them."

"They would need someone to break the pen open," Alain said.

"I don't break things, Alain. The Mechanic rule is repair and replace. That's what we would have to do, but repairing and replacing a world? I think that is beyond the capability of Mechanics."

"But if Mages and commons also help," Alain said, "you could do this."

"Me? Oh. Sure. Mari's going to save the world." She laughed shortly. "I'm...what's her name? That daughter of Jules! Is that why you're hanging around with me?"

"I thought you did not want to speak of—"

"You're right. I don't." Mari took a deep breath, glaring across the harbor, upset that she had introduced the topic of their relationship into the discussion. "Alain, I can't fix anything unless I get someone to listen to me. Someone besides you, that is. I need proof. I need...I need a dragon."

"I cannot—"

"Not a real one, *and don't say it*! One of the fake dragons that is doing this damage. Would you like to go dragon hunting with me? Tonight?"

Alain nodded without hesitating. "A friend helps."

Mari smiled. "Yeah. But it might be dangerous."

"Then I must be there with you."

Stars above, if only this could work. It can't. You know that. Focus on the job, Mari! Remember what happens to him if he's caught with a Mechanic. You can stay just a friend with Alain and help him change enough that he can meet some girl who can be a lot more than that to him without also endangering him. She ignored the pang of distress that thought brought to life. "All right. Let's go case the job." Alain gave her a questioning glance. "That means look around the barge area before it gets dark."

She stood up and they started along the waterfront once more, just as some sort of loud argument erupted nearby. Ignoring the debate, Mari nonetheless heard it quickly escalate into a fight. A crowd swelled in the area with amazing rapidity as laborers rushed to see the combatants, so that before she knew it Mari was struggling through a dense mass of people trying to rush past her and Alain.

A powerful arm suddenly came around her waist, pinning her arms to her sides, while another arm came around from the other side to clap a hand over her mouth. She gripped her bag. Alain had vanished in the mass of humanity. Mari felt herself being lifted and pulled back with the flow of the crowd toward the buildings and alleys that lined the waterfront, barely able to struggle and unable to cry out.

CHAPTER FIFTEEN

Mari tried to elbow her captor in the side but couldn't get her arm free. She tried to bite the hand over her mouth but a stout leather glove protected it. She kicked backwards, getting in some jabs to the ankles of whoever had grabbed her, but he was wearing heavy boots that protected his shins. Mari's kicks made him stumble, but he kept a firm grip on her.

They were fading into the crowd. Mari lost sight of where she had been. She had no idea where Alain was. Then they backed through a doorway. The door started to close, caught on something, then slammed shut, leaving Mari and her captor in the dimness of a room illuminated only by a heavily curtained window, the sounds of the brawl outside now muffled.

"Get her," someone grunted. Hands grabbed her own, forcing her arms back as her captor released his grip slightly. The bag dropped from her hand. Mari twisted, slipping one hand free and swinging a punch that caused one of the kidnappers to back away hastily.

The big man's grip tightened again. Mari felt a sense of despair. There were at least two other men in here, and she had no way to get in a good blow at any of them. Once she was tied up she would be helpless.

"She's supposed to have a gun," the big man stated. "Search her."

One of the others placed his hands on Mari, pawing her and

grinning as he saw Mari's outrage. "What's the matter, girl? Not used to men feeling around? Maybe you'll like it."

That did it.

Mari twisted again, surprised at her own strength and surprising her captors. Her leg came up and she planted her boot in the gut of the man who had been trying to search her. As he fell backwards with a grunt of pain, the other men shouted angrily, but under their cries Mari heard a familiar voice whose tones conveyed calm and confidence even though they carried no emotion.

"Close your eyes."

Hope blossoming inside her, Mari squeezed her eyes tightly shut. A moment later bright light flared in the room, dazzling even through her eyelids. The cries of the men holding her changed to distress. A thudding noise resounded, then the arms of the big man holding her finally relaxed as he fell, almost pulling her down with him.

Mari spun, her angry gaze fixed on the third man, who was stumbling around blinking. Mari pivoted on one foot, leaning back and bringing her other leg up in a kick that slammed into the man's stomach and bent him over, gasping for breath. A moment later she landed a hard kick on the man's head, snapping him back and to the side, where his head struck a wooden beam. He fell and lay still.

That left at least one. But as Mari turned to face the first man she had kicked, she saw Alain hurl himself forward, hitting the man in the chest and forcing him back through the window. Glass shattered as the curtains billowed, and the noise of the riot outside suddenly jumped in volume. Alain stood up and looked out the window, one hand raised slightly, then backed away. "He is running," he explained dispassionately.

"You couldn't get a good shot at him?" she asked, trembling with reaction, fear, and anger at the kidnapping attempt. She stared at Alain, who appeared to be completely unfazed by the recent crisis.

"I could easily place the heat upon him," Alain said. "I chose not to, even though he is nothing. I did not think you would want me to."

She got control of her breathing, remembering the bodies of the bandits in the Waste who had been struck by Alain's heat. "You're right. For a moment there I did want to hurt him, even after he stopped being a danger to me—to us," Mari admitted. "But that would have been hard to live with. Where did you come from?"

"Later. We must leave this place. These three might have more companions nearby."

"Right. Good thinking." Mari looked down at her captor as she bent to pick up her bag. He was a big man, as she had guessed, wearing common laborer's clothes and now lying unconscious on the floor. "Did you do that? What kind of spell was that?"

Alain held up a paving stone from the street. "I made use of part of the illusion."

She couldn't help grinning. "You used an imaginary rock to hit my imaginary captor on his imaginary head?"

"Exactly. You are learning much wisdom," Alain said with absolute seriousness. "It is important to see the illusion around you and employ it in the service of your goals," he said as if reciting a lesson. "Do you know that shadow who held you?"

"No," Mari said. "I don't think I've ever seen him. I didn't recognize the other two, either."

Alain yanked open the door and Mari followed him out. The fight seemed to be spreading and overwhelming the city guards in the area. There would be no timely help from that quarter. Turning, she and Alain ducked and dodged their way along the front of the buildings until out of the mess, finally getting clear of the riot and hastening down the waterfront before stopping to rest in a place where they could see if anyone else was coming at them. But no pursuit could be seen.

Mari realized she was shaking with reaction again and tried to calm herself. "Nobody told me Dorcastle had a kidnapping problem."

"No one told me of that, either," Alain observed, his totally emotionless voice sounding inappropriate rather than confident now.

"I doubt that anyone tries to kidnap Mages," Mari said. "Not more than once, anyway. I, on the other hand, seem to have started attracting kidnap attempts like a magnet."

"What is a mag-net?"

Mari fumbled for an explanation for something she had never needed to explain. "It's a piece of metal that attracts other metal using invisible lines of force."

Alain actually betrayed a flash of interest. "It employs power to bring other objects to it? I did not know any part of the illusion could do such a thing."

"No," Mari said. "It's not Mage stuff. It's electromagnetism, which is an invisible force that...uh...makes things...happen. Why does something that's part of Mechanic training and knowledge sound so much like what you've said about your Mage work? That's weird. But a person can't employ electromagnetism directly just by...thinking about it. We need equipment to do that. Um...what did you do? How did you get into that room without being seen?"

He shrugged. "A protection spell. I used it at the caravan, if you recall, when getting water. It causes the light to bend around a Mage instead of revealing the Mage. The door almost caught me coming in, but no one seemed to notice."

"Bending light. Sure. Why not? And that flash of light?"

"Another spell," Alain replied. "Changing the darkness to an equal measure of light."

"Sort of the opposite of what you did at Ringhmon? Thank you, Alain. I don't know what that man and his friends were planning, but I'm very grateful you stopped them. You're the most wonderful—" *Stop it! Stop it! Don't say it! He's a friend, that's all he can be! He just saved you again and you can't repay that by clinging to him at the cost of his own well-being!*

Her thanks seemed to embarrass the usually impassive Mage. "I am very...happy...I was there to stop them, though it would be important to know why they wanted you."

"There are a couple of obvious possibilities." How could she be speaking so calmly about this so soon after the event? Alain must be wearing off on her. But she couldn't pretend any longer how much safer his presence made her feel. And for good reason. He had just proven again how cool and capable he was in an emergency. Just thinking about that made Mari want to smile at Alain. "They might have been after any girl for purposes I don't want to think about," Mari continued. "Or they might have been after me. They took advantage of that fight to grab me."

Alain shook his head, frowning slightly in thought. "The sudden fight, the rapid growth in the crowd, the swift development of a riot, singling you out quickly. I see in the illusion a pattern of planning. I think it more likely that it was all arranged to cover your capture."

She stared at him. "That would require a lot of work, and I assume a fair amount of money. Do you think they know who I am?" By now Ringhmon could have hired agents to try to kidnap her again, though this time for purposes of vengeance.

"If they knew who you are," Alain said, "they would have used more shadows to ensure your capture."

"Alain," Mari said, "if you're trying to reassure me, or compliment me, you're doing a terrible job. No one tried to get you?"

"No. I believe some commons tried to block me as I saw you being taken. I would have lost sight of you quickly if they had succeeded. But once I bent light to hide myself, they could not see to obstruct me and I easily got past them. I did not fail this time. Those in the caravan died, but I saved you." He hadn't talked about the caravan since they had left the site of its destruction, but unless she was mistaken, what he had just said meant a great deal to the Mage.

"Of course you did," Mari replied. "And you also saved me from that dungeon in Ringhmon, if I may remind you. You don't need directions to act, you can take charge in an instant when you need to, and you think through what you're doing even during a crisis. You're really good at saving people, Alain."

"As are you."

"I guess. When I'm not getting them into situations where they need to be saved. Now what? Do you think we should hide?"

The Mage shook his head again. "If they know who you are, they will search and lie in wait. It is better to go on the attack, to gain and use the initiative, rather than let them set up another attack on us."

She grinned. "Are you still game to go dragon hunting?"

"Yes." Then Alain turned swiftly and stared out into the city. "I sense Dark Mages."

"Sense them?" Mari asked, looking around quickly.

"Yes. I told you that a Mage can feel when other Mages are not too far away. We are taught ways to hide our presence from other Mages, but it is not my strongest skill by any means, and when I cast those spells it would have advertised my presence very clearly."

"But you didn't think Dark Mages were involved in this dragon stuff."

"No," Alain agreed. "But they could be in the city, and attracted to the violence as a possible source of profit. They might even strike at me to weaken my Guild, or attempt to kidnap me to extort ransom from my Guild. Or they could be hired to threaten you."

Mari nodded, running one hand through her hair and wondering how many other threats against her would materialize. "Maybe I shouldn't have burnt down the city hall in Ringhmon. But you can tell when a Dark Mage is close?"

"I should be able to, yes."

"All right. That's one more thing we have to keep an eye out for. Let's get out of here before someone else attacks us."

❋　　❋　　❋

The barges which floated down the Silver River into Dorcastle, carrying the crops grown on the farms of the Bakre Confederation and the goods built in the workshops of Danalee, rode the last stage of their journey through a series of locks which carried them past the rushing waters where the Silver River plunged down past Dorcastle into the harbor. Once safely at sea level, the barges went to an inner harbor surrounded by warehouses. There they tied up alongside lengthy piers, offloading their cargo and awaiting imports from the sea-going ships arriving at Dorcastle. Once loaded again, the barges would undertake the long, arduous journey back up the Silver River, completing the circle of trade that enriched Dorcastle and much of the Bakre Confederation.

But that circle had been broken lately, as the ships already there remained in Dorcastle's harbor and new ships stayed away for fear of the dragons terrorizing the city. The warehouses were packed to the brim with cargo waiting to go out to sea, and nothing was coming in to go back up the river. As a result, the number of barges had grown steadily, until the inner harbor was filled with them and their increasingly restive crews.

Alain and Mari had chosen a place on top of a flat-roofed two-story building where they could sit unobserved and watch the inner harbor area. As the sun sank, the workers at the warehouses left for their homes, leaving the sailors on the barges where they lived. Some of the sailors who still had a little money to spend wandered into town, looking for entertainment in the nearby inns, but most stayed on their boats, huddled around small cooking fires in the boxes of sand that served as the barge kitchens. Alain could hear Mari muttering angrily to herself occasionally as the night wore on and the sailors sat up talking, gambling, and singing. She had been on edge ever since the attempt to kidnap her. In a Mage that would have been improper, but since Mari was a Mechanic, Alain could not fault her. And if someone in Dorcastle already knew or suspected who Mari was, that she was the daughter named in the old prophecy, her reactions actually displayed great composure in the face of such a threat.

By midnight, almost all of the sailors had packed themselves off to sleep. A trickle of foot traffic still existed as party-goers wandered back in twos and threes. "Do sailors ever sleep?" Mari grumbled.

"It is growing quiet," Alain reassured her. "We can move soon." He had noticed that the Mechanic was much more impatient than the Mages he was used to associating with. Apparently she felt time pass in a different way, speaking of short periods as if they held great importance and must be measured exactly. Alain had refrained from asking Mari about that tonight, however, as she had seemed very irritable on the subject of how much time had gone by while they watched the sailors.

He felt a lingering urgency himself from the vision of the oncoming storm. Was that what drove Mari as well? The same sense that danger loomed and must be dealt with?

Seeking some subject to distract her, he looked upward, seeing the tapestry of the stars standing out brilliantly against the black of night. "You do not believe that Mechanics came from the stars, as your Guild claims?"

She gave him a cross look, then took on a more companionable expression with an obvious effort. "Didn't we talk about that once? Officially, yes, we're the superior beings from the stars. I personally think it was just made up to make the Guild seem more powerful or mysterious or whatever. Aside from our skills, we seem to be just like everyone else."

"Do you know of any other group who believes they came from the stars?"

"No." Mari's expression changed to curiosity. "Why are you asking? I mean, that would just be a ridiculous myth."

"Perhaps." Alain gestured upward. "There is an oddity in history. You asked me of the last few centuries when we talked of Tiae and other events, but before that we know of the oldest cities, places like Landfall the Ancient, Larharbor, and Altis, which were of course much smaller when they started. And we know when people left those cities to found new ones. But nowhere does it say where the people of the oldest cities came from."

"They came from..." Mari waved a hand vaguely. "Around those places."

"There are no older towns, no settlements, no ruins. Only the oldest cities. I checked on that when I went through Landfall. There are no signs of any human presence older than the city itself, and the oldest portions of the city show planning. It was not the haphazard growth which happens when no authority is ordering events."

She gave him a perplexed look. "Really? That's sort of strange. How could a city full of people just show up from nowhere? It makes me wonder if maybe the Western Continent really exists and they came from there. But if there is such a place, and people were there, why haven't they kept coming?"

"Or perhaps they came from the stars?"

"I'd need some proof of that." Mari shook her head. "I'm not sure what difference it would make, anyway. Say we did come from the stars. Why would that matter now?"

Alain considered that. "I do not know. I have a feeling that it is somehow important, but cannot say why. At the least it would mean that, somewhere among those stars we see, there are others looking up at us as we look upon them."

She stared upward. "That's sort of wild to think about. Do you know that you can be almost poetic at times, Alain? But there's the same problem as I mentioned before. If we came here from the stars, why hasn't anyone else come here from there?"

"It could be the journey is too long or too difficult."

"That I can believe. How far away are the stars, anyway? The Guild discourages any actual study of the heavens." Mari gave him a sharp look. "I wonder what's up there that I'm not supposed to see? I can't believe it matters, but if it doesn't, why doesn't the Guild want people studying the stars? I know someone who wanted to build a far-seer that would let them view the moon better." Calu, enthusiastic as he outlined the design for a scaled-up version of what Mechanics used to see longer distances on land and sea. Calu, abashed as Senior Mechanics tongue-lashed him for improper experimentation and wasted effort. "He wasn't allowed."

She dropped her gaze back to the rows of barges alongside the piers, then stood up and stretched, stiff from the long wait. "We'll have to leave questions about the origin of everything for another time. It's as quiet as it'll get. Let's go for a walk."

"All right." Alain saw the smile that she turned on him as he used her phrase. He had guessed that Mari might be pleased to have him say it. How strange it felt to correctly anticipate the emotional reaction of another.

He stretched out his muscles as well, then followed her down the fire stairs on one side of the building. Once they reached the ground, he had to speed up to walk beside her, as Mari started off at a rapid pace. She might complain of others looking to her for direction, but Mari had a habit of taking the lead. "We might want to walk slower so we do not seem so obvious," Alain suggested. Everyone else they had seen in the area for a while had been ambling along as if they had no need to be anywhere soon.

Mari grumbled something under her breath, but slowed her walking. "Thanks for pointing that out."

"Thank you for listening to me," Alain said.

She gave him a startled look. "That's right. Your elders don't listen to you, either. I'm so grateful that you listen to me that I forget how important it is for me to listen to you."

"Even when you forget, you listen," Alain said. "That is important to me."

Mari mumbled something, looking embarrassed, then made an obvious effort of focusing back on the barges.

"What are we looking for?" he asked. "Just a barge? There are many."

She took a moment to answer as she thought it through. "We want a low-riding barge. You can see most of these are riding high because they've offloaded their cargo. But the one we want would still have a lot of heavy stuff aboard." Mari hesitated. "I'm not sure what else. When we see any low-riding barges, we'll take a closer look and maybe spot something else."

They started down the piers in turn, moving quietly past barge after barge, the only sounds the creaking of wood and the gentle lapping of the inner harbor's waters, punctuated by an occasional snore from aboard one of the barges. The barges varied a bit in size, and were painted different colors which were hard to distinguish in the darkness, but otherwise were distressingly the same.

After going down two piers and seeing nothing, Mari stopped and looked angry. "This is going to take all night."

Alain, agreeing with her, scanned the inner harbor. He paused as he got a glimpse of shadows moving between the barges two piers down from where they were.

"What is it? Do you see something?" Mari asked.

"Wait." He watched carefully, finally rewarded by another sight of a dark shape moving along the water. "A barge is underway, but it is headed toward the warehouses, not the harbor."

Mari craned her neck to see, then beckoned to Alain. "Come on. There's no good reason a barge should be moving at this hour. Maybe that's who we're looking for."

It was not easy to move quickly along the piers without making noise, but they managed it, reaching the end just in time to see a barge riding low in the water ease inside the broad, open doors of a warehouse that like some others extended out over the water and contained an enclosed dock. As soon as the barge's stern cleared the doors, they were silently swung shut.

"That's it," Mari breathed. "It's got to be." She starting walking at a fast pace toward the warehouse, Alain following despite his doubts about the wisdom of so openly approaching a possible enemy position.

Reaching the large building, which was partly made of wood and partly of masonry, Mari kept going until she found a small side door giving access to the inside. "Locked. Like that's a problem." She pulled out something from one of her jacket pockets.

"Mari," Alain said in a low voice. "What are you doing?"

"I'm going to pick this lock, then I'm going inside this warehouse to find the proof of what's really going on here," she muttered, going to one knee and examining the lock as she had the ones in the dungeon of Ringhmon.

"But there are those inside. Those crewing the barge and those who operated the doors, at least. Possibly more."

"Yeah." She had brought out one of her tools and was applying it to the lock. "So?"

Alain tried not to stare at Mari, who was patiently working away at the lock. "There may be more enemies inside that warehouse than we can deal with," he explained.

"I don't hear a crowd in there," Mari replied, her voice stubborn.

"They could be quiet."

"We'll be quiet, too."

"Wait," Alain said. "Mari, this is not wise. I was told to evaluate a foe before attacking. We have no idea how many we could be facing, what weapons they might have— "

"We have to have better evidence if we're to convince anyone that the barge and this warehouse are involved with the so called dragon attacks!" Mari insisted. "We need proof. We need proof that no one can deny. Everybody keeps telling me that I don't know what I'm doing and refuses to listen to me! What's in here can change that. We need to know what it is."

"This could be very dangerous," Alain said.

She paused, eyeing him. "How dangerous? Is that a guess? Or your, um, foresight?"

Alain hesitated. The temptation to say whatever he wanted to say was strong. And, after all, his misgivings might be the result of his foresight. But he knew that was not the case, and Alain knew he did not want to lie to Mari even if truth did not exist. "It is a guess. My assessment."

"Alain, I respect that," Mari said. "I do. But my guess is that we need to check this out and we need to do it now. I got attacked *again* today, so I do feel a little urgency to learn exactly what I'm dealing with here."

"Mari..." What was the right word to use? When it was not a command but a request? Mages never used such words. But Alain remembered being in the dungeon in Ringhmon, recalled Mari asking for his help in getting her tools. She had used the word. "We should go carefully. Please."

"You said please?" She looked at him, then away. "What did that take? Are you really feeling that much concern about this?"

"Yes. For you."

"That is so not fair." Mari ran both hands through her hair, looking down. "Alain, I'm not planning on charging into there and making noise and everything. I want to scout it out. Carefully. Just like you said. Maybe I've been rushing things a little just now because success is so close. I can feel it. But I will be careful in there. You're feeling emotions and they may be a bit overwhelming. I am flattered that you're worried about me. But this is important. Don't we need to know who is after me and why?"

"Yes," Alain agreed.

"Whatever is in there is very likely to be the kind of evidence, the kind of proof, that no one can pretend not to see, or stuff into a drawer and forget about. This isn't just about me." Mari paused, her expression shifting to distress. "I've learned that things are being ignored. Very important things. If my Guild doesn't start dealing with those things, doesn't start admitting some problems exist, then...then this world will be like a boiler with too much pressure inside. Sooner or later, it will explode."

He looked down at where Mari crouched next to the lock. "As Tiae has?"

"Yes. Like we talked about earlier. Like Tiae. Or like those animals in the pen." She pointed to the door. "But if I can get strong enough proof, it might be enough to change things, to start changing things here. I just want to fix what is broken. That's what a Mechanic should do. Will you help me, Alain?"

As he listened to Mari's earnest words, Alain thought of the storm in his vision sweeping down upon the second sun in the sky. What happened now would either help Mari fight that storm, or perhaps put an end to the future only she could bring. What happened now could perhaps doom the world illusion to the eventual fate of Tiae and worse.

It did not matter, his Mage training told him. The world illusion did not matter. What mattered to him was the young woman who knelt by the door, the shadow who called herself Mari. A shadow the storm would utterly destroy to prevent her from bringing the new day of hope to this world.

The elder had said that his choices mattered, and now he understood just how much that was so. Part of him wanted to stop Mari, to try to keep her safe no matter what, but that would be selfish, an act like that of the Mage elders who clung to power. Mari would insist on trying to help others no matter what Alain did. He understood her well enough already to know that.

Alain remembered the graves of his parents and thought of countless other parents dying if that storm swept this world, countless children dying as well or left unprotected, while the Mage Guild and the Mechanics Guild fortified their Halls and held out as long as possible against the bedlam that the world had become before they, too, fell. How much time was left before that storm struck?

He knew that no matter what his training told him, he would not allow such a thing to happen if he could help prevent it. And the only way he could help prevent it was by helping the daughter of the prophecy, no matter how much he feared for her safety. "I will help you," Alain told Mari. "Not just because it is you who ask, but because you seek to do the right thing."

She smiled in a way he had not seen before. "You know what the right thing means, now?"

"Yes. I will help you do the right thing. But do not forget that there are limits to my powers," Alain added.

"I know. All you can do is walk through walls and bend light and stuff," Mari replied in her sarcasm voice, still smiling at him. "Listen," she said, earnest again, "I've been thinking. We survived the attack on the caravan. That took both of us, working together. Then we got out of the city hall in Ringhmon together. Separately, we couldn't have done that. But together our skills add up to something more than just a sum. I really think that. Because Mages and Mechanics don't work together, do they? Never. Something designed to handle a Mage isn't very good at handling a Mechanic, and something a Mechanic can't handle a Mage can . You and I work together, so we can handle anything that comes up."

He nodded to her. "Yes. Mages and Mechanics working together. You have already done this."

"We've both done it." Mari grinned and pumped her fist in triumph at Alain's agreement. Turning back to the lock, she worked again for a few moments until a soft click announced her success. Before opening the door, Mari knelt by her bag, putting on the holster which held her weapon, then her Mechanics jacket over that. "Do you want to get into Mage gear?"

"My robes? No. If we are seen, if they do not already know who you are, it will be better if no one knows a Mage and a Mechanic are side by side."

"Good point." Taking the weapon in one hand and leaving her empty bag on the ground, Mari eased the door open slowly, sliding in as soon as the gap was large enough.

Alain slipped in behind Mari, who carefully closed the door behind them. They were in a narrow open lane running next to the wall, facing a tall barrier of wooden crates in various states of dilapidation. Mari listened intently, then gestured to Alain, leading him to the right.

The crates proved to be stacked into walls two crates deep, with passageways of varying widths running between them in a mazelike arrangement. The height of the crate stacks also varied but was generally well above their heads, blocking off sight. Higher up, the flickering light of oil lamps reflected off of a lofty ceiling. Alain could hear voices and the occasional sounds of large objects being moved. Mari, using those noises to orient herself, cautiously led the way through the maze.

They were close to the sounds when Mari paused and went to one knee, examining something resting on a crate. The object was metal and looked to Alain like a Mechanic device. "No makers' marks," she whispered. "No workshop codes. My Guild didn't construct this."

"Then you have found what you sought?"

"A small part of it," Mari said.

She headed closer to the sounds while Alain looked around, seeking any trace of warning from his foresight or other senses.

Finally they reached what must be the last wall of crates. Mari pointed upward, and they carefully climbed the wooden crates, trying not to make a sound. Reaching the top, Alain crawled with Mari along the top of the crates until they could see the rest of the warehouse.

A large area opened up ahead, leading to a dock with a small wooden pier to which a barge was tied up., The big warehouse doors leading out to the open water were still sealed. On the opposite side of the open area was what must be the main door of the warehouse, providing access to one of the roads on the landward side. Within the open area and on the barge, a group of commons, men and women, were working. The sides of the structure on top of the barge had been taken down so that what was within it could be seen.

Mari pointed to one object after another, murmuring just loudly enough for Alain to hear. "Steam boiler. Collapsible funnel for the steam boiler, so they could raise it when needed and lower it the rest of the time and no one could see it. Winches powered by the steam. I wonder if it also ties in to a propulsion screw beneath the barge? That would really help them move around. What do you think?"

"I think I have understood about one word in five of what you are saying," Alain replied.

She grinned, then pointed again. "See those iron-tipped timbers? Braces. That's what made those marks on the cliff face and provided stand-off so the barge didn't get caught in the collapse of the rail trestle. And look at those. Hooks shaped like really big claws on the end of the cables that the winches pull in. We've found our dragons, Alain. Those people down there are working on it, but they're not wearing Mechanics Guild jackets. We've found our Dark Mechanics." She pointed to one side, where a big man stood. "Doesn't he look familiar?"

"It is the same one who tried to kidnap you earlier," Alain agreed. "The one I knocked unconscious." Her certainty about what they were seeing impressed him, even though he could not grasp her descriptions of what they had found. But the objects in the barge were definitely Mechanic work. Alain took in the many Dark Mechanics below, not liking the odds if they were discovered. "Should we go?"

Mari chewed her lip, plainly reluctant. "I'll have to convince a bunch of other Mechanics to come here, but if I can get even one or two others to see this, it should be the lever I need. It's the best I'll get unless we steal that barge."

"You wish to steal the barge?" Alain asked, trying to think up a plan that might succeed in doing that.

"No. I'm not that crazy," Mari said. "But if there was any way to do that it sure would—"

Both of them froze as someone banged loudly on the main entrance to the warehouse. The commons in the warehouse stopped their work, staring silently toward the door, then all of them produced weapons of various kinds. A woman who seemed to be in charge beckoned to two others who had grabbed crossbows, then walked to the door, a knife at ready.

Alain could not see the woman's reaction when she peered through the door's security peephole, but he did not have to. "There is a Dark Mage there. At least one," he murmured to Mari.

Mari frowned at him. "The Dark Mechanics are working with Dark Mages?"

"I doubt that. Even Dark Mages are Mages. They disregard Mechanics, considering them beneath notice."

Anything else Mari might have planned on saying was cut short as the leader of the Dark Mechanics opened the door. Alain could just make out a lean, middle aged man with a hawk nose. He did not wear Mage robes, but the power that hung around him announced his status clearly to another Mage. "A strange place to find dragons," the Dark Mage announced impassively.

The Dark Mechanic leader shifted her hold on her knife so it was ready to stab. "You've got a very short time to convince me not to kill you."

The Dark Mage shook his head. "My comrades would take that poorly, and you do not want that. We hold this place in the palms of our hands. Should we choose to close our hands, you will all die and lose all that is here." The emotionless monotony of his voice was in strange contrast to the threatening words.

"You're a Mage," the Dark Mechanic spat.

"That should not bother you. You already have a Mage here."

Alain saw all of the Dark Mechanics start with surprise. His efforts to hide his presence from other Mages clearly had not been effective enough. "The Dark Mages sensed me," he breathed to Mari. "They have been following me. That is how they found this place. They may have been watching us for some time."

"Great," Mari muttered back. "We've been chasing Dark Mechanics, and Dark Mechanics and Dark Mages have been chasing us. Do they know exactly where you are in here? Is this anything like the thread?"

"No, it is very different. They can sense my general location, but that cannot lead them directly to me. They know that I am inside the building. If I use a spell, they will be able to find me."

"Let's not do that, then," Mari said.

Down below, the leader of the Dark Mechanics was glowering at the Dark Mage. "A Mage?" she said scornfully. "Here? That's a lie, but since you're a Mage, that's no surprise. What do you want?"

"A piece of the action," the Dark Mage said with emotionless calm. "We have been wondering who was behind these dragon acts, and now we know. If you do not wish us to inform others—perhaps the Mage Guild in this city, or the Mechanics Guild—you will agree to pay us half of whatever you make. Half before expenses."

Dark Mages, Alain thought, must know a great deal about money and such things as paying. But the Dark Mage's offer did not sit well with the Dark Mechanic. Even from where he was Alain could see the Dark Mechanic's face darken with anger. "No deal. Because killing you would be a distraction, I'll agree to give you one tenth. After expenses. Not a single bit more."

"One half."

"One tenth!"

"One half."

Snarling, the leader of the Dark Mechanics swung her knife forward, but her target vanished as the Dark Mage invoked a concealment spell. Alain could see the Dark Mage still, as a pale pillar of fire that marked his use of power. That pillar leaped back as the Dark Mechanic fruitlessly swung her knife through the space where the Dark Mage had been. With a growl of disgust, the Dark Mechanic slammed the door, locked it, and faced her comrades. "Get everything together. We have to move it all tonight, as fast as possible."

"What if those Mages try anything?" one of the others asked.

"Just get moving! Get a good head of steam up on the barge!"

As the Dark Mechanics began running around, Alain tapped Mari's shoulder. "We must leave quickly. I sense a Mage preparing a spell of great power somewhere nearby."

She gave him an alarmed glance, then wriggled backwards to drop back to the floor. Alain followed, staying close as Mari moved quickly back toward the side door, trusting the noise the Dark Mechanics were making to cover the sound of their retreat.

"Hey! Who the blazes— ?"

Alain saw a Dark Mechanic staring their way from the end of the lane they were in.

The Dark Mechanic shouted again. "There are some commons in here! No, one of them is a Mechanic!"

Mari brought her pistol up, but the Dark Mechanic dodged away and out of sight. Mari took the next right, then kept ducking through the maze of crates, running. Alain followed, hoping that Mari had some idea where she was going.

As it turned out, it was in the wrong direction. They burst out into the open area, where Dark Mechanics were turning to look, point and raise weapons. Behind them Alain could hear other Dark Mechanics pursuing them through the crates.

He would have hesitated then, deciding on a course of action, and been quickly trapped as the Dark Mechanics closed in. But Mari moved instantly, not pausing at all. "Come on!" she yelled, grabbing Alain and running full out for the main door.

Crossbows sang and bolts tore past, thudding into walls or crates. A Dark Mechanic reached the entry first, holding a knife at ready. Still running, Mari raised her pistol and the Dark Mechanic scrambled away, yelling. "She's got a pistol! Shoot her!"

As they got closer to the door, Mari gasped with anger. "I forgot. It's locked."

"I will take care of it," Alain replied. "Keep running!" Concentrating despite the weapons being aimed at them and the solid door coming rapidly closer, Alain managed to make a section of the door vanish just before Mari reached it.

Mari made a disbelieving noise but went through the opening as another crossbow bolt tore into the door frame. Alain followed right behind as they ran onto the darkened road in front of the warehouse, letting his spell relax so that the door would reappear behind him. It would take the Dark Mechanics a few moments to get the door unlocked, allowing them time to—

Alain reached out and pulled Mari to an abrupt halt. She glared at him in disbelief. "We need to get away. Why are you stopping us?"

"Because of that," Alain advised, pointing down the road. The Dark Mage he had sensed at work had completed his spell.

Mari looked that way, then stared, her mouth falling open.

CHAPTER SIXTEEN

"It is a dragon," Alain explained. "An actual dragon. Not a very big one, but still dangerous." The creature's head did not even come up to the top of the warehouses on either side, so it was only about the height of three people. But its armored scales winked in the dim light and its powerful hind legs drove it toward them as the dragon charged, the huge claws on its smaller forearms extended, its powerful tail raised behind to balance it.

Mari spun around and yanked Alain back toward the warehouse entrance. "Can it breathe fire?" she gasped as they ran.

"How could a dragon breathe fire? They are just very large and powerful creatures, as you see. We discussed this."

"I'm having a little trouble concentrating on past conversations!" Mari yelled.

Dark Mechanics had managed to unlock the door and were spilling out of the warehouse in pursuit of Mari and Alain when she ran full tilt into them, bulling through the startled enemies before they realized that their quarry had changed direction.

The dragon roared as it sighted the Dark Mechanics, who stood paralyzed for a moment before stampeding back through the entry as well, the last ones slamming and relocking the door, then bracing themselves against it.

Mari and Alain ran across the open area and had just about reached the crates again when the door and the surrounding wall burst inward in a mass of splintering wood, followed by the dragon. The Dark Mechanics who had tried to hold the door shut flew in all directions, some hitting the floor to lie still and others stumbling to their feet and limping frantically away.

Crossbows were firing again, the bolts glancing harmlessly from the dragon's scales. One of the Dark Mechanics had produced an old Mechanic weapon and fired, the crash of the shot followed by a clunk as the projectile struck the dragon and fell harmlessly to the floor.

Dark Mechanics were running in all directions as the dragon snapped at anyone within reach. But then the creature caught sight of Mari and Alain and with another roar sprang after them.

"Why is it chasing us?" Mari screamed as they ducked in among the crates again.

"It saw us first," Alain explained. "Dragons are not very intelligent. I told you that as well." She gave him a murderous look. Perhaps it was not the best time to remind Mari that he had already told her things. "It will keep after its target until that target is destroyed or for as long as the dragon can move."

"Tell me you're not serious!" Mari jerked to a halt as the shape of the dragon loomed before them, its head above the level of the crates as it searched the open aisles between. Catching sight of them, the dragon roared, revealing a mouthful of daggerlike teeth as it slammed into the intervening crates to try to reach them.

Mari stood her ground, her expression determined, holding her weapon with both hands as she fired several times, the sounds of the shots echoing deafeningly from the crates around them. Her projectiles glanced off the scales with bursts of sparks, just as useless against the dragon's armor as the weapons of the Dark Mechanics had been.

Mari's attack had caused the dragon to pause for a moment, giving Alain time to concentrate. He built as powerful a fireball as he could manage in the time available, then placed it against the monster's head.

Nearby wooden crates exploded into flaming fragments as the dragon roared with pain as well as fury this time. The scales on one side of its head had been blackened with heat, but it did not seem to have been hurt badly.

Mari grabbed Alain again and pulled him along into the maze of crates, taking lefts and rights in quick succession. They ran past some of the Dark Mechanics, also fleeing with no more thought of trying to catch intruders. "Was that your best shot?" Mari gasped as she leaned against some crates to catch her breath.

"Do you mean was that my most powerful fire? Yes," Alain admitted. "I still need to grow my abilities."

"Great. My weapon can't kill it and neither can yours." Mari stared forward, her face intent. "It's going to keep after us until it's dead?"

"It is not alive—"

"Answer the question!"

"Yes," Alain said. "It will kill or destroy anyone and anything else that gets in its way before then, of course. If we survive long enough, the creature's spell will expire even if it has not been destroyed."

"How long is long enough?"

Alain spread his hands. "Perhaps a few days."

"That's way too long." Mari paused as a hissing sound came to them over the sounds of the dragon crashing through the crates. "I thought you said they didn't hiss."

"That is not the dragon," Alain said, trying to identify the sound and failing.

"It's the steam boiler on the barge," Mari gasped. "The Dark Mechanics fired it up before this mess started and they've forgotten about it." Her eyes lit with hope. "We've got another weapon, Alain."

"We do?"

"Yeah. We just have to survive long enough to get to it." As if summoned by her words, the dragon's head appeared, darting down toward them, crates splintering and flying to either side as it lunged. Mari held her weapon in both hands again, now looking stubborn as well as scared, aiming carefully as the dragon reared back for another strike.

She fired a single shot.

Alain saw the projectile from Mari's weapon hit just beneath one eye and shatter, fragments pelting the dragon's eye. It screamed in rage and pain, the sound so intense the air itself seemed to pulse with its power.

"Go left!" Mari urged, darting past the creature's blinded side as she grabbed Alain once more and led them through a couple of more turns before skidding to a halt as they faced a solid wall of crates. "We're dead."

"No." Alain concentrated, even though his strength was draining rapidly. For a moment he wondered if he could manage the spell, but as his fear for Mari peaked he felt her presence more strongly, felt the thread between them, and sensed a small additional surge of strength from somewhere. An opening appeared in the crates before them. Mari dashed through the opening, Alain following. Moments later he heard the dragon crashing around in the area they had left, trying to figure out where its prey could have gone.

Mari headed back into the open area, running toward the barge. The leader of the Dark Mechanics, scurrying past in another direction, turned to face them with a livid expression and opened her mouth, but when Mari pointed her weapon at her, the Dark Mechanic wheeled away and ran.

With a leap, Mari jumped onto the barge's deck, running to the big Mechanic creature she called a boiler. Alain followed, seeing the dragon's head where it was floundering through the crates, hurling aside broken wood and the occasional Dark Mechanic as it searched for Mari and Alain. But they and the barge were to the monster's left, unseen thanks to the damage done by Mari's last shot.

Mari was crouched near a very large barrel which radiated heat, her hands spinning some wheels attached to it or on things leading into or out of it. "Wire or rope. We need wire or rope," she gasped.

Alain looked around, faded memories of his earliest years on his parents' farm coming back to him. He spotted a coil hanging from a hook. "Will this do?"

She grabbed it gratefully. "I hope so." Hastening to one side of the barrel, Mari started winding the rope around something high up, over and over again until all of the rope had been used up, then knotting it hastily.

Alain took another look at the dragon, which had reduced most of the crates to splinters and was digging through the remains while the few surviving Dark Mechanics near it tried to crawl away.

Mari came up beside Alain and grabbed his arm, not to direct him this time but apparently for comfort. Her face was very pale and her eyes frightened, but she spoke with forced calm. "All right. I've opened the fuel valves all the way. The pressure in that boiler is going up fast, but I closed off the steam exhaust pipes and I've tied down the relief valve. When the pressure gets high enough the boiler will explode with enough force to hurt even something like that dragon. I hope."

"You are frightened of this boiler," Alain said.

"Alain, an over-pressured boiler is incredibly destructive. It may well kill us instead of the dragon, but it's our only chance."

Alain nodded. "How do we get the dragon here when your device explodes?"

"If the boiler is close enough to blowing, having that monster step on it or crash into it will finish the job," Mari explained. "As to how to get it here, I was hoping you knew how to do that. Being that you're my expert on dragons."

"The only way to get it here is to show it a reason." Alain nodded again, this time slowly, not having to think through his decision. "One of us must act as bait, so I will—"

"*No!*" Mari shouted. "You will not act as bait! You can't judge when the boiler is close to blowing, and I won't let you die saving me! Nor will I leave you or anyone else to face something like this alone. Is that understood, Alain? If that's what we have to do, then I'll do it while you go—"

It was Alain's turn to interrupt. "I cannot allow you to die saving me. I will not leave, either."

She glared at him, then unexpectedly smiled in a sad way. "You're as stubborn as I am, Alain. We'll do it together. All right? When I give the word, follow me and run like your life depends on it, because it will." Her hand shifted from his arm, reaching down to clasp his hand tightly.

They waited, Mari glancing back at the Mechanic device behind them. Alain took a firmer grip on the bag containing his robes, surprised that he had not lost it during all of the running and fighting. He could feel the increasing heat coming off the boiler and hear it roaring and hissing ever louder. Metal pinged and groaned in a way that sounded more frightening than the dragon did.

Her hand gripped his, and even amid the fear and danger he marveled at the feeling that came with that contact. *If we die holding hands in this way, will we enter the next dream together?*

Mari took one more look at the Mechanic boiler, bit her lip, then looked at him. "I'm going to say this because in another minute we may be dead, and I don't want to die not having told you. I love you."

Before he could reply, or even try to grasp her words, Mari had aimed her weapon at where the dragon was still rooting around in the mess of broken and battered crates. "Hey, ugly!" she yelled. "Come and get some!" She fired, the projectile sparking off the side of the dragon.

Its head jerked around, the right eye finally focusing on Mari and Alain, then the creature leaped out of the wreckage around it and dashed straight for them.

Mari stood, her face paler than ever, her hand holding the weapon shaking. Her other hand still gripped Alain's. "Now," she breathed, then burst into motion like a scared cat.

Alain tried not to slow them down as Mari scrambled over the deck of the barge, the dragon roaring as it came on behind but its cries not matching the rising thunder from the Mechanic boiler inside the barge.

The dragon was almost to the barge when Mari reached the bow. "Dive deep and stay down!" she yelled as they jumped.

The water swallowed them into a strange silence and cold, the noise of the Mechanic device and that of the dragon muted and distorted. Alain had lost his grip on Mari when they hit the water, but he did as she said, stroking downward until he reached the mud of the bottom and trying to hold himself there.

The world shook.

A wave of pressure swept across Alain, hurling him tumbling through water suddenly opaque with mud swept from the bottom. Half-stunned by the force of the wave, Alain struggled to reach the surface. He broke it, taking in a deep lungful of air, wondering why the lights inside the warehouse were all gone, and only slowly realizing that he still had a death-grip on his bag.

Heavy objects were splashing into the water around him. Alain looked upward, baffled, seeing stars in the night sky through a massive hole framed by shattered fragments of the warehouse roof. Pieces of the warehouse flung high into the air were still falling back to the ground.

Looking around, Alain saw that the warehouse walls were also shattered. The entire part of the barge above the waterline had almost vanished, and the pier it had been tied to had been reduced to matchsticks.

Off to one side, the massive bulk of the dragon twitched, then lay unmoving, apparently hurled there by the force of the Mechanic boiler's explosion.

Where is Mari? Alain looked around frantically. Finally spotting a dark jacket, Alain lunged that way through the water.

Mari was floating on her back, more badly stunned than Alain had been. But her eyes were open and focused. "Are you all right?" he gasped.

"Uh...yeah." He helped her to the pier, where they painfully climbed up the remains of the wood to the floor of the warehouse. Mari glanced back at the dead dragon and the wreckage. "This is why you don't tie down relief valves on boilers," she said in a voice almost as calm as that of a Mage, as if she were giving a lecture.

"How did we survive?" Alain wondered.

"The boiler was above the water when it blew, so almost all of the force vented above and to the sides, unfortunately for the dragon and fortunately for us. I did plan on that, you know." Mari shook her head and looked around. "We've got to get out of here before people come to investigate this. Are the Dark Mages still around?"

"I do not sense any nearby. If any of them had come close to the warehouse, they probably regretted it when your Mechanic boiler exploded."

"Yeah. Come on." They staggered to their feet and stumbled through the wreckage. Getting out was fairly simple, since most of the warehouse walls had been blown out. People bearing torches and oil lights were running toward them, and Mari led Alain off at an angle. More people appeared, though, coming their way fast. Finding a dark alcove, Mari pulled Alain in with her, waiting as rescuers dashed past heading for the warehouse.

They were close together inside the alcove. Alain could feel her body moving as Mari tried to catch her breath, could feel the warmth of her. He felt an urge to pull her even closer and fought it off only with great difficulty. Then Alain heard her breath shudder.

"You stayed with me," Mari whispered, and a moment later one of her hands grabbed one of his again.

"I would not leave you to face danger alone," Alain answered, wondering once more at the sensations inside him from her touch.

Mari's voice turned despairing as she held his hand tightly. "I am in so much trouble."

"No one can blame you for what happened in the warehouse."

"Oh, you big, dumb, wonderful Mage, I'm not talking about the warehouse. Do...do you like me? A lot?"

"Yes, Mari."

"Oh, no," she groaned.

"You said...on the barge...you said..." He could not seem to get the words out.

"Yeah. I did."

"Did you...?"

"Yeah. I meant it." Her hand released his and both arms came around him, her hug so tight as to be almost painful. "But, Alain...oh, blazes...we can't."

His mind filled with a roaring in which the only thing outside himself was her. Alain's arms came around her loosely, awkwardly. He had not held anyone in so long, not since being taken by the Mages, that he was not sure how to do it.

The moment ended as Mari abruptly broke her grip on him. "We... we should go," she said as she stumbled away.

He followed, wondering what had just happened, as they went out into the growing crowd on this roadway. In the dark, the fact that they were soaking wet wasn't obvious, and they were able to move through the onlookers until the crowds thinned out and Mari could find a deserted street.

Only then did she lean against a wall, looking at Alain with a wan smile. "Do you know, back when I was taking Basic Steam Engine Mechanics the instructor told us 'Never tie down a safety valve. The only one of you who would ever do that is probably Apprentice Mari, but I hope even she will avoid doing it just to see what happens.' And I did do it!" Mari said with a forced laugh.

Alain had been taught so stringently not to laugh that he could not summon the same hilarity even amid the elation of unlooked-for survival, but he was barely able to avoid smiling. "Our elders should be impressed by what we accomplished, but somehow I do not think they will be."

"You're amazing, Alain!" Mari's smile became rueful. "I can't believe we survived that. Go ahead. Say it."

"Say what?" Alain asked.

"You know what I mean! You were right. Going in that warehouse was a dangerous thing to do."

Alain shook his head. "Yes, but together we were able to handle the danger, and the Dark Mechanic threat to you in Dorcastle has very likely been eliminated. You were also right."

"I was also right? Ohhh nooo." Mari had lost all of her attempt at humor, once again sounding as despairing as she had when they were in the alcove together. "You have the perfect chance to say 'I told you so,' but instead you find a way to say I was right, too. What's the matter with you, Alain? You listen to me, you believe in me, you respect me and you care about me. You're honest and smart and brave and resourceful. You never ask for anything for yourself and you're always there when I need you. Where are your flaws? You were supposed to have *flaws*. Do you have to be *perfect*? Except for what I can fix, that voice and that face that doesn't show anything?"

"I am not perfect," Alain objected. "All of those things you said, they are true of you. You listen to me, you believe..." He had trouble bringing out the words for a moment. "You are also smart and brave, and can do anything, it seems. You have saved me when it seemed impossible. Mari, do you know how hard it is to slay a dragon? Any Mage who can do so earns great respect. We have survived. I do not understand why you are upset."

Mari shook her head. "I'm unhappy because I wanted to find those flaws so I could find reasons not to feel...like I do. I wanted to learn about all of the things wrong with you. And you just wouldn't cooperate. This can't work, Alain! It can't happen! Don't you know that? What will your Guild do to you if they know about me? Tell me the truth."

He knew some emotions were showing on his face, knew she could see bewilderment and something else, something he could not comprehend, but he could not control his expression at this moment. "It did work, Mari. We have found those behind the dragon illusion, we have destroyed their creation and the place they worked from—"

"That's not what I'm talking about." Mari was slumping against the wall now, her expression distressed, her eyes fixed on him. "You *know* that's not what I'm talking about. And you're not answering my question."

His stomach seemed to be tying itself into a knot. "I..."

"Do you feel anything?" She was pleading now. "Am I being a total idiot? You said you like me. Do you? Do you know what that means? Are there emotions still buried down inside you or have I just imagined that?"

"I...feel." He stared back at her, wondering what his face revealed.

"It's my fault, isn't it? You were all right before you met me, you were a Mage and you were happy."

It was Alain's turn to shake his head. "I am still a Mage. I was not happy. I did not know what happiness was. I had forgotten. But now I have met you and I remember some things and feel other things that—"

"No!" Mari turned her face away from him. "Don't say it. It's impossible. Now answer my question, Alain. What will your Guild do to you if they learn that...that a Mechanic is in love with you."

"That would be a cause for discussion," Alain said. "Cause to decide if I could exploit the situation for the good of the Mage Guild. Cause to debate what should be done to her. But I would be eliminated as a danger to the Mage Guild if my Guild learned that I was...in...love... with a Mechanic."

"Are you really?" Mari asked, her eyes searching his. "Stars above, you are. I've messed up everything."

She seemed to need some praise, some commendation to make her feel better. Alain, who had been taught as an acolyte never to say nice things, cast around for anything, saying whatever he could think of. "You do not mess up all things. You have defeated the dragons of Dorcastle." She almost smiled. He could see it. What else to say? Discuss her abilities, just as if she were a fellow Mage. "You are a very dangerous person, Master Mechanic Mari."

Mari finally turned a sad smile on him. "Maybe I'm more dangerous than I ever realized. I never thought of myself as the sort of girl who could ruin a guy's life. Didn't anyone ever warn you that girls can be dangerous, Alain?"

"I have often been warned lately how dangerous girl Mechanics can be."

"You're dangerous, too. In all the good ways and all the bad ways." She shook her head. "Alain, we're talking about a relationship that endangers your life."

"It endangers yours as well. That is more important."

"No, it isn't." Mari covered her face with both hands. "I really have to think. Not here. Not now. Alain, you need to get back to your Guild Hall so you don't get tied into this, and I need to call my Guild Hall so they can get some Mechanics down here to take over what's left of the warehouse. There's no telling what Mechanic devices might have survived the explosion."

"And your fellow Mechanics will get to see the dragon," Alain added, still desperately trying to make her feel better.

"Yeah." Mari managed another smile. "Those Dark Mechanics were pretending to be dragons, and an actual dragon came in and whomped them. How's that for poetic justice?" She sighed, reaching into her jacket. "Good thing I had this in a waterproof pack. I hope the shock of the boiler explosion didn't break it. Um, you're not seeing or hearing anything, all right?"

Alain nodded. "Yes, Mari."

Bringing out a dark box as long as her lower arm, Mari held the box near her mouth, then spoke as if talking to someone. After waiting a while, she talked into the box again. Finally Alain heard the faint sound of someone answering her, as if that person was in the box but also far away. Mari and the box voice talked for a while, then she put the box away. "That's it, my...Alain. You need to be gone before the other Mechanics get here." She sounded very weary as well as sad now.

"How will I know you are safe? If I see someone coming, how will I know they are your friends?"

She thought about that. "Go somewhere where you can see me. I'll stay here. If I see the people I expect to see, I'll wave. So when you see that wave, you'll know everything's fine."

"I will do as you say." Alain felt a terrible reluctance to leave, overpowered by emotions he had forgotten how to deal with, or never learned to deal with. For a moment, Mari's status as the daughter of the prophecy meant nothing. For a moment, only she mattered. "Mari, I did not know that I could ever feel like—"

"*Don't*, Alain. *Please.*" She saw his face. "Oh, I'm so sorry. I've been so selfish. I wanted you around because I trust you and because you make me happy and now..."

"I make you happy?" Alain asked, unable to believe what he had heard.

"We can't— Yes."

Alain hesitated. "You do not seem happy."

"I'm unhappy because you make me happy," Mari sighed. "If I wasn't so glad to be around you I wouldn't be so upset."

"I do not understand."

"For once, I don't blame you," she said. "I feel very confused, too. I need a little time, Alain. You need...you need some girl who can fly on a giant bird with you."

"Why cannot you be that girl?" he asked.

"Firstly, because I think it's impossible for a bird that big to actually fly, and I can prove it using equations, and secondly, because your fellow Mages will kill me. After they kill you." Mari made a confused gesture. "This is just like me. I can't fall in love with some regular guy, a Mechanic or even a common. I have to fall in love with a Mage. But sometimes love means giving something up, Alain. And we may have to do that. I need to think and I need to see how my Guild reacts to what's happened tonight and what I learned. When I can talk, I'll leave my Guild Hall and be somewhere on one of the walls. Can you still find me?"

Alain nodded, wondering why his insides felt so heavy. "Always."

"Always." She repeated the word softly, staring into his eyes, then took a deep breath. "We...we'll talk. I promise. I have to... What am I going to do? I don't know yet. I'll be on the walls somewhere, in a day or so. Maybe three. I promise. Maybe by then..." Mari shook her head. "Tell your Guild that the dragon problem should be solved. That should make you look good, right? Now you'd better go. I don't know how long it'll take the other Mechanics to get here."

"You will be safe?" he asked.

"I'll be very careful," Mari said. "I promise."

He hesitated, looking at her, wanting to say more, but Mari bit her lip and shook her head again, and Alain turned and walked away, turmoil filling him. He walked fast, trying to outrun something even though he did not know what it was, until he reached a place where two adjacent warehouses left a shadowed gap between them. Alain went to the gap, sliding into the deeper darkness and gazing back at where Mari waited.

He finally had time to think. He had not worn his Mage robes, but he had been forced to use some spells. Someone in that warehouse might have seen enough to realize that Mari had a Mage working with her. Did Dark Mages know enough of the prophecy to realize what that would mean? Did the Mechanics Guild?

Mari stood on the deserted road, the dark of her Mechanics jacket blending into the raven of her hair and both matching the shadows so that she seemed to be fading into the night. Time passed slowly, but eventually Alain heard the sounds of numerous people approaching through the otherwise silent area. Moments later, a group of Mechanics came into view, moving quickly.

Mari raised her arm and waved slowly and deliberately, holding her arm aloft an extra-long time before letting it fall.

He stayed a while longer, watching as the Mechanics reached Mari, waiting until the entire group headed back toward the ruins of the Dark Mechanic warehouse. As the last Mechanic vanished from sight,

Alain pulled out his Mage robes, soaking wet inside his bag, and put on the dripping garment. It would dry on the long walk to the Mage Guild Hall, and the wetness and the cold might help distract from the strange sensations filling him.

Mari had said she loved him. Why had it made her sad? Alain knew emotions and relationships only as negatives, as distractions which his elders had sought to drive from the spirits of every acolyte, the greatest error any Mage could fall into. But even though he felt terrible right now, he also felt a remarkable sense of joy. Love was very bizarre.

Alain paused in the street, held his hand before him, and concentrated. Intense heat flared above his palm. When its power had peaked he sent the ball of fire high above to vanish into the sky over Dorcastle. *Is this strange feeling actually love? I believe that it is. But I have not lost my powers. I feel instead strength beyond anything that I had before. What road is this I have found?*

How can I do what is right to protect the daughter of the prophecy, to stop the storm, if all I can think of is Mari?

He struck off for the Mage Guild Hall through a night which seemed darker than before, wondering how he would explain knowing that the dragons of Dorcastle had been vanquished.

CHAPTER SEVENTEEN

By the time the next morning that Alain found himself standing before another Inquiry, he still had not come up with a good explanation. He could not make out the shadowed faces of the three Mage elders, but he was certain the old female Mage was not among their number.

"We have confirmed your report that the Mechanics were involved in this dragon incident, Mage Alain," one of the elders said in a voice that held no warmth, no approval or gratitude, just the emotionless tones of a Mage.

A second elder spoke, her voice actually emptier of feeling than that of the first elder. "How did you learn of this?"

"I was at the inner harbor last night, having spent much time in meditation." If he was going to make up a story, it might as well be one that cast him in a good light. "I saw Mechanics fighting among each other, and thought more knowledge of this incident would be important to the Mage Guild. I used a concealment spell to move among them and saw one of their creations which could have done the damage lately attributed to dragons."

"How fortunate that you were in the proper place to do this," the third elder said dispassionately. "Were you in the company of a female that night, Mage Alain?"

Alain paused. "A common.–She—"

"You were in the company of this same female through much of the day."

Had they been watching him? Or was it a guess? He had best assume they knew. "Yes."

"You wore the clothes of a common, Mage Alain. Why?"

They had been watching him. But he still had an acceptable explanation to offer. "I desired physical companionship, the company of a female."

"We do not doubt that part of your story, Mage Alain." The elders spoke very quietly among each other, so that Alain could not hear, then the first addressed him again. "Physical needs can distract from wisdom, especially in young male Mages. We know this. The Guild accepts that Mages must find means to satisfy physical distractions. But we also know that this female common resembled the Mechanic you were with in the desert and in Dorcastle."

They knew a great deal more than he had expected. Alain's attempts to fabricate a story were diverted by speculations about how badly he might be punished. About whether he would leave this room alive. It surprised him not at all that the overriding worry in his mind was not fear over his own possible death but rather fear that he might not be able to tell Mari what had happened to him. What if she thought he had lied, had decided to walk away from her? "The female did resemble the Mechanic," Alain finally said.

"Do you desire that Mechanic, Mage Alain?"

Lie. Lie better than he ever had before, or see himself dead before this day ended. "No." Had the single word been as emotionless as it sounded to him? "She is a Mechanic."

"Exactly. A shadow, an enemy of our Guild, a creature who no doubt seeks to destroy your powers. Do you understand this, Mage Alain? You have sought a taste of that which is forbidden, using a female common as your vessel. In one so young such behavior will occur, but it must not occur again. It could lead you into the arms of the Mechanic herself, and if once she ensnares you then you will never be free again, and your powers will dwindle to ashes. Do you understand?"

Alain fought to keep elation from showing. The elders had misinterpreted what they had seen. "This one understands."

"And the Dark Mages?" one of the elders asked. "You saw their dragon?"

"Yes, elder. Its remains were in the warehouse used by the Mechanics."

One of the elders let some glee into his voice. "A perfect opportunity. We will tell all that the dragon was used by our Guild to halt the schemes of the Mechanics." The other elders made noises of agreement.

The woman's voice held no hint of feeling as she once again addressed Alain, though. "You saw the devices of the Mechanics?"

"I did."

"You say you understood them?"

"No, elder." At least this did not call for a lie. "I saw items which resembled the claws of dragons. But the other Mechanic devices I could not understand at all."

"You studied these devices?" another elder asked.

"No. They made noise. They created heat. That is all I know."

"It is all any Mage needs to know," the elder declared. "The Mechanic tricks might have harmed you, but in that at least you acted wisely by avoiding them. Despite your errors, your service to the Guild has been valuable, Mage Alain. But an issue remains."

He waited, trying to reveal nothing.

"You have been about Mechanics often of late. You have revealed a fascination with one of their females. Our inquiries show that this female may be young, but she is still very dangerous."

It felt strange to hear the elder using the same words which Alain had employed last night, but not with the intent of praising Mari. Alain confined himself to a nod, not sure what his voice might reveal.

"You are to inform your elders immediately," the elder continued, "if this Mechanic attempts to attach herself to you again, or if you see her even at a distance. If she proves to be a danger to our Guild, if she once again seeks you out, then she will be eliminated as a warning to the Mechanics. They will have no proof, but they will know who did this thing."

Alain surprised himself, his voice sounding so very, very unemotional as he heard a conditional death sentence uttered against Mari. "This one understands."

"Mage Alain," the third elder said. "The Guild will not tolerate dangers to it, in any form. No Mage must tolerate the presence of a Mechanic. Do you understand?"

"This one understands." That had been a direct warning to him, and perhaps a veiled reference to the prophecy. Obey, or else. Stay away from Mechanics, or else. He remembered one night a few years ago, a rebellious acolyte driven past endurance who had tried attacking an elder, long knives flashing in the night, another elder warning Alain: *"All enemies of the Mage Guild must be dealt with."* But now he feared for himself less than he did for Mari.

"You are dismissed."

Alain walked from the room, part of him noticing with some surprise that his gait was steady despite the tremors he felt inside. *They will kill her if they see her with me. Even if they do not realize she is the daughter. They cannot know that yet, or I would not have left that room alive. But if we are seen together again, they will suspect, and if they suspect then they will kill her. Mari was right. I must leave her. Not to protect myself, but to protect her. She cannot bring about the new day, she cannot stop the storm, if she dies. No matter what pain it brings me, I must ensure Master Mechanic Mari is safe. And the only way to do that is not to be anywhere near her until my Guild ceases to watch me.*

He thought of her waiting on the wall for him, and his resolve wavered. *I must warn her. That also I must do. Then we will part, for Mari must not die on my account.*

The new day, stopping the storm that threatened this world, had dwindled in significance inside him. All that Alain could think of was that he had found happiness, and now he must cast it away.

✳   ✳   ✳

Mari sat in an uncomfortable chair before a long table deep within the Mechanics Guild Hall of Dorcastle. Sitting at the other side of the table were three Senior Mechanics. The man Saco, the woman who had belittled her at the wrecked trestle, and a third man Mari hadn't seen before. The door behind Mari was thick and had been closed tightly after she entered the room. She took another look at the expressions of the Senior Mechanics facing her. *If this isn't what a prisoner feels like, it must be close. You would think I was one of the Dark Mechanics instead of the person who uncovered them.*

The woman spoke in a formal, detached voice. "This proceeding is convened to resolve questions regarding the actions of Master Mechanic Mari of Caer Lyn in the city of Dorcastle the night before."

The male Senior Mechanic whom Mari hadn't seen before spoke brusquely. "What led you to the inner harbor last night?"

Mari kept her head up and eyes on the man as she answered. She had nothing to apologize for and wouldn't be intimidated. "I'd been looking into the acts supposedly carried out by dragons. I conducted an independent inquiry, examining the evidence available, and concluded that the barge docks probably held the answer to events which had been causing harm to the Guild by restricting trade in this city." She had been rehearsing that statement in her head ever since last night while she waited for her fellow Mechanics to arrive. She had known it would be necessary, and it had also been a way to try to avoid thinking about Alain.

Senior Mechanic Saco glared at her. "What made you think you had any right to conduct an independent inquiry?"

"I had no alternative. My attempts to discuss my theories with the leadership of the Mechanics Guild were rebuffed. Since Senior Mechanics refused to listen to me or to respond to formal requests submitted using proper procedures, I was forced to take action alone for the good of the Guild." *Let them put that in their record of the proceeding.*

Apparently none of them wished to pursue that angle, though. Saco frowned at her as he changed the subject. "Alone? You say you acted alone? Your report is extremely vague on how the boiler in the warehouse came to explode, and how you managed to survive that."

Mari met his gaze, keeping her face composed. "As I said in my report, the people in the warehouse were distracted by a visitor while getting up steam. Apparently they let the pressure get too high. I was far enough distant to avoid harm when it blew."

"We found the relief valve for the boiler," the third Senior Mechanic stated in a hard voice. "It had been tied down."

Mari nodded, determined to tell the truth where she could. "I did that while the people were distracted."

"Did you have any help?"

"Tying down the relief valve? No." As she had phrased it, the answer was literally true. Mari thanked the luck that had left Alain's presence at the warehouse last night unknown to her own Guild. How could she have explained the identity of a mysterious ally there?

"How did you come to be soaking wet when the Mechanics from this Guild Hall met you?" the female Senior Mechanic asked.

"I dove into the harbor to protect myself from the blast. I know steam boilers, and I could tell when that one was about to explode."

The woman's stare pinned Mari. "Then you are willing to swear that no other Mechanic aided you in this? That there was no other Mechanic accompanying you at that warehouse last night?"

That one was easy. "I swear there was no other Mechanic aiding me last night," Mari said. "There was no other Mechanic with me at the warehouse, not until Mechanics from this Guild Hall arrived in a group to meet me."

"Were there any commons with you? One or more?"

"No. I swear there was no common with me." They wouldn't ask about Mages. Mari was sure of that. The possibility would not even occur to them.

They didn't. The three Senior Mechanics exchanged glances, none of them looking happy, then the woman nodded. "The proceeding is closed. Master Mechanic Mari, you are ordered by authority of the Guild Master not to say anything to anyone regarding any of these events. You are to forget them. They did not happen."

There it was again. She had found so much proof, she had been hoping it would change something, but... Mari took a deep breath. "I respectfully ask for an explanation of the Guild's policy in this matter."

"You have your orders," Saco noted in a cold voice.

"Yes, sir. But I can best serve the Guild if I understand the Guild's policies and instructions, and I do not understand this."

The third Senior Mechanic shook his head. "Your reputation precedes you, Mechanic Mari."

"Master Mechanic Mari."

"Certainly. The point is, you're always asking questions instead of doing what you're told. From this point on, that changes. Do you understand that?"

Mari took a couple of slow breaths. "Yes, sir."

"Are there further questions?"

She couldn't help herself. She knew she shouldn't, but she couldn't help herself. "Yes, sir."

The third Senior Mechanic looked incredulous, but Saco gave Mari an insincere smile. "Go ahead."

"The contents of the warehouse, sir." *Careful, Mari. Careful how you say this.* "They—"

The woman interrupted. "By order of the Guild Master, the warehouse held nothing."

Mari stared at the three Senior Mechanics. *Nothing.* She hadn't even tried to bring up the dragon's carcass, impossible to miss, knowing the Senior Mechanics would ignore the existence of the remains. "Those who were in the warehouse—"

"There was no one in the warehouse except some commons who died in the accident."

"—and escaped before the explosion—" Mari tried to continue.

"There is no one who meets that description."

What had happened to them? Had they escaped the city? Or been taken into custody by the Mechanics Guild, disappearing as completely as Mechanic Rindal had?

Mari swallowed and tried one more time. "The boiler that exploded—"

"There was no boiler."

The boiler we just talked about no longer ever existed. Because its existence would be inconvenient. "So we pretend that something real doesn't exist? How does that make us any better than the Mages?"

Saco leaned forward, the false smile gone. "That is a treasonous statement."

"No, sir! I want the best for my Guild! I am loyal to my Guild! But something is wrong. Something is wrong with the world! If we don't change— "

"Change?" the woman demanded. "Think through the consequences of change," she advised Mari in the tone of a teacher speaking to a not very bright student. "Think what would happen to this Guild. Think what would happen to this world. Think of the upheaval of all that we know, to be replaced by what? Do you know? Can you even guess? You're eighteen years old, girl! You don't even have a good grasp on how things are yet. How can you say that altering the system our ancestors created would be a good thing? How can you say they were wrong?"

Mari stared back at the woman. "Things are breaking," she said as calmly as she could. "If things were breaking on a machine, I would analyze the problem and find out what needed to be fixed."

The woman smiled insincerely. "That is a good attitude for a Mechanic. You would also call in a specialist, correct? Someone who knew more than you did about that particular machine. And you would listen to them, as you must listen to us now. Learn. Grow. With time you'll come to understand why things *must* be this way. For the benefit of all."

The female Senior Mechanic leveled a finger at Mari, her face suddenly as stern as the stone in the walls of Dorcastle. "You've got real gifts, girl. Your skills as a Mechanic are obvious, and achieving Master Mechanic status at your age was a remarkable achievement. You could have a great future in the Guild, *if* you take advantage of the offer you're about to get."

The woman leaned back. "Because you've done the Guild a service in Dorcastle, and because of your undeniable skills, the Guild is willing to forget any of your recent words and actions which contradict the rules and guidance the Guild expects us all to live by. But only if you vow to remain silent on events here and to abide by every Guild rule and guidance to the letter."

Mari looked back at the three Senior Mechanics, thinking through her choices, seeing in their faces that her earlier fears had been true. The definition of treason to the Guild was far wider than she had once believed, far wider than had ever been publicly stated. Treason involved anything that the Senior Mechanics and the Guild Master didn't want to deal with, anything they wanted to ignore, anything that might rock the boat. The leadership of her Guild would silence anyone who threatened the way things were. Possibilities which Mari would never have considered a couple of months ago now seemed all too real. Professor S'san must have known the sort of dangers which Mari would face, but what good was the pistol S'san had given her against threats like these? The weapon had helped save her and Alain in the warehouse, but what use was it against a threat from her own Guild? *It is not to be depended upon as a first resort, or a second, or even a third. Your greatest assets will always be your mind and your ability to act on wise decisions. Fail to make proper use of those assets, and the weapon cannot save you.*

Listen, learn, and obey. That was what the Senior Mechanics facing her were demanding. Just like when she was an apprentice. Maybe what was needed now wasn't a weapon or the tools of a Mechanic, but the tools of an apprentice. *In the event of emergency, take all necessary actions to minimize damage and loss of life.* One of the first basic rules an apprentice learned. It certainly applied now.

Mari nodded to the Senior Mechanics. "I vow to abide by every Guild rule and regulation, and to say nothing about recent events."

But I'm not saying for how long.

Saco leaned forward again. "Your vow includes the things you said a short while ago. You don't say them again. To anyone. Not even yourself."

Mari nodded, knowing her voice was trembling with anger but hoping the Senior Mechanics would read that as fear. "I vow not to speak of those things." *For at least a few minutes.*

"What about Mages?" Saco insisted. "Do you have questions about them?"

Mari stared back silently for a moment, images of Alain tumbling through her head. She had spent some hopeful moments last night wondering if perhaps her Guild would be open to learning more about Mages once it had proof the Dark Mechanics existed.—Perhaps—her fantasies had briefly soared—they would even offer a Mage refuge if he were willing to tell other Mechanics the things he had told her. But the proof of Dark Mechanics had been ruthlessly suppressed. That offered no reason to believe proof of Mage abilities would be treated any differently.

And if they knew she loved a Mage?

If these Senior Mechanics were willing to threaten a fellow Mechanic, they would surely treat a Mage with no mercy at all.

If he stays around me, somebody will kill him, either another Mage or a Mechanic. All right. I love him. That means this time I let him go. I can't let him die because of me. "No," Mari said out loud. "Why should I question the Guild's position on Mages?"

"Even though you spent time in a Mage's company?" Saco pressed.

"After the caravan was destroyed? I already explained at Ringhmon that nothing happened except a shared road. I did what I had to do then to survive," Mari said. "I know what I have to do now to survive."

She knew how she meant that, but Mari also knew they would interpret the statement as one of surrender.

"Good," the female Senior Mechanic declared as Saco leaned back again, not hiding his disappointment. "It's nice to see that you are finally learning. Be aware that the Guild's mercy is limited. There will be no second chance. You know the penalty for violating such an oath."

Mari nodded. "I understand."

"Then I declare this matter closed," the woman said. "No one here is to speak of anything which we have discussed."

The woman gave Mari a polite smile, as if Mari had just entered the room. "I have good news for you." She pushed a sheet of paper toward Mari.

Mari managed to pick it up without revealing her tension. "A contract. On such short notice."

"Yes. We knew you would be pleased at this opportunity to further serve your Guild. Fair travel, Mechanic Mari."

"Master Mechanic Mari."

"Of course. Master Mechanic Mari." The woman indicated the contract. "You'll notice that your services are needed on a priority basis, so you will have to leave Dorcastle as soon as we can make travel arrangements."

Mari looked down at the contract. "Thank you. I look forward to leaving Dorcastle...so I can continue serving my Guild." If they had noticed her brief pause, they gave no sign. The woman indicated that Mari could leave, and the three Senior Mechanics began talking in low voices.

Mari stood up, opening the heavy door and walking out into the hallways of the Guild Hall. Familiar hallways, following the standard floor plan for every Mechanics Guild Hall. She had walked down essentially identical hallways countless times.

Not since she had been eight years old and newly arrived at the Guild Hall in Caer Lyn had Mari noticed just how restricting those hallways could feel, how instead of giving a sense of security could create a sense of being confined. How the shadows and the alcoves could easily hide someone watching, or someone waiting with a weapon at hand. It was funny how the world around her could alter even when its outward appearance hadn't seemed to change. Alain would tell her that it was just a matter of how you looked at an illusion.

Mari squared her shoulders and walked steadily down the halls, determined not to show any sign of fear. Who could she talk to? No one here, that was for sure. Any Mechanic possibly sympathetic to her would be watched, and every Mechanic here had doubtless been warned again about associating with Mari.

But if any Senior Mechanics plan on taking down Master Mechanic Mari, they'll find that I'm not that easy to stop. Everything else I once thought true may now be in doubt, but I still believe that. I still believe in myself.

And I still believe in doing the right thing even when it costs me. Things need to be fixed. I need to fix them if no one else will. But first I need to play nice for a while, get the Senior Mechanics off my back and find more people I can trust.

Someone I can trust.

What am I going to tell Alain when I have to say goodbye?

Mari stood inside a turret on the battlements of one of Dorcastle's walls, leaning on the edge of a narrow firing slit. She looked down to the sea, where ships were once again leaving harbor, riding low in the water with their holds packed full of cargo. The wind blew hard from along the coast, buffeting flocks of sea gulls screaming over scraps of food. Picking the lock on the gate leading into this bartizan hadn't been too difficult, and no one could see her in here, concealed by the darkness inside the turret.

A chip knocked out of the stone fortification marred one edge of the firing slit. The chip had weathered to the same appearance as the rest of the stone, only its imperfections revealing its origin. A crossbow bolt, or maybe the bullet from a Mechanic rifle, had struck here a long time ago, during one of the those battles Alain had spoken of, while Imperial legions and Confederation soldiers were spilling each others' blood in the streets below. Mari stared down at those streets, wondering how many commons had died across the centuries for the purpose of maintaining the stability the Mechanics Guild desired.

Wondering how many might die within a few more years, if this world were indeed heading for some kind of horrible crack-up.

A footstep sounded nearby, and Alain was beside her, appearing out of the shadows so suddenly that Mari wondered if he had used that concealment spell. The Mage's face, which she had come to know as unrevealing of feelings, reflected concern now.

"Hi, Mage Alain," Mari said softly, fighting an urge to wrap her arms around him and hold on tight. *If you hold him, if you kiss him, you'll never be able to let him go. For his sake, Mari, keep yourself under control.*

Alain bowed his head toward her. "Greetings, Master Mechanic Mari. You have chosen a good place to meet. We will not be seen here."

"It's nice to know I made one good decision in the last few weeks. Is your Guild spying on you?"

"Yes," Alain said. "We have been watched, but this time I came carefully."

"Yeah, I'm certain that my Guild is watching me, too. Like I'm a criminal." Mari shook her head. "Are you all right? With your Guild, I mean?"

Alain considered the question. "They suspect me of being attracted to a Mechanic. They are right, but so far lack proof. They do not suspect that I love you, or who you are, but I have no doubt of what they will do if they discover either of those things."

"Oh, blazes." Mari lowered her head to rest her brow against the cool stone of the fortification. "I have ruined your life."

"You have given me back my life."

She straightened up, swiveling her head to stare at him. "I have to leave. I have a new contract. I'm not allowed to back out of it and... and I really think it's for the best anyway. I have to lie low for a while." Mari couldn't see his eyes clearly enough to tell what emotions might be revealed there.

Alain's voice stayed steady, though. "You are right. The Mage Guild is watching you. It would be unsafe for you if we were seen together. They would know what that meant."

She let out a long, slow breath. "I've found a man who keeps telling me that I'm right, and I have to give him up. Are you staying in Dorcastle?"

"No. I must leave soon as well. My own contract is far to the north, in the Free Cities."

"The Free Cities," Mari repeated, her own voice tight. She seemed to be having trouble breathing, but she got her next words out. "Alain, you must promise me that you'll take care of yourself. I don't want to see you hurt. Not physically and not...any other way."

"It is too late for that," Alain said. "I once again feel such hurt. I do not regret that, because it also brought me the ability to feel the happiness that you brought me."

She looked at him again, blinking away tears, as Alain actually tried to smile reassuringly at her. He didn't do a very good job of it, but he was trying. "At least I learned a few things about dragons, right?"

"Yes. The things that you learned may be useful again."

"I hope not. I don't want to run into any more dragons."

His voice tensed. "There are many dangers you must face. Dragons may not be the worst of those. You know this."

She shook her head, staring out the firing slit again. "You could be a little more comforting. I don't know nearly enough, Alain. So many things are wrong. I have to do something, try to fix things. But I don't know what to do."

"You will learn."

She laughed, the sound soft and bitter. "I can learn. But I will have to play by my Guild's rules while I try to figure out what to do next. Blazes, Alain, how did I mess everything up so badly? I must be the biggest idiot that Dematr has ever seen. Thank you for not blaming me, but you'd probably be happier if we'd never met."

"No. That is not so," Alain said. "My world is brighter. Every shadow seems more real now."

"You mean other people?" Mari asked. "Won't that— Can you still do that spell stuff?"

"So far," Alain assured her. "I do not know why. The thread that connects us gives me a new strength, a strength which I believe saved us in Ringhmon and perhaps here at Dorcastle. Wisdom says this cannot be."

Mari exhaled heavily. "I'm beginning to suspect that a great deal of the wisdom you and I have been fed isn't all that wise, though I can't imagine how something that isn't there can make you stronger." She swallowed and looked away, not able to stand seeing him there, so close, knowing he would be gone soon. "You ought to go. Before we get caught, before somebody sees us together."

"Be careful, Mari. You know the storm that threatens. I would not leave if it were not the best way to protect you for now. But even though the thread between us will fade with distance, even if it becomes too weak to sense at all, still I will find you again when the suspicions of my Guild have subsided."

"What?" Mari glared at him through her tears. "I'm trying to say goodbye to you! Forever. Because otherwise you would be in too much danger. Don't come looking for me. Don't die because of me."

Alain looked down, then back at her. "You are more important than I am."

"*Don't ever say that! It is not true!*"

"You know it is," Alain replied.

"I don't know any such thing," Mari said, her voice still fierce. "Why do you keep saying things like that?"

"You know why. We both know why it must not be spoken of. Farewell, Master Mechanic Mari of Caer Lyn. Until next we meet."

"No! Go away and stay safe! Farewell, Mage Alain of Ihris!" *I love you.* She heard him begin to move away, but kept her gaze fixed stubbornly out to sea.

Then he stopped. "Mari."

"Get out of here, blast you! This is already too hard!"

"I see something." She spun to look at him. "My foresight," Alain continued, staring into the shadows of the turret. "You and I are on this wall, again, not inside this fortification, but along the parapet. Time has passed. A few years, I think. We are older, but not by much. It feels as if a great deal has happened. We stand side by side and a mighty battle rages around us."

Mari looked into the darkness but saw nothing. "What else? What else is there?"

"We wear similar armbands of a strange design." Alain blinked. "The vision is gone. The way we stood with each other spoke of much history between us. We...we stood together against the storm of battle," he said, the last words coming out slowly.

Her heart seemed to pause, then beat rapidly. "What are you saying? That we're certain to be together again?"

Alain shook his head. "There is no certainty. I saw myself in the vision as well as you. The vision is but a possibility, a chance that something may come to pass, should we make the decisions which lead to it. Should we both live long enough to reach that place and time."

"What decisions? When?"

"I do not know."

"*You don't know?* Oh, that's just *great!*" Mari burst out angrily, then pointed an accusing finger at him. "I'm ready to break my heart and say goodbye forever to the only man I have ever loved, and then one of your blasted Mage spells shows up and tells me maybe something could happen if we both do the right things, but there's no telling what those things are. Do I get that right?"

"Yes, but— "

"Thanks for nothing!"

"Mari, it shows that we can survive that long. The chance exists, despite all perils. We were together, and you were still alive, still fighting. There is hope."

"I don't want to fight!" Mari said.

"But this vision tells us that our decision today is the right one," Alain insisted. "It sets us on the path to that day."

"To that battle?" Mari drew in a shuddering breath. "Who were we fighting?"

"The storm," he replied, as if that answered everything.

"Fine. We were together. So I want that future, Mage Alain. A future with you." She took a step closer to him, then managed to halt herself. "You were right, I guess. I will see you again. Someday. Somehow. You had better make the right decisions, do you hear me?"

He looked at her. "We will face many choices, any one of which made wrongly could bring an end to that possible future I saw. I will do my best. I also want that future with you, and you will have need of me in the new day you must bring to pass."

"I already need you," Mari said, "but I keep getting the feeling that you and I are talking about two different things sometimes. What new day? What storm?"

Was that a flash of puzzlement that appeared in Alain's eyes? "But you said—" His voice broke off as Alain suddenly looked down and to one side, then over in another direction. "Mages approach. They seek me. They must not find you. I must go now to lead them away."

"Alain, what—"

But he was moving, gliding silently through the shadows and out the gate, leaving Mari glaring at the empty shadows inside the turret.

You blasted Mage! Why do I keep thinking there is something you're not telling me? No. It's more like something you think I know, but I have no idea what it is. Fine. Right now I have to leave to keep you safe, so I'll do that. But I will see you again, and we will be together, and I will find out what this "new" day stuff means, and I will fix the problems that I am finding, no matter what any of those things take, and no matter what I have to change.

I'll change the whole world, if that's what it takes.

Mari gazed once more at the chipped stone of the firing slit and felt a shiver run through her as she remembered Alain speaking of them being in a battle. She tore her eyes from the token of old wars and looked out over the harbor again, past the works of humans and on to the restless waters of the Sea of Bakre.

To the north, she could see storm clouds forming.

ABOUT THE AUTHOR

"Jack Campbell" is the pseudonym for John G. Hemry, a retired Naval officer who graduated from the U.S. Naval Academy in Annapolis before serving with the surface fleet and in a variety of other assignments. He is the author of The Lost Fleet military science fiction series, as well as the Stark's War series, and the Paul Sinclair series. His short fiction appears frequently in Analog magazine, and many have been collected in ebook anthologies Ad Astra, Borrowed Time, and Swords and Saddles. The Pillars of Reality is his first epic fantasy series. He lives with his indomitable wife and three children in Maryland.

FOR NEWS ABOUT JABBERWOCKY BOOKS AND AUTHORS

Sign up for our newsletter*: http://eepurl.com/b84tDz
visit our website: awfulagent.com/ebooks
or follow us on twitter: @awfulagent

THANKS FOR READING!

*We will never sell or giveaway your email address, nor use it for nefarious purposes. Newsletter sent out quarterly.

Made in the USA
Middletown, DE
21 January 2021